AL-SAADIQ BANKS
BLOCK PARTY3
BRICK CITY MASSACRE

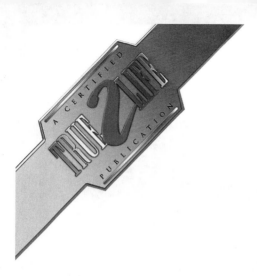

Block Party 3
Brick City Massacre

For information contact:
True 2 Life Publications
P.O. Box 8722
Newark, N.J. 07108

Website: www.True2LifeProductions.com
Author's E-mail: Alsaadiqbanks@aol.com

ISBN: 978-0-974-0610-5-4

ISBN: 0-974-0610-5-0

Printed in Canada

"I still pray Allah,
   forgive me for my actions,
  'cause I think Muslim,
   spit gangster but act Kafa."

— Beanie Siegel

Rapper
"B Coming: I Can't Go On This Way"

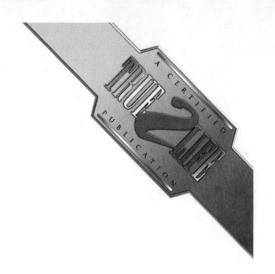

AL-SAADIQ BANKS
BLOCK PARTY 3
BRICK CITY MASSACRE

///// CHAPTER 1 /////

The loud noise of the helicopter rumbles through the airwaves as it makes a landing directly in the middle of the street. A short stocky man hops from the passenger's seat of the cockpit and makes his way toward the back, as the crowd of spectators watch in awe. The man pulls a short Asian woman by her hand and leads her from the copter. Just as she stands to the side, a tall Caucasian woman is being pulled from the copter.

Seconds later, a towering man, wearing a green prison jumpsuit jumps from the copter. He ducks down low in fear of being struck by the spinning propellers. He grabs both women by their hands and drags them away. Cameras flashing brightens up the extremely dark block. The man drags the two women up the stairs of Sugar Rays' Lounge. "This way, Sir," the bouncer says as he leads them across the thick black carpet that extends from the top of the steps down to the curbside.

As he's entering the building, he peeks around cautiously. The sound of loud clapping and cheering rips over the music. The sound of the music fades away and the loud noise of the crowd increases. "Welcome home!" they all shout simultaneously. The Mayor's smile brightens up the room as he lifts his arms up high in the air, accepting the admiration. His heart is touched by the many banners that he sees spread over the walls. They read, 'Welcome Home Mayor.' Not only are banners posted up everywhere. Damn near everyone in the building have on welcome home t-shirts as well.

"Mayor, come to the stage!" the deejay shouts into the microphone.

The Mayor shakes his head negatively while waving his hands in the air. He lowers his head in a shameful manner.

"Mayor! Mayor! Mayor!" the crowd shouts, cheering him on. Suddenly the bashfulness vanishes. He's always been a sucker for the spotlight.

"Come on!" the deejay demands.

He feels like he owes the people this, especially since they all are here to welcome him home. He grabs both women and lead them across the packed room. He claps hands throughout the crowd, which is opening up for him as he struts through confidently. The women are just as happy to see him. Desperateness fills their eyes as they pull and tug on him, treating him like the ghetto superstar he is. Seeing him free is like a breath of fresh air. Each female secretly thinks that she'll be the lucky woman to share his spotlight.

He finally makes it to the stage, where he seats the women side by side at a small table in the corner. The microphone is handed to him. He stands there silently until the ranting and raving stops. He clears his throat. "Look ya'll," he says as he lifts his hands high in the air, crossed over one another. "No shackles!" he shouts as he spreads them apart. The crowd goes into an uproar, cheering away. After the cheering dies down, he speaks again. "I told ya'll they couldn't hold me. I'm free!" he shouts arrogantly before slamming the microphone onto the floor. He walks away in the midst of all the hand clapping. The deejay plays the song "Free As a Bird" by rapper A.Z.

The Mayor takes a seat at the table where the two women are sitting. As soon as he's seated, both women take a seat on opposite sides of his lap. He turns to his right and gives his girl Liu a soft sensual kiss. He feels so grateful to have had her in his corner. She did the entire bid with him like a true trooper. Even though at times he felt her getting weak, she never turned her back on him. For that, he plans to give her the world and everything that it has in it.

He slowly turns to his right and he gives Megan a wetter and more passionate kiss. He misses her so much. In all the years he only saw her twice. Once was in the beginning of his bid and the other was at his mother's funeral. Although they had no contact, his love for her never faded away. He hates the fact that he had to cut his ties with her. He only did it to save her from going to prison.

"I love you," she whispers into his ear.

"I love you, too," he mumbles with a smile. He can't believe that he's finally reunited with the two loves of his life. He vows that he will never be separated from them ever again.

He looks up and is surprised to find crowds of people swarmed around him. He stands up and greets everyone with love, one by one. While hugging, he peeks over the girl's shoulder and there he sees his brother Dre standing a few feet away from him.

Dre winks at him. "I love you, Lil Bruh" are the words that the Mayor sees roll off of his lips.

"I love you, too, Big Bruh" he mumbles.

One Hour Later

After conversing and entertaining, the Mayor is now ready to leave. He struggles to get up from his seat due to the many glasses of champagne that he has consumed. The Mayor has never had a sip of alcohol in his life. He planned to take one sip in celebration but one sip led to three bottles.

His women both grab him by an arm and pull him from the seat. He staggers slightly. "Hold up," he slurs. "I want to make an announcement," he says as he walks toward the center of the stage. He grabs hold of the microphone and holds it high in the air, giving the deejay the signal to stop the music. Once it's completely quiet, he clears his throat. Everyone watches attentively as they wait to hear what he has to say. He rocks back and forth, trying to balance himself. "Special announcement," he says loud and clear. "On today May 21, 2007, I, your former Mayor am resigning from office. From this day on, I will no longer be the Mayor of this beautiful city." The mouths of all the spectators are stretched wide open as they stand there with confusion. "I've been elected for a new office," he mumbles. "I'm now the president. The country is mine!" he shouts arrogantly.

His big brother Dre can't believe his ears. His brother's arrogance has made him furious. He rushes to the stage and snatches his brother by the arm. "What the fuck is wrong with you?" he whispers in his ear as he pulls him close. "Are you a fucking idiot? Do you realize the Feds may be in here, watching and listening to everything you say and you gone make a foolish ass statement like that?"

"The Feds?" he asks in a high pitched voice. "The Feds," he repeats. "Who gives a fuck about the Feds? Not me. It's obvious that they can't hold me. I got Tony Cochran on my side," he says as he looks to his right, where his lawyer sits calm and collectively. "Tony!" the Mayor shouts. "Tony! I made you famous!" he shouts arrogantly.

Dre snatches him even harder, leading him out of the club. "You got a second wind. You was almost finished. Don't be ignorant. Take it as a blessing."

"A blessing?" the Mayor asks. "I am taking it as a blessing. You're right, I was almost finished, but God had another plan for me. He didn't want to finish me off...you know why? Because my work out here wasn't done," he says as his brother drags him through the doorway. "The streets are nothing without me. Look at the conditions of the hood. I'm the poster boy! Without me, guys have no direction. My presence is missed. The streets need me. Look around...niggas driving fake Bentley 300ms, and Magnums and Chargers, all type of bullshit and it's accepted," he says with despair in his voice as he points to the many cars that are parked in the area. They don't know no better," he whispers. "When I was home, niggas peeped me to find out what garments were hot...what vehicles were in. I set the standards. "Me," he adds as he pounds on his chest. "It's all my fault. I take full blame. I left these guys out here with no direction; nobody lead to follow. I have to set the records straight. No, you can't wear that outfit. No, you can't play cloudy-stoned jewelry that you buy from the bullshit jewelry stand in the middle of the mall. No, you can't drive American cars. No, you can't wear country ass platinum grills in your mouth. Look, they looking to a fucking white boy for guidance. Who the fuck is Paul Wall to tell niggas in my city that it's alright to get a grill in your mouth? That's some 1988 shit!" he says furiously. "I have to reestablish all of the standards. I have to give them guidelines to set their goals to. My lifestyle motivates them. I have to give them something to strive for. It's the least I can do. They're begging and pleading for guidance," he cries arrogantly. Dre, can't you see this? It's my obligation to them."

Dre can't believe his ears. He had no clue that his brother was this far gone. Dre wonders if he really believes this or is this just his arrogance speaking out as usual. "All those years away and you still learned nothing? You're still living for the people. That shit almost got your life taken away from you and you come back out with the same mentality? One day you will learn that the same people that you're living for, trying to impress, is the same motherfuckers that are going to get on that stand and bury your ass in trial. Telling everything they know. The people don't give a fuck about you. They just build you up to tear you down! They gone be here while you here and they gone be here when you gone. When you leave they'll just gossip about another nigga. That's it," he says sternly. "Ay, man, I'm all for getting a dollar but I don't do shit for the people. As long as I get my cut, I'm good," Dre whispers sternly.

"That's all you want is your cut?" the Mayor asks sarcastically. "It's way too much money out here to be made. Yeah, we getting our cut, but fuck our cut. See, me and you different. Yeah, we from the same bloodline but our hearts

7

beat to a different drum. You content with getting whatever you can get. Me, I want the whole pie!" he shouts as he's being dragged down the black carpet-covered steps. "Fuck just getting a break in the action. I am the action!" he says arrogantly.

Dre leads him to the curbside, where the two women stand waiting patiently. The Mayor's eyes damn near pop out of his head when he sets them on the beauty of a vehicle that's parked a few feet away. "Ooooh," he cringes as the sensation fills his body. "Damn," he whispers to himself as he walks toward the front of the vehicle. The triple black Phantom Rolls Royce sends a chill up his spine. He stands at the front of the car, just enjoying the view. His attention is snatched by the license plates, which blow his mind. They read, 'The Mayor.' "Ungghh, unghh, unghh," he sighs to himself as he walks toward the back where the chauffeur awaits his entrance. "Dre, you crazy for this one," he whispers as he passes his brother.

"Get in the car, man," Dre replies hastily.

Liu gets in first, while the Mayor follows hesitantly. Once he's seated in the middle, Megan slides in right next to him. The chauffeur gets inside and begins to slowly pull off.

"Hold up! Hold up!" the Mayor shouts to the driver as the back window slides down. The driver slams on the brakes abruptly.

The Mayor looks to the curbside where a crowd of people stand huddled together. "Dre!" he shouts. "There are millions of dudes in the prison system dying to get home so they can do them. Some will get another shot at it. Others are never coming home cause they got life. They forever niggas. If you gon' be out here bullshitting and wasting space you might as well trade places with one of those forever niggas. You know my motto...go hard or go home! Them cocksuckers held me down for a few summers. I'm about to go hard! Let me know what you gon' do," he says arrogantly. "If you gone do it, nigga, do it. If not get out of the way. You always screaming about the Feds. Them boys got they job to do and we got ours. No matter if you're only getting your cut or you taking the whole pie, they draw it up the same on your paperwork, so you might as well do you!" he shouts. "Driver, pull off...get me outta here!" he shouts furiously to the chauffeur.

"Count!" a voice yells from afar. "Count!" the voice repeats. "Blackhead, wake up...Count!"

The Mayor's eyes stretch wide open, staring directly at the ceiling. He looks around slowly. He looks down at himself. His green jumpsuit brings him back to reality.

"Count!" the Marshall shouts loudly.

"Damn," the Mayor says to himself. It was all a dream. "Damn..it felt so real," he says as he sits up on the edge of the cot. He pounds his fist into the palm of his left hand furiously. "Damn!"

The Mayor often dreams of being on the street. He wishes he were home so he can take back over the town and bring order and guidance back to the streets. He knows no one can do it like him, not even his brother Dre. At this point, the Mayor has a great deal of animosity toward his brother. He feels that Dre is going against his instructions. When he turned the 'After Party' connect over to Dre there were certain rules that he was supposed to abide by that he didn't. It's been about two months and Dre has yet to reach out to him and handle his end of the bargain. Sure Dre has been taking care of him financially, but that's only half of their deal. The Mayor has tried to contact him several times with no success. He often asks himself, how his brother could backstab him. He feels so betrayed and double-crossed. He also feels disrespected and hurt. He's sure if he were on the street things would be playing out differently. He's come to the realization that the only reason that he's being played is because he's behind the wall. He feels that his buttons are being pressed because people think there isn't much he can do under these circumstances. He plans to show them all, even if it's the very last thing he does. "Damn," he shouts. "I gotta get the fuck outta here." I'm ready to do me, he thinks to himself.

///// CHAPTER 2 /////

Dre rolls his eyes with disgust as he passes the female who stands to his left. Just as he grabs hold of the door knob, she speaks. "Bye to you, too," she says in a sassy tone.

Venom bleeds from his eyes as he looks at her. If looks could kill, she would have been dead a long time ago. This is Dre's former girlfriend of six years. Her name is Cindy. Dre hates the ground that she walks on. He tries hard not to show it, but it's almost impossible not to.

His only reason for being here is the fact that he had nowhere else to be paroled to. Before his mom died she was living in Colorado, which left Dre with nowhere to turn. He searched high and low with no success. He was left with no other alternative but to turn to Cindy for help.

While incarcerated Dre promised himself that he would never ever speak to her again in life. She made the first two years of his bid a living hell. Not even a month into his bid, Dre got the word from the street, that Cindy had picked up and started another relationship. The worse part was Dre was friends with the guy. As many people that informed him, he still couldn't believe that their six year relationship meant nothing to her. That relationship lasted no time, but she immediately picked up another and another. She spread out through the town like a plague. She bounced from hustler to hustler. They used her up until she wasn't worth anything.

He realizes that 15 years is a long time for a woman to wait for a man. The problem that he has with her is that she never kept it real with him. She denied her affairs all the way up until she got pregnant with her son who is now 12 years old. Each and every time he looks at her son, he's forced to relive the nightmare.

Dre looks her over from head to toe. He can't understand why he was initially attracted to her in the first place. They say that beauty is in the eye of the beholder. Right now, he doesn't know what eye he was looking at her through back then.

Dre told Cindy over and over that the dudes she cheated on him with were never into her. They were more into him. The fact of who he was raised her stock in the town. Their sole purpose for dealing with her was to gain points for stealing his girl. Even after being kicked to the curb so many times, she refused to believe that.

Dre also hates her for the fact that he left over $200,000 with her and during his bid, he couldn't get a dime of it from her. She rode around in brand new cars, wore expensive clothes and took vacation after vacation, while the man who funded it all could barely get her to accept his phone call.

"Bye," he says with a phony smile.

Dre steps out of the house and walks toward the curb. In one hand he lugs a laundry bag and in the other he carries a briefcase. He stops in his tracks as he stands behind the black Cherokee Hemi Edition. He lifts the hatch up and dumps the bag into the rear of the vehicle. After slamming the hatch shut, he quickly dusts off his clothes. Dre is looking very sharp and neat. He more fits the description of a Wall Street guy than a drug dealer. His black custom fit suit and briefcase is enough to throw anyone off.

He hops into the jeep and starts it up immediately. As the jeep is warming up, he pulls the visor down to take a look at himself. He stares into the mirror conceitedly as he cracks a smile at himself. He looks over at the console where he sees an open bottle of water, which he picks up and pours a palmful into his hand. He quickly rubs the water over his hair back and forth. The water makes it look curlier than it actually is. He then licks his lips and winks at himself before closing the visor.

Dre is on his way to meet with the 'After Party' connect. The duffle bag in the back is filled with dirty money instead of dirty clothes. In total, the bag holds $65,000 in cold cash. Things have been running so smoothly for Dre these past couple of weeks. In fact, things have been going so good, he has managed to ease himself of the 'just coming home' fear. He finally feels comfortable enough to get his feet wet. Up until last week, he was solely depending on the customers that Ahmir left behind with ILL Wheel and Dusty.

The $65,000 will buy Dre one kilo at $45,000 and it will cover the chemist's fee of $20,000. Dre was quite hesitant in the beginning because he knew very little about heroin. Now he zips through a kilo a week with ease. Dusty and ILL Wheel are good for about 4 or 500 bricks from the clientele that Ahmir left behind.

Dre has managed to steal himself some out of town clientele of his own through the many people that he's met while in prison. He now feels it's time to spread his wings a little. It should be easy because over the course of the 15 years that he's been in prison, he's been in a total of 40 federal prisons across the country. His bid started out in Fairton, where he did one year. From there he was shipped to upstate New York, where he changed prisons almost every four months. After his New York tour, he was shipped to Pennsylvania where he was bounced around from prison to prison until he covered almost every prison ground Pennsylvania had to offer. He thought that was the worse place until they shipped him off to the Midwest, where he spent a couple of years in Milwaukee.

The Feds' main purpose in shipping the inmates around is to prevent them from ever getting comfortable enough in one place to get organized. The federal prisons are filled with powerful guys from all across the country. They have access to anything illegal that you can imagine. The government realizes that if these guys get together and start networking, there is no limit to the things that they can do.

Their plan may have worked while Dre was in the system, but now that he's free, it's a whole different ball game. At the time he was being shipped around, he felt he was living a nightmare, but now he sees it differently. Throughout the majority of the spots where he was incarcerated, he connected with some real power dudes. His focus now is to connect all the dots he made while he was locked up. He'll concentrate on the out- of- town moves, while his squad covers all the in town moves. Actually, he doesn't give two fucks about the in town moves. Rubbing elbows with hustlers from different places and listening to their different methods of getting money made him realize how spacious the world really is and what the game really has to offer.

He doesn't have the slightest interest in getting money in the town. This is more of his brother's idea. Dre's plan was to only use Newark as a foundation just to put him in a position to service the rest of the world. At this point, he has achieved his goal. His feet are somewhat planted. Dre constantly tells his brother that he wants to cut all ties with anyone from the town, but the Mayor is so into controlling everything that he debates without hearing Dre out; which is the reason Dre has been avoiding him. He figures, if he stays away from the Mayor long enough, his passion to take over the town will die down and he will just live happily off of the cut that Dre breaks him off after every flip.

He's so concerned with taking over Newark, not realizing how much money they can get without even dealing in Newark. Dre realizes that Newark is all the Mayor knows and that's why he's so stuck in his ways. Dre, on the other hand, has another view; never shit where you eat. He learned that during his prison bid. He learned that lesson the hard way and he plans to never fall into that trap again. He plans to use all his out-of-town plugs to his advantage. The biggest mistake the government could have made was giving him the opportunity to meet powerful dudes from all across the land. That's one mistake he's sure he'll capitalize off.

While incarcerated, he thought about and analyzed a lot. He saw where a great deal of the inmates took their fall. Arrogance and flamboyance was 99 percent of the inmates' downfall. It was there that he made a vow to himself that he would play the game differently once he came home. So far he's been sticking to the script. To the naked eye, he looks like the average working class 'Joe Schmo'. He leaves his home every morning at 7:30 dressed in a business suit, just as all the other working class men do. Never in a million years will anyone believe that he's responsible for a small percentage of the dope that floods the city. With the help of Latif and Mu-Mit, Dre is sure that small percent will increase drastically.

Twenty Minutes Later

Dre parks in the far left corner of the huge parking lot and he walks into Outback Steakhouse on Route 22 in Union. After being escorted to the table by the waitress, Dre slams his briefcase onto the table and pulls his laptop from inside. While waiting for his food to come he kills time by surfing the internet. His phone rings, disturbing the silence. "Yeah?" he whispers. "Ah, hah," he agrees. "Got ya," he says before hanging the phone up. That call was the 'After Party' connect informing him that they're five minutes away.

One hour passes and Dre still sits at the table alone. He's devoured his lunch totally. After paying the waitress, he snatches his briefcase from the table and walks casually out of the restaurant. As he steps into the parking lot, he slows down his pace. He sneakily peeks around, being extra careful of his surroundings just to make sure nothing or no one looks suspicious.

After making sure that the coast is clear, he walks up the middle aisle of the parking lot, in the total opposite direction of where he parked. He pulls his key ring from his pants pocket, holding it high in the air as he presses the alarm. Suddenly the lights of a gold Windstar van illuminate the area. He approaches the van and hops in quickly. Before pulling off, he quickly peeks behind him at the backseat, where he sees four huge cardboard boxes. It's no puzzle; the boxes are filled with heroin.

He quickly backs up and zips out of the parking lot. He peeks to his right, just as he nears the parking space where his Cherokee was parked but is now empty. This is how Dre and the connect operate. They have duplicate keys. The connect pulls into the parking lot with a van full of work and he leaves with a car filled with money. The entire process is all Dre's idea.

Dre picks up his cell phone and begins dialing. "Yeah," he says into the phone before hanging up. Another thing he learned, the less phone conversation, the better. Just in case the Feds are listening on the line, they hear nothing, they know nothing.

After riding about five minutes east on route 22, Dre slows down and steers toward the right lane. He turns into the entrance, right next to White Castle. He cruises to the back of the carwash, where the employees greet him. He jumps out quickly. "Exterior only...silicone on the tires!" he screams to the Mexican. The Mexican jumps inside and pulls off as Dre watches cautiously. He watches all the way up until the van is inside of the glass cubicle getting shampoo lathered onto it. Dre then walks through the door where he pays the woman at the counter.

As Dre steps out of the building, something strange appears before his eyes. There are a row of four vehicles spread across the front of the car wash getting vacuumed. The first vehicle is a Mitsubishi. The second is a Toyota. The third vehicle is a gold Windstar van and the fourth one is also a gold Windstar van. Dre stares at the vans. They're identical. Is the first one his? Or is the second his?

As he nears the two identical vans, a beautiful white woman appears from the right side of the building, stealing everyone's attention. Her long blonde hair blows in the wind vigorously as she steps like a thoroughbred. The sun bounces off of her beautiful emerald green eyes. Her short tight mini-skirt hugs her broad hips. Her long sexy muscular legs put Tina Turner's legs to shame. She's packed with beauty but her double D cups are the main attraction. Her low cut silky blouse suffocates her huge breast.

Dre and the gorgeous woman meet directly at the back of the vans. She looks him up and down once before hopping into the van at the end of the row. Dre automatically hops into the alternative van. There they sit side by side. Dre peeks behind him only to find the backseat of his van completely empty.

He quickly looks over to her and stares into her sexy eyes. She bats her long eye lashes twenty times within one second before she winks at him and smiles devilishly, exposing her pearly whites. He winks back at her before pulling off and zipping down the highway, leaving her sitting there with over 800 bags of After Party in her backseat. Whew! he says to himself, while wiping his brow. That's only half the battle. He does realize that in this game, anything can happen. This means, he can't classify this as another successful pick-up until his female accomplice calls him and informs him that she's made it to safety.

Minutes later, Dre cruises along Morris Avenue in Union. Just as he makes the left turn into an office building parking lot, his phone rings. He hits the intercom button. "Yes?" he shouts.

No one replies. The sound of numbers being dialed gives him confirmation that she's safe and sound.

"Yes?" he shouts angrily, playing it off just in case unwanted listeners are on the line. Dre moves cautiously. Those 15 years in prison took so much out of him. That's time that he can never get back. He refuses to ever do another day in prison, so he knows he has to move accordingly. He's no fool. He does realize that the Feds expect him to go back to the streets. Knowing that, he's forced to move wisely and calculate his every move.

Dre pulls into the first empty parking space that he sees. He grabs hold of his briefcase and jumps out. He diddy bops over to the building and into the elevator. He hops off at the 10th floor. He enters the first door to the right. The gold plated name tag on the door sparkles brightly. The words, 'Tony Austin, Attorney At Law' are in bold lettering.

Dre opens the door and steps inside. "Hello, Mrs. Austin," he says loud and clear as he approaches the area where the secretary sits.

"Mrs. Austin?" she asks in a sassy manner. "What did I tell you about that? Mocha...call me Mocha," she insists.

Dre laughs and continues to walk toward the back. He steps into the tiny office, and sits behind the desk. Never in a million years did he ever think he would be sitting behind anyone's desk. Thanks to the Mayor, Tony gave Dre a job as his personal assistant. It all ties in well because while Dre was away in prison, he studied as a paralegal. He studied that field solely for the purpose of giving some of his time back, but it all worked out well because this is the perfect front for him to use as he takes over the world.

///// CHAPTER 3 /////

The driver of a hunter green Cherokee Sport cruises through the intersection of Central Avenue and Seventh Street, while the three passengers lock their eyes on the champagne colored 750 BMW that is pulling up to the pump slowly. Just as the vehicle stops, the passenger hops out, running toward the convenience shop.

"ILL Wheel, lemme out right here!" Latif shouts from the back passenger's seat. ILL Wheel stops short, just past the building. "Meet ya'll in the front!" he shouts as he gets out and slams the door.

"Go ahead, go ahead!" Mu-Mit says anxiously.

ILL Wheel zips through the entrance and cruises the lot, before pulling up behind the BMW. He passes the BMW slowly. He cuts right in front of the car to the pump as if he's about to get gas. He backs up within a few short inches of the BMW.

"That's good, that's good," Dusty shouts from the passenger's seat. It's a wonder that he can even speak at this point, being that he's so high off of the 'Wet'. The weed dipped in embalming fluid has him on cloud nine.

"Ready?" Mu-Mit asks Dusty as he's pulling his ski-mask snug over his face. He then grips the .357 that he holds in his hand tightly.

Dusty pulls his skull cap down over his dreadlocks, and ties his red bandana around his face. Only his eyes can be seen through the small opening in between the cap and the bandana. "Yeah!" he confirms.

"Let's go!" Mu-Mit shouts as he forces the door open. Dusty hops out right behind him.

Mu-Mit runs rapidly toward the driver's side of the BMW, while Dusty runs to the passenger's side. They both stop short at the front quarter panels of both sides of the vehicle, out of each other's way.

The driver's eyes stretch wide open from fear. He quickly attempts to reach for his gun but it's already too late. Dusty begins firing first. Boc! Boc! Boc! The glass shatters instantly. Two shots land in his lap while one bangs him in the chest.

Mu-Mit follows. Boom! Boom! The first shot pierces through his neck, and the other rips through his chest. The windshield caves in and glass disperses everywhere.

Dusty continues firing. Boc! Boc! Boc!

Cars begin zooming out of the gas station, with the nozzles still attached to their cars. Loud screaming roars from every direction.

Mu-Mit steps closer. Boom! Boom! He fires banging the man in the head twice back to back. His body folds over lifelessly into the passenger's seat.

The man's passenger sees all the mayhem from inside the convenience store and decides to play hero. He forces his way out the door, with his gun held high. He fires rapidly, aiming in the direction of Mu-Mit and Dusty. Boc! Boc! Boc! Boc!

The man is so busy watching them that he doesn't hear Latif sneaking up

15

behind him. Latif reaches out with his left hand. He yanks the man to him by his hood, while simultaneously resting his 44 Magnum on the back of the boy's skull. Boom! Boom! The man tumbles over face first onto the asphalt. Latif grabs him by his shoulder and turns him over onto his back. Boom! Boom! He fires with the intentions of finishing the job off. Both shots rip through his face caving it in from the impact. Blood gushes instantly.

Scccuuurrrrr! The Cherokee Sport burns rubber as it comes to a halt in front of Latif. "Come on, let's go!" Mu-Mit shouts from the backseat bringing Latif back to reality. He hops in as instructed.

Just as he's getting in ILL Wheel notices a string of police cars zooming up Central Avenue at top speed. Before Latif can even close the door, ILL Wheel takes off. Scccuurrr!

"Oh shit!" Latif shouts as he hears the sirens sounding off.

"Go, go!" Mu-Mit shouts nervously.

ILL Wheel zips recklessly through the red light at the intersection, totally disregarding the heavy flow of oncoming traffic. He presses play and rapper Rick Ross' 'Push It to the Limit' blares through the speakers, forcing ILL Wheel into a zone.

Latif looks behind him. The police cars are about a half a block behind them. Nervousness fills his body, as he pictures himself standing before a judge for a double homicide. "Go!" he shouts as he looks in the front seat, where he sees Dusty laying back as cool as a fan, as if he has no worries in the world. Although he does have a huge amount of confidence in ILL Wheel's driving, his coolness does not come from the confidence. At this point he is not sober enough to worry. He's so high right now, that he doesn't even realize what they have just done or what they're actually up against. He just sits there dazing straight ahead, eyes wide open. His mind is as blank as can be.

ILL Wheel zips through the intersection of 11th Avenue and Seventh Street, honking the horn like a maniac to warn any oncoming drivers. "Push it to the limit!" he shouts as he approaches 12th Avenue, where he busts a wild right turn. He zooms up the block and makes a quick left up 8th street. He quickly drops the jeep into first gear and takes off even faster.

Mu-Mit looks back behind them and realizes that the police are damn near glued to them. He can't actually believe that he's in a stolen car, in an actual car chase. He's never been in a stolen car in his life, let alone a car chase. Normally, he's on the sideline shouting how stupid the young kids are, and here it is today, he's riding along with the stupid young kids. Go figure! There is no way in the world, we're getting away from them, he thinks to himself. We're going to prison, he thinks to himself. He quickly thinks of the time he's going to get for this double homicide. With his jacket, it's impossible for him to beat this. He just beat the last two on the strength of God. And now here he is all over again. God spared him and now he feels like he smacked him in the face. He's sure his punishment will be tormenting. He refuses to allow himself to be at the court's mercy again. "Fuck that," he whispers to himself, as he pulls a glove from his inside pocket and dumps six shells onto his lap. He peeks behind him and sees that the cars have not even bent the corner yet. He quickly reloads his gun. He slams the barrel and spins it around. "I ain't going back to prison," he whispers to Latif.

ILL Wheel busts a wild and crazy turn right into 13th Avenue schools' playground. The playground is extremely busy. It's lunch time and the playground is covered with small children. He begins mashing the horn to get the kids attention who occupy the playground. The kids and their teachers scatter hysterically. ILL Wheel speeds through the playground. As he approaches the entrance of the gate, he steps on the accelerator to get more power. He busts through the gate onto Ninth Street.

Latif realizes what is on Mu-Mit's mind and he's with him 100 percent. He quickly reloads his weapon as well.

Mu-Mit nods his head up and down.

Latif sees the seriousness in Mu's eyes. He feels him totally. There is only one problem. They both have a problem with young boys. They don't trust them as far as they can throw them. "I knew we should have handled this by ourselves," Latif whispers only loud enough for Mu-Mit to hear. "These niggas gone tell," he whispers.

Mu-Mit stares him directly in the eyes. "After we get out of the hole, we bang them too," he whispers almost silently. "We ain't got no choice," he adds.

He makes the quick left and zooms into the direction of South Orange Avenue. That shortcut just gave them a two block lead. ILL Wheel makes the right turn onto South Orange Avenue and floors it all the way up, not stopping for anything. "Push it to the limit!" he sings along with Rick Ross. He looks down at the dashboard and is excited to see that he's exceeding 120 miles an hour. "Push it to the limit!" he shouts once again.

Latif is right. Maybe they should have handled this beef themselves. It's way too late to think about the would haves, should haves. The point is they didn't handle it alone, and now they have to deal with the consequences. Using ILL Wheel as the driver was all Mu-Mit's idea. He feared a situation like this coming about and he didn't trust his own driving skills enough.

The instructions for the man's murder were given to them several months ago, but they couldn't seem to catch him. Finally they got a tip from someone of what he drives and where he lives. This morning, they waited in front of his house for almost five hours, and when he finally decided to come out, there just happened to be a car accident directly in front of his building. Instead of taking a chance and creeping up on him in traffic, Mu-Mit decided to tail him until they could get a clear shot at him. The trip to the gas station was as perfect as can be. He made their job just that much easier.

The Mayor told them that he wanted the man dead and that's what it had to be. Apparently, when the Mayor was arrested, a few guys in the town still owed him money. Everyone else paid their debt except for this man. He figured the Mayor was never ever going to hit the streets again, so why should he pay him. He owed the Mayor for 200 bricks, which was equivalent to $60,000 at that particular time.

The Mayor sent message after message to him yet and he still would not pay the money back. Finally, the Mayor sent word for the man to turn the money over to his lawyer. He lied to him telling him that his lawyer refuses to represent him if he doesn't come up with more money. He also told him that the money he owed was his last opportunity for freedom. Even after hearing that, he still refused to pay, which left the Mayor with a bad taste in his mouth. The Mayor said the man felt that his life was in his hands and he still didn't turn the money over. That means he couldn't care less if the Mayor was dead or alive. He didn't care about the Mayor's life which gave him no alternative but to care less about the man's life. The Mayor promised himself right then, he would get even, and now he has.

ILL Wheel makes the left turn up 18th street and zips up the block recklessly. At the corner, he makes a quick right up 15th avenue. He speeds up the block in record breaking time, running every red light in sight. As he gets to the top of the hill, he peeks to his left before jumping onto the entrance of the parkway.

Both Latif and Mu-Mit look behind them and is happy to see not a cherry top in sight. ILL Wheel has managed to shake them off of them. Phew! They both sigh simultaneously as they loosen the grip of their guns.

"Push it to the limit!" ILL Wheel sings as he slows down the vehicle. He drives up the highway following the speed limit. Not only has his expertise gotten him out of yet another hectic situation, he also saved him and Dusty's life without even knowing it.

///// CHAPTER 4 /////

Dusty sits in the driver's seat of his cherry red Dodge Charger SRT. He watches ahead of him as his cousin walks across the street towards a black Monte Carlo. Dusty and the driver of the car lock eyes with one another. Neither of them wants to back down and look away. Dusty's cousin hops into the backseat of the vehicle, interrupting their staring match.

"Punk mufucker," Dusty laughs to himself as he takes a huge pull of the 'Wet'. He holds the smoke in his mouth, allowing the chemicals to fry his brain. He coughs hard as the smoke chokes him terribly.

The tension between Dusty and the dude comes from the fact that Dusty is Blood while the other guy is Crip. Neither of them can stand each other but the 'After Party' brings them together. The dope is so good that the man is willing to put their color difference to the side just to get his hands on it. They both refuse to deal with each other or even speak to one another which is why Dusty's cousin is an important factor. He's neither Blood nor Crip. He's neutral which is why he's able to be the liaison.

Dusty's cousin hops out of the Monte Carlo just as Dusty exhales another huge mouthful of smoke. He crosses the street casually. As he hops into the car, the pungent odor almost knocks him out. "Here," he says as he drops the bag of money onto Dusty's lap.

"You counted it?" Dusty asks as he watches the Monte Carlo pull off. He has his hand on his gun the whole time. He doesn't trust them the least bit. Their eyes lock with each other once again. "Fucking Brab," Dusty mumbles under his breath with a smile.

"Yeah, I counted it. $6,250," he whispers.

The man just bought 25 bricks of After Party. Dusty charged him $250.00 a brick. The fact that he's Crip is the reason that he pays an extra $35.00 per brick. Dusty normally sells the dope for $220.00 a brick, making a profit of $40.00 for him and ILL Wheel to spilt. In this case the liaison has to be paid. His cut is $25.00 per brick. Dusty pockets the extra $5.00 profit. He considers it as the Crip paying homage to him. At the end of the day, the extra change ends up as more G-Smoke money.

Dusty takes another pull as he dials numbers on his phone.

"Yo?" ILL Wheel answers.

Dusty coughs violently. "Uhmm, uhhmm," he clears his throat. "Yo!"

"What up?" ILL Wheel asks.

"It's all good," Dusty claims. He calls ILL Wheel just to let him know that the move has been made successfully and he's safe and sound. Neither of them like the fact of dealing with the Crip because they don't trust them but at the end of the day it's all business.

////// CHAPTER 5 //////

Days Later

The white 2 door G-35 Infiniti cruises down Lyons Avenue, looking attentively in search of a parking space. After locating one, the young, gorgeous, beautifully proportioned girl hops out of the vehicle slowly. About a half a block behind her, an all black Cadillac STS parks and sits idly. The Cadillac draws attention due to the huge swirls of thick white wax that covers it.

The driver of the Infiniti walks toward the rear of the vehicle and snatches the door open. She snatches the Bloomingdales' shopping bag from the backseat, slams the door shut and prances her way toward the six- story building that sits across the street. She hits the bell and the buzzer sounds off loudly.

The sound of the buzzer awakens Dusty. He walks out of his room in a complete daze. The 'Wet' has him walking around in a blur.

ILL Wheel passes by him on his way to the door. He hates to see him looking like this. Just his presence has irked him to no end. Stupid mufucker, he thinks to himself. "Looking just like a feign," he mumbles as he passes him. He rolls his eyes with disgust, but Dusty ignores him. Just as ILL Wheel gets to the door, the bell rings again. He peeks through the peak hole and quickly opens the door. At her entrance, her cute baby-face, dimple-indented smile disappears and an ice cold stare appears. She passes the bag off to ILL Wheel and takes a seat on the sofa. ILL Wheel quickly dumps the contents onto the table. He automatically begins counting away. "300 hundred bricks?" he sighs. "He bugging!" he shouts furiously.

Week after week Dre has been slowly decreasing their workload. They've gone from getting 1,000 bricks a week to 300 bricks a week. A great deal of the original clientele that Ahmir left behind has disappeared for whatever reason, but ILL Wheel and Dusty were still managing to be consistent with their flow. The majority of their clientele is gang affiliated. They distribute the dope throughout the town, mainly to other Blood gang members. The number of bricks that they do is far beyond fair, but Dre is sure they can do more. Their lack of real business sense is a big obstacle for them. The flow they have has nothing to do with them. The 'After Party' is so raw that anyone can get rich off of it. It sells itself. All you have to do is have it and the rest is clockwork. Dre is sure he can find someone better to hold that position, but he doesn't, because of the promise he made to Ahmir, to take good care of them. The Mayor's say so is important as well. If not for the Mayor, Dre would have left them alone and taken his entire show on the road, without dealing with anyone from Newark. His game is finally taking off. He went from having no heroin clientele at all to being in a position where he can move more than 500 bricks a week on his own. The bigger his clientele gets the less work he gives Dusty and Ill Wheel. Dre is also decreasing the amount of bricks he gives them because when he deals with them he cuts a portion of his profit. He can't charge them top dollar due to the promise he made to Ahmir. So the more dope he gives them, the less profit he makes in the end. At the rate that he's moving, before they know it, they may be getting a weekly workload of 50 bricks.

About ten minutes later, the female exits the building and quickly walks toward her car. She pulls off quickly. Just as she reaches the corner, the Cadillac pulls off behind her. She makes the left onto Elizabeth Avenue and races up the block, while the Cadillac tails her about a half a block away. At the very next traffic light, the Infiniti gets into the left turning lane, while the Cadillac pulls up side by side with it. She looks over to her right, in the direction of the Cadillac, and nods her head once, gesturing to the driver that she's alright.

The dark tinted window of the Cadillac rolls down slowly. Once the window is halfway down, Mu-Mit peeks his head up and nods back at her, before quickly hitting the button for the window to roll up.

At the change of the light, Mu-Mit proceeds up the block slowly with no determined destination.

"So, let the sideshow begin. Hurry, hurry, step right on in!" Latif sings from the passenger's seat of the Cadillac. "Can't afford to pass you by. Guaranteed to make you cry," he sings along with the tune of Blue Magic, which blasts through the stereo system. "See the man with the broken heart, whose cried a million years," he whines, totally pissing Mu-Mit off. "So many tears," he whispers as he pats the short, twisted braids that are spread over his head.

Mu-Mit watches him secretly out of the corner of his eye. A look of aggravation appears on Mu-Mit's face instantly. Latif has decided to grow dreadlocks and Mu-Mit despises his decision. He feels like Latif is trying to emulate the young boys. Just watching him play around with his twists pisses him off to no end. He rolls his eyes with disgust. "Yo!" Mu-Mit shouts.

Latif is in his zone. He continues singing as if Mu hasn't said a word. "It will only cost you fifty cents to see! What life has done to those like you and me!"

"Yo," Mu shouts again. "Ain't that the boy, Parlay, right there?"

"So, let the side...Where?" Latif asks, while scanning the entire area.

"Up front, at the light."

"Latif's cool-out zone has been broken. He looks up and there he sees a silver convertible 650 BMW. "Yeah, that's the fag ass nigga. Slide up on 'eem."

Mu-Mit swerves the Cadillac to the right, dipping around the sitting traffic. He quickly races to the traffic light. Just as they pull parallel to the BMW, the beautiful passenger sees them through her peripheral and turns to look directly at them.

The automatic window of the Cadillac begins rolling down slowly, while Latif sits on the edge of the seat anxiously. He points at the driver, gesturing for the female to tell him to look over. She does so and the driver looks directly over.

The window slides down slowly. "Sa'Laikum!" he shouts at the sight of Mu-Mit.

Mu-Mit doesn't extend the greeting. He acknowledges him by headnod, while tightening the strings of his doo rag. Mu-Mit encounters guys like him on the street and in prison. They're guys who run to Islam for protection. He feels that they figure by greeting him with the Salaams, he'll hold back from moving out on them. How wrong they are? Mu-Mit's philosophy is; you can't mix halal (good) with haram (bad.) If you're a Muslim who is dealing in any type of haram, then he'll never spare you.

"What's going on, Daddy?" Latif shouts aggressively with a devilish smile on his face. He's smiling but the tension is evident. The sight of the boy is pissing Latif off gravely.

"Not too much. You know...the same ol shit. It's a roller coaster ride! You go up...you go down, ya know?"

"Yeah, yeah," Latif interrupts. "But what's good, though? You looked into that?"

"Indeed," the boy says casually. "It was definitely what you said it was. I been meaning to get at you but I been running crazy, feel me? What's your number again? I need to get with you in a couple of days."

"9734446624," Latif calls out with a smirk on his face. Right now, he feels played. This is about the tenth time that he's given this dude his phone number. At this point, he's sure the boy has no plans of calling him. He just asks for the number to get them out of his face and brush them off.

After hearing about how much money Parlay is making, Dre instructed them to reach out to the boy, offering him the 'After Party' at a decent rate. At this time, Parlay controls about 50 percent of the dope flow running throughout the town. Dre realizes how much of an asset Parlay will be. The only thing is Parlay doesn't see it that way. Latif and Mu-Mit wanted to get at him a long time ago but Dre being the fair dude that he is, wants to give him the chance to jump on board on his own without force.

"Mu, Sa'Laikum!" Parlay shouts. This time Mu doesn't even acknowledge him. He stares straight ahead as if he hasn't said a word.

Latif sits back in his seat, while Mu-Mit cruises off at the change of the traffic light.

"Yo, I'm about ready to jump on that bitch ass nigga, right now. Who the fuck he think he playing with? Bitch ass nigga," he whispers. "How the fuck these bitch ass niggas be holding these positions? Nigga soft as toilet tissue, and niggas following his bitch ass lead. One thing though, we have to get some info on him. I know that nigga loaded. We gone make that one beneficial for all of us. We gone kill two birds with one stone. We gone peel his shit back, to get him out the way, but at the same time we gone find out where that bread at too, fuck that! Man, I tell you, I can't wait for Big Bruh to give us the word. He be bullshittin' though. Giving motherfuckers too many chances. I say, you offer the nigga the smack one time. After that, he either with us or against us! Fuck that! I tell you one motherfucking thing! As soon as he gives us the word, we cleaning this shit up! Operation shutdown!"

///// CHAPTER 6 /////

Fort Dix, New Jersey

The pleasant smell of Spanish cuisine fills the air, resembling more of a fine restaurant than a jail cell. In the center of the tiny table there sits the remaining contents of the feast. The foods range from Paella and Filet Mignon, to 15-inch lobster tails.

There's no special occasion. This is just an ordinary supper in the Mayor's dorm. Every night the smell of good home-cooked food rips through the air, filling the prison. Inmates will do anything just to get a portion of these left-overs. Even some Marshals sneak past the room for a sample.

The Mayor lies across the top bunk, holding his belly. He's so stuffed that he can barely move. "I'm full as a bull, right now!" he shouts. "I gotta stop eating like this," he whispers. "You gone have me walking around, 300 pounds," he says to the inmate who is lying across the bottom bunk.

The man doesn't reply with words. He just snickers. These two have shared the room for over a year now. The man was already here when the Mayor got shipped here. In the short time, they've managed to develop a strong bond. In fact, this is the only inmate the Mayor deals with wholeheartedly.

In the beginning, neither of them would say a word to each other but after a few months they began to speak more and more. Before they both knew it, they were sharing some of their inner most thoughts with each other. The Mayor truly respects his wisdom and truly looks forward to the elderly man's late night beat downs, in which the man tells tales of some of the things that he's seen in his life. Sometimes these fables will go on until the wee hours of the night. The majority of the time, the stories put the Mayor to sleep. That coupled with the huge meals. The Mayor has grown accustomed to the man's cooking as well. With the man's cooking skills and his perception of life, he reminds the Mayor so much of his father. Although no one could ever replace his father, he's surely a good fill-in at times.

The Mayor has a soft spot for the man. He has no love on the outside and no income whatsoever. When the Mayor first got shipped here, the man was struggling. He barely was able to survive throughout the month. The Mayor's good heart made him reach out to the man and offer him food, but the man's pride and huge ego made him refuse. That made the Mayor gain even more respect for him.

He no longer struggles though. The Mayor being shipped to this room is the best thing that could have ever happened to the man. He now lives like a king. Anything that the Mayor orders from commissary, he orders double. Any clothes or food that comes from the outside, there's always a package for his bunkie. They even have their own televisions, due to the fact that the Mayor got sick and tired of watching 'Telemundo.' At first they would alternate shows until the Mayor could no longer take it. He heard so much

Spanish in the first couple of months that he can actually speak the language.

The Mayor asks for nothing in return for his hospitality. The good home-cooking is more than enough. "Where did you learn to cook like that? Did you always know how to cook?"

"Cook?" the man asks sarcastically. "The only thing I cooked back then was cocaine, Papi," he laughs. "I was never home long enough to cook. I learned to cook while on the inside. Eating enough of the disgusting prison food, will turn anyone into a chef," he laughs.

The Mayor closes his eyes and his mind begins to wander. He wonders what his future actually holds for him. He's actually given up on making it out of prison but there are times that he considers the possibility. His lawyer tells him he'll get him out. He hopes for the best, but plans for the worse. He feels that it's safer that way. He thinks of his bunkie who has been on the inside for close to twenty years now and will finish his life off in someone's prison. The Mayor truly admires how the man takes it in stride without ever complaining, sort of like the way he does. He's told the Mayor, ever since the judge sentenced him to life; he erased the outside world from his mind. Chills run through the Mayor's body every time he considers that.

Minutes pass and a sniffling sound from the bottom bunk interrupts the Mayor's thoughts. "Yo?" the Mayor calls out. The man doesn't reply. Instead he just sniffs again. "Benderas? You alright?" the Mayor asks as he peeks his head over the edge of the bed, staring onto the bottom bunk, where he sees his bunkie crouched over, reading a letter.

The man keeps his face buried in the paper, trying to hide his tears from the Mayor. He quickly hands over a photograph, just to get the attention off of him.

"What's this?" the Mayor asks as he reaches for the photo. He then lays back on his bed and stares at the photo. Got damn, he says to himself as he lays his eyes on the most beautiful woman that he's ever seen in his life. He's had beautiful women in his life but nothing he's had can compare to this one. Seeing her dressed in an oversized prison jumpsuit almost breaks his heart. Prison is no place for a beautiful woman like this. It's evident that her place is strutting up someone's runway, somewhere

The waving of the yellow paper at the foot of the Mayor's bed catches his attention. He rises up and grasps it quickly. He immediately begins to read it.

Papi, I hope this scribe reaches you in the best of health and spirits. I know it's been several months since I last wrote but please forgive me. I had to get into my bid. I must admit, in the beginning it was hell. I didn't believe I could make it another day, but each day it got easier and easier just like you said it would.

You know, a lot of things you told me as a child I couldn't understand, but now as an adult, I understand it all perfectly clear. I remember you would always say, 'Don't marry the man you love. Marry the man that loves you.' It made no sense to me back then, but now it makes all the sense in the world. I should have listened. If only I could turn back the hands of time, I would listen and take heed to every instruction you've ever given me. I wouldn't be here today. You know how the saying goes, 'A hard head makes a soft a..' As a little girl, I never imagined prison being a part of my future. I never even considered it. In my young eyes, prison was a place for bad people who did bad things, and I wasn't bad at all. How did I end up here? I ask myself over and over. Did love lead me here? Or was it stupidity? How could my heart deceive me like that? At what point does a woman stop and analyze the situation.

Papi, everyday I think about the situation. I gave my heart to a man who probably never loved me from the beginning. Doing this bid would probably be a lot easier if the circumstances were different. If I was here for standing up and holding it down for a man who would do the same for me, I could stomach it a little better, but unfortunately I'm not.

I thought you said loyalty and honor was a good thing? I believed you and look what it got me? Life in prison. Of all the things I chose to listen to, why did it have to be that? You said loyalty and honor would carry me through life. You didn't say it would get me life.

Papi, please forgive me for lashing out. It's not your fault. I take full blame for my actions. It's these steel bars. They're eating away at my mind and my soul. I can't take it anymore. I can't finish my life here...if so, I'd rather die right now. It's driving me crazy. I have to get out of here.

After that sentence, the words on the page start to get blurry from the many tear stains that cover the last lines of the page. The dried-up stains are hers. The fresh ones belong to her father.

Papi, I want to go home. I have to get out of here. The last line reads. A total of ten tears fill the bottom of the page. That's three old ones and seven new ones. Ooops, make that twelve. The Mayor has added two of his very own. The letter has managed to rip through his stone cold heart. Signed, Miranda A.K.A. Your Little Princess A.K.A. Like Father Like Daughter.

The Mayor hands the letter over the edge of the bed. He then lays back with his eyes closed. He would love to say something to comfort the old man but nothing seems to come to mind. He puts himself in the man's shoes. He wonders how he lives with that burden on his shoulders. The old man has told him bits and pieces of how she ended up in prison. The Mayor is totally against snitches and he'll never openly admit it but he wishes the girl would have rolled over. If she had, he would understand it totally.

"Reality has set in," the man whispers. "She's breaking down. I've never heard words like that come out of her mouth. I can feel her weakness through the pages. It's scaring me. You know...when my little princess was born, I said to myself, this must be God's punishment to me for all the wrong that I have done to women. Trust and believe, I never wanted a daughter. When me and my wife were at the doctor's office looking at the sonogram on the screen, I asked him over and over if he was sure that it was a girl. Each time we went to visit him, I would ask him to check again, hoping the sex of the baby would change. Unfortunately, the sonogram was correct. When my wife delivered that beautiful little girl, I cried like a baby. I wasn't crying with joy. I was crying from fear. I think of all the manipulating I've done to woman, all the lies I've told, all the games that I've played, and all the hearts that I've broken. And just to think that she would have to go through that type of pain and hurt. I couldn't imagine anyone hurting my baby like that. I asked God is she my Karma? From the day she was born, I made a vow to myself to protect her from any pain that she would endure. I promised myself that I would teach her the game and make her strong where no man could ever play games with her and hurt her. At a young age I tried to give her the survival package that I thought she would need to get her through her life. I taught her to be stone cold and to never back away from anything or anybody. I taught her to stand up and take full responsibility for her actions. I taught her to play by the rules, and that she did. It's too bad that the rules I taught her to play by, were my rules. I was a drug dealer. She was a child. Look what I did? I created a monster. I made her too strong and now look...it ain't no turning back. I messed up. It's all my fault. My little princess will spend the rest of her life behind bars all because I added all the wrong ingredients. Women are supposed to be soft and loving, not heartless and stone-cold. Now she has to pay for my mistakes. Just because I chose to gamble my life away with the law, she has to suffer. If I had lived the life of a square, I would still be home to protect my little princess. Because I didn't, my princess was left on the battlefield all alone to defend herself. I swear to you, if I had it all to do again, I would pump gas at Exxon for $2.00 an hour," he claims. "It's all fucked up and guess who fucked it up?" he asks. "Me, that's who," he whispers before wiping the tears from his eyes.

Those words touch the Mayor's heart. He tries to think of something comforting to say, but nothing comes to mind. All of a sudden a light bulb goes off in his mind. He nods his head up and down for a few seconds before speaking. "I got the answer to your problem," the Mayor whispers while nodding his head up and down. "I got just the man to fix all of this for you."

///// CHAPTER 7 /////

Dre just got off the Benjamin Franklin Bridge approximately 15 minutes ago and his program is already in effect. "Yo," he whispers into his phone as he sits parked in the parking lot of McDonalds.

"Yeah," the man on the other end replies.

"Where you at?" Dre asks. "I'll be there in about twenty minutes," he lies as he already sits in their designated meeting place. "I'm getting off of the Ben Franklin, right now."

"Oh, ok. I'm already enroute. I should be getting there a few minutes before you."

"Bet," Dre says as he hangs up the phone. He looks toward the back of the parking lot where he spots a space at the far end of the lot. He immediately pulls off and parks his Cherokee in between two huge trucks that look like they may be abandoned. From the looks of the thick dirt and debris that cover them, they have not been moved in years. Between the trucks you can barely see Dre's jeep. "Perfect," he mumbles under his breath.

Ten minutes later, a black big body Impala pulls into the McDonald's parking lot. The driver can't be seen on the count of his dark tinted windows, yet Dre knows exactly who it is. It's his man, Peanut. Dre and Peanut did time together in the Feds. Neither of them could hardly wait to get home and connect. Dre has never heard anything but good when it comes to Peanut. He's a money getting dude, who the entire Philly seems to love and respect. Dre is sure he's the perfect man to use to slide into this city and take it over. Dre is so sure that with this smack and the power Peanut has, they can make some real money together.

Dre's phone rings. "Yeah?"

"Yo!" Peanut shouts. "I'm here. Where you at?"

"Aw man, traffic crazy," Dre says as he scopes the entire area, paying close attention to any cars that maybe following Peanut. "We might have to meet somewhere else closer to where I am," Dre says as he sneakily pulls out of the parking space and exits the lot from the opposite exit.

"Where?" Peanut asks.

"Uhmm, lemme see," Dre says slowly. "Alright, how about Popeyes?"

"That's cool."

"How long will it take you to get there?" Dre asks already knowing exactly how long it will take.

"Man, I'm about 15 minutes away from there. That's all the way across town from here."

"Alright then, I'm pulling into the parking lot right...now," Dre lies as he cruises along Broad Street. "See you in a minute," Dre says before hanging up the phone.

Minutes Later

Peanut turns into the parking lot of Popeyes. He pulls out his cell phone and begins dialing but he gets no answer from Dre. He then parks in the center of the lot and continues to call. Dre sits parked across the street with his cell phone in his lap as it rings back to back several times before he answers. After scoping the area for a few minutes, he finally answers. "Yeah?"

"Dre, what up?"

"Yo...change of plans. Shit ain't looking right over there. Meet me at, Church's Fried Chicken," Dre says as he cruises away.

"Psst," Peanut sighs. "That's all the way back across town."

"That's where I'm at," Dre says as he speeds up Broad Street.

"Alright," Peanut says as he hangs the phone up with frustration.

Dre can hear the frustration in his voice, but he could care less. It's safety first for Dre. He realizes that each move can very well be his last move. He's weighed the options, either frustrating his client or get trapped off and finish his life off in prison. That in no way was a hard decision to make.

Minutes later, Dre parks in the middle of the block. Just minutes later, the Impala turns onto the block. Dre watches carefully, making sure no one is tailing Peanut. Dre paid special attention to every car that came in behind Peanut at the last two meeting spots. If any familiar car pulls in behind him he's sure something isn't right. He switched locations just so he can keep track of any unwanted followers.

Dre's phone rings. "Yeah?"

"I'm here," Peanut says. "Where you at?"

"I had to circle the block," Dre lies as he sits there staring attentively. "I'll be right there in two minutes," he says before hanging up.

After watching for another two minutes, he now feels a certain amount of assurance. He picks up his phone and dials. "Yeah," he shouts into the phone before hanging up. Seconds later, he watches the entrance as the white Infiniti cruises the block and parks directly behind the Impala. Lil Mama exits the car and walks casually toward the Impala. In her hand, she grips a Macy's shopping bag full of After Party; 100 bricks to be exact. She jumps into the Impala and gets back out in a matter of seconds. She quickly walks back to her vehicle with empty hands.

Dre sells Peanut the dope for $225.00 a brick. Dre is giving him the dope on consignment, which is why he's charging the extra $25.00 for each brick. Peanut is in no position to pay for the dope up front because he's only been home for a matter of days now. He wrote Dre about two weeks ago stating that he was on his way in. As soon as he touched, he made the call to Dre. Dre didn't hesitate to make his way to Philly. Today marks their very first move and he's sure bigger and more lucrative moves are to come.

The girl gets into her vehicle, while the Impala cruises away. "Mission complete," Dre mumbles under his breath.

///// CHAPTER 8 /////

One Week Later

ILL Wheel pushes Dusty's door wide open. The terrible odor of feet seeps out of the room almost knocking ILL Wheel off of his feet. Mounds and mounds of dirty clothes are piled up everywhere.

"D!" he shouts. "D!" he calls again. ILL Wheel could have sworn that he heard Dusty come in late last night but he thinks maybe he could have left back out. Suddenly a mound of clothes moves. It's Dusty turning over. He coughs loud and hard in his sleep. "Yo, D! Get up, nigga. D!"

"Huh?" Dusty replies in a groggy voice. He lifts up slightly but has to lay his head back down on account of his painful headache.

"D, I need that money. The broad on her way over. You got that money for the fifty, right?"

"Yeah," he says in an agitated manner as he gets up from the floor. He looks a mess. His clothes are wrinkled and tacky looking. He looks like he just crawled up out of a sewer.

He walks toward the door with his eyes half closed. He grabs the top of his head attempting to alleviate the pounding but that doesn't work. You would think that he would be used to the pain by now being that he wakes up like this every morning. The pain is excruciating yet and still he continues to smoke routinely.

"Headache, huh?" ILL Wheel asks sarcastically. "Still smoking though," he smiles. "You ain't gone learn."

"Whatever," Dusty mumbles under his breath as he exits the room.

Minutes later, Dusty searches his room high and low for the nine thousand dollars that ILL Wheel is waiting for. He's searched his car thoroughly and still can't seem to remember what he did with the money. The "Wet" has fogged up his memory. The last thing that he remembers doing last night is serving the boy the fifty bricks. After making the score, he stashed the money in the car and started up his night. He remembers going to the 'Twenty Grand Bar' and that's when everything becomes a blur. His smoking session started right then. He remembers nothing after that point. He doesn't know who he linked up with and he doesn't have the slightest idea when he got home or how he got home. Slowly but surely the smoking is destroying his mind and he doesn't even realize it.

"Dusty!" ILL Wheel shouts. "The damn girl down stairs! I need that!" he shouts from the living room.

"Damn," Dusty whispers to himself. How the fuck did I lose nine thousand?" he asks himself. Sure he's misplaced money before but never this much. He's lost a few hundred here and there or misplaced a couple of bricks but never fifty brick money.

He's absolutely frustrated. He knows that if he lets ILL Wheel know this he will never hear the end of it. The bell rings interrupting his thoughts.

"Damn," he sighs, realizing that his time is up.

"D!"

"Here, I come!" he replies hastily as he pulls his dresser drawer open. He digs inside the drawer, retrieving nine stacks from his personal stash. For the life of him, he can't remember what happened to the money but what he does know is he's definitely made a costly mistake.

A Few Miles Away

Dre sits there desperately as he listens to the phone ring with no answer. This makes his twentieth call of today. He's been calling the 'After Party' connect for an entire week to no avail. For the life of him he can't understand why they haven't been answering or returning his calls. This is so unlike them. He wonders if they have encountered some type of problem. He thinks maybe they got knocked off. That is the only answer he can come up with. That alone is enough reason for him to stop calling. He assumes that if they're locked up, their phones are in custody and they're probably tracing all the numbers that call them. Knowing this, he's sure that it will be smart to stop calling them, but his curiosity won't allow him to do so.

He's been without work for 4 days now and it's driving him crazy. His team is crying for dope and he can't deliver. He's gotten accustomed to the 60 grand a week profit and the thought of losing this week frustrates him gravely.

He dials the number again and prays silently as the phone rings away. "Please, let them pick up," he mumbles. "Fuck!" he shouts with despair. Another call interrupts the line. A sense of hope fills his heart as he thinks that it may be the connect. "Hello?"

"What up?" the caller asks.

Dre automatically recognizes the voice. It's his man Peanut from Philly. He's managed to breeze through his workload in a couple of days and has been trying to re-up ever since. "Nothing!" he shouts.

"Damn, Dre, what's the problem?"

"Who the fuck knows," he says. "Yo, I'll call you later!" Dre shouts with frustration before slamming the cell phone onto the floor. "Stupid motherfuckers!" he shouts. Now he's pissed off. He just has to get to the bottom of this. He needs to know exactly what's going on with them.

///// CHAPTER 9 /////

The Mayor stares coldly at the female visitor from across the table without saying a word to her. The look in his eyes almost melts her away. She can sense how furious he really is. She slouches down in her chair with fear. She doesn't know the Mayor well but ever since she was a small child she has heard nothing but treacherous stories about him. Sometimes she wonders how she got herself all tied up in this mess. Dre uses her to relay messages back and forth between him and the Mayor due to the fact that he refuses to have any contact with his brother. He wants their ties to be limited if none at all is possible. The last thing he needs is for the Feds to find out that he's been speaking with him. They'll automatically assume that he's picked up from where the Mayor left off.

"A visit, finally, huh?" he asks sarcastically. "Is that what I had to do to get a visit?" The Mayor quickly remembers that the girl is only the messenger and is completely innocent to the entire matter.

He peeks around nervously; making sure no one is eavesdropping on their conversation. "Listen, I'm going to keep this visit short and brief. Right to the point," he whispers. "Tell Big Bruh, he's breaking my heart," he says with sorrow in his eyes. Tell 'em that I've been waiting for months for him to come through and do what he said he would do. I can't wait anymore. Tell 'em he gave me his word and I believed him. Promises are not made to be broken. All we have is our word. Tell 'em I got everything lined up already. All my players are in position. They're all just waiting for me. He's making me look like a liar, like I'm faking jacks. I keep telling them this week, this week. They starting to lose faith in my word. Up until now, everything that I ever said, I would do, I've done. I don't make promises, I make dreams come true. But now thanks to him, my word has become suspect. I refuse to allow anyone to demolish my character," he says sternly. Tell 'em the plug moves at my command, and without me there's no deal. Tell 'em if I can't play, I'll mess up the entire game," he says arrogantly. "Listen, word for word. Don't miss a syllable," he demands. "You hear me?" She nods her head up and down. "Tell 'em, there are a couple of guys who he has to get in touch with. I want him to give everyone of 'em an offer that they can't refuse. Tell 'em, I already know the majority of 'em will cooperate, just by mention of my name, but I'm sure some will go against the plan. Tell 'em to be fair...give everyone a chance to play. Go against the plan? You already know," he says with his eyebrows raised high. "Tell 'em, no second and third chances. I know him," he adds. "Tell 'em, no one is exempt from this. From here on out, the city is all ours or we burn it down," he says as he stands up and backpedals away from the table. "Listen closely...Parlay, Craig C, Infra-Red and Doughboy. They on the top of the list. Lil Mookie, O, and Jay," he says as he stops short. "You got it?"

"Yes," she whispers as she stands to her feet.

"Tell 'em, either they with us or they against us. Operation Shutdown is officially in effect."

One Hour Later

The female visitor and Dre get off at the Newark Exit. During the entire one hour ride, neither one of them said a word to each other, due to the fact one of Dre's golden rules is never to talk inside of cars.

Dre makes the quick right into Dunkin Donuts. "Come on," he whispers as he snatches the key out of the ignition. Once they're inside they order and seat themselves along the front window.

Dre takes a small sip of the coffee as he peeks around cautiously. "Ssssip," he slurps. "Well...what did he say?"

The young girl then repeats word for word everything that the Mayor told her just as if she had recorded it. Dre listens carefully as she's speaking. He shakes his head from side to side with a look of disgust on his face.

Dre doesn't take his little brother's threat lightly. One thing he knows about his brother, he does exactly what he says he will do. He's definitely a man of his word. Furthermore, he's the most stubborn person Dre has ever encountered. Ever since he was a kid, it was either his way or no way, and he's always been a sore loser. Dre has tried his hardest to avoid doing what his brother wants him to do because he expects Dre to make some moves that he totally opposes. He fears that the moves will only dig the Mayor into a deeper hole. He now knows that the only way he'll be able to continue getting money, he'll have to give in to him. As much as he hates to do it, he has no other choice. "Stubborn motherfucker," he whispers sternly.

///// CHAPTER 10 /////

Dre sits at the small candlelit table, outside of Voro in South Orange. To the right of him sits, Latif, and to the left sits Mu-Mit. They're sitting close but they have to strain their ears in order to hear him speak over the loud music. He takes a huge gulp of the seltzer water, just to wet his whistle. He clears his throat. "Unghh um. Dig, I spoke to Lil Bruh and this is how it's going down," he whispers. "He wants the town. I'mma keep it real with ya'll...I really don't want no parts of this fucked up city but...ya'll already know how he is? It's his way or no way. He made it perfectly clear, that if we don't abide by the rules, he's cutting off our lifeline, bottom line. With that being said, it's time to play ball," he says as he peeks around suspiciously. "I got a list of a few names of cats ya'll need to get in contact with. Holler at them one by one. I'll give it to ya'll at 180. Ya'll offer to them at 220 a brick and let's see what comes out of that?

"Hmphh," Latif sighs as he looks away with frustration on his face.

"What up, La?" Dre asks. "You got a problem with something I said? Let me know? Put it on Front Street. That's why we're here at the round table," he whispers as he smacks the table with the palm of his hand.

"Yeah, I got a problem," he admits staring Dre straight in the eyes. "I'll tell you what's gon' come out of it...nothing. These young motherfuckers doing them. They ain't gone be trying to hear no old head motherfuckers coming out here changing the rules and dictating to them how shit is gon' be. The only thing these punk mufuckers respect is pressure. I say we run all these sucker ass niggas out the town and just do us."

"And how we gone do that?" Dre asks sarcastically. "By murdering everyone in the town?"

"If we have to," Latif replies sternly.

"Then you'll have a massacre and no one will be able to get money," Dre replies. "Listen, that route ain't gone get us nothing but 100 years apiece. The key to this whole shit is doing it smoothly. If we gotta crack a couple of asses along the way, then so be it," he says holding his hands palm up in the air. "But if we don't have to, that's all the better."

"Dre, man, I'm with La," Mu-Mit adds. "You talking about a day that no longer exists. That shit played out. Young niggas already rich doing it their way. If you think they just gone stop doing what they already doing and turn their entire game over to us, then I'm here to tell you...you living on Fantasy Island."

Dre hesitates before speaking. "I don't see it like that," says Dre. "I look at it like this...we got the best smack on the planet. Why would they go against that? If they're smart, they'll get with us."

"Yeah, keyword...smart," Mu-Mit replies. "How you gone think logical, when you dealing with niggas who don't use logic? Ignorant mufuckers only respect ignorance. That's the only way you'll get their attention. You have to let them know that we're not bullshitting. You gotta show them. These young mufuckers don't care nothing about what we used to do. In their minds we ain't nothing but a bunch of washed up old heads trying to get another run. And they ain't trying to hear that. It's their turn."

"Hey man, we all been around for a while," Latif reminds. "Think of all the successful niggas you done seen," says Latif. "Do you know why Akbar was successful? Cause he didn't give a mufucker a choice...that's why. There was no option. You give a mufucker a choice, he gone always choose the alternative. Ak had the right idea. If you gone work, you gone work with him, bottom line. Just like Lil Bruh. He didn't give options either."

"You're correct in that aspect but look at both of the examples you just gave. Neither one of them are successful because they're both behind the wall. You know why? Greed and ego. You can't control it all. When you start putting that type of pressure on dudes, you don't give them no choice but to put the boys on you," Dre says.

"That's a whole nother khutbah," Mu-Mit says casually. "Pressure ain't got nothing to do with these niggas telling. These weak ass niggas gone do that either way," Mu-Mit replies. "These fag motherfuckers gon' do that, if we put the pressure or if we continue to let them do them. It's just who they are. It's how they're bred. I blame that on the fag ass Italian boy, Sammy the Bull. He made it alright to snitch."

"See, ya'll got a different mindset when it comes to this," Dre replies. "I ain't mad at ya'll though. Ya'll are murderers and you're thinking how murderers should. Me, on the other hand...I'm a money getter. Both are essential to make a complete team. One without the other is useless. That's why we need each other to operate as a unit. Ya'll stick to the murder and leave all the thinking up to me," Dre says as he pats his own chest. "That way we can all be successful in getting this money. How does that sound? At the end of the day, we're all trying to get a dollar, right or wrong?" Both Latif and Mu-Mit both agree by head nod. "Ok, then this is the deal...Lil Bro gave the word that he wants all projects and housing complexes throughout this town. Baxter Terrace, Stephen Crane, Bradley Court, Pennington Court, all of 'em. Street corner activity, we have no concern with, unless," he says as he holds his index finger high in the air. "Unless, they're making some real noise. We step to all the key players. Hopefully, they'll roll with us. If they don't, then we have no choice but to roll over them. That's when all your murdering mind set comes into play," he laughs. "I thought I'd never ever say these words in my life but from here on out, Brick City is ours. Like Lil Bro said...if we can't have it all, then we burn it down," he says with a determined look on his face. At this time, 8 p.m., June 12, 2007, operation shutdown is officially in effect," he whispers sternly.

///// CHAPTER 11 /////

Mu-Mit sits sprawled across the park bench inside of Military Park on Broad Street. He sits there patiently. The sight of Latif pacing back and forth is driving him crazier by the second. They've been here for almost two hours now, stalking their prey.

From the park, they have a clear view of the silver CLS Mercedes Benz which sits across the street. The Mercedes belongs to Jay. Jay is one of the players on the top of the Mayor's list. Mu-Mit and Latif had to do their homework to track him down and get the low down on him. They managed to find out that this project complex is only his base. This project produces about a 75 brick-a-day flow. Still and all this complex is only the foundation to his enterprise. His real bread and butter come from the many bricks of dope he soars through on the wholesale tip.

Finally, the moment that they've been waiting for has arrived. Mu-Mit spots the frail man limping up the block. They were told that he can be recognized by the limp in his walk, which is the aftermath of a neighborhood shootout that he had gotten into.

"That's him," Mu-Mit says as he quickly rises up from the bench. Latif's eyes stretch wide open with anxiousness. He immediately starts stepping. "Hold up, hold up, easy," Mu-Mit says.

Slowly they both cross Broad Street. The heavy flow of on-coming traffic makes it quite difficult to do so. As he approaches his car, they pick their step up, in order to catch up to him. Just as he grabs hold of his door, Latif shouts, "Jay!"

Jay turns around abruptly. A look of confusion is on his face as he studies the two foreign faces, trying to figure out who they are. He has no clue of who they are. He sneakily places his hand underneath his shirt, as he backs away from his car, giving himself room to maneuver.

Latif realizes what he's doing. "Easy, Daddy!" he shouts. "Peace," he says as he lifts his shirt up, allowing him to view his empty waistband. He raises his hands high in the air and spins around slowly. "We come in peace," he whispers as they stand face to face with about twenty five feet in between them.

Mu-Mit has managed to get onto the sidewalk where he stands on the passenger's side of the vehicle. From where he's standing he has a clean shot at the man.

Jay attempts to watch both of them, back and forth. He quickly snatches his gun from his waist and holds it close to the back of his thigh.

"Easy, easy," Latif says sternly.

Mu-Mit has already beaten him to the draw. "Don't even think about it," Mu-Mit says as he aims his gun high.

Jay turns around, staring straight into the barrel of the .44 cannon. Now he stands there baffled.

"Listen Daddy, we ain't here for no drama. We come in peace. Let's put these pistols away before we all get knocked off out this motherfucker? You Jay, right?" Latif asks hoping that hearing his name will make him feel some type of comfort.

"Who you?" he asks with major aggressiveness in his voice.

"Pardon me, let me introduce myself," he says as he extends his hand for a handshake. "I'm La."

"La, who?" Jay asks as he leaves Latif's hand dangling in mid-air.

"Ay man, put the gun up, first and foremost," he says as he snatches his hand out of the air. "Ain't no need for them. Mu, put it away. Show him we ain't on no bullshit. Mu-Mit slowly tucks his hand inside his pocket, but Jay still keeps his gun concealed by his thigh.

"Yo, who you?" Jay asks furiously.

"I'm Latif. You know the Mayor?"

"The Mayor?" he asks in a high pitched voice.

"Yeah, from up the hill. 'Block Party,' Mayor."

Block Party, Jay thinks to himself for a second. "Oh yeah, what about him?"

"Well, he sent us to come rap to you. He wants to let you know that everything is everything. He's back in business."

"And?" Jay asks defensively. "What that mean to me?"

"Ay, I'm just relaying the message. Apparently, ya'll had some type of business arrangement back in the day?"

"Yeah, you said it right. Back in the day," he repeats.

"Listen, Daddy, you taking this all wrong. He ain't on that King of Newark shit this time. He got a different approach," Latif lies. "Every man has his own right to do him. Either you roll or you don't have to. He told me that ya'll had a rapport and he thinks that you would probably be more than willing to hear him out. It's simple as this...I don't know what your situation is right now, but the boy got it good. You already know how he do? The smack is a 10 all over the land. Ain't nothing on the street fucking with it. He already doing him in a few spots but the boy want to stretch out a little bit. All I ask is, take a couple of samples and let it do what it do? Your choice," Latif whispers while digging deep inside of his pocket, retrieving a brick. He slowly hands it over to Jay. "It ain't gone hurt to check it out. I'm telling you, ain't nothing out here better, trust me. And price wise he gone corner the market. He's willing to give it to you at 200 a brick. Hopefully for the benefit of all of us, you won't refuse."

Jay hesitantly grabs hold of the brick. He reads the words "The 'After Party' that is printed across the top bag of the tiny square package. His mind quickly wanders back to the days when the Mayor was on the street. He used to buy work from the Mayor. Although the Mayor didn't give him a choice back then, he still had no problem with it because it really was the best dope in the town. Today is different though. He has a choice. He no longer has to buy dope unless he chooses to do so. He's his own man now, with his own squad who moves at his command. He may not have the money the Mayor had, but he does have some power. He has a good mind to throw the dope back into Latif's face, but his curiosity wants to know how good the dope really is. For all he knows this could be the dope that the town needs right now. With the overflow of garbage dope on the street, this might just be what the game has been missing.

"Just see what it do," Latif says. "You got a number, so I can check up on you?"

"Check up on me?" he asks sarcastically. "You ain't gotta check up on me. I don't owe you shit," he whispers. "I'll be around. I ain't hard to find. I'm right here in the projects all day, everyday," he says arrogantly.

Latif snickers at his tough, arrogant talk, but it's really pissing him off immensely. "I got you, playboy," he smiles. "So, I'll come back through in a day or two, alright?"

"Ay, whatever. That's up to you," he says as he snatches his door open. He holds his gun tightly until he's seated inside of his vehicle. Seconds later, he peels off, leaving them with stupid looks on their faces.

A frown quickly appears on Latif's face. "I swear to God on my Momma, I hope he go against the plan. I see right now, this shit ain't gone work. Begging and pleading with these arrogant, sucker ass niggas. I can't do it! Somebody else gon' have to handle that part. Just call me in when it's time to shut a mufucker down. One day...that's it. That's all he got. 24 motherfucking hours. If he don't put in a mufucking order within 1440 minutes, I'm peeling his shit smooth back," he says sternly as they proceed across the street furiously. "Please God, let this nigga go against the plan?"

▗▛▗▛▗▛ CHAPTER 12 ▗▛▗▛▗▛

Attorney, Tony Austin steps out of Miami International Airport. His white linen suit is extremely crinkled from his constant tossing and turning during his flight. Even full of wrinkles he looks extremely fashionable. His Louis Vutton printed flip flops matches his luggage perfectly. Stylish aviator shades protect his eyes from the hot beaming sun. The silk printed Louis Vutton handkerchief that is tied around his neck, makes him resemble, Thurston Howell from Gilligan's Island.

Just as he steps onto the curbside, his car service pulls up and he hops right on in. "Exotic Car Rentals on Biscayne Boulevard, Playboy," he yells.

Meanwhile back in Newark

Tony's wife, Mocha walks beside her good friend, Sincere as they board the airplane at Newark International Airport. Mocha holds Sincere by the waist as she takes baby steps using her aluminum cane as an aide.

Sincere has been like this for many years now, yet Mocha still hasn't gotten used to it. Seeing her best friend in this condition breaks her heart more and more each day. The bad part is, she takes all the blame for the situation. Oh how she wishes she would have stayed out of Sincere and Suave's business. If only she would have left Sincere alone instead of persuading her to creep around on Suave while he was locked up.

Cheating was never a part of Sincere's makeup. She was so happy and content with Suave. Suave was the first man that she ever had in her life and if it wasn't for Mocha, he would have probably been her last and only man. Mocha now realizes that all the while, she was actually jealous of the relationship Sincere and Suave had. At that time she couldn't understand it because she didn't have a clue of what real love was about. She has always been girl number two and she was perfectly fine with that. Well at least she thought she was. In her eyes, men were put on this earth only to spoil and cater to women and that's all she expected from them. Now, it's completely different though. She appreciates and respects love to the fullest, thanks to her husband, Tony. He's made her the happiest woman in the world. She's completely happy until reality sets in that she's responsible for destroying her best friend's life. She always wonders how life would have been for the two best friends if the tragedy never occurred. She could picture it so clearly. Both of them would be happily in love with their husbands, living the American Dream.

They finally get seated in the First Class section of the airplane. Sincere hasn't traveled since the tragedy. Being on an airplane again takes her mind back in the day when she and Suave were traveling the world. Before she was nineteen years old, Suave had already taken her places the average women could only dream of going. "Hmpphh," she sighs quietly. Oh how she misses her love, Suave. As the tears begin to pour down her face, she turns toward the window to hide from Mocha.

Mocha hears her sniffling. "Girl, I know you not crying again?" she asks with a broken heart. She's quite sure that she is though. Sincere has been crying for almost a year now, since Suave walked out on her. She's been in a state of depression ever since. "Girl, stop crying?" she begs. "It's gone be alright," she says with her mouth but not even believing it herself.

"I hate my life," Sincere cries.

"Don't say that. It can be worse."

"Worse?" Sincere asks sarcastically. "What could be worse?"

"Death."

"Death would be better."

"Stop it, Sincere, please!" Mocha pleads.

"Mo, I look back at my life and ask myself how did I get in this situation. This wasn't supposed to happen to me. I was a good faithful girl. I stood by my man all the way through. How did I ever get mixed up in all of that mess? I'm not a cheater," she cries. "How? How?" she asks. Tears begin pouring down Mocha's face as well. She can't reply with words. She just pats Sincere's back for comfort.

"How could Suave just up and leave me like that?" she asks. "Oh, what am I talking about? I broke his heart, that's how" she laughs goofily. "Still...he knows how sorry I am for doing that. I hate him for leaving me like this, but I understand him. Look at me, I'm crippled. Who wants a crippled ass wife who is cripple because she chose to cheat on her dude instead of keeping it real with him. He told me that my condition haunted him. He said, looking at me was a constant reminder of the situation. It got so bad, that he couldn't even look me in the eyes. How could I do that to him? He was a good man at that," she cries. "Suave is any woman's dream come true, but I messed up. How could I hurt him like that? He was all I had, Mo. Why did it have to go like this? Huh?"

"Girl, I don't know. I wish I had the answers but I don't," Mocha cries. Mocha hates that Suave left her but deep down inside she can't blame him.

"I knew the day would come when he would say those words to me. Ever so often, I would have nightmares about him telling me that he couldn't do it any longer. I tried to prepare myself for the day because I knew it was coming, but when it did, all my preparations meant nothing. Mo, he's all I had," she cries.

"You got me," she whispers. "Stop crying, girl," Mo says crying harder than Sincere at this time. She continuously pats Sincere's back. "Don't cry no more," she begs.

"I can't help it."

"Yes, you can...just try. Promise me one thing?"

"What's that?" Sincere asks.

"Leave all your tears right here in Newark. No crying in Miami. That's what this vacation is all about. We're going down there to relax, girl. No stress, no worries. Just us on the topless beach, letting it all hang out," she smirks, attempting to make Sincere laugh. "Tanning and drinking Mojitos."

Sincere laughs as Mocha hoped she would. "I ain't gone promise you topless," she admits, as she looks down at her beautiful set. "No crying, but topless...I can't promise," she laughs.

Three Hours Later

Tony struts gracefully out of Prime 112 Steak House. He steps toward the street, where the most beautiful vehicle in the world awaits him. The canary yellow Ferrari sits there with the top dropped, glistening like a precious diamond. He snatches the door open and sits inside. Seconds later, the engine roars like a lion, breaking everyone's attention, causing them to stare. As he sits there revving the engine up, he pulls from the center console, an 8-inch Zino Platinum Cigar and sticks it inside his mouth. After lighting it, thick clouds of smoke fill the car instantly.

He peels out of the parking space recklessly. Scccuuurrr! He quickly presses play on his CD. The voice of Steppenwolf blares through the speakers. He blows out a mouthful of thick smoke. "I was...born to be wiiiild!" he shouts at the top of his lungs as he speeds up Ocean Drive.

A Few Miles Away

Mocha escorts Sincere to the passenger's side of the candy apple red Lamborghini. Sincere slowly seats herself, while Mocha places the cane on the floor of the car. Mocha then jumps into the driver's seat shortly after. She automatically hits the stereo system. 'Don't you wish your girlfriend was hot like me," rips through the speakers loudly. As they cruise up the block, they both sing along.

Mocha turns the volume down at the end of the song. She then quickly begins dialing numbers on the cell phone.

"Yes Wife?" Tony answers in a playful manner.

"Where you at, nigga?" Mocha asks in a playful manner.

"Where I'm at? Where I'm at?" he replies in a playful manner as well. "I am where I am!" he shouts. "MIA...You already know!"

"I know that, fool! Where at in MIA? You know what I mean."

"On 14th Street."

"On 14th Street? What's over there?" Silence fills the air. Tony doesn't say a word. "Hello! I said what's over there?"

"Nothing, just cruising," he replies.

"Cruising my ass, nigga. Why you hesitate to answer?" she questions. Her jealousy takes over. She doesn't play when it comes to her Tony. Her insecurities always seem to get the best of her and make her act like this. She's so afraid that karma will bite her on the ass. All the happy homes that she has messed up in her heart breaking days, stealing and cheating with women's husbands makes her afraid that someone will step in and take the only man that she's ever really loved. "Motherfucker, where you at?"

"I told you on 14th," he whispers, sounding extremely guilty of something.

"For what?" she questions hastily. "Nigga stop playing with me. What's on 14th?"

"I gotta ride past the Women's Detention Center," he whispers.

"Women's Detention Center? For what?"

"I gotta see somebody," he mumbles.

"Oh hell no!" she shouts. "We're not here for business. Didn't you say this was vacation? Ah, ah," she sighs. "You lying nigga. I should have known this was work related.

"Nah, Mo...I just gotta go holler at somebody. This is vacation," he claims.

"Whatever," she snaps before hanging up in his ear.

"Mo," he shouts before he hears the dial tone.

"Uh, someone is jealous," Sincere teases.

"Damn right, bitch," Mocha laughs. "I'll be got damn! That motherfucker know I don't play with his ass. I'll kill him and a bitch." Both Sincere and Mocha laugh.

30 Minutes Later

Tony sits patiently in the visiting hall of Dade County Women's Detention Center. Suddenly his attention is caught by one of the most gorgeous sights that he has ever laid eyes on. Through the many women prisoners that are huddled at the door, attempting to enter, one stands out far from the rest.

All the women prisoners scatter to their separate tables, where their families have been awaiting them, except for one. She stands in the center of the room with a look of confusion on her beautiful face. Her smooth, bronze colored skin glistens like an angel. Her jet black silky hair drapes over the shoulders of her orange prison jumpsuit, which hugs her broad hips and bowlegs tightly. Prison has given her ten extra but well proportioned pounds that have fallen in all the right places.

"Miranda Benderas?" Tony shouts as he stares at the beauty that sets before his very eyes. She has all natural beauty. Standing here in an orange jumpsuit with no make up, she's still more gorgeous than any supermodel that he's ever seen.

She steps toward him at the sound of her name. As she gets closer to him, Tony extends his hand to greet her with a handshake. He's speechless. His professionalism disappears. Never has he seen a woman this beautiful in all his life. She attempts to pull her hand away, but Tony has a tight grip on it. Her beauty actually has him mesmerized. A, a...attorney, Tony Austin," he stutters foolishly. Finally, he lets her hand go and they both seat themselves at the wooden table.

"Who are you? How do you know me? Who sent you here?" she questions arrogantly, putting up this huge tough girl front.

"Slow down, Mami," he laughs, finally regaining his composure. He has now regained his confidence. "One question at a time," he smiles, showing his newly polished pearly whites which damn near blind her. "Who am I? Let's just say, I'm your lifesaver. We're going to give this time back by way of appeal. Your father hired me to get you out of this mess and that's what I'm going to do," he says to her as he looks her dead in the eyes, melting her away. The Mayor actually hired Tony to get her off. He felt so bad for her father, that it was the least he could do.

"Thank you, thank you," she says as the tears flow from her eyes. Tony grabs both of her hands attempting to comfort her. His tight grip reassures her and gives her a sense of hope.

"No more tears...I got you, Mami," he says arrogantly. "Wipe your eyes, girlfriend. It's over. You can bet your pretty face on that," he mumbles under his breath.

///// CHAPTER 13 /////

Dre slowly cruises up South Orange Avenue. The blazing sun beams through his windshield, almost blinding him. He makes the quick right turn onto South Center Street. He admires the beautiful homes as he passes them. Just as he passes his mark, he slows down. After the oncoming traffic passes he makes a left turn and drives cautiously up the driveway of a beautiful, one family home, which is about the size of a small mansion.

Dre has to stop short mid-way up the driveway due to the many cars that block the passageway. He gets out and walks slowly toward the backyard. The first car he passes is a beautiful Porshe Carrera, then a Porsche 911, and the third and final vehicle is a Porsche Cayenne Bi-Turbo SUV. The alley looks more like a Porsche dealership.

He stops short at the end of the alley. His eyes are drawn to the huge in-ground pool with the overhanging diving board. The clear blue water sparkles beautifully. Dre then admires the two lifeguard chairs that set on a hill above the pool. The back of the first chair reads Emily, and the other reads Frank. The backyard even has a miniature golf course.

Dre stands there just scanning the beautiful yard until his eyes land upon a more beautiful sight. About fifty feet away from him there's a body of milky white skin sprawled across a lawn chair, which sets in the corner of the yard. Embarrassment fills Dre's heart when his eyes are drawn to the perky pink nipples of the woman's enormous breasts. He quickly turns around attempting to make his exit out of the yard without her knowing that he's seen her. Just as he turns around. "Dre!" the sweet voice sounds off, startling him. He turns around as slow as he can. Through the corner of his eye, he can see her sitting up on the edge of the lawn chair. By now he's fully about-faced and there he finds her standing there shamelessly with her breasts still exposed. She turns around giving him the mooning of a lifetime as she bends over to slide her flip-flops on her feet. The thin spaghetti strap of her g-string runs up the crack of her huge, rounded rear and disappears.

She turns around, walking toward him. Her huge breasts bounce heavily. "Just sun bathing," she whispers. "Trying to darken this pale white skin of mine," she laughs, exposing her beautiful smile. "Why were you leaving?" she asks.

"Uh, uh...I thought you were sleep," he lies. He quickly lowers his gaze to keep her from seeing the lust that may lie in his eyes.

She wraps a towel around her neck, allowing the ends to drape over her breasts, attempting to cover them but she'll need two of those towels to do that. There's barely enough towel to cover them. Her pink porno nipples peek from behind the terry-cloth.

As she struts towards him, he can't help but stare at her gorgeous body. She struts with the confidence and the sexy swagger of a porn star. They lock eyes. Her emerald green eyes, slightly closed are extremely sexy to Dre. They spell out pure freak.

"Dre, baby, this way," she says as she leads him into the house. Dre's breath is snatched away at the entrance of the lavish home. Antique furniture floods the house. Expensive paintings cover the walls, and thick area rugs cover the floors. The huge mahogany grand piano steals Dre's attention. As a child, he wanted to be a famous piano player. He even took lessons in school. Disappointingly, he went from playing keys to slinging keys, killing his childhood dreams. Oh how he would love to just sit at the piano and play a few tunes.

"Baby, c'mon," she calls interrupting Dre's thoughts. She leads him down the steps to the basement. The finished basement has all the contents of a fitness center; wall to wall mirrors, treadmills, stair climbers, a ping pong table and any other piece of exercise equipment imagined. A Plasma televisions hangs from the corner ceiling of each wall.

She makes her way through a door, where she stays for a couple of minutes. She reappears, lugging a huge cardboard box in her hands. "Unghh," she sighs as she drops it to the floor.

Dre bends over and digs inside. There sits over 4,000 bags (800) bricks of After Party. The package was just delivered a few short hours ago. Dre and Emily made the move together as usual. Dre felt so good getting his hands on the work again. The Mayor made him give him his word before contacting the plug and giving them the official ok to serve him again. Dre hated to do so, but he knew he had to in order to get back to business.

Dre pulls from the box, 250 bricks and dumps them into a plastic shopping bag.

"Dre, baby do you think you'll need to come back tomorrow?"

"Shit, I hope so...why?"

"Because my husband comes back tomorrow and I think he'll be home most of the day."

"I may," he says slowly debating back and forth with himself. "I'll take a couple more, just in case," he says as he grabs hold of another 50 bricks.

"If it's going to inconvenience you, don't worry about it."

"It's no inconvenience," he lies, knowing damn well he doesn't have a place to put the rest of the dope. He never likes to have work in his possession. He figures the less you have it in your possession the less your chances of going to jail are. He'd rather take what he needs when he needs it.

"Never mind, don't worry. Even if he's home I'll come up with something," she states. "He doesn't question me like that. I can tell him anything."

"How long will he be in town for?"

"I'm not sure. He's coming to town for some convention. I think he's leaving back out in a couple of days though. The sooner, the better," she sighs.

Dre snickers at her remark.

"What?" she laughs. "Well, it's the truth. Who needs him here? His only purpose here is his checkbook," she laughs. "It's all business," she adds sarcastically.

"You're crazy," Dre laughs.

"Not crazy," she replies. "It's all about stability, baby...that's it. "Look at me," she says as she spins around sexily. "You thought a beautiful girl like me married an old fart like him for love? I'm afraid not," she mumbles. "My parents raised me to marry for stability not for love. That's the problem with your African Americans. You're so stuck on that love shit. Love can't pay the bills. Nothing plus nothing equals nothing. Tina Turner said it best. What's love got to do with it?" she smiles devilishly.

Twenty Minutes Later

Dre pulls into the parking lot of Rite Aid. As soon as he parks, a man who appears to be in his mid-thirties hops into Dre's passenger's seat. "Dre, what's going on Baby?" the man says with a look of despair in his eyes.

"It's all green!" Dre replies. "What's going on with you?"

"Shit...Wifey bugging, 4 kids eating up all the food, outgrowing their clothes by the day, wife credit card bills charged up to the max," he complains. "Bitch had the nerve to disrespect the kid, talking about I gotta get a J.O.B!" he laughs.

"Nah?" Dre laughs.

"Yeah," he confirms, nodding his head up and down. "That bad," he snickers. "Man, I been home for six months already and I ain't had $2,500 in my hand at once yet. I been getting a lil bullshit dope from my nephews just to keep a couple of dollars in my pocket. And they taxing the shit out of me, $325 a brick. Stepping on my fucking neck. That ain't no room to do shit but take it to the ground. I been on the block hand to handing."

"Fuck outta here," Dre says. "On the block, where?"

"Riverside," he mumbles casually. "The projects."

"Wow! Z, it can't be that bad?"

"I ain't have no choice. Man, I come home to nothing. I had to do something. No where to turn. Man, I didn't know shit was fucked up like it is. All my niggas either knocked off or dead. A few of them dudes still around, but the ones who are, they squared the fuck up on me, working and shit. They ain't got shit to give me. Shit crazy! When I left I had the whole town on smash and to come home to taking packs from my lil nephews? Man!" he grunts as he shakes his head from side to side with despair. "I had the gun to my head, ready to blow my brains out, right when you called," he jokes. "I'm broke, busted, but I can be trusted. Please tell me something good... Anything?" he begs.

"Ay man, the nightmare is over. I'm home now. I told you I was gone take care of you. What, you thought I was bullshitting? I don't talk just to hear myself talk. It's time to sing a different tune now. We gone make it happen. You been away for seven years. It's time to catch up," Dre says staring him in the eyes. Dre can see the starvation in his eyes.

"When, when?" he says in a high-pitched voice. "I can't take another day of this shit."

"Say no more," Dre says as he hands the plastic bag over to him.

His eyes light up like a Christmas tree. "What you got in here?" he says with a cracking voice.

"The key to your happiness," he smiles. "50 bricks."

"50? Thanks, thanks," he says with gratitude.

"Eat, nigga. Give me back, $250 a brick...12-5."

"No doubt. Man, I should be able to breeze through these in a few days. Niggas been waiting for me. I just ain't have shit for them."

"Well, now you do," he says sarcastically. Dre digs into his pocket retrieving a stack of bills. He peels off a short stack and hands it over to the passenger. "Here."

"What's that?"

"Twenty-five hundred," he says casually. "Now you can't say you ain't had $2,500.00 at once. That's my coming home present to you."

The man sits there quietly for a matter of seconds. "Thanks."

"Don't thank me again, Z. Just get money. Now get the hell outta my car before we both go back to prison," Dre laughs.

"Yo, I'll hit you when I get halfway through them," Zaid says as he's getting out.

"Yo, hold up. I almost forgot," Dre says. "Here," he says as he passes his man a cell phone. The man looks at the phone in a baffled manner. "From here on out, only call me from this phone. Never use this phone when calling anyone else. You hear me? This is for us and no one else? Ok?" Dre plans to give everyone on his squad a phone just for them to politic on. This way this line will be clean of any other business that they may be involved in. He feels this will eliminate the risk of the Feds getting onto him for some other situation that he may not have anything to do with.

"Got you," he says before slamming the door. "I love you, nigga," he whispers. He then skips to his car like a kid with a bag full of candy.

Dre watches carefully as the car with the out-of-state plates exits the parking lot. The man is Dre's boy from Delaware. They spent about a year together at FCI Schuykill, in Pennsylvania. All the while they were knocked off, they planned on coming home and hooking up and now the day has finally come. "Delaware down," Dre mumbles under his breath.

Dre meets with another client in the parking lot of ShopRite. The man slams the door after sitting down in the car. He slams the door so hard that he almost shatters the passenger window. He damn near dives into Dre's lap with excitement. He plants the wettest kiss on Dre's cheek, giving Dre the shock of a lifetime. "Muaaahhh! I love you, nigga! No bullshit. You changed my fucking life," he says with excitement on his face. "That shit is the truth! Man, listen to me... you got a gold mine on your hands. You hear me? I got the town on smash! That shit right there putting everything to shame...no competition. Everybody trying to get their hands on that shit!" he shouts. "Boy, I owe you!"

Dre smiles modestly. "Ay man, it is what it is."

"Man that shit shutting shit down!"

"Why wouldn't it?" Dre asks arrogantly. "You know if I stand behind something it has to be official. You know I ain't gone just put my name on some dumb shit." he says as he hands over the work. He hands him a cell phone as well. "This phone here, is our line only. Don't call anyone else from this line. You got me?"

"Got you," he answers casually, barely paying attention to the phone. "How many bricks you got in there?" the man asks as he grabs hold of the bag.

"That's , 200, right there. Just give me the 50 money on the next ride," Dre says casually.

"Bet nigga...will do," he says as he hands a bag full of money over to Dre. "Here, that's 30 cash($30,000). Give me about three days," he whispers. "I'll be right back at you, my nigga."

This is Dre's man from Harlem. They spent about two years together Upstate New York. He's from Harlem, but he makes his living out of town in Binghamton, New York. He's been home for close to a year now after doing four years. Dre got in contact with him a week and a half ago. His first flip was 50 bricks. His flip has increased to 150 bricks in just 10 days, thanks to the 'After Party'. Dre plans to build the man up to 500 bricks a week. He's sure he can do that in no time. All the man has to do is play his position and do what Dre tells him to do. The rest is clockwork. He plans to move him up the ladder slowly, increasing his workload a little at a time. Dre is sure his man knows how to play the game on the level that he's used to playing on, but Dre plans to teach him how to play on a bigger scale. The man may know how to play checkers, but Dre will now teach him to play chess. He will teach him the game slowly, step by step, making sure that he doesn't miss a step, and learns every aspect of the game as he climbs the ladder of success.

"Yo, Bee, I don't know how much of this shit you got, but whatever you do, put something to the side for me?"

"Don't worry, I got you, Daddy. This shit unlimited, trust me."

"This the same shit, right?" he asks with a desperate look in his eyes. "You know how mufuckers be doing, giving you the good shit in the beginning, then once they get you hooked, they start feeding you the garbage." Dre doesn't even reply, but his eyes say it all as he looks at him as if he's just said the dumbest shit in the world. "Alright, well, I'll be back in about 2 days. Be ready!"

"No question," Dre replies.

"Alright, let me get out of here, one!" he shouts as he rushes out of the car.

Ten minutes later, Dre parks in front of Carvel Ice Cream on South Orange Avenue in South Orange. This is his last move for the day and he dreads this one the most.

The middle aged man hops into the car. "What's up?" he whispers.

Dre doesn't reply with words. He only acknowledges him by head nod. He pulls five bricks from his pocket and passes them over to the man without ever looking at him. He just continuously stares straight ahead, hating that he's even dealing with this client.

"Alright, take care," the man says as he exits the vehicle. As he bends over to get out, Dre notices a 40 Millimeter handgun sitting inside of a leather holster, peeking from underneath the man's shirt, on his right hip.

"Pssst," Dre says as he shakes his head from side to side.

The man slams the door shut and Dre pulls off quickly. "Stupid, stupid, stupid," he mumbles as he cruises up the block.

⫻⫻⫻ CHAPTER 14 ⫻⫻⫻

Next Day

The Mayor lies back in his cell, with his feet propped up on a small refrigerator, as he watches King of New York. He repeats word after word as actor Christopher Walken speaks. The Mayor knows the words to every gangster movie ever made. Ever since he was a little boy he would watch and study Mob flicks. He would analyze them and break everything down to a science. He bases his life on these movies. You can't tell him that he's not an organized crime boss. "No Blackjack, no nothing," he says as he whispers right along with the words that come out of Christopher Walken's mouth.

A shadow zips pass The Mayor's cell, grabbing his attention. Seconds later, a man appears at the doorway. The Mayor squints his eyes to get a clear picture. It's his main man, US Marshal Jackson. Ever since he aided the Mayor with the murder of Mob boss, Vinnie Balducci, he's established a certain amount of comfort with him.

The Marshal peeks from side to side nervously, making sure no one is watching. He then gives the Mayor a head nod.

The Mayor rushes to the opening of the cell. "What up?"

"Here it is," he whispers as he passes the Mayor the five bricks of 'After Party' that he got from Dre yesterday.

Just holding the dope in his hand gives the Mayor an instant hard-on. Dre hated to give the Marshall the dope. He only did it because he gave the Mayor his word that he would. Dre doesn't trust the Marshal the least bit but the Mayor on the other hand tried hard to reassure him that the Marshal is cool. Dre can only hope that the Mayor knows what he's doing.

The Mayor stares at the 'After Party' stamp. "Once again, it's on," he sings to himself as he thinks of the money he's about to make. A small percentage of the inmates here in Fort Dix are heroin addicts. He has so much faith in the 'After Party' that he's sure guys who are not addicts will become addicts once they get their hands on it. He already has it all set up. He has his team in order already, just waiting to get their hands on the dope. One bag on the street is $10, but in here the same bag goes for $40. Here he stands looking at $2,500 worth of dope, but in here it values at $10,000. What a come up, he says to himself. "If a nickel bag gets sold in the park, I want in!" he repeats with passion. "You guys got fat while everyone starved in the streets," he laughs satanically to himself. "It's my turn!"

//// CHAPTER 15 /////

ıy night and Ringside Sports Club in Jersey City is extremely ̣ ̣ ̣ ̣ ̣ ̣ ̣cu as usual. Women fill the place, but men still out number them 3 to 1. Huddles of small packs fill the bar.

One particular table sticks out the most because of the 20 bottles of champagne that occupy the area. The group consists of five males and eight females. The women sip the champagne while the men gulp away on Remy.

"One more bottle of Remy!" the handsome looking young man shouts to the woman behind the bar. "And bring the check too! I'm about to break out. I gotta get in. Wifey bugging!" he shouts with a smile. Right now he's as drunk as can be and it shows in his face.

The barmaid comes over and sits the bottle of Remy on the table. He then snatches the check from her hand. "$3600! Got damn!" he shouts while digging in his pocket. He peels four stacks from the 15 stacks that he has. "Keep the change!" he shouts in a cocky manner. "Damn, I didn't know we drunk that much," he says just the way he does every week. He's a regular here. He's the main attraction at Ringside. His name rings bells throughout the town and everyone seems to love him.

"I'm out," he says standing up. He rocks back and forth until he gains his balance. "Damn," he slurs. "I'm fucked all the way up," he laughs. Everyone at the table joins in with laughter.

"Nah nigga, you can't leave yet. You gotta crack the Remy at least?" Sha suggests.

"Hell no. I'm done."

"Come on man. Just one sip," Sha says. "Just one for the road?"

He gives in easily. "Alright, just one," he says before he turns the bottle up to his mouth. He gulps for seconds before pulling it away from his mouth. "Aghhh!" He frowns his face while shaking his head from side to side. "Damn!" The crowd bursts into laughter. "That's it. Your boy done," he smiles. "Later ya'll!" he shouts before walking away staggering.

In between taking his baby steps, he has to stop in order to regain enough balance to take a few more steps. It takes him all of ten minutes to make it to the door. He walks slowly to the corner to his right. He stands there rocking back and forth. He stands at the corner, just looking at his R class Mercedes wagon. He's too drunk to walk, let alone drive. No one who has any real concern for him would allow him to drive under these conditions.

Only twenty steps away yet he feels like he's so far.

"Come with me, Hail Mary. Run quick see, what do we have here," Latif sings along with Tupac's 'Hail Mary.' "Now, do you wanna ride or die? La dadada, la la la la."

The ringing of Mu-Mit's phone interrupts Latif's zone.

"Yeah?" Mu answers.

"Now," the voice whispers into the phone.

Mu-Mit doesn't reply. He just hangs up the phone in the man's ear.

48

"What up?" Latif asks anxiously.

"He's on his way," Mu informs as he turns around to see where the man is. "Yep, there he go."

"I'm getting out," Latif says.

"Nah. Wait 'till he get closer to his car."

The anxiety is ripping through Latif's gut. His heart is pounding and his mind is racing.

The man has managed to stagger his way to his car. Not even six steps away from his door and he decides to take a leak. He stands at the trunk, rocking back and forth.

"Now," Mu-Mit demands. Latif dashes out of the car like a race horse. In less than 4 seconds he's within arms reach of the man, who has his back facing Latif.

The drunken man feels a shadow over his shoulder and begins to turn around. "Ah ah," Latif says. "Don't turn around," he warns, while resting the gun on the back of the man's skull. "Don't move," he whispers. "You already know what it is," he says as he digs his hands into the man's pockets. He stuffs the man's money into his own pocket while peeking around. The drunken man goes against the rules and decides to turn his head around, disregarding Latif's wanrning. Latif smacks him across the back of the head with the gun. "What the fuck I say?"

"Aghh," the man sighs.

"Boom!" the .357 sounds off. The slug rips into the back of his head. The man drops to his knees instantly. He's in shock. He doesn't realize what just happened. Everything goes pitch black. The shot to his head has blinded him. He crawls around trying to find his way. "Boom! Boom!" Two shots slam into the top of his skull, forcing him to collapse onto the ground face first.

Latif kicks him just to measure his resistance. His body doesn't budge which tells him that the deal is sealed.

Latif then trots to the car and Mu-Mit peels off casually. Latif peeks around making sure there are no witnesses.

One Hour Later

Mu-Mit and Latif sit parked behind Penn Station. They watch attentively as a man hops out of a Ford F-150 pick-up truck that has just pulled up right in front of them.

Latif quickly gets out of the car, leaving the door wide open for the man. "Get in the front," Latif demands as he hops into the backseat.

The man pulls several stacks of money from his pocket as soon as he's seated. "Here," he says to Mu-Mit.

Mu-Mit quickly fumbles through the money counting ten stacks total. "How niggas was acting?"

"Everybody out there crying like a motherfucker. You know how it goes. Crocodile ass tears. Niggas don't really give a fuck. Put your face on a t-shirt, and wear it a couple of days and it's a wrap. Not giving a fuck about the nigga just wearing the shirt as another outfit. I know a lot of niggas is happy though. He got a lot of work left out there on the street. A lot of niggas came up!"

This is one of Mu-Mit's associates. He's from Jersey City. They met each other down Rahway prison. He uses Mu-Mit from time to time to come through and clean up his dirty work. The man was just murdered for being in his way.

"Yeah, I hated to do it to him, but he ain't give me no choice. Everything was cool. We moving like 200 bricks a day in my building in between two shifts. Shit was good! And here comes this nigga with the $7 bags. Fucked up everything. I pulled him to the side a few times, but he acted like he wasn't beat. What was I supposed to do?" he asks.

"What you did," Mu-Mit replies. "Nobody knows you had a problem with him right?"

"Nah, nah. We was just in there drinking together. As a matter of fact, I'm the one who souped him up to take the last drink," he informs them. "Man, they don't have a clue. I done heard ten different stories before I left. First it was a robbery. Then it was a a connect that he beat back in the day. Then it was the Bloods. Then it was his man who got knocked off and he let him sit in jail on a bullshit bail. Then it was this broad's husband. Man, they don't know shit."

"Good, Mu replies. He fumbles in his pocket, retrieving a brick of 'After Party'. "Here," he says as he hands it over. "That's the situation I told you about. Grade A, top quality."

"Word? What's the number on it?"

"Well, on the real to real, we getting it at 180 a brick, but I'm sure we can put something together where all of us can eat?"

"No question. As long as it's the right shit," Sha says.

"Oh, ain't no doubt about that. It's definitely the right shit."

"So, let me get a reading on it and I'll get back with you, alright?"

"Absolutely."

"I'm gone. Ya'll be safe," he says as he's getting out of the car. "Thanks!" he shouts from the sidewalk.

"No need for thank you's. We bigger than that. Anything come up, just holler. We'll be right there."

"Bet," he says as he backpedals away from the car.

Latif hops into the front seat.

Mu-Mit quickly peels $5,000 from the ten thousand and hands it over to Latif.

Latif quickly piles the 5 stacks onto the stacks that he took from the man before he robbed him. The man had over $11,000.00 on him. They made almost $12,000.00 apiece for twenty seconds worth of work. "Who said there's no business like show business?" Latif asks while wearing a big smile.

///// CHAPTER 16 /////

Days Later

Dre stands in the center of Red Hook Projects in Brooklyn New York. It's 7 a.m. and the projects are packed like a summer evening. People swarm the court like there's a parade going on. Dope feigns pour in from every entrance. Total confusion are the two words that best describe the scenery. Dope-feigns scatter around, zipping in and out of the courts. Each corner is packed with customers bent over with their noses buried deep in the small packets of dope. Other feigns are huddled up with syringes dug deep in their veins.

Dre has never seen anything like this in all his years of hustling. He can't believe his eyes. The customers look so deteriorated, almost like something from the movie 'Dawn of the Dead.'

He looks over to his right, where a young teen age boy stands with his back up against the wall, with a bag in his hand. In front of him is a line which consists of about 100 customers. They're lined up perfectly, like they're in a soup line. "Here, Auntie, take two. Let me know what it do?" the boy says as he hands the woman two bags of dope.

"Thank you, baby," she shouts. "What's the name of it?"

"After Party. It's fire! That's what we gone have out here from now on. Check us out!"

"Sure will," she says as she runs away with lightening speed.

"One per person!" the boy shouts as he passes the next man in line a bag. "Keep it moving! Don't crowd me. I got enough for everybody!" he adds.

They've been giving away samples of the 'After Party' for nearly two hours now. This was all Dre's idea to come out here the busiest shift of the day to pass out free samples.

His man Smooth, runs these projects. He told Dre that he moves almost 100 bricks per day of the dope that he already has. He claims that nothing can touch the dope that he's getting. He and Dre developed a tight bond in prison but even their friendship won't get in the way of his money. No way will he cut off his current connect to get dope of a lesser stature from Dre just to make Dre happy.

Dre has already given away 8 bricks. He only plans to give away 10 bricks in all. Sure, he loses $2,000 but the kickback will be incredible. He has total faith in his product. He's sure the 400 or 500 customers that get hold of the 'After Party' will not only come back, but they will also spread the word to every dope feign and dope seller that they know. He's sure the 100 brick a day clientele Smooth has can double overnight.

"Dre, come here!" Smooth says as he stands with a raggedy looking elderly man.

Dre walks over quickly. "What up?"

"This my main tester, right here. He knows dope and I trust him to keep

51

it real. The rest of these mufuckers gone say it's the truth just cause we gave it to them for free. I gave him a bag to see what it is," he says to Dre. "Buck, how is it?" Smooth asks the old man. Right now the old man is in the middle of a huge nod, where his head is damn near touching his knees. "Buck, he shouts as he taps the man to wake him out of his nod. "Wake up, mufucker! How is it? Keep it real, too."

"Anghhh," he whines with his eyes still closed. He pinches his nostrils 4 times consecutively before speaking. "Anghhh, like I said. It's good...real good. A little too strong, though."

"Huh?" Dre asks, shocked at what he's hearing. He's never heard that before. "Too strong?"

"Angghh, yeah," he says as he rocks back and forth with his eyes closed. "Soon as I hit it, it rushed straight to my brain. See, I like the dope to sneak up on me. Anghhh, usually when it hits like that, it don't hold you...don't last. It hit hard then it fades away. With this shit, right here, smack to the brain."

"How about the drain?" Smooth asks.

"Anghhh, the drain there too. The drain came quick," he whines.

Dre is completely baffled. "So, you don't like it?"

"Anghhh," he whines. "I love it. Like I said, the drain there," he sniffs. "And the hit, too. I ain't had nothing like this since the eighties. Anghh, if you ask me, might can stand another hit. Angghhh..trust me. I know dope and this shit is pure heron! Angghhh," he whines as he fades into another nod.

"Buck," Smooth says as he taps the man again. What's better, this or that Oriental Pleasure?" Smooth asks as he prepares himself for the answer.

"Angghh, Oriental Pleasure ain't got a shot against this. Oriental Pleasure is good but this shit great. Anggghh...I rate this a solid 10 plus."

"Yeah?" Smooth asks, looking at Dre with a slight smirk on his face. "Knock it off, Buck. Ain't no dope out here a 10 plus. You told me that yourself?"

"Anggghh...10 plus. Like I said, I ain't had dope this pure since the anggghhh...eighties."

Dre throws his hands high in the air, feeling victorious. "I told you, ain't nothing fucking with this," he gloats. "You had a lot of faith in that shit you got," he teases.

"Man, I'm telling you, that Oriental Pleasure is fire.

"I don't know," Dre smiles. "You heard the Old Timer...this is great. Ay man, my work here is done," Dre says arrogantly. "I proved my point. Need I say more?" he asks as he walks away.

Ten Minutes Later

Dre and Smooth walk out of the projects onto Myrtle Avenue. "Dig," Dre whispers. "Look down the street on your right," he instructs. "You see the white Infiniti?"

"Yeah, yeah."

"My little girl in there. She got 50 bricks in there for you. I'm leaving them here with you. Just pay me the $10,000 tomorrow. How that sound?"

"Sounds like a plan."

"I'm out," Dre says as he steps toward his jeep. "What time should I expect your call?"

"In the PM!" he shouts as he steps down the block.

"Later, Daddy!" Dre says as he gloats like a champion. He's connecting the dots just like he knew he would. Damn, I love it when a plan comes together," he says as he hops into his Jeep.

////// CHAPTER 17 //////

The Mayor stands at the desk in the Essex County Jail, where he's getting processed. He just arrived a few minutes ago. His purpose here is to go to a court for an old charge.

He stands there patiently as the officers complete his paperwork. An officer speaks. "You want to wear these up?" he asks as he holds a pair of shower slippers in the air. "Or are you going to take your chances and wear those up?" he asks as he points to the Mayor's sneakers.

The Mayor is completely dumbfounded. "Excuse me?" he asks.

"Do you want to check your sneakers in?"

"Check my sneakers in?" he asks sarcastically. "Why would I want to do that?"

"Just a question," the officer replies.

"Those are nice. You might want to check those in," a female officer interrupts. "It can get kind of crazy up there."

The Mayor snickers, before rolling his eyes at her. "I always take my chances in everything I do. Take me up, please," he begs.

Meanwhile on the Streets of Newark

Mu-Mit cruises into Bradley Court as Latif looks around in search of a particular face. It's hard to do so on account of the heavy traffic which swarms the courts. Huddles of young boys are all over the place. Packs of people crowd the stoops while feigns run back and forth.

"You see him?" Mu asks.

"Nah," Latif replies slowly as he continues to look around. "Nope. Hold up. I think that is one of the young boys from the other day. Stop!"

Mu-Mit stops while Latif rolls down his window. "Playboy!" Everyone in the crowd turn toward the car. "Ay, Doughboy out here?" Their facial expressions change from playful to serious instantly. They all just stand there without responding. "Doughboy ain't around?"

"Who?" one young boy replies acting as if he doesn't have the slightest idea of who Latif is talking about.

"Dough," Latif replies, simplifying his name, attempting to make them think that he knows him well. He hopes this will make them feel comfortable enough to tell him where Doughboy is.

Another young boy finally replies by shrugging his shoulders. "We don't know no Dough," he replies casually, turning his back on Latif. The boys pick up their conversation as if Mu and Latif aren't even there.

Latif is getting more and more furious by the second. Suddenly a familiar face approaches them, slightly easing Latif's mind. "Hey, what's up, Baby Boy?" Latif says as the boy steps toward the crowd, counting a stack of money. The boy only replies by head nod. "Dough around?" Latif asks.

"Nah," he replies quickly without any eye contact at all.

Latif and the boy met early last week when they came through looking for

Doughboy.

"Ay, did you give him my number?"

"I gave it to him," he replies arrogantly.

"And what did he say?" Latif asks.

"Shit," he replies sarcastically. A few boys in the crowd snicker at the remark.

By now, Latif is pissed off with the entire situation. He can't believe that he's actually allowing these young guys that are only a third of his age to talk to him as if he's nobody. He laughs under his breath, but he's furious. "Yo, tell him I came back through, alright?"

The boy stands there looking Latif dead in the eyes without saying a word.

"Pull off before I be done murdered one of these pussies," Latif whispers to Mu-Mit. Mu cruises off slowly. "Man, I swear for God in heaven, these young mufuckers gone make me act a fool!" Latif shouts as Mu-Mit smirks, shaking his head from side to side. "These fag ass niggas ain't got a clue of how ugly I can get. I was two seconds away from sticking my gun down his throat. These young mufuckers tough as hell when they in their little packs. Catch them by themselves and they grow titties and ass right before your eyes. All the bitch comes out. These young niggas disrespecting me like I'm a square from nowhere," he mumbles. I don't believe this shit!"

"Yooooo!" Mu-Mit hears in the distance, causing him to look in his rearview mirror. There he sees a man standing behind them, waving for them to come back. "Somebody calling us back."

"Where?" Latif questions as he turns around in his seat. "Back up," he says as he grabs his 9MM from his waistband and tucks it in between his thigh and the seat, still holding it tightly in his grip.

As they're backing up, the short stout man backpedals out of their path, giving them room. Mu-Mit halts while Latif rolls down his window. Once they're before him, Latif and the man lock eyes.

The man breaks the silence. "You looking for Doughboy?" he asks as a crowd of young boys form a circle around him.

"Yeah," Latif replies, while nodding his head up and down.

"For what?" he asks arrogantly.

He's nothing like Latif expected. Latif expected a big stocky man, and he's nothing but a short fat baby-faced kid. His rounded belly and his puffy cheeks make him resemble Fat Albert. Soft as pudding, Latif thinks to himself. "You Dough?"

"True! What's good?"

"Ay, what's going on Baby Boy? I been looking all over for you. You a hard man to catch up with."

"Looking all over for me, why?" he asks with signs of agitation in his voice. "You know me?"

"Come on man, knock it off," he laughs. "Who don't know Doughboy?" Latif asks, stroking his ego. "I need to kick it with you?"

"Kick it then," he replies sarcastically.

"I was thinking more on the one on one tip. Everything ain't for everybody, you know?"

"Don't mind them. This all family right here."

"I mean, I feel you but this is business."

Doughboy laughs. I don't even know you. We don't have no business.

Latif is really getting frustrated now. He tries to ignore the boy's last statement. I'll get out and we can step to the side and kick it?" he asks. Latif can easily say what he has to say in front of them, but he's almost sure of how the boy will react. He's sure the boy's ego will make him say something that he will find offensive and at this point he can't take any more disrespect. Latif knows exactly what it is. Doughboy is showing off for his little followers. He's hoping that if he can get him alone to the side, he'll be able to cut into the real Doughboy. He's positive this is only his representative. He can look in his eyes and tell that he's nothing but a chump.

Doughboy shrugs his shoulders and raises his hands in the air, gesturing for Latif to get out.

Latif sneakily slides his gun across the seat to Mu-Mit who grabs it tightly. Just as Latif closes the door, he extends his right hand to Doughboy. "Latif," he says sternly as he grips the Doughboy's hand with a manly grip squeezing Doughboy's soft and pudgy hand. Latif grips his hand and gently leads him away from the crowd. "Yeah, I didn't want to talk in front of them," Latif says just as they approach the front of Mu-Mit's car. "You know, everybody's business, is nobody's business?" Doughboy just nods his head up and down. "Like I said, I'm Latif. I know you're wondering why I been looking for you?"

"Nah, not really," he laughs.

Latif looks at him with pure venom in his eyes. If looks could kill Doughboy would be a dead man. Once again, he has to laugh his anger away. "Anyway, I don't know you from a can of paint, but your name keeps coming up in our circle. You're making a lot of noise in the town. Word on the street is you're the guy. We were just wondering if there is anyway we can hook up and maybe expand the network a little. We got a few things brewing, and you doing you...together we can turn it up." Doughboy frowns his face, but Latif continues to speak anyway. "You might have heard of us and what we doing? We got the After Party? Doughboy stands there with a blank look on his face. "You ever heard of it?"

Doughboy shakes his head from side to side with his hands in the air palm up. His facial expression shows that he doesn't have the slightest interest in this conversation.

"Well ask around. It's fire! I'm wondering what I can do to be a part of what you got going? Trust me, it will benefit everybody. It's the best shit on the street. I'm in position to give it to you for $220 a brick.

"220," Doughboy laughs. "Let me keep it real with you, OG. This is a dead end conversation, headed nowhere fast," he smiles. "220 a brick is absurd. I do me. I ain't no little nigga. As you can see, I'm a big boy. I can give it to ya'll for $165 a brick. "You might wanna come holler at me," he says arrogantly.

His reply totally shocks Latif making him feel like he just crashed into a brick wall. He's at a loss for words. He fumbles around in search of a reply. 165, he thinks to himself. "But what is the quality like? I'm sure it ain't nothing like the work we got."

"It's whatever I want it to be. I go to the table myself. I turn up the volume or lower it whenever I feel like it."

"I'm willing to bet even when you got it all the way turned up it ain't nothing like we got. Just take a brick and pass it out? See what it do? Lemme get it for you," Latif suggests as he begins to walk toward the passenger's side of the car.

"Nah, nah. Don't even waste your time Old Head."

"Old Head?" Latif says to himself.

"On the real, I ain't gone waste no more of your time or mines. I ain't gone pass out the samples," he whispers. "I'm sure it ain't gone do nothing, cause I ain't gone let it do nothing. I'm good," he smiles, extending his hand for a handshake. "Nice meeting you though."

"Likewise," Latif replies with a devilish smirk on his face.

"Be good man," Doughboy says as he backpedals away, leaving Latif standing there alone. He stands there frozen for a second, not believing the outcome of this meeting. Latif is so embarrassed at this point. He hops into the car feeling degraded and humiliated. Never in his life has he ever felt so disrespected. He looks at Mu-Mit, while shaking his head from side to side. "Young boy just talked to me like I was Eddie Spaghetti. He just played the shit outta me," he laughs. "Oh shit! I never thought I'd see the day when a fag ass nigga like him looks me in the eyes and tells me, fuck me. I gotta respect it though. He kept it funky. In so many words he told me to go fuck myself. I gotta respect his courage, though," he laughs. "Yeah, I respect his courage, but his arrogance just signed his own death certificate."

////// CHAPTER 18 //////

Next Day

Dre sits at the table in the kitchen of the cozy little Bronx apartment.
Sitting directly across from him is his man Chico. They did a short bid
together at FCI Greenville, in Illinois. Chico served an eleven year sentence.
Originally, he was sentenced to life, but miraculously he was able to give back
a great deal of his time through appeal.

Chico's beautiful wife walks away from the stove, holding two plates in her
hands. She places a plate in front of each of them. "Gracias, Mamita," Chico
whispers, as he smacks and palm grips a cheek of her voluptuous behind.

"Thank you, much," Dre says as he lowers his gaze. She acknowledges
him by nodding her head before leaving the kitchen.

Chico then bows his head saying grace over the food, while Dre follows
his lead. "Amen!" he shouts.

"Amen," Dre whispers, before sticking his fork into the hefty plate of Cod
Fish and rice.

"Listen," Chico says with a mouthful of food. "I checked out the material
and everybody likes it…no complaints. The only complaint I have, is the
price. There's no way in the world, I can pay that price for it. Look, I got three
spots here in the Bronx. Watson is my slowest spot, and the least I do there
is 100-150 bricks a day, 10-20 bricks at a time. I send all my small customers
there. The other two spots are for my big customers, 100, 200 bricks. They
come from everywhere, Buffalo, Connecticut, Boston, even New Jersey. I'm
good for at least four or five hundred bricks a day. If you can play the number
game with me, we can make a lot of money?"

"500 bricks a day, Dre thinks to himself. Got damn! He never imagined
those types of numbers. He thinks back at his days of selling cocaine, and
hates the fact that he's wasted so much time. He figures he should have
changed over a long time ago. Sure he made a lot of money selling cocaine,
but heroin is a different game. The stakes are so much bigger. The profit he
makes in just one week with the 'After Party', he would have to hustle damn
near two months to make selling cocaine. He just thinks of all the time he
has wasted, but he's sure now that he's found out where the real money is,
he'll definitely make up for all that he's missed. He has to come up with a deal
that Chico can't turn down. In all reality, he's well aware that he needs Chico
more than Chico needs him. He refuses to blow this deal. "Chico, you already
know. Everything is negotiable," he laughs as he swallows his food. He peeks
over his shoulder just to make sure that Chico's wife has not come back into
the room. "Talk to me, baby. Tell me what you need me to do to make this
thing happen? You tell me what number is feasible for you? What can you
pay?"

"Dre, I can't tell you that. It's your food. What I will tell you is this, as you
know, my brother runs this operation. I was the boss back then, but I come

home and he's a big man. I can't make a decision without him. We get a lot of work, but really the quality is only so so. It can be a whole lot better. It's nothing like what you have. But we don't pay for it. We get everything on consignment. I want to work with you, but you have to keep all that in mind. Trust me, there's a lot of money that can be made."

"Alright, give me a few days, let me sit down with my people and find out what's the best we can do?" Dre's mind begins to race. All that comes to his mind is the huge clientele that Chico claims to have. If he's telling the truth, he has a damn near 3,500 brick a week clientele. Damn, I have to pull this one off, Dre thinks to himself.

Meanwhile in Essex County Jail

The Mayor sits in a corner all alone. He skims through a Robb Report Magazine, just to pass the time away. Reading about exotic cars and lavish lifestyles seems to ease his mind and relieve his frustrations. He reads this magazine faithfully. It's been a great help to him through his bid.

It's so loud in the dayroom that he can barely get into his magazine. Every couple of words that he reads he has to peek back and forth due to some type of distraction. The young men act like pre-school kids. They run back and forth, screaming out at the top of their lungs. The Mayor is so frustrated with them. He can't wait to get back to Fort Dix.

Being in here around these young boys is far worse than being in prison. The new 23 hour lock down program is like capital punishment. This is his first time out of his cell all day. He has just 25 minutes left before he'll be locked down again. It's enough to drive a man insane.

In all his years of jailing, he's never seen the county jail in this state. Through his many visits, he's never felt so out-of-touch. Usually, he knows almost everyone in the building and if he didn't, they knew exactly who he was. Right now, he feels like a foreigner in his own city. He's never seen any of these guys around, anywhere. When he was doing him, they were probably 10 or 11 years old. Most of them are barely 19 years old, and it shows in their behavior.

"Ah shit!" The Mayor hears a young man shout. He looks up in the direction where the voice came from, only to find a young guy sitting in front of the television. "Turn that shit off! I ain't watching no fucking, Brab!" the boy shouts. Seconds later, all the guys that surround the television turn their backs on it, while others in the room cover their eyes with their hands.

The Mayor is baffled. He doesn't have a clue as to what is going on. He looks at the Snoop Dogg video in a state of confusion.

"Fucking Brab!" one boy shouts. The Mayor finally figures out what all the commotion is about. The majority of the population on this tier are Blood gang members and they refuse to watch Snoop Dogg's video because he's a Crip. The Mayor can't believe this. He's never seen anything like this. He shakes his head from side to side with laughter. What has our city come to, he asks himself.

"All dogs, up top, down low to the gate!" the Mayor hears as one young man screams at the top of his lungs. In a matter of seconds, everyone runs to their gates watching attentively. They do this every time a new person steps into the jail. They're curious to find out whether he's a Blood or a Crip. The frail man steps nervously up the corridor. Fear is written all over his face as he looks straight ahead afraid to look anyone in the eyes.

"550 (non-gang banger), from my hood!" echoes from the top tier. "He good!" the man shouts from afar. "Shawn! What the hell you doing in here?" the boy asks.

The frail man looks up and the fear vanishes from his face. He feels comfort in knowing that he knows someone in here. "Some bullshit! Child support!" he shouts.

Everyone walks away from their gates angrily. Boredom appears on their faces immediately. They were hoping to have some fun with the new person.

Just to think, this man is in here for a misdemeanor and he's placed in here with a bunch of savages where he can easily lose his life, the Mayor thinks to himself. He shakes his head with disgust at the very thought of it. He then buries his face back into his magazine. He turns the page and his eyes set on to the most beautiful thing in the world to him. Tears damn near come to his eyes as he views the new Maybauch Coupe. "Damn," he mumbles under his breath, as he stares at it with pure admiration. Just as he pictures himself behind the wheel, his euphoria is interrupted by a tapping on his shoulder. He turns his head slowly, stopping at his shoulder where the young man's hand rests. He then looks up at the young man whom is standing directly over him. He then looks back at his shoulder gesturing for the boy to remove his hand from his shoulder.

"What's popping?" the young man asks.

The Mayor stares him directly in the eyes without responding. The frail young man appears to be about eighteen years old. He fits the description of almost every young man in here with his long dreadlocks.

The man finally removes his hand from the Mayor's shoulder. "I like them sneakers," the boy says as he points to the Mayor's hi-top black leather Pradas. "Prada, right?" he asks. "Them shits will look good on Blood's feet."

The Mayor automatically thinks of what the officers said to him about checking his sneakers in. He can't believe this. He hates to even think that this young boy even has the heart to step to him in this manner. He sure hopes this isn't what he thinks it is. "You don't want these. They got murder written all over 'em," the Mayor says as he looks at his magazine, pretending that the guy isn't even standing over him.

"What's up?" the boy asks.

The Mayor folds his magazine and looks the boy in the eyes. "Listen man, not right now, alright?" the Mayor says sternly. "I'm over here doing me, go back over there and do you. Please?" he asks.

"I said, them will look real good on Blood's feet."

"And I said, these got murder written all over 'em," the Mayor says arrogantly. "Baby Boy, I suggest you find somebody your own age to play with. I'm a grown ass man."

"And?" the boy asks in a cocky tone.

The Mayor laughs in his face. "Listen Bee, you don't know me, but trust me when I tell you, I'm a different type of beef," he says in a calm manner, standing as he's talking. He towers over the young boy by at least eight inches and outweighs him by about 70 pounds. He's shocked to see that the kid still isn't backing down after seeing the disadvantage. Instead the kid gets more excited. "Fall back before it's too late," the Mayor laughs.

"Bdddddaaatt, bdddaaaaat!" the boy shouts loudly, while the Mayor stands there baffled. As he peeks around he sees everyone getting up from their seats. He quickly realizes that he's just made the call. It's on, he thinks to himself. He sees about 15 men approaching him. He has no time to waste. He quickly snatches the boy by his collar with his left hand, while lunging his right elbow into the boy's throat, followed by a right uppercut that shifts the cartilage in the boy's nose. The boy attempts to put up a fight but the Mayor is way too strong for him. The Mayor knees the boy in his testicles, taking all the fight out of him. As the boy bends over grabbing his jewels, the Mayor spins him around and wraps his arms around the boy's neck. He gasps as the Mayor tightens his huge biceps around his throat, cutting off all of his oxygen. The Mayor's adrenaline pumps up as he's surrounded by 20 Bloods. "Back up!" he shouts to them as he tightens his grip. "Back the fuck up!"

"Anngghh," the boy gasps.

"Back the fuck up!" the Mayor yells furiously, looking like a madman. He squeezes tighter. "Back up before I kill his ass!" he threatens as he tightens his grip even more.

"Anghh," the boy gasps for his life.

"Pussy, you better tell them to back up?" he shouts into the boy's ear as he backs up against the wall so no one can get behind him. He peeks back and forth trying to keep his eyes on the entire crowd.

All of a sudden The Mayor spots a box cutter in the hand of one of the young boys. Nervousness fills his heart. Being cut or stabbed is one of the Mayor's biggest fears. "Oh shit," he mumbles to himself as the man swings the blade recklessly. In the nick of time, the Mayor ducks his head against his captive's back, and turns him around using him as a shield. The blade zips across the boy's face causing blood to pour like a waterfall.

The man swings the blade once again, missing the Mayor's head by a few inches.

"Break it up, break it up!" the Mayor hears in the background. He peeks over his captive's shoulder, only to see about ten six feet tall huge, correction officers dressed in riot gear, coming to his safety. Never has he been this pleased to see officers. "Break it the fuck up!" they shout as the Mayor's opponents back away from him. "Let him go!" the officer shouts to the Mayor as they surround him. "Let him go!"

The Mayor peeks around cautiously, just to make sure they have the situation under control. He looks around in search of the blade yielding man. After locating him far in the corner, the Mayor loosens his grip and slams the boy to the ground. He lays there gasping for air while blood jumps from his face. The Mayor spits directly in his face and kicks him brutally in the ribs. The officers rush in. The Mayor lifts his hands high in the air. His eyes are full of rage.

"Blackhead!" the Mayor snaps back into reality as he hears his government name being called. "Blackhead," he hears again as he sees the white woman dressed in a business suit standing at the gate. "Bring him to my office!" she shouts furiously to the officers.

The officers don't hesitate to snatch the Mayor off of his feet, dragging him toward the gate. The Mayor laughs. "Look at your man. He all fucked up. I told him to fall back, but he wouldn't listen. It'll take a thousand of you little punk motherfuckers to hold me," he teases. "Ya'll barked up the wrong tree. Ya'll done fucked with the right one this time. You can't imagine the problem you just created for yourselves. Ya'll some disrespectful young niggas, but I'm just the one to teach ya'll some manners."

"You spilled Blood, now you're Alpo...dog food. Blood rules," one boy says with a satanic smile on his face.

"Don't nothing or nobody rule me," the Mayor smiles. "You better ask somebody. You fucking with a nigga that's over your head."

He nods his head up and down, making the Mayor even more furious.

The Mayor laughs as well to cover up his rage. "Laugh now, cry later," he whispers as the officers escort him through the gate.

As they're riding the elevator the Mayor replays the entire situation back in his mind. He never thought he'd see the day when someone would step to him in that manner. The fact that they're kids makes it even worse. Although, they're only children and they don't know any better, he still has to make them pay for their actions. "Yo, ease up off of me, Playboy," the Mayor says to the officer to his right, who has an extremely tight grip on him. "I ain't going nowhere," he says as he gives the officer the coldest look. The officer immediately loosens his grip.

After getting off of the elevator, they walk through a series of gates until they finally make it to a door. The officer taps the door lightly.

The sound of a woman's shoes tapping against the hardwood floors echoes loudly. Seconds later, the door is snatched wide open. The woman's emerald green eyes attract the Mayor's attention like a magnet. Rage and fury lies within her eyes, making her resemble a witch. As soon as they lock eyes, he automatically lowers his gaze, dropping his eyes to the floor. He secretly looks her up and down. Her tight pin-striped slacks grip her hips and her voluptuous thighs. Her enormous breasts ooze over the top of her silk blouse, exposing massive cleavage. Her blonde hair is pinned up in a tight pony-tail. Her beauty shines through underneath the mean look that she's displaying.

"I got him from here," she says with a fierce look on her face. "You can get back to work," she snaps.

"Are you sure, Warden?"

"More than positive; carry on!" she shouts hastily.

"Yes, Maam," the officer whispers as they walk away leaving the Mayor standing there. This is the Warden. Everyone in the building hates her. They nicknamed her the Wicked Bitch of the East. She shows the racism that's in her heart every chance she gets. She's a middle aged Italian woman with an old school Italian code. If you're not Italian, you don't count. She makes all her employees feel like slaves.

She snatches the door wide open, gesturing for the Mayor to come in. "Listen to me, I don't care what you do in any other jail, but when you're in my house, you will abide by my rules!" she shouts as he's walking in. She slams the door behind him.

"Knock it the fuck off," he whispers with rage.

They stand there face to face as she looks up at him. Her mean look changes to an inviting smile. "How did I sound? Did I sound believable?" she asks. "What happened down there?" she asks while the Mayor just stands there quietly. "I saved your black ass," she laughs. "You owe me big," she teases as she points her finger in his face.

The Mayor is still furious. "No, you saved them," he says arrogantly.

"I don't know," she smiles as she comes closer to him. She grabs him by his collar, pulling his face closer to hers. She mimics a dog by snapping at him, gripping his lower lip with her teeth. "Grrr," she growls. "I miss you," she whispers, before locking lips with him.

He's not even indulging in the kiss. He lets her do all the work as he stands there full of rage.

"Baby, I miss you so much," she says as she rests her head on his chest. She follows that with a tight hug. She lifts her head, and in a playful manner she pushes him backwards using all of her might. He stumbles back onto her desk. She clears her desk quickly. As soon as his back touches the desk, she damn near rips his jumper off of him. Her aggressiveness is turning him on.

As she's pulling his jumper down to his knees, she's greeted by his fully erect manhood. It's calling her name and she can't help but to answer it. She strokes it violently a few times before jamming it into her mouth. "Uhhm," she whispers as she drops to her knees. She slurps as she looks upward into his eyes. She slurps louder as she sucks harder until his entire shaft is wet from her saliva. She stops for a brief second, long enough to speak. "Baby, I miss you," she whispers, with saliva dripping from her mouth.

No time for talking, he thinks to himself before grabbing hold of the back of her head and shoving himself into her mouth. She strokes him with her hand while planting soft kisses all over him. The intensity is driving him crazy. He brings himself closer to her mouth. He digs his finger-tips into the edge of the desk, to keep from making noises. She licks him up and down as if it's a huge lollipop. Her tongue-twirls are freaking him out, making him weak. Finally, he gets a burst of energy that brings him to his feet. Once his feet are firmly planted, he snatches her pony-tail, forcing her head backwards. There she sits on her knees. Her head is laid back with her mouth wide open. He slowly penetrates her mouth and thrusts in and out with gentle strokes. He pulls her hair harder as he speeds up his stroking. He jams his free hand down her blouse, gripping her firm breast. This gets him even more excited, causing him to stroke faster. His impact is knocking her backwards. She has to grab hold of his ankles just to keep her balance.

He tightens the grip on her ponytail, pulling her onto her feet. He turns her around, facing her desk. She quickly unfastens her slacks, and forces them down to her knees, as he bends her over the desk. He's so anxious that he doesn't even have the time to pull her panties down. He just slides them to the side enough to force his way inside of her. He plants his hand in the center of her back, pinning her to the desk. He starts off with hard short strokes which make her tight firm rear roll like tidal waves. He palm grips her cheeks, spreading them apart as he begins to manhandle her. The feeling is rather painful, but the pain only stimulates her more. He follows up with a series of long strokes, teasing her tremendously. "Give it to me," she moans, as she backs up closer to him, ramming herself against him. The loud clapping noise drives him wild, causing him to pound harder and harder. He can feel his load creeping up on him, but he's not quite ready to unload. He's not done with her yet. He closes his eyes and tries to think of something else to prevent him from ejaculating. Not yet, he thinks to himself as he pounds away. He tries to imagine a big red apple in his mind, hoping that will take his mind off of what is actually going on. Even that doesn't work on the account of her moaning and gasping. He opens his eyes and stares at the wall before him. He focuses his attention on her name tag. Emily Annuci, Emily Annuci," he mumbles under his breath over and over just to forget the erotic sex that he's indulging in. He grabs hold of her tiny waist and digs deep before slow grinding, with their bodies almost glued together. She starts to grind against his direction, yet and still their rhythm is totally in sync with each other.

Suddenly his knees buckle. Just as he's about to shoot his load, he backs up, pulling himself out of her. He releases. "Aghh," he grunts almost silently, as he falls onto one knee. He's drained. He just kneels there attempting to revitalize himself.

The faint sound of crying interrupts his relaxation. He looks up at Emily, who is still lying face down bent over the desk. Oh boy, he thinks to himself. Here we go with this shit all over again, he thinks as he slowly stands up and takes a step toward her. He reaches over, grabs her by the arm and lifts her from the desk.

Her face is covered with tears. He gets frustrated at the sight of her weeping. They've been through this several times prior to this. He's told himself time after time again that he should stop having sex with her, but he's afraid that if he stops she won't assist him anymore and he needs her at this point. She is a valuable player of his team. "What now?" he asks with no compassion at all.

"Nothing," she cries.

"Nothing, then why are you crying?"

"We have to stop this," she weeps. "I tell myself over and over, I'm not having meaningless sex with you anymore," she cries. "I've been your sex toy for over five years now. I refuse to play this game with you any longer."

This alarms him. He's sure if she cuts their sexual relationship off, she'll also cut off all of their business ties. He thinks quick. He has to keep her on his side. "Em, come on. We've been through this a million times already and you're still bugging?"

"I'm not bugging," she cries. "I'm good enough to have sex with you, but I'm not good enough for you to be with me?"

"Em, you're a married woman," he reminds her.

"Don't give me that shit," she snaps. "I've already told you that I would leave him in a heartbeat. All you have to do is say the word."

"Em, you talking crazy. I will never let you leave your husband on the strength of me.

"Don't give me that shit," she snaps. "It's not about me or my husband. It's about you and your two bitches," she cries as she pulls her slacks up and fastens them.

"Look we've been through this already. I told you, now is not the time. I got too much shit going on," he whispers. "But if you feel like this is just meaningless sex, then I can't and won't keep trying to change your mind. You gone believe what you want to believe. You know what's better for you," he adds. He quickly realizes how much of a gamble he's taking by talking to her like this, but she's giving him no choice. "Do what you gotta do," he mumbles. He's on a roll now. "If you want to cut our ties, I understand," he says as he turns his back on her and walks away from her. He's hoping she'll play into his hands.

Seconds later, he hears her stepping toward him. Her arms wrapping around him, tells him that she's falling right into his trap. "Baby, I'm sorry," she cries.

He realizes that he has her, but he can't give in too easily or she'll try this again. He wants her to believe that he's willing to cut it off if she's going to continue to carry on like this. He attempts to pull away from her but she hugs him tighter. "I'm sorry," she cries. He snatches away from her. "Babe, don't do this to me. I said I'm sorry," she pleads as she follows closely behind him. He turns around and looks her directly in the eyes. He shakes his head from side to side with disgust. "It's not me," she cries. "It's my heart. I want you to myself."

The Mayor looks at her without replying for a matter of seconds before applying more pressure. "If you can't handle this, then you're right, we gotta let it go."

"No," she says. "I love you," she cries as she buries her head in his chest, hugging him tightly.

He pushes her off of him. "Where is it?" he asks with no emotion.

She walks over to her desk. She digs deep into her purse. She pulls her hand out, holding three bricks of 'After Party'.

He walks over, takes them out of her hand and tucks them inside the front of his boxers. "How are things moving out there?" he asks as he pulls up his jumper.

"Good, I guess," she replies. "Dre doesn't say much, but I assume things are going good. He moves back and forth consistently and just the other day the workload increased double."

"Good," he replies. "Listen, I need to get over to the 2 Building. My man over there waiting for these," he says as he pats his waistband where the dope lies.

"Ok," she replies. "Let me get the officers to take you over there," she says as she picks the phone up from her desk.

In a matter of two minutes, there is a tapping on the door. She quickly tucks her blouse into her pants and ruffles her hair while her and the Mayor walk toward the door.

"Listen, that incident that just happened down there." he whispers.

"Uh huh, what about it?" she asks.

"I need the names of every person involved in that. I need their pictures as well," he adds. "All right?"

"Uh huh," she replies as she nods her head up and down. She grabs hold of the door. Before snatching it open she speaks. "What about us?" she whispers. He turns toward her with a blank look on his face, just staring into her eyes. He leans over, grabs her face and plants a reassuring kiss on the top of her forehead. "I gotta go," he whispers.

She snatches the door open and like magic the Wicked Bitch of the East reappears. "Take this prisoner to the 2 Building!" she demands. "Listen…no more bullshit out of you!" she shouts out to the Mayor.

The Mayor ignores her as if she hasn't said a word to him. As he's being escorted down the hall, he thinks of how valuable a player Emily is to him. She's been on his team now for over five years. He met her several years ago during a county visit. Back then she was only Lieutenant of Corrections. His name rang so much in the county jail, that when he finally came through, all the guards just wanted to get a glimpse of the living legend. Both female and male officers damn near rolled out the red carpet for him. Every female officer secretly wanted a shot with him, but he chose to roll with Emily. It made sense back then. With Emily being the Lieutenant, she was in a position to help him do whatever he needed to do while in their system. He's so happy that he chose her because now look, she's the warden, controlling all movements in this system. What a smart decision?

///// CHAPTER 19 /////

The Next Day

Mu-Mit and Latif cruise along the busy block. They finally found someone who is willing to accept their offer. "Listen," Latif says from the backseat of the car. Latif and Mu-Mit are old heads who play by the rules. Both of them have done so much dirt in their lives that they never allow anyone they don't know and trust to sit behind them in a car. They've taken so many guys for the deadly ride that they know better than to ever leave themselves open like that. "We're in a position to do big things. We have way more than enough work. There's no limit to the moves that you can make. It's only 25 bricks today but I don't see no reason why that 25 can't turn into 125. If you know anyone around town that wants to get their hands on this, just turn us onto them. I'll make it beneficial for you, trust me."

"True!" the boy shouts.

Latif fumbles through the stack of money. Fifty-five hundred, right?" he asks.

"Yep! What time ya'll go in?" he questions. "I'm sure I can bang these out before tonight. I mean, I can wait until the morning, but I like to have my shit ready the night before. I come out early as hell, like 5. I like to catch that early morning rush," he adds. "Shit be banging out here on Baghdad!"

"You can hit me, whenever. We'll come out. Don't worry!"

"Bet!" the young boy shouts. "Right here. Let me out, right here."

Mu-Mit stops short, allowing the young boy to hop out of the car. He jumps out, zips through the alley and disappears. Latif hops right in the front seat immediately.

"You heard that mufucker?" Latif asks. They call this shit Baghdad. These young mufuckers crazy. Watch too many movies," he laughs as he quickly separates the money into three piles on his lap. "Here," he says as he hands $500 over to Mu-Mit. He then pockets his $500 before stuffing Dre's $4,500 into the glove compartment. "Not bad, for 9 in the morning, right? We get about four more young niggas like him and we'll be ok!" he shouts with excitement. "I don't need a lot. Two thousand a day, is fourteen thousand a week. I'm good! I don't see no reason why we can't sell 100 bricks a day throughout the town with this fire we got?" he says while looking at Mu-Mit. "Where the fuck Jesse at? He said he was going to be on the corner. Hold up, hold up. There he go!"

Mu-Mit steers the car toward the right, and stops directly in front of the small crowd of dope feigns that huddle up alongside of the curb. The filthiest, ashiest one of them all steps out of the crowd.

"Jesse, come here!" Latif shouts.

The man runs over to the car. "What up, La?" he asks while sucking on the 25 cent dope feign (freeze pop). He turns the freeze pop up high in the air to suck the remaining juice from it. After tossing it away he removes the wash cloth from the top of his head and pats his face dry.

"Get in." he demands. He jumps in with no hesitation. "Circle the block," Latif suggests. "Here!" he shouts as he passes 10 bags of dope to the backseat where Jesse is. "That's the bundle I promised you. I shouldn't even be giving you no dope. I'm making matters worse. Just adding more fuel to the fire. You need to get your shit together. It's time!"

"I know, I know," Jesse mumbles.

"If you know, then what you waiting for? Get your mufucking mind right!"

"I'm about to, word up," he mumbles as he stares at the bundle of dope in his hand. It's calling his name.

"Jess, you gotta want it."

Shut the fuck up, Jesse thinks to himself. He can't wait to sniff the dope. This conversation is taking way too long. Please let me the fuck up outta here, he says in his mind.

"I ain't preaching to you. I'm just keeping it real with you, cause I love you."

Latif and Jesse are childhood friends. They were best friends all the way through school. After they graduated, Latif started running the streets, getting high and getting into all types of trouble until he finally caught a bid. Jesse on the other hand, never got into any trouble, but being around Latif destroyed his life. He started getting high just following Latif's lead. By the time Latif came home Jesse was strung all the way out.

"I love you, too," Jesse whispers, hoping that will be the end of their conversation.

"Ay, what you told ol boy?" Latif asks.

"I just told him that I had got hold of some fire, called After Party. They all trust my judgement. They know I know good dope."

"So that lil nigga run all this out here?"

"Nah, not like that. It's broken off into a few squads. They have different dopes out here. No one man don't run this. They all getting paid."

"So imagine if all that was going into one pot?" Latif says. "Listen Jess, we can filter this shit through you. Fuck them young niggas! We can have this shit to the neck. Fuck selling bricks! We can take this shit to the ground, loose, bag for bag," he says as he thinks of the profit they can make. "Me and Mu can push them mufuckers up outta here and you can put you a little crew together. We can get this paper."

"Sounds good," Jess sighs.

"Nigga it is good!"

"It ain't that simple, La. Them young niggas ain't having that. They crazy!"

"Crazy? Crazy? Them mufuckers ain't crazy! I'm crazy! Nigga just tell me you're ready and I'll show you how simple it is! You ready?"

"Chill, La," he whispers.

"Nigga just say the word! Is you ready?"

Meanwhile in the Essex County Court Building

The Mayor sits in the front of the crowded courtroom. He sits before the honorable Judge Jones. She looks like the sweetest woman in the world, but the Mayor has been told that she's a beast. The fact that she's a black woman scares him even more. Through his many courtroom experiences, he's learned that sometimes it's better to stand before Caucasians than to stand in front of your own people. For some strange reason they seem to be harder and give out tougher sentences. He blames it on the fact that they have something to prove.

Today's case is quite critical for the Mayor. He caught the charge making a sale which consisted of 100 bricks. The police caught him and his co-defendant right in the middle of the transaction. The incident took place many years ago, but the Mayor's attorney was able to prolong it. There were more important cases that he wanted to tend to first before stepping into this one.

The Mayor rubs his hands across the pants leg of his jumper to wipe off the sweat that has accumulated in his hands. He's so nervous yet continues to maintain his confident persona. He peeks over to his left, where he sees his two least favorite people in the entire world. There sits the two federal agents, Dumber and Dumbest. Dumb is not here today. Word has spread out throughout the prison that he's on sick leave. Rumor has it that he's dying of kidney failure.

As much as the Mayor hates them, he kind of misses seeing him. He's been absent the last two court dates the Mayor had. He was sure the other two would be here just as they're at every other courtroom appearance that he has. They sit in the far corner, side by side. The Mayor and Dumber lock eyes. After a 20 second stare-down, Dumber blows a kiss at him, hoping to agitate him. The Mayor smiles at him to cover up his anger.

Suddenly, the Mayor hears someone entering the courtroom. Hoping to see his attorney, he looks behind him. Walking through the huge double-doors is his co-defendant, his pregnant wife and his attorney. They were here already but they stepped out. Now here it is they're returning and Tony still has not arrived. The Mayor has gotten used to Tony arriving in the courtroom late, but it still aggravates him.

More nervousness fills the Mayor's heart when he sees the look of fear that his co-defendant displays on his face. The pregnant woman takes a seat in the middle of the courtroom while the man and his attorney walk toward the front.

The judge speaks. "Mr. Blackhead, I can't wait any longer. I have given your attorney more than enough time. We will now proceed," she snaps. "Court is now in session!" she shouts as she bangs the gravel.

The Mayor sighs as he watches the prosecutor stand up. The Mayor listens attentively as the prosecutor tells all the details of the case. The Mayor's heart pounds in his chest as he hears the prosecutor try to finish him off. The Mayor looks around, and notices that everyone is listening attentively as the prosecutor attempts to put all the blame on him. In this case, the Mayor totally understands why he's doing so. The Mayor has much more to lose than his co-defendant has. If the Mayor is found guilty, he can face up to 20 additional years. His co-defendant on the other hand, this is his first and only charge. If he's found guilty, he's facing about 10 years.

The prosecutor finally stops talking. The judge looks at the Mayor, displaying a look of coldness. "Blackhead, in the above matter, how do you plead?"

The Mayor stands up slowly, staring straight ahead. Just as he's about to speak a loud noise erupts from the back of the courtroom, breaking everyone's attention. The double doors swing open wildly as Attorney Tony Austin bursts into the room, just in the nick of time.

"Not guilty!" he shouts from across the crowded room, causing everyone to turn around in their seats to look at him. He struts confidently. He flashes a slight smirk at the Mayor followed by a confident wink of the eye. "Your honor, I gravely apologize to you and the court for my tardiness," he lies as he unbuckles the top buttons of his turtle skin blazer, exposing his white v-neck t-shirt. The judge rolls her eyes with disgust at the fact of how informal he looks. His matching charcoal grey turtle skinned cowboy boots bang against the floor loudly as he struts up to the front of the room.

Tony stands shoulder to shoulder with the Mayor as he extends a closed fist out to the Mayor. The Mayor accepts the greeting by banging his fist against Tony's. "What up?" Tony whispers.

"You," the Mayor replies.

"Not guilty?" the judge questions. "Mr. Blackhead, you are aware that by pleading not guilty, you wave all chances of your original plea if you're found guilty after trial, right? You lose trial and you face up to 18 years. You are aware of that, correct?"

The Mayor hesitates before speaking. Another 18 years, he thinks to himself. Whew, he sighs silently. He feels so close to being free, yet reality sets in showing him how far away he really is. "Yes Maam," he says loud and clear.

"So knowing that, you're still willing to go on with this?"

"Your honor, my client is fully aware of the consequences," Tony interrupts.

"Counsel, at this time I'm speaking to Mr. Blackhead. I would appreciate it if you speak when spoken to in my courtroom. When I'm speaking to you, I will address you as Mr. Austin," she barks in a humiliating manner. "Mr. Blackhead, are you still willing to go further?"

The Mayor turns to Tony before speaking. The Mayor is shocked at the cocky smile Tony is wearing, after the judge just tried to humiliate him. "Yes Maam," he answers, turning toward the judge.

"Mr. Hall, how do you plead?" she asks immediately thereafter. The Mayor's co-defendant stands up slowly. Fear sets on his face. "Guilty," he mumbles, with a squeaky crackling voice.

Fury sets on the prosecutor's face. In no way did he expect this outcome.

"Your honor, may I speak?" the co-defendants lawyer asks as he stands up.

"Proceed!"

"Your honor, my client pleads guilty to all charges. The evidence was found in his possession. He admits that it was his and he was negligent to inform Mr. Blackhead of what he had on his person. He was totally ignorant to the matter."

The judge's face turns stone-cold. She stares at the man with rage. Mr.

Hall, is this true?"

"Yes," he whispers.

"Mr. Hall, are you admitting to these charges willingly or have you been coaxed into doing so?"

"It was mines. He was only giving me a ride home," he lies.

"With that being said, you do know that you face up to ten years, correct?"

"Yes, Maam," he whispers.

Loud crying sounds off. The pregnant woman covers her mouth to muffle her crying.

"Recess!" the judge shouts.

Two Hours Later

Mr. Hall's attorney sits parked in his Range Rover, in the parking lot of Tops Diner in Harrison. Sitting in the passenger's seat is Mr. Hall's pregnant wife. She's been crying now for almost two hours. The attorney is immune to this behavior. He's been down this road so many times before this. He blasts the tunes of radio station CD 101.9, just to tune out the sounds of her crying.

Suddenly, the sparkling beauty of a vehicle comes ripping into the parking lot. The fire engine red Bentley GT coupe speeds recklessly through the lot. The golden interior makes the car resemble strawberry shortcake. The car comes head on towards the attorney's truck. As it is approaching, the high beams are flashing brightly. "I'll be right back," the attorney says as he exits his vehicle.

As the attorney walks toward the car, Tony leans back, almost melting into his butter soft leather seat. He rolls his windows down to allow his cigar smoke to flow out of the vehicle. The attorney gets in and plops into the passenger's seat. "Beautiful piece," the attorney admits.

"Ah, it's ok," Tony says modestly. "How is the pregnant chick doing? Did you get her calm yet?"

"Nah, not really. She's still crying her head off."

Tony reaches into the back of the vehicle retrieving a small Gucci shoe bag. "Here," he says as he hands the bag to the attorney. "Seventy five thousand…as promised. All hundreds," he adds. "And here is yours," he says as he hands an envelope over. "Fifteen thousand, thanks for everything. I owe you! Anything that I can assist you with in the future, I'm here."

Some may call this dirty business, but Tony calls it fair game. Freedom doesn't have a price tag on it. The Mayor was willing to pay anything to beat this charge. Tony came up with the idea of propositioning the man. Just so happen they caught the man at the perfect time, when he was totally hurting for cash. His hunger gave him no choice but to accept.

Seventy five thousand is only the profit off of a kilo and a half for the Mayor, but to Mr. Hall it means provisions for his wife and his expecting baby. The man traded four years of his freedom for a week's worth of profit for the Mayor. The Mayor was so desperate that he would have given the man any amount that he asked for. Luckily for them they caught the man when he was in a terrible state. He's been down on his luck for the past two years now, and with his wife pregnant and out of work, the offer seemed that much sweeter. When propositioned by his attorney, he barely hesitated.

Not only did he score 75 grand, Tony assisted them with the case, coaching the attorney into getting the man the best deal possible. Basically Tony used the attorney as a puppet. Thanks to Tony's expertise, the man should be freed in a little over three years.

"So, what about the back-end?" the attorney asks.

"Everything goes as promised. Every 1st of the month, her rent check of $1,250 will be in her mailbox for the entire time that he's incarcerated, alright?"

"Sounds good," the attorney replies as he opens the door to get out of the vehicle.

"Again, anything you need, just holler at me," Tony says before taking a huge puff of his cigar.

"Ok, good day!" the attorney shouts before slamming the door.

Tony blasts the volume of rapper Jay Z's "30 Something." He goes into a deep zone, nodding his head violently as he sings along. "Thirty is the new twenty, nigga I'm on fire still!" he sings along. "Ya'll young boys is like fire drills…false alarms!" he shouts before taking another puff.

He leans his head back, exhaling a mouthful of smoke. While watching the smoky rings spinning in the air, he just thinks of the success that he's having with the Mayor's charges. For so many years, he's been telling the Mayor that he was going to free him, but at times he didn't believe it himself. He just didn't want his client to lose hope. At the current time he can actually smell freedom for the Mayor. Just a couple more victories, he thinks to himself. He peels off burning massive rubber, leaving a trail of smoke behind. "Just a couple more victories!"

///// CHAPTER 20 /////

One Week Later

Mu-Mit cruises up the block while Latif speaks to the young boy who is leaning low in the front seat. "See, I told you to ride with me and now look? You copping 75 bricks," he says trying to motivate the young boy.

All last week the boy purchased 25 bricks faithfully everyday. Today is his first time buying this amount.

"Yo, I should be hitting you tomorrow night," he says as he hands over the bag which consists of $16,500.

Both Latif and Mu-Mit are impressed with his growth, but what they don't know is that the young boy collected money from seven other dope dealers to come up with the money. The dope is so good that he shuts everyone else down while he's out there. Every customer who comes through wants the 'After Party' or nothing. Frustration made them come up with the idea of putting their money together in one pot.

"Let me out, right here," the young boy demands. Mu-Mit stops abruptly and the boy hops out quickly. "Next day!" he shouts as he runs away from the car.

After Latif jumps into the front seat, Mu-Mit rides up the block. Latif immediately begins counting through the stacks. "Yo, pull up on Jess," Latif demands. Mu-Mit stops short at the corner. Latif honks the horn and Jesse runs over. Latif quickly hands him 5 bags of dope in compensation for plugging them with the young boy.

"I'll see you tomorrow," Latif says as Mu-Mit pulls off leaving Jesse standing at the curbside.

20 Minutes Later

Latif finally finishes counting through the stacks of money. "Here," he says as he hands Mu-Mit his profit of $1,500. He quickly lays his own profit onto his lap before stuffing Dre's $13,500 underneath the seat. "Boy, I love the dope game!" Latif shouts. "Feels good to be on the other side. God knows, I spent enough money with dope dealers. Now it's time to get some of mine back! I can't believe this shit!" he shouts with joy. In just one week of fucking with the young boy, I stacked 5 grand. Can you imagine if he start copping 100 everyday? Man, we'll be on our way! Yo, we got to get on the ball. It's money out here on these streets! These fag ass niggas stopping our flow though. We gave them long enough. It's now or never!"

"Indeed," Mu-Mit confirms. I ain't never been one for the talking, shit," he whispers. You know me, I'm a quiet nigga."

"I'm with you on that. Fuck the talking shit. It's time to make some real noise now! Fuck what Dre talking about. We gotta go over his head. We gave everybody fair enough warning. We asked them to take the dope and they refused. Now, they don't have a choice! It's time to roll over these sucker ass niggas!"

///// CHAPTER 21 /////

Chico stands bent over the pool table in deep concentration. "Two ball, corner pocket," he says clearly, before tapping the ball gently. It happens just as he calls it. "Game!" he shouts as he makes his way toward Dre who is seated at a table in the corner. "Primo, que pasa!" Chico screams. "Dimelo (Talk to me), tell me something good," he whispers.

"Chico, what's the deal baby," he replies while shrugging his shoulders.

"Mami, Corona con Limon," he orders from the waitress. "Primo, you drinking?"

"Yeah, coke with lemon."

Una coca cola con limon y una corona con limon," he says to the woman while taking a seat right next to Dre.

"Talk to me, Primo," he whispers.

"Chico, Chico, baby...you busting my balls," he smiles. "I got it all figured out though. I'm a businessman. That's what I do...business. You know my motto everything is negotiable." Chico sits there quietly, listening word for word. "I ain't gone pull no wool over your eyes. You my man. I'm laying it all on the table for you," he claims. "I'm getting the work at $135 a brick," he lies. "I know you said you banging at 200-215 a brick. Meet me at 160. Lemme at least make a quarter? I know that ain't too much to ask?" he laughs.

Chico shakes his head with despair. "Primo, Primo, I dunno. We got guys from Boston who buy 500 or 600 bricks at a time. No way, we can tax them for $200. We sell it to them for $165-$170 a brick."

Damn, Dre mumbles under his breath. He was so sure that Chico would jump at that offer. Greedy ass Dominican, he thinks to himself. He should have known better. He learned a lesson with dealing with Dominicans back in his cocaine days. He remembers going over to the Washington Heights one particular time with $100,000 cash. The connect wanted $20,500 per kilo. Dre wanted five but he was short $2,500. He was 100 percent sure that his connect wouldn't turn him down for 2 measly thousand dollars but he was totally wrong. He begged the connect to give it to him for 20,000. Not only did he refuse, he let Dre walk out of the door with 100,000 in cash. It was then that Dre learned the value of business and he also learned how greedy Dominicans can be. "Come on, Chico, this ain't the coke days, baby," he teases. "It's all about a quick flip. Don't be like that. You know we talked about this shit down the way...how greedy ya'll Dominicans can be," he smiles. "You know how ya'll do...trying to make ten thousand dollars off a joint," he laughs. "Trying to get rich off of one pie," he jokes. "Need 5 points, huh? Fuck a point and a half, right?" He smiles but deep down inside he means everything he's saying.

Chico smiles from ear to ear, realizing that everything Dre is saying is the actual truth. "Primo, come on, baby. I know it's a new day," he laughs. "A quarter profit is cool on 500 bricks. We can live with that. Meet us at 150 and we got a deal," he says looking away in the direction of the waitress who is on her way over to their table with the drinks.

Dre can't believe that his man is actually greedy enough to try and play him out like this. He told him that he gets it for $135, yet and still Chico has the nerve to ask for it at $150, leaving him with a $15.00 margin. Dre shakes his head with disgust at the thought of it. It's a good thing that he did lie about the price he pays. If he had told the truth, that he pays $115.00, Chico would have wanted it at $125. Dre can't believe it but he definitely understands it. It's all business.

Dre quickly begins calculating in his mind. 3500 bricks at $35 profit equal $122,500 profit a week. Damn, he thinks to himself. Dre decides to take his chances at getting a little more. It's not that he needs more, he's only trying to get more for the simple fact that Chico is acting so petty. "Chico, I'm at $135, let a nigga eat a little, damn. I can roll with a 20 cent profit. Meet me at 155?" he begs.

Chico sits quietly for a second, while he does his own calculations. "Fair enough," he mumbles. "It's a deal," he says, holding his glass in the air. "To good business!" he says as he taps his glass against Dre's.

Yes, Dre cheers to himself. "So, when you're ready to roll, just holler…I'm here," he says casually, trying not to sound too excited.

"Let me call my brother," says Chico. As he's on the phone, Dre is adding up the profit again. He figures 3500 bricks a week at $40.00 profit equal $140,000 profit a week for himself and $192,500 for the Mayor. Got damn, he thinks to himself. This is the type of moves that he's told his brother about, but for some reason the Mayor won't pay attention to him. He's told the Mayor time after time again, that he shouldn't limit himself to Newark. Maybe after receiving damn near $200,000 profit from one client will change his mind and make him see the big picture. If that doesn't do it, Dre is sure nothing will.

Chico hangs up the phone. "We ready. He says he'll take things slow to start with. I told him that you're real people, but you know how it goes? He wants to do things his way. He wants to go light the first time around, just to make sure everything is on the up and up."

Oh boy, here comes the bullshit, Dre thinks to himself. He had a feeling the shit Chico was talking was all gas. "No problem," Dre whispers, trying to conceal the attitude that is building up quickly. All this negotiating, trying to talk him down and now that they agree on a number, he wants to pull back. Dre is becoming angry at the thought that Chico has been wasting his time.

"How fast can you have 1,000 bricks ready for me?"

"A thousand?" Dre repeats. That's going light, Dre thinks to himself. "Well, I'm light right now. I'm lucky if I got 200 bricks left. Shit moving like that," he says as he snaps his fingers. "I can't keep it. Just as fast as I get it, it's gone," he claims. "At the latest, I'll be back in position in about two days."

"Good enough," Chico says arrogantly. "My brother is worried about your reach. I told him, you're the number one guy over there, but he's afraid that you may not be able to supply us with the amount we need. He's afraid to cut the other connect off, then find out too late that you can't handle the workload. He doesn't want to burn a bridge. Primo, I vouched for you. Please don't make me look bad." he pleads.

"Make you look bad?" Dre asks sarcastically. Don't even worry about that. You'll make yourself look bad before I make you look bad. Tell him he can burn the bridge, tear it down, even bomb the bridge," he says arrogantly. "I can cover any order. I have this shit in excess…more than I know what to do with. All I ask is that you call me at least two days before…that's it. Just don't wait until the last minute to place the order."

"No problem," Chico replies. "We'll be waiting for your call in 2 days. You need the money up front? I can have the $155,000 brought here to you just in case you need it to make the connection on your end?"

He's really reaching right now, Dre says to himself. Dre realizes what he's doing. Chico thinks that Dre is a middle man who needs his money to make the plug, and then take his profit off of the top. "Nah, that's not business. I give you the work, you give me the money. That's how I roll. No pressure for anyone. It's all business," says Dre as he winks at Chico in a cocky manner. "It's all business, Daddy. See you in two days."

///// CHAPTER 22 /////

Two Days Later

It's 2 in the morning. The young man rolls over in the bottom bunk in the Essex County Jail. His urge to urinate has awakened him. He gets up and walks over to the toilet. He stands there with his eyes half closed as he's urinating.

After he's done, he stretches and yawns. He peeks to his right, where a small package sits by the entrance of his cell. He slowly walks toward the package. He's extremely curious to know what it is. Once he gets there, he taps it with his foot. A piece of white paper is attached to the box. He bends over and picks up the box. He kneels down as he reads the letter. It reads: What's up, Gangster? They say be careful what you ask for 'cause you just might get something that you really don't want once you get it. You asked for those sneakers over and over, even after I told you that you really didn't want them. You insisted, so here they are. You got them. They're yours now. Wear them with pride. Keep one thing in mind though. Remember what I told you. These sneakers have murder written all over them. These sneakers are a gift from me to you. Don't worry, it's nothing. I paid for them. The only thing you have to pay for is the taxes that come with them.

The letter is signed, The Mayor. The last lines of the letter reads: P.S. If you can be seen you can be touched.

The young boy sits there with confusion. He doesn't have a clue what this letter is all about. He opens the box and his questions are answered. Lying in the box is a brand new pair of Prada sneakers. They're the exact pair that the Mayor was wearing when he came here for court. The Mayor instructed Emily to buy them and place them in the man's cell.

Ink on the receipt catches the boy's attention. The price of $375.00 has ink slashed through it. Right next to the price the words, "Taxes is equal to your life" is printed boldly.

The man wonders how the sneakers got in his cell. He can't help but wonder what this means. Suddenly nervousness sets in. He feels like he may be in some type of danger. Little does he know his assumption is correct.

///// CHAPTER 23 /////

Rahway State prison

Visit is just ending. The last inmate hugs his wife tightly. "I love you," he says as he pulls away from her. "See you next week," he says as he backpedals away from her. As he passes the garbage can, he drops an empty soda can and a potato chip bag into the can.

The prisoner lines up behind the rest of the inmates who are getting searched. The officers pat them down quickly, finishing the line up in no time at all. "Mike Mittens, the officer shouts. "Step up!" Mike does as he's instructed. As he's being searched, he peeks through the corner of his eye, where he sees the inmate cleaning the visit room. Mike Mittens secretly watches as the inmate dumps the contents of the can into a huge plastic bag. The man peeks around cautiously before grabbing hold of the potato chip bag that Mike Mittens threw away. He looks inside just to make sure he has the right bag. Bingo, he thinks to himself as he sees three bricks of dope lying in the bottom of the bag. He then lays the bag on top of the pile of garbage.

Before stepping through the doorway, Mike Mittens looks the inmate in the eyes and gives him a head nod. The man returns the head nod.

Anxiety fills Mike Mittens gut. He can't wait to get his hands on the dope. He plans to circulate the dope throughout the entire prison. He plans to sell each bag for $50. His profit will be $10 a bag. The rest will go to the Mayor.

The Mayor gained so much respect for him. Mike Mittens could have easily testified against him during the murder trial, but he didn't. Mike's loyalty to the game solidified a spot in the Mayor's heart. The Mayor promised Mike that he would take care of him. Now that the Mayor is back in position, he can now show Mike his appreciation by breaking bread with him.
Meanwhile at Trenton State Prison

The middle-aged man stands against the wall accompanied by his wife and his three small children. "Say cheese," the cameraman says before snapping away with his camera.

As the family is walking away, the man shakes the cameraman's hand. "Thanks," he says as he grips the photographer's hand. Through the handshake, they transfer a brick of dope. The photographer conceals the dope in the palm of his hand as he takes the next picture.

Once visit is over, the photographer will make sure the inmate gets his dope back. In just this one visit, ten bricks of dope have been smuggled into the prison, which will earn the Mayor $20,000 in cash at the end of the score.

The Mayor's plan to control the dope market inside the prison is coming together slowly but surely. Dre hates the idea of making one and two brick moves but the Mayor insists that he does so. The Mayor has a bigger plan, but he knows he has to crawl before he can walk. He has it all figured out. If he can move just five bricks a week in twenty five prisons, he scores a quarter of a million dollars a week, from the prison system alone. Currently, he's distributing his dope throughout six different prisons, but he has many more lined up. $250,000 a week is his short term goal. His big picture is controlling every prison that he has a contact in.

In The Bronx

Dre stands in the kitchen of Chico's apartment, while Chico examines the duffle bag filled with dope. "One thousand, right?" he asks

"Indeed," Dre replies casually.

"One second," Chico says as he's walking out of the kitchen.

He returns shortly holding a shopping bag. "Here, Primo," he says as he hands the bag over. "That's $155,000. All one hundred dollar bills. Count it," he demands.

"How much you say it is?" Dre questions.

$155,000," he replies.

"Count it for what?" Dre asks in a confident manner. "It is what you say it is. I take your word for it."

Chico smiles from ear to ear. "Listen, 500 of these are already sold the minute I get them to the spot. My peoples from Ohio is waiting for them right now. I'm sure, I'll be done with the rest of these in no more than a day and a half. Put the order in for another 1,500 now, so we can get it as soon as we're done. We can't wait. My brother hates to go a second without work."

"Don't worry, I got you," Dre says confidently. His confidence comes from him knowing that he has enough work stashed to supply Chico for the rest of the week. After speaking with Chico the other day, Dre put in an order of 6 kilos. This was his biggest flip thus far. At first he was a little hesitant but he quickly shook his nervousness. He has it all figured out. He hates to count his chickens before they hatch, but he can't help but to calculate what his profit will be if the week goes as planned. If Chico buys the 3,500 bricks he claims he will buy, Dre is sure he can shake the remaining 1,300 with the rest of his crew. His Philly, Delaware, Brooklyn, and Harlem plugs are good for at least 700 bricks together. ILL Wheel is good for another 300. Latif and Mu-Mit's movements are slow but they account for at least 200 bricks. Anything that is left over, Dre will save for the Mayor and his prison movements. If all goes well, he can profit $250,000 this week easily.

Dre hops into his jeep and starts it up. He dumps the bag of money onto his lap. As he's skimming over the stacks, his favorite song comes on. He sings along with singer Akon. "If you want to, we can supply you! Got enough work to feed the whole town. They won't shoot you unless you try to come around and try to stomp on our ground. Cause we taking over, one city at a time! Said we taking over one city at a time! Said we taking over one city at a time!"

///// CHAPTER 24 /////

Days Later

Dre stands at the window of Tony's spacious office, just enjoying the view. Suddenly, the door squeaks as it opens. Tony enters casually, dressed in his golfing attire. "You sure you don't want to get a couple of holes in with me?" Tony asks. "Golfing is good for the mind," he adds.

"Nah, I'm good," he replies with a slight smirk on his face. "I'll catch you the next time," he says a he walks over to Tony's desk, where he retrieves his briefcase. He quickly pops the latches open and stacks of money are exposed. "Altogether, that's $215,000.00," Dre informs. "165 of that is for my brother and the other 50 is for the Miami chick."

Dre had a very lucrative 2 weeks, despite the fact that Chico and his brother didn't move their estimated workload. Instead of moving 3,500 bricks as they said they would, they only moved 2,500. The rest of Dre's team accounted for another 800 bricks. All in all it was still a good two week period for Dre and the Mayor. Both of them made an approximate profit of about $165,000 apiece. This has been their best so far. In all Dre's years of hustling he's never scored like this. He's certain this is only the beginning though because he hasn't even got in contact with all of his candidates yet.

Dre had plans of coming home and turning it up, but never in his wildest dreams did he imagine doing it like this. In just a few short months, he's accumulated money that some hustlers don't see in a lifetime. His main goal is to stay focused though. He knows that if he allows himself to get caught up in the fascination of the money, he can be blindfolded by it. He has to stick to the script and continue to make wise decisions. If not, he knows, with the capacity of the moves that he's making, it can cost him his freedom forever.

"Ok," Tony whispers. "I'll make the deposit on my way to the course."

The Mayor ordered Dre to give his profit to Tony after every score. Tony has several accounts set up for the Mayor. Tony also sees to it that Liu and Megan are both taken care of. They both receive monthly allotments of $20,000 on the first of every month.

The Mayor feels total comfort in letting Tony handle all of his finances. He trusts Dre just as much, but he realizes Dre is playing the same game, which means anything can happen, on any given day. He has to be sure that his money is safe at all costs.

Dre hates the fact of how much faith his brother has in Tony. Dre doesn't trust him the least bit. In his eyes, Tony is nothing but a slick, money hungry attorney. He feels that the Mayor has it all wrong. He looks at Tony as a friend when he should be looking at it like business. Dre tells the Mayor over and over that Tony is only out for the dollar, but the Mayor denies it each and every time.

Dre watches him cautiously and he only deals with Tony for whatever business they have with each other. Although Tony does know a great deal of their business, Dre discusses very little with him. He figures the less he knows the better off they are. One thing Dre is sure of is if the Feds ever come for them, Tony will get pressed on. Dre is sure Tony will give them up in a heartbeat if his back is pushed against the wall. Dre has heard of so many stories where that has been the case. No way in the world does he expect Tony to mess up his life for two drug dealers. Keeping that in mind, Dre plans to keep Tony as far away from his business as he possibly can.

Meanwhile In Newark

Mu-Mit's Cadillac sits parked on Central Avenue and 8th street as their meeting is in progress.

"Baby Boy," Mu-Mit says aggressively. This is the first time Mu-Mit has said a word to the young boy. Mu has a plan of his own. He sees a way that they can capitalize off of having the boy on their team. "I got a proposition for you. We got a little situation and we was wondering if you could help us out."

"What's up?" the young boy asks from the front seat.

"Dig, your block jumping. Everybody eating except me and La. We selling it to ya'll at 220 and we getting it for 210," he lies. "We splitting 10 cent profit a brick, five apiece. That ain't no room to do shit with. It's like we doing this shit for the hell of it. We taking a lot of risk for damn near no paper," he adds. "If you can help us, we would appreciate it. If you can't, I understand that too," he whispers. "But we gone have to stop moving out though, cause it ain't worth it for us, understand? I mean we a team, now. Ain't no one sided business with us. One hand has to wash the other. That's the only way any of us is going to stay afloat. If me and La sink, then we ain't gone be able to get the fire to ya'll, understand?"

"What you need me to do?"

"We can't live off of $10 profit between the two of us and we don't want to raise the price on you and fuck up what you got going. So, all I'm asking is whenever you cop, we hit you with a few extra bricks. Then when you done with yours, just bang a couple of ours for the same price you bang yours for? Only a few, here and there, nothing major. Nothing to take no real money out yo pocket. You figure, 5 or 10 bricks every time you cop. That will balance everything out. What it take like, 2 hours to bang 10?"

I knew there was gone be some bullshit in the game somewhere. Slick ass Old Head, he thinks to himself. I should have known better than fucking with slick ass old heads. "Something like that," he whispers. The boy thinks about Mu-Mit's proposal for a quick second. In no way does he want to go without this work and he would hate for them to raise the price. They've put him in a tight spot, giving him no other alternative. "Aight that can be done."

"Good looking, fam," Mu says as he starts to cruise up the block. "See, I told you, La," Mu says, winking at Latif. "I was telling La that you wouldn't mind helping us out."

"No doubt," he mumbles. "So, ya'll definitely gone have something tomorrow, right?" the boy asks desperately.

"For sure," Mu replies. "First thing in the morning," he says as he pulls over on 11th avenue. "We'll hit you as soon as we get it in our hands...aight?"

"Fo sho," he replies as he starts to exit the vehicle.

As Latif is getting into the front seat he scans the empty block. It's extremely quiet today. All the young dope dealers are standing around wearing long, saddened faces. Things have picked up tremendously out there and they hate the fact of having no work today. The thought of someone else's block getting their money, disappoints them. They could have easily called up one of their other connections, but they refuse to do so. The 'After Party' has them spoiled. When they have the 'After Party', they do less grinding and they still make more money. All they have to do is scream the name and the dope sells itself, unlike other dope they've had. They have to damn near force the customers to buy it from them. "Aight, Babyboy in the a.m.!" Latif shouts.

Mu-Mit pulls off slowly after the young boy slams the door. He walks away with his head hanging low.

"Damn, Mu why you tell him we don't have shit? You just blew $2,000 profit apiece. We could have made the profit today and started that new shit tomorrow?"

Mu-Mit shakes his head from side to side. "Trust me on this one, La. You living for the day or are you in this shit for the long haul? Look at these niggas faces. Not having the dope is making them sicker than the dope-feigns. They only been without for a few hours now and look at them. Can you imagine how they feel when the feigns walk away from them, cause they ain't got the 'After Party'? It makes them sick to their stomachs. Let them go dry for a day or two. We ain't gone have none tomorrow either."

"Come on, Mu."

"Trust me, baby. Yeah we blow $4,000 profit but guess what? When they go dry they'll appreciate it more. Then when we give them our shit to mix in, they won't have no problem with doing that for us. They'll do whatever we want, just so we don't pull the plug on they ass."

"Makes sense," Latif admits. "It definitely makes sense," he whispers.

///// CHAPTER 25 /////

The Next Day

Dre sits in the passenger's seat of the Infiniti. "Good to go," he says to himself as he closes the secret stash spot underneath the dashboard. "Listen, Lil Mama, you can take your girlfriend with you for the ride. I know 14 hours of driving by yourself is kinda rough, but whatever you do, do not let her know what you're going down there for, hear me?"

"Yes," she replies submissively.

"Here," he says as he hands her a stack of money. "This is $2,500. That's your gas, toll and hotel. As soon as you get in town, book yourself into the first decent hotel you see. Make yourself at home, find a mall and do you, alright?" he asks as he gets out of the car.

"Got you," she whispers in a low tone.

Dre slams the door. "Drive safe and be careful. Don't bullshit here in the town too long! Get the girl and bounce. I want you on the road no later than 10:30," he says as he smacks the roof of the car. "Hit me as soon as you touch!" he says as she peels off slowly. "Don't forget, park the car," he whispers.

Twenty Minutes Later

"Yo, hold the fort down, ya'll. I'll be back in about 4 or 5 days," says Dre from the backseat of Mu's Cadillac. "It's 200 bricks in there, alright? See ya'll when I get back."

Latif holds the bag of dope in his hand. He quickly calculates his profit of $4,000. Just the thought of it makes him want to get out and pound the street. He is so ready to drop the dope on his young boy, but Mu-Mit insists that they wait one more day. Latif understands where Mu is coming from, but he just hates to slow down their process of getting money. If they had other plugs, it wouldn't be such a problem. They could easily make a dollar for themselves, here and there. Unfortunately, they have nowhere else to dump the work, but they plan to fix that problem, real soon.

Hours Later

Dre lays back in the First Class section of the airplane. He's exhausted. It's only 12 noon and he's already done more that the average man does all day.

He opened up his day with a 150 brick score, followed by a 200 brick score from two of his clients. All his ends are tied for the week, now he has business to tend elsewhere. "ATL, here I come," he mumbles to himself, as he lays his head back for a quick nap.

Meanwhile In Fort Dix

The Mayor lies back on his bunk, reading through his stack of mail. He receives an abundance of mail daily. Today is no different; letters from Megan and Liu, a few official court documents pertaining to his many cases, and the rest are letters from guys begging for handouts from him.

As much as the letters annoy him, he still looks forward to reading them.

The Mayor hardly ever ignores any of the letters. The letters come from inmates all over New Jersey. They are from different dudes that the Mayor has come in contact with over the years in the prison system and on the street. Some are little favors like, paying for their girlfriend's rent, relative's mortgages, or kid's school clothes. Some even ask for his help in paying their attorneys' fees. All in all, the Mayor's good heart makes him do whatever he can possibly do in aiding them. He can't stand to see someone helpless in a crisis, which is why he has no problem spreading his fortune.

For all these years, he's had no problem helping these guys. Now he just has been reaching out to each and everyone that he's helped over the course of the years. Slowly but surely, he plans to put all of them on his payroll.

The Mayor grabs hold of the very last letter. He looks at the name and return address carefully. "Damien Bryant," he says to himself, trying to see if the name rings a bell. He can't figure out who it can be. The name is foreign to him. He then looks at the return address once again. "Big Sandy, he says to himself. "Inez Kentucky? He says without a clue. His curiosity is driving him crazy. He rips the envelope open quickly.

It reads: I know you have no idea who I am, so let me formally introduce myself. My name is Damien 'Manslaughter' Bryant. Don't let the return address fool you. I'm from Newark 'Brick City'. I was shipped here two months ago. The stop before this was in California. After being convicted of nine homicides and conspiracy of over twenty more, I was labeled a menace to society. I'm being charged with capital murder. At age 25, they're trying to end my young life by giving me the death penalty.

That's a whole different story, though. My purpose in writing you isn't to talk about me. This letter is about one of my little Homies. The word was spread from Essex County Jail to Big Sandy about an incident that took place where an altercation broke out and my blood was spilled. It was explained to me that the Homie stepped out of line and you took it upon yourself to discipline him. It was also brought to my attention that a threat was made to the Homie by you.

The Mayor is getting more furious after each line. He wonders how they got his information. It's obvious that they have done their homework on him as well. He truly can't believe this. Who the fuck these young motherfuckers think they're dealing with, he asks himself. He's pissed, but he does respect their heart. He wonders if it's courage or pure stupidity. He humors them by reading further.

I know and respect the level that this war can go onto, which is why I'm willing to swallow my pride and do something that I've never done. I'm waving the peace flag. You made a statement to the Homie 'if you can be seen, you can be touched.' Are you invisible?

The Mayor is terribly disgusted now. This threat has taken him to the next level.

Immediately after hearing about the incident, I bounced your name against a few prison walls, from Kentucky back to the Bricks. I realized that the Homie stepped in a mess and may be up to his neck in shit. I'm responsible not only for that Homie, but approximately 800 more. If this situation isn't handled properly, it can turn into a disaster. Can you imagine Bin Laden going up against Fidel Castro? Disaster right?

The Homie is only a baby and he's way too young to respect your gangster. I'm responsible for him, so I'm pleading to you on his behalf. If you can find it in your heart to forgive the Homie, it would be appreciated. I can have him write you a formal apology and hopefully we both can forget that this ever happened.

From one gangster to another, I give my word to you. We will not make another move, but if attacked, I will have to command my army to retaliate. This is not a threat, just an act of defense.

I'm a businessman first and I realize that nothing is free. I would love to put this small situation behind us. If you feel disrespected and reject my plea, I understand wholeheartedly. I'm asking you as a favor to me, to let the Homie slide. Trust me, he will be disciplined accordingly. In return, me and my army are here at your disposal.

It's signed: "Manslaughter" A.K.A. The Black Charles Manson.

The Black Charles Manson, the Mayor repeats to himself, while laughing. Who the fuck does he think he is, the Mayor asks himself. Furthermore, who the fuck does he think I am. It's obvious that he doesn't have a clue of who he's up against, but I will show him. He laughs satanically to himself. "I will definitely show them."

///// CHAPTER 26 /////

Hours Later

Dre sits in the lobby of the Hyatt Hotel. Lil Mama just dropped him off here. He sits there casually as if he actually is a resident at this hotel. He and Lil Mama are actually booked in the Intercontinental Hotel, which is directly across the street. Dre lied to his man telling him that he's at this hotel, not wanting him to know his real whereabouts.

Dre's purpose here in Atlanta is to hook up with his man Casper. They met each other years ago in FCI Ashland. Casper is a guy Dre believes to be highly reputable. He landed a bid for a sale of 2 kilos to a federal informant many years ago.

Dre got in contact with him about three weeks ago through a mutual friend. Dre wasn't in a big rush to come here at first. After hearing how good Casper was doing, his curiosity dragged him down here. He just hopes that the trip is well worthwhile because he can think of a million other productive moves he can be making back home.

Dre's phone rings. "Hello?"

"New York, what up, my nigga? Where you at?" Casper yells into the phone.

"I'm in the lobby," Dre whispers. He gets pissed off at the sound of Casper's voice. He's always hated the fact that Casper calls him New York. Casper means no harm. He's just gotten used to it. In the Feds, being that people come from all over the world, a lot of times they're nicknamed by where they're from. Although, Dre is from New Jersey, southerners tend to classify anything up North as New York.

"Alright, I'm pulling up...right now. Come on out!"

Dre stands up, facing the doorway. Through the huge glass, all that's visible to him is a huge chrome grill which is coming up the entrance path. He can't decipher the make of the vehicle, but he can see that it's a shining beauty. Dre faintly sees Casper's pitch black face behind the steering wheel.

The vehicle parks directly in front of the hotel, blocking up the entire entrance. Everyone in front of the hotel can't help but stop and stare at the huge, stainless steel colored 4 door Bentley Flying Spur. The loud noise of the stereo gives them no other alternative but to focus on him. The attention drives him wild causing him to bop his head crazily to the tunes of rapper, Maino. "Take a picture...click, click!" he shouts at the top of his lungs. "My life is a movie! My life is a movie!"

Butterflies automatically fill Dre's belly. He steps almost in slow motion toward the vehicle. The attention of the people makes Dre extremely nervous. Unlike his brother he hates the spotlight.

"What's good, nigga!" Casper yells from the driver's side window, causing even more attention. Dre hurries to the car and hops in quickly. His face is red from embarrassment. He lays down in the seat, real low, with shame.

Something about too much attention always makes him nervous. He's so paranoid, that he always thinks he's being watched. Knowing he's being watched makes him even more uncomfortable. "What up, nigga?" Casper shouts as he extends his hand for a pound.

"Ay man, it's all good," Dre mumbles very casually as he looks into Casper's sleepy looking eyes.

"Good to see you, man," Casper says with a wide tooth grin, exposing his platinum smile. A chunky diamond encrusted grill fills his mouth. The rainbow reflection blinds Dre more and more after each word that Casper spits out. Huge chunk jewelry also covers his wrist and fingers, complimenting his dark skin well.

Casper pulls a wash cloth from the console and begins pat drying his huge bald head. "What up, talk to me?"

"Calm down…take it easy," Dre laughs. "You still extra hyper, huh?"

"Ay man, ain't nothing change! I'm the same nigga in the prison or out the prison," he says arrogantly.

Dre peeks around and notices that everyone's eyes are still glued to them. "Pull off from here," he suggests.

"So, what's up, nigga? When you check in?" Casper asks as they cruise away.

"I been home for a few months now."

"Aight!" Casper shouts with unnecessary joy. "How shit been going for you?"

"Shit alright. I'm doing fair for a square," Dre says modestly. "Not like you…Bentleys and shit," he teases.

"This ain't about shit! Nigga, life is good!" he shouts, staring straight into Dre's eyes.

"I got eyes nigga. I can see. Either you doing it, or you got a hellified bluff game." Dre laughs.

"Bluff game? Nigga, never that! You ain't seen nothing yet," he says sarcastically. "I can show you better than I can tell you. I told you, when we were in Kentucky, if them crackers ever fuck up and free me, I had something for they ass. Didn't I tell you that?"

Dre responds by smiling.

"You been to ATL before, right?"

"Nah, never," Dre admits with shame. Dre has spent a great deal of his life in prison. He never actually got the chance to soar the land. The most traveling that he's done has been when he was being shipped from institution to institution. The furthest that he's been away from Newark on his own is Virginia Beach.

"I got you. Let me give you a little tour."

Minutes later, they pull up to a huge mansion. "That's the big house, right there. That's my rest," he claims. "Well, one of them that is," he says arrogantly.

Dre is quite impressed. Yeah?" he asks, nodding his head up and down.

"Yeah," he whispers. "You don't know ATL but this block is the shit! Jermaine Dupri and Janet live on that end. Dwayne Wade got a spot right there, and Will Smith got a spot right behind me. We meet in our backyards every morning. I'm surrounded by millions nigga! I told you life is good! I'll show you the rest of the city first, then I'll show you the inside. Before we go, peep the garage," Casper boasts as he hits the remote garage opener. In the dual garage there sits a yellow Diablo and a snow white CL 550 coupe, Mercedes. "Nigga got toys, too," he shouts as he pulls off.

Two hours have passed and throughout their tour Casper has shown Dre two other homes that he claims are his along with four other homes that he says he bought for his babies' mothers. The cars he claims he bought for the women range from BMWs to Porsche trucks. Dre has never known Casper to be a liar, but all of this seems to be just a little too much to believe.

Their tour ends at a warehouse on a little dead end block. Casper parks directly in front of the warehouse in between a Range Rover and a Bentley GT. "Come on!" he shouts as he hops out of the car.

Dre is hesitant at first, but he follows Casper's lead. "What's this?" Dre asks as Casper presses the code on the door.

"Hold up, you'll see," he smiles. Casper leads Dre up the steps and the closer they get to the top, the louder and more clearly the music gets. Casper opens the door at the top of the stairs and the loud, pungent smell of marijuana seeps into the hallway, almost knocking him off of his feet.

Suddenly the sound of a woman's beautiful voice zips through the airwaves. Dre bops his head to the smooth R and B vibe.

"You like that, huh?" Casper asks as he closes the door behind Dre.

"She hot," Dre admits. "Who is she?"

"The next Mary J," he says. "That's my artist," he brags with a smile, pointing to the glass covered booth in the corner of the room.

Artist, Dre says to himself. Ok, now it all makes sense. This explains everything. He assumes that Casper must be doing it big in the record business. "Ok, what's her name? She got hits already?"

"Shit yeah! She got a bunch of hits, but she ain't out yet. I just signed her. Her name is Deja Vu. She won't be out until next year this time. Watch out for her. She gone make a lot of noise."

"You got other artists?"

"Yeah, I got a bunch of artists. I'm still trying to put everything together though."

Dre is now back to square one. All new artists and no hits yet. It doesn't make sense to him.

Casper sits down. "So, talk to me, New York. What's the deal? What you know good?"

"Nigga how many times I gotta tell you, I ain't from New York?" Dre asks with a smile on his face.

"My bad, man. It's a habit," he laughs. I been calling you that for ten years. How you expect me to change up now? "New York, New Jersey, whatever… what's good?"

Dre peeks around cautiously before speaking. "The *heron*," he mumbles. "I got it good, but from the looks of it you already doing you."

"Yeah, I'm doing me, but I'm playing a different game. You know me, I'm multi-talented. Name the sport, I can play it," he smiles.

"What game you playing now," Dre asks curiously.

"I'm on the powder side. You know that's my love. That's all I know."

"Oh yeah...like that?"

"Yeah, like that! Lovely too," he adds. My network is crazy. Dig the twist, 1000 birds a month. I'm getting em at 12- 5 apiece and banging 'em for 16- 5. I got a ten man squad. Each of them responsible for a hundred joints a month. Do the math...that's 4 million dollars profit a month."

Damn, Dre thinks to himself. Casper's flow makes his seem like petty street corner activity. "That's serious," Dre mumbles.

"Tell me about it!" Casper says sarcastically.

"Damn, you came all the way up?"

"Yeah," he agrees, nodding his head up and down.

"That's hell a flow. All that to the neck?"

"Nah, you know I don't do nothing without my main man Che-Che. As a matter of fact, I owe it all to Che-Che."

"Yeah? What's up with Che? Where is he?"

"Che chilling. That nigga ain't even in the country. He's in Dominican Republic living like a king. He over there building castles and condos and shit. Nigga begging me to come over there, but you know me...I love the hood!" he laughs. "Fuck that!" he shouts. "He comes back here one weekend out of the month. That's it. Man, Che-Che hit the mufuckin jackpot! He fucked around and went over there and got a Dominican Princess, you hear me? She the prettiest shit you ever seen. Bitch don't speak a word of English. Mufuckin Che-Che learned enough Spanish to ask the bitch to marry him," Casper laughs. "Come to find out the bitch father that dude. The rest is history. Papi plugged Che-Che into a mufucker in Miami who got unlimited joints. We took it from there and now we got a multi-million dollar network. That's 2 million for me and 2 million for Che-Che," he informs.

"Wow," Dre sighs.

"Enough about us. What's good on your side, though?"

Dre is hesitant to answer. Casper's story is a hard act to follow. He's almost embarrassed to even bring up his activity.

"Talk to me New York?"

"Man my shit is peanuts compared to what you doing," Dre admits. "It's almost no need to discuss my shit. I came down here thinking I can change your situation. Your situation don't need no changing," he smiles.

"Well, maybe I can change yours then? Tell me what I can do? Just name it? I owe you. You took care of me in Ashland. Now what can I do to repay you?"

"Well, here's nothing," Dre says with shame. "I'm getting smack at a fairly decent number. The work is Grade A. It's starting fires everywhere I put it."

"Say no more," he whispers. "You sold me on it. Where is it?"

"Casper, knock it off baby. You don't need it. Your plate is full."

"You right. I don't need it, but you know me. I'll do anything for a friend. I got a team of niggas. Just tell me the number and I'll give it to them...that simple. 10 phone calls and and we can flood ATL, Texas, Chicago and Louisiana."

"I'm plugged into over 20 cities and about 7 states. I got long arms," he says sarcastically. "Use my reach. You brought some with you, right?"

"Yeah," Dre mumbles.

"Well, get it. "Do you need me to take you to go and get it?"

"Nah, I can get it brought here."

"Do it, then. Make your call and I'll make mines. Let's get the party started! You my man. My connections are your connections. Use me up!"

///// CHAPTER 27 /////

Next Day at 12 noon in Atlanta

Here Dre stands in Casper's studio once again, while Lil Mama waits outside for him. Casper called Dre early this morning, telling him that it's very urgent that they meet.

"The food," Casper says. "They love it. The hundred bricks you gave me…it's gone already. I don't know where you got it from, but boy you got the recipe! Tell me you brought more?"

"Yeah, yeah. I got more," Dre replies. "150 more."

"150 more? 150?" he asks with a look of agitation on his face. "I thought you said you brought some dope with you?" he says sarcastically. "That ain't no dope. That's just a tease for my boys. That ain't even enough to rip through ATL. Check, this how we gone do it. How much I owe you for the hundred?"

Dre quickly thinks of a price for Casper. He can't hit him over the head, knowing that he's only moving the dope as a favor to him. "I'm usually at $180 a brick for it, but I can't charge you that. Just give me $165 a brick for it."

"Nah, baby, this business. This your hustle. I'll give you, your price."

"Nah, Cas," Dre refuses. "165."

"I insist," Casper says sternly. "100 is 18,000, right? Another 100 is another, 18,000, right? That's 36,000, plus 9,000 for the 50, which comes out to $45,000.00," he calculates quickly. "This is what we gone do. Give me five minutes and I'll have the change here for you. You can get back home, make your move and get me some real dope down here. Fuck New Jersey! You can set up shop, right here. I got a stash house, in a nice clean down low area. I'll clean it out and you can move right in. You ain't never gotta go home. Trade your New Jersey Nets jersey in for an Atlanta Hawks jersey. The Nets stink anyway," he teases. "Listen, I'm gon' get you rich down here. You ain't gotta touch shit but paper. You my man, you kept me up, while we was bumped. I gotta take care of you. Dig, what is it gone take for you to get 2 or 3,000 bricks down here? I can put the money up for you?"

His last statement sits in Dre's mind. Apparently, Casper thinks that Dre is a small-time middle man. Dre smiles slightly, but his ego is a little crushed. He feels good to know that Casper is more than willing to help him, but he hates the fact that he thinks that he's struggling. His ego makes him want to clear it up, but one thing that he's learned is the less a person knows the better. Knowing that, he just sits there listening as Casper continues to speak.

"I got a half-a-M (half a million dollars) for you. You can go up there and cop like 3,000 bricks. I'll send one or two of my guys up behind you. Get the smack, load my cruisers up, and send my boys on their way. You can fly back down here, whenever you get the time. Your paper will be here. I got you."

Dre listens attentively. Casper has it all figured out. He makes it seem so simple. Casper is willing to give him $500,000 for 3,000 bricks. He starts to calculate in his mind. He can easily do just what Casper says and he can make an easy $155,000 profit up front, no waiting. "Sounds good," Dre mumbles to himself.

"Sit tight while I set this all up. My girl will bring the paper to me. What you need a half?" Casper asks nonchalantly as if a half a million dollars is nothing to him.

"Nah, Casper. You can just pay me for the 250. I'll make a way to get the work here," he says as if he doesn't have total control of his operation.

"You sure?" Casper asks as he starts dialing his phone. "You sure?" he whispers. Dre replies with a head nod. "Yo!" he shouts into the phone. "I need fifty stacks over here right now!" he shouts into the phone recklessly. Asap!" he yells. In the studio!" he shouts with no regard.

Dre's stomach muscles cringe as he listens to Casper talk carelessly on the phone. He can't believe his ears. He would think that after all the years he spent in the Feds, he would at least have learned to stay away from the phones.

"Trust me when I tell you, you about to blow! I'm gon' see to that," he whispers sternly. You gon' get filthy fucking rich, fucking with me…watch," he says arrogantly.

///// CHAPTER 28 /////

In Newark

"Here you go," Latif says as he hands the young boy in the front seat a bag filled with dope.

"How many is this?" he asks.

"A hundred," Latif replies. "The 75 you ordered and the other 25 is what we discussed."

"Twenty-five," the boy whispers in a disappointed tone.

"Yeah, no pressure," Latif blurts out. "When ya'll finish with ya'll's, just squeeze ours in alright?" he says as Mu-Mit pulls alongside of the boy's older model, Chevy Lumina.

The boy hands Latif the bag of money. He then tucks the bag of dope underneath his shirt. He cracks the door open. "I should be hitting you by tomorrow night," he claims.

"Alright, we here," Latif says in a calm manner.

"Alright, one!" the boy shouts leaving the door wide open for Latif to get in the front seat.

As Mu-Mit pulls off, Latif begins separating the money.

"What I tell you?" Mu-Mit boasts. "We gone come up off the young boy. You figure, if he just bang 100 a week for us, that's like $27,000 profit… 13- 5 for both of us. Not to mention, the $4,000 profit we make off of every hundred they cop," he says.

Latif quickly does his own calculations. "Yeah," he agrees. "This gone be a come-up, right here. You a genius," he laughs.

Mu-Mit makes the right turn onto South Orange Avenue. As he creeps through the intersection, his passage is cut off by a group of men, who are taking their sweet time to cross the street. One of the men sticks out like a sore thumb amongst the crowd. He's quite neater in appearance than the rest of the shabby looking feigns. "Look!" Latif shouts. "Mufucking Salaam!"

"Damn sure is," Mu-Mit agrees. "Lemme fuck with him," Mu smiles. He revs the engine up and slams on the brakes, just short of smacking into the man. Huuuuurrrr! Mu-Mit rests on the horn.

Latif cracks the window open. "Move the fuck out the way!" he shouts, hiding behind the dark tinted glass.

Salaam struts slowly, trying hard to peek through the glass but to no avail.

"Nigga, don't make me get the fuck out!" Latif shouts.

"Who that?" Salaam whispers to the crowd. All of them reply with a shrugging of their shoulders.

"Back up on 'eem," Latif demands. Just as they get within feet of the crowd, Latif rolls the window down. "You got a problem with something I said?" Latif asks, while staring straight at Salaam.

Salaam smiles at the sight of Latif's face. "Fuck you!" Salaam shouts in a playful manner.

"You was petrified," Latif teases.

"Petrified?" he asks as he walks toward the car. "Nigga that word ain't even in my vocabulary," he smiles. "Ay, man, what's going on?" he asks as he shakes Latif's hand, which is stretched out of the window. He peeks his head inside the vehicle to see who the driver is. The glare of the sun makes him have to strain his one good eye in order to see clearly. Ever since a kid he's been blind in one eye. His eyes stretch wide open with joy. "Aw, hell no!" he shouts. Mu-Mit! What's going on? Aw man, ya'll two mufuckers together? That's trouble!" he laughs. "I know ya'll can't be up to no good. I know ya'll up to something! I want in!" he smiles.

"Jake the motherfucking Snake!" Mu-Mit shouts. "What up?"

Salaam's real name is Jake but the streets nicknamed him 'Jake the Snake'. He's one of the sneakiest, slimiest dudes to ever walk the streets of Newark. He made his living by robbing street corner hustlers. The only purpose his stick-ups served was fulfilling his cocaine habit.

"Ay man, you know how it goes…they keep feeding me the same old soup. They just warming it up," he smiles. "Aw man, there is a God!" he shouts. "I ran into the right motherfuckers!" he shouts as his bad eye twitches non-stop. "Ya'll just the mufuckers that I needed to see. Where ya'll headed? Ya'll got a minute or two?" he asks desperately. "Let me the fuck in?" he begs. Mu-Mit pops the locks open for him. "I know ya'll up to no good," he smiles as he sits down. "Tell me something good," he begs as he slams the door shut.

"Jake?" Mu-Mit says, totally disregarding his wishes of being called Salaam. Mu-Mit will never call him by a Muslim name being that he is not a Muslim. In fact Mu-Mit is probably the only guy who has enough heart to go against his wishes. "You just coming home?"

"Nah," Salaam replies. "I been home now for almost a year. I just been staying under the radar. Next month will be a year that I been home. Last month, I celebrated my first birthday on the street in 17 years," he brags. "I ain't been home for a year since I was a kid," he further boasts. "I been home, just been real low, sneaking in and out. I'm down in Asbury. Been there ever since I got out. Met me a good lil girl, during my last bid. Good girl," he emphasizes. "Held a nigga down. Anything I needed, she was there. Knocking the doors down for visits. Good girl, man. Bitch fatter than a Sumo wrestler, but she a good girl," he laughs. "Take care a nigga too..to the fullest but the money done got low, that's why I'm back up here. "To make a short story even shorter… the bitch got her hands on a big lawsuit, but I done breezed through her bank account. I'm fucked up! Man, but later for that shit! What's up with ya'll? What ya'll know good? I know ya'll got something going on. I'm starving! Nigga, let me eat with ya'll. Break bread with a nigga?" he begs.

"I wish, we had something going on," Latif replies. "Shit dark on our side."

"Bullshit!" Salaam replies. "Mufuckers riding through the town in Mercedes and shit. Ain't no way in the world, ya'll two mufuckers allowing that shit unless ya'll getting a cut. Nigga, fuck the bullshit! You know, I know!" he laughs.

Latif's new business mind comes into play. "What's going on down Asbury?" he asks, thinking of moving some 'After Party' throughout the town. "Any money down there?"

"Any money down there?" he repeats sarcastically. "Any money?" he repeats. "Them mufuckers down there getting rich. It's mega money down there! And they selling straight garbage. Garbage coke, garbage weed, and garbage dope! I don't know how they getting that shit off? If a mufucker come through with some good shit, they can take over everything." Latif's mind begins racing. He looks over to Mu-Mit, nodding his head up and down. "Exactly," Salaam replies, thinking that they have the same idea in their mind. "And I know all the key guys. I know who doing what and where they doing it at. Guys out there love the shit outta me, too. They think I'm the hottest thing since pants with pockets. I been down there, just scoping everything out, waiting for the perfect time to make my move. I'm gon' tear that whole fucking town upside down," he says devilishly. "I just been sitting back, trying to put it all together. I don't want to miss a beat. I want to hit everything back to back, before they even realize what's going on. I'm not going to give them time to retaliate. I been ready to move, I just wasn't in a position, feel me? No manpower, no artillery, but now that I found ya'll, it's the perfect time. A nigga can get rich down there. All ya'll gotta do is say the word and we can go down there and do us. I know shit we can hit tonight!" he says with joy in his eyes. "What's up?"

They sit quietly for seconds before Latif speaks. "I'm with you but I got another angle. True story, we got a goldmine. We got a monster on our hands. It's the dope of a lifetime. You turn us onto them niggas and we can flood the town with this shit. We all eat!"

"Flood the town?" he asks sarcastically. "What the hell you talking about? When the fuck you became a dope dealer? What the fuck the world coming to?" he says in a jokingly manner. "You done bumped yo mufucking head. We ain't no dope dealers! We wait around for a mufucker to make it so we can take it from 'eem. Flood the town? You on some bullshit. I'm telling you that I know where mufuckers got hundreds of gees stashed, waiting for us to come and get it and you talking about going down there, risking getting knocked off, selling some mufucking dope? Uhmm, uhmm, uhhmm," he sighs. "Un-fucking-believeable! I know niggas we can hit one time and score the bread that it will take a lifetime to make selling bags of dope. Bro, before I turn you onto them, I'll act like we never had this conversation. Fuck that! I ain't waste all that time, kissing up to them and planning shit for nothing. All the while, I was rocking them mufuckers to sleep, not prepping them to sell dope to them. Fuck that!" he shouts furiously.

"I feel you," Latif says. "But this shit too good to be true."

"Jake you know me," Mu-Mit interrupts. "I ain't never had the patience for that hustling shit, so you know it must be something to hold my interest. This shit fire! We got the recipe."

"Salaam, I'm telling you, we can all get rich, man. Six months from now we can all be sitting back somewhere. Paper up to the gods," he smiles.

"Man, I hear ya'll but I can't do that shit. Six months ain't promised to none of us. I damn sure ain't trying to be going to nobody prison for slinging dope," he laughs. "That ain't my game. I don't know shit about it and ain't trying to learn about it at no 45 years old. The only thing I know to do with *heron* is sniff it or shoot it," he admits. "I ain't got ten years for them crackers."

"Salaam, you missing the point," Latif says. "You ain't gotta do shit. All you gotta do is hook us up with the people. We will do the rest.

"Man, I been working on this shit too long. I got the whole shit mapped out. I can see it now, we go down there on some hustling shit and one of them poo-put ass niggas get knocked and put us up in the mix. That's all I need is to catch a federal beef. With my jacket, they'll finish me off. I'm sure I will get the L. It's too many snitches down there. Them mufuckers will tell on they Mama!" he shouts. "We go down there and do shit my way, we ain't got to worry about that shit. We get in and out like the bandits that we are. And it ain't gone take six months either!"

Mu-Mit pulls back onto South Orange Avenue

"Salaam, give it some thought," Latif says as he scribbles his phone number onto a matchbook. "Here's my number," he says as he passes the matchbook over the headrest. "If you change your mind give us a call. I'm telling you nigga, we can pop off!"

"On the real to real La, I ain't even considering it. I ain't even gone lie to you," he says as he grabs hold of the matchbook. In my eyes it ain't even worth going down there selling bag for bag. The town too small. Niggas don't last long down there. Just my luck, the first move we make will be the last," he laughs. "I can't believe this shit," he smiles. "Ya'll mufuckers trying to sell dope. What the world coming to? I never thought I would see this day," he says as he drags himself out of the car. "Well since ya'll got a goldmine, I'm sure ya'll doing more than alright. Let me hold something?" he begs. "I'm fucked up!"

Both Mu-Mit and Latif knew this was coming. You fucked up and don't have to be," Latif says. "Your situation can change overnight."

"Man, please with that shit. Knock it off, already!" Salaam shouts. "Nigga my ribs touching. Just lemme hold a couple of dollars. I'll get it right back to you when I make my sting, nigga," he laughs.

Latif peels off two one hundred dollar bills from his stash. "Here."

"Thanks baby. I'm definitely gone give ya'll a call. Hopefully when ya'll come off of that bullshit and come back to reality ya'll will be ready to get with me." he says as he's closing the door. He peeks his head back inside the vehicle. "What about you Big Muslim? You got a couple of dollars for a nigga?" he smirks.

"Jake call us," Mu says disregarding his begging. He pulls off slowly leaving Salaam standing on the curb.

"Yo, that will be a good look if we can get down there, right?" Latif asks. "We can tear that shit down too!"

Dollar signs flood both of their minds.

///// CHAPTER 29 /////

One Week Later

Dre stands in Weequahic Park, near the monkey bars. He's just finished doing his routine morning workout. He started the morning off by running the track and after that he did a couple sets of pull-ups and push ups. Right now, he's just pacing back and forth trying to regulate his breathing. He stops pacing near the lake on the wooden ledge.

As Dre is standing there watching the waves of the water roll peacefully, he thinks of the offer his man Casper made. He's been debating back and forth about it ever since he left Atlanta. Casper made him the proposition of a lifetime. He's sure he can capitalize off of Casper, but a part of him is unsure. Casper is the connection he needs to make this thing happen a little bit faster. The plugs he has are very much needed, but it can be extremely dangerous as well. In the short time that Dre was around Casper he noticed how sloppy Casper moved. Casper's reckless phone conversations, sloppy moves and his flamboyant lifestyle are all the things Dre tells himself he wants to stay clear of. Dre has to stay on point because he realizes that all those characteristics derive from having riches. The more money a dude makes the more arrogant and cocky he becomes. Even they start to believe that they are invincible. They actually believe that there is no situation that their money can't buy them out of. Dre begs to differ. In the FEDS he has bumped into multi-millionaires who have life. All the money in the world can't buy their freedom for them. Keeping that in mind, he plans to stay as humble and modest as he possibly can.

Dre thinks of all the money he can make with Casper on his side. He's sure a quick run with Casper can be worth at least a cool million. That will put him right where he needs to be. He has been weighing the options day after day. His greed tells him to go for it, but his heart tells him to pass up on it. This has been one of the hardest decisions he's ever had to make. Casper's back to back phone calls make it even harder to deal with. So far he's been doing a great job in stalling him, but Casper's persistence is making him weak.

Dre is almost sure that Casper is already in the middle of an investigation, if not he will soon be. Dre knows that there is no possible way that Casper can be making moves of that magnitude without the Feds being aware of him. The last thing Dre needs is to be dragged into a situation that Casper has already created for himself. Knowing all of this, a part of Dre still wants to try his luck. Greed makes a man lose his common sense.

"Maybe I can sneak in, get a couple of dollars and sneak back out," he whispers to himself, knowing that will never happen. One thing he's sure of is once he starts rolling, the only thing that will stop him is the Feds knocking on his door.

Dre's phone interrupts his thought process. "Hello?" he answers hastily.

"New York! What up?" Casper yells into the phone. "Nigga I told you, you got the recipe. You bullshitting. You left here a week ago. What you gone do? You done started these niggas up. They love that shit! Money down here waiting for you. If you ain't gone move on it, get it for me. I'll run with it. What you gone do? I need 2,000 bricks right now!" he shouts recklessly.

The word bricks rip through Dre's ears. His stomach bubbles from queasiness, as he entertains the thought that Casper's phone could be tapped. "Hello!" he shouts into the phone.

"Yeah!" Casper shouts clearly.

"Hello?" Dre repeats acting as if he can't hear Casper. "Hello?"

"Yeah!"

"I can't hear you. We got a bad connection. Hello?" he says before hanging up the phone. He stares at the phone, shaking his head from side to side. He can't believe Casper's negligence. This phone call could have easily just put him in harms way. It could easily land him a conspiracy charge. "Damn," he sighs. He thinks of doing another bid and he trembles at the very thought of it. This phone call just helped him make his final decision. He draws back and launches the cell phone high into the air like a football. "Fuck that!" he mumbles as he watches the phone splash into the sparkling water.

Meanwhile In Fort Dix

Benderas walks toward the Mayor who is lying on his bunk, engaging in a deep conversation with Liu. "Mail," he says as he drops a stack of letters onto the foot of the bed along with a box.

His curiosity leads him to rip the box open immediately. He's shocked to see the Prada sneakers before his eyes. "Liu, I'll call you back," he says hastily as he hangs the phone up. He quickly grasps the letter from the bottom of the box. He anxiously begins reading it. The Mayor is surprised to see that the letter is the formal apology from the kid in the County Jail as promised to him. He respects the fact that he's a man of his word, but he still refuses to let this matter ride. The young boy stepped out of line and his pride won't let him disregard that fact. Furthermore, the entire County jail knows of this beef because it was done in the public eye. The apology on the other hand is done in private which means no one will ever know about it.

Image is everything to the Mayor. He feels that if he lets this matter go untouched, he'll lose the reputation that took all of his life to build. "Good try, but not good enough," he mumbles to himself.

The Mayor has already thrown the line out there. He's sure in no time, he'll be getting confirmation that not only the young boy has been dealt with, but his leader as well. The Mayor understands that in order to destroy an army you must demolish the head first. Little do they know, it is way too late for their apologies.

The Mayor slams the box onto the floor and grabs the very first envelope from the pile. Just by pure coincidence the return address is from Inez Kentucky. It's from the kid, who calls himself Manslaughter. It reads.

"What's banging Homie? If you are in receipt of this letter, then I assume that you have already gotten the package. I'm not one for a lot of talking so, I will keep this letter short and brief.

As I said before, I hope that you can find it in your heart to forgive the little Homie for he not know. Also, as you can see the sneakers have been returned to you in the same condition as they were sent out from you. They were never worn so I don't think that it's fair for him to have to pay for them.

I kept my word by sticking to my end of the deal. Now I ask you from one gangster to the next, can we get pass all of this? Let's turn this negative situation into a positive? I told you before, I have over 800 followers. In the short time between this letter and the last, my army has increased by approximately 250 soldiers, which means I have control of over 1,000 men who occupy every prison in this nation. Which means it can either be a disaster or it can be beneficial for the both of us. If you can let this situation pass, I will be more than willing to be of any assistance that I can be to you.

The ball is now in your court. I'm here waiting for your reply, but if by chance I never hear from you, I will take it that you're denying the treaty.

All is well that ends well.

Signed "Manslaughter" A.K.A The Black Charles Manson

The Mayor laughs to himself, but deep down inside he's furious. He looks at the letter as the young boy copping out but he also takes some of it as if he's making threats. He realizes that the boy doesn't want trouble, but his pride won't allow him to admit that. Instead he slides sneaky threats within the pleas that he's copping.

The Mayor rips the letter in half furiously. At this point, there is nothing they can say to him to hold him off. They have barked up the wrong tree and now it's time for them to pay the penalty.

/////// CHAPTER 30 ///////

Tony and Dre sit patiently inside of the private plane, waiting for their departure at Teterboro Airport. They're on their way to Florida. Today marks Miranda's first court appearance with Tony as her representation.

Dre really doesn't want to go, but Tony begged him to come along. Dre's mind was dead set against it, but he came because he took Tony's persistence as a sign. He thought maybe Tony was saving him from some type of disaster without even knowing it. If he had stayed at home and gotten into some type of trouble later, he would hate himself forever. At this point, he's just taking it as a sign from God.

Dre looks around at the many beautiful private jets that are flying into the air and he can't help but to dislike Tony even more. Just to think that his brother's money is funding this type of bullshit. He now truly believes that Tony is using his brother to support his lavish lifestyle.

He has to bite his tongue just to keep his mouth shut at this point. Suddenly the urge takes over. He can't hold back any longer. "Damn baby, you doing it," he smiles with hate in his heart. "Private planes and shit," he adds. "I know this baby cost you a pretty penny, huh?" he asks.

Tony smiles modestly. "I wish I could afford my own plane. Me and four other attorneys that I went to law school with all chipped in for this. It all works out well. We take turns taking it out."

"Good answer," Dre says to himself.

"I hardly ever take it out."

Tony's answer makes Dre feel a little at ease, but he still can't stop now. He's on a roll. "So, honestly speaking…what are my brother's chances of actually getting freed?"

Tony wonders for a second where this question comes from. The sarcasm in Dre's voice makes him know exactly where Dre is going with this. "His chances are about as good as any other man who is going against the federal system," he says sarcastically. He then pauses for a second or two. "It's all a gamble and the good thing is he's willing to take the gamble. Let me tell you something. I deal with each client differently. I move according to the pulse of the client's heart. Some clients have very little heart and others like your brother have the heart of lions. My heart beats to the pulse of theirs. When dealing with your brother I'm forced to take risks that I would never take with other clients."

"Why? Because he has more money to burn?" Dre asks sarcastically.

Tony looks him in the eyes. His remark has him pissed, yet he keeps his composure. "It's not about a check, if that is what you're insinuating."

"I'm not insinuating," Dre replies. "We're just kicking it. We can kick it, right?"

"Sure," Tony says with a smile on his face. "I would be bullshitting you, if I tell you I have not made a lot of money as your brother's attorney. And I'm no bullshitter," he adds. "I will tell you this though…any other attorney would have been 50 percent richer. Ask your brother, I have done just as many cases for him in good faith as the ones that I charged him for. If you think, it's only about a check you are totally wrong. Me and your brother have built a relationship. If your brother was to go dead broke today, I would still fight for him in the same manner.

Your brother came to me at the end of his rope with nothing to lose. I'm proud to tell you at this point he has everything to lose. In the beginning I laid it all on the table for him. I told him, I'm not God. I can't promise a miracle, but I can promise you that I will fight as if it's my own life on the line. He knew exactly what he was up against, yet he was still willing to go on. I keep it real with him. I let him know when he should roll and when he should fold."

"Ok, so should he be rolling or folding, right now? Again, what are his chances of being freed?"

"Nothing is 100 percent, so I have to go with 75 percent. We've ripped through so many cases, and just the other day I just received a letter pertaining to a major case. I have not even told him about this one yet because I don't want to get him too excited. Some evidence has been suppressed; which brings us that much closer. There is only one thing I'm worried about though. What makes your brother's case different from other similar cases is, normally with a case of this magnitude there are so many co-defendants to use to finish off the top guy. The good thing with this is your brother rarely dealt with people outside of his immediate team. His main lieutenant, Black would have been the ideal co-defendant in this case. He knew everything from the monies made to the murders. Unfortunately for Black, but fortunately for us, he was murdered along with another co-defendant during a street war that was going on during the investigation. Only one living man was indicted Thomas Howard. Currently, he's out on bail. Apparently, he comes from a well to do family and they were in a position to put three houses up on his behalf. He was set free, but he wears the home detention monitor. They have no one else to put up against your brother, so I'm sure they will use him. At this point, he's our only obstacle. If it wasn't for him I would feel totally comfortable in going through with this and leaning on the courts mercy. I'm just not sure exactly what he will say to distract the jury, understand?"

"Indeed, I do," Dre says casually, nodding his head up and down. "Indeed, I do."

"I'm not concerned with him because I'm prepared for any games that they may play. All I need you to do is to stay clear of your brother. One little slip up on your end can blow this for us. I've worked too hard to allow new issues to set us back. At any cost, there should be no contact between you and him. I don't need any snooping around to lead back to him. You keep him clean and I'm almost sure, I can get him freed. You feel me?'

"I feel you," Dre whispers with certainty.   Over two and a half hours pass and the car service has just picked Tony and Dre up from Opa-Locka Airport in Miami.

"Can you speed it up, please, Sir?" Tony requests. "I can't be late," he sighs as he takes a quick glance at his watch. His anxiety is killing him.

Nervousness fills his gut. Being nervous is normal for him before any case but never has it been this bad. He blames it on the fact that this is his first time ever working in this state. New Jersey and New York are different. It's like his own backyard. He knows the majority of the judges and the prosecutors on a personal level. He knows who he can do what with and who he can not. His nervousness today reminds him of his first few cases, straight out of law school. The cockiness he's gained over the years has hidden itself today.

"Damn," he sighs as he rubs the sweat from his palms.

Dre watches him closely. Never has he seen him act in this manner. He's a nervous wreck right now. "Hey, what's up?" Dre asks trying to loosen him up. "So, what's the story with ol girl?"

"Um, at home this would be a story with a happy ending. I would have the home court advantage. You know how it goes when you play at the other team's home. You don't know the dead spots on the floor or you're not used to the heating system in the gym," he laughs. "And to top it off, the officials are all against you, making bad calls just to help the home team win," he adds. "It's a typical story though…young girl is head over heels in love with gangster boyfriend. He commits a string of crimes, mainly robberies which all end in homicide. They come down to Miami and the boyfriend murders the girls' godfather who happened to be a kingpin. They trace her from a car she rented. They arrest her and he gets ghost. She was offered a conspiracy charge if only she would tell his whereabouts and testify against him. She holds it down for whatever reason. She doesn't mumble a word."

"My type of broad," Dre interrupts.

"Nah, Dre," he refuses. "This is what you call a Murder Mami," Tony laughs. She's the most beautiful thing you will ever lay your eyes upon, which makes her all the more dangerous. Drop dead gorgeous!" he smiles. "Currently, she's facing life. They have no witness to the murder and no weapon. What they do have is a chauffeur who testifies that he picked them up from the airport days before. They also have a half empty glass of liquor with her DNA on it, which put her dead in the mix of the murder. Apparently, she and the godfather were drinking together right before the murder. Needless to say the man was found half naked."

Dre analyzes the story before speaking. "So, you think the boyfriend came in and killed him because of what it looked like?"

"Nah," Tony replies sarcastically. "I think together they planned this caper. She reeled him in with sex and her boyfriend came in right before."

"Her Godfather, though? Could she be that scandalous?"

Tony throws his hands in the air. "Ay," he sighs with his eyebrows raised high. "Straight smut, but I got a job to do. It's a dirty job, but someone has to do it. Now my duty is to go in here and recreate this woman right before the court's eyes. I will do my best to make her look as innocent as I possibly can."

"So, you think you can pull it off?"

"It's not a matter of thinking. It's about going in there and making it happen. No script, just pure free-styling. Look no briefcase, no nothing," he says as he looks down at his lap. "All I can do is let it flow from the heart. I'm gon' freestyle today just to feel these guys out. Wish me luck?"

"Good luck!"

Just fifteen short minutes later and it's already Showtime. Tony and Dre are walking through the double doors of the courtroom.

Tension fills the air. It's so quiet in here that Tony actually just heard a pen drop. All the attention is focused on them as they step up the aisle. Tony looks up front in search of Miranda. He quickly spots her silky hair from afar. "This way," he whispers to Dre.

Dre is so nervous right now. This is his first time stepping foot in a courtroom in years. Just being in here gives him the runs. His stomach is extremely queasy. He hates being in courtrooms. He can't even watch Court TV. At this point, he actually feels like he's the one on trial.

"Hello Benderas," Tony says as she quickly turns toward him.

"Hello," she whispers softly.

Tony looks into her puffy, swollen eyes. Tear drops flood her eye lids. "Miranda Benderas this is my assistant Mr. Blackhead," he introduces.

"Hello," she whispers with a head nod.

"Got damn," Dre says to himself. Drop dead gorgeous is an understatement, he thinks. "Nice to meet you," he whispers.

"Dre, you take a seat in that row," Tony suggests as he points to the bench one row behind them. Tony slides right next to Miranda. She's sniffling and crying. Tony wants to comfort her and tell her to stop crying, but her tears are good in this situation. Maybe the judge will see the tears coming from her pretty face and get sympathetic.

Miranda sneakily looks Tony up and down. His lack of professionalism scares her. Never has she seen an attorney not dressed in a suit. His multi-flavored polo golf shirt and orange polo safari jacket makes him look more like a Ralph Lauren mannequin than an attorney. And to add more insult to injury, he has the nerve to have on jeans and a casual driving shoe. She can't believe her eyes. Just to think that her life is in his hands frightens her tremendously. She hates to judge a book by its cover, but he looks young and inexperienced.

The door of the judge's chambers squeaks as it opens. The courtroom becomes even quieter as everyone awaits the judge's entrance. Tony's heart pounds as he sees a set of black hands grip the door. He quickly realizes that the fact that the judge is black can work for him, just as well as it can work against him. He watches closely as the short slender man makes his way to the chair. Tony does a quick analysis of the man. He only stands about 5 feet 2 inches tall, which scares Tony dearly. If he has the 'short man complex', Tony is sure he will be a problem. His dorky walk, thick bi-focal glasses, and his huge overbite make him resemble a character from 'Revenge of the Nerds'. His overall thoughts are it can be either one of two things; either he's as green as a golf course or he's as tough as nails. He wonders which one is the actual truth.

"All rise!" the bailiff shouts. Everyone scuffles to their feet.

"Be seated!" the judge says in a deep voice. He then gives a head nod as he sits down.

"First case, Supreme Court versus Benderas!"

The prosecutor stands quickly and begins reading from his stack of papers. Tony listens attentively. He peeks over at Miranda who he notices is trembling like a leaf. After a few minutes of the run-down, the prosecutor finally stands there in silence.

"Defense!"

Tony stands up confidently at his cue. Here we go, he says to himself trying to psyche himself up. As he's rising, he nudges Miranda softly with his elbow. He winks at her arrogantly. "Good morning, your honor," he says loud and clearly, staring the judge dead in the eyes. "My name is attorney Tony Austin and I represent Miranda Benderas," he says confidently.

The judge stares at him coldly. He sits quiet for a matter of seconds before he blurts out, "Excuse me but what did you say your name is?"

"Tony Austin, Sir!"

"I apologize, uh, Mr. Austin but do me a favor, please?"

"Excuse me Sir?" Tony asks with confusion.

"Step to the middle of the aisle, please?"

Tony steps to the middle of the aisle as he's instructed to. He's clueless to what this is all about. He stands there as the judge looks him over from head to toe. He feels like a science project the way all eyes are glued on him. At this moment, he feels like a huge spotlight is beaming down on him.

"Mr. Austin, you are an attorney, correct?"

"Yes, Sir?" Tony replies. Tony thinks he understands. He's been through this before. People look at his youthful face and they don't believe that he's an actual lawyer.

"I thought you said that," he says sarcastically. "But from here I couldn't decipher if you are an attorney or the Lucky Charms Leprechaun," he says with a smirk on his face. Laughter fills the courtroom, embarrassing Tony gravely, yet he remains cool. "Mr. Austin, this is the state of Florida. I'm going to assume that you're not aware of how things work here. That's better for the both of us, because if I assume that you don't care then I'm forced not to care," he smiles. "I don't know how you Yankees operate in New York, but while here in Florida, in my courtroom, you will come dressed like an attorney. He snickers with a cold smirk on his face. "Sports blazer, sport shirt and jeans are not acceptable in my courtroom. I'm going to give you two weeks to get your wardrobe together. Court adjourned! Get a new date for two weeks from today," he says harshly.

"Your honor?" Tony blurts out. "Please? I've just flown for three hours to get here from New York. Please?"

"See you in two weeks," the judge says with no compassion.

"Your honor, please? Just give me one hour?" Tony begs. "I was running late and I didn't have time to change. I didn't want to disrespect your court and come in late," he lies hoping the judge will give him time to go and purchase a suit from somewhere.

"So, you rather disrespect my court, walking in here with jeans on?" he asks sarcastically. "Mr. Austin, you never get a second chance to make a first impression, remember that. See you in two weeks."

"Your honor, please?" Tony begs desperately. His huge ego has been crushed. He realizes he has to swallow his pride in this matter. "Please, your honor?"

"Two weeks, Tony Cochran," he smiles.

Tony Cochran, Tony says to himself. Oh, that explains everything. The judge is already aware of who Tony is. Tony now realizes that this will be one of his tougher cases. He's sure the judge has something to prove. He's going to do everything in his power to make this situation difficult.

"Bailiff, remove Mrs. Benderas from my courtroom.

Miranda rolls her leaking eyes at Tony with pure disgust.

Tony stands there in humiliation as they escort Miranda out of the courtroom in full shackles. Never has he been this embarrassed in his entire life.

///// CHAPTER 31 /////

Days Later

It's 10 a.m. and Dre is already on his grind as usual. His morning has started off beautifully. Instead of breakfast he had a 100 brick move followed by a 150 brick move; making it a $50,000 morning. And still in no way is his belly full.

Dre stands in the living room of Chico's Bronx apartment. Chico called Dre two days ago, stating that they need to meet immediately. The reason for the emergency meeting, Dre has no clue. It's been really bugging him to find out what the problem is. Did the work fall off? Did someone come to them with a better price? These are the questions that continue to pop up in his mind.

As he's busy driving himself insane, Chico comes walking into the room as another man follows closely behind.

Chico stands within a couple of feet of Dre, while the man stands directly behind him. "Primo, this is my brother Gardo. Gardo this is Primo."

Dre extends his hand and Gardo accepts. Dre looks into the man's eyes which are stone cold. His face shows no emotion. He appears to be totally different from Chico who is friendly and outgoing. This man appears to be very anti-social.

He snatches his hand away slowly and tucks it back into his pocket. He lowers his gaze onto the floor.

"Chico, what up?" Dre asks anxiously. "Is there a problem with the work?"

"Ah no, Primo. There's no problem with the work. My brother wants to speak with you," he says as he looks toward his brother.

"Poppo, we have a small problem," he says in a low hoarse voice. Dre has to strain his ears just to hear him. "The problem isn't the material itself. It's Grade A, top quality. I have no complaints as far as that goes," he admits. "As you know we have customers who come from all over, Boston, Connecticut, Syracuse, everywhere. My problem is ever since we switched over to the 'After Party', we have been losing some of our clientele. I couldn't figure out why at first because the work is good. I have customers from Brooklyn and Harlem who have not come to me in weeks. The other day my people from Connecticut told me that he ran into a few people who have the same stamp. Days later, I heard it again from another customer. It seems like the stamp is popping up everywhere. I don't know if you are dealing with these people or your connection is seeing all these people, but it's hurting my business. We sell it to our customers for 180 to 220 a brick. There's no reason for them to come all the way here to get it from us, when they can get the work right there. Even if it's a couple of dollars more expensive there, it's still more convenient."

Dre nods his head up and down, agreeing with Gardo totally. Hearing this makes Dre proud. It feels good to know that his work is not only stretching out, but it's making noise as well. On the flip side of that, this can be bad because the sound of Gardo's voice tells him that he can easily be on the way to losing a prominent client. "I understand," he agrees. "So, tell me what I can do to fix this problem? I can't drop the price any lower," he says defensively.

"No, I don't expect you to. "The number is great," he says. "We need our own stamp."

"Your own stamp?"

"Yeah, we're good for at least 3,000 bricks a week. I think we're valuable enough to have our own stamp?"

"Indeed. That's easy. I was scared," Dre admits. I thought we had a real problem," he laughs. "Just tell me what name you want and it's done."
Meanwhile In Newark

Mu-Mit and Latif sit inside the 2007 Chevy Impala. As they're sitting here parked, they're watching down the block attentively. Anxiety fills both of their guts. Latif grips the .357 in his hand tightly. "Now," Latif demands, giving Mu-Mit the word to pull off. Mu pulls off at a normal speed, trying hard not to draw any unnecessary attention to them.

As Mu-Mit proceeds down the block, he accelerates more and more. "Let me out, right here," Latif says as he tugs onto the strings of his hood, drawing it tight. He draws it so tight that not only can anyone not see inside, he can barely see outside of it.

As Mu-Mit slows down at the corner, Latif peeks around, one last time, just to make sure there are no witnesses in the area. As far as he can see, the coast is clear. "I wanna get him once he gets inside," Latif says referring to the man who is standing in front of a barbershop, lifting the gates open. Just as the man sticks his key into the door, Latif hops out of the car. The man steps inside the barbershop, just as Latif hops onto the curb of the sidewalk.

He trots quickly toward the barbershop. His adrenaline is pumping hard. As he approaches the glass door, he can clearly see the man from across the room. He stands about twenty feet away with his back facing the door. He's looking up at the huge flat screen television which hangs from the ceiling.

Suddenly, Latif rushes through the doorway, drawing his gun simultaneously. The noise startles the man. He turns around quickly to face the gun toting Latif. His eyes stretch wide open with fear. "Owww!" he screams with a high pitched voice. "Oww!" he screams again as his eyes set onto the huge .357 magnum.

Latif doesn't hesitate to pull the trigger. Boom! He fires aiming at the man's chest. His torso caves in as the bullet penetrates his mid-section. The strong impact forces him backwards. Boom! Latif fires again. The man trips over the barber's chair and lands against the barber's station in a sitting position. Latif steps closer to him. He hovers over top of the man. The man looks up at Latif desperately with pure fear in his eyes. Boom! He fires once again. The slug tears into his forehead. The loud noise of an explosion sounds off as his head bangs against the wooden station. Thick blood pours from his mouth as he shivers uncontrollably. Boom! He fires again. The bullet rips through his shoulder, making his body do a flip flop. He lands flat onto his stomach. At this point, he's as still as can be. Latif stands over him with his gun still aimed at the man. He's waiting to see the slightest movement but there is none. He's as dead as can be. Latif looks the man up and down and can't help but notice the electronic anklet which wraps around his ankle.

Boom! He fires once again, just to seal the deal. He then takes off toward the door. He tucks his gun inside his waistband, before stepping outside.

He peeks around cautiously as he quickly steps to the getaway car. Once he's seated, Mu-Mit pulls off slowly.

Back In the Bronx

"Here it is, right here," Chico's brother says as he hands Dre a rubber stamp. "This is our old stamp," he informs.

Dre reads the bold print. "Death Certificate," he whispers to himself. "That's a hell of a name," he admits.

Chico steps into the room, carrying a duffle bag in his hand. He dumps it onto the table right in front of Dre.

Chico's brother speaks again. "That's $465,000.00." In total, this money pays for 3,000 bricks. Chico and his brother pay for 1,500 and Dre fronts them 1,500 on consignment. Half of this money is for last week's tab and the other part is a down payment for this week's work.

"Dig, it's gonna take me a couple of days to get the new stamp up and running. I have a lot of work left that I need to shake before I can holler at my people. I mean, unless you want to take these until they're done?" he asks knowing damn well that they don't want to go a day without work. He has approximately 3,600 bricks left. He ordered them with them in mind, knowing that it was about time for them to re-up. Now that they want to switch stamps, he may be forced to move the work amongst the rest of his squad. That will slow his process down tremendously.

"We'll wait," he says modestly, shocking Dre with his answer.

Damn, Dre thinks to himself as he thinks of the two weeks this will set him back. "You sure? This could take about a week. I have a lot of work to move before it's time for me to re-up."

"Yeah, I'm sure. I can't take no more of that. It's hurting my business."

Dre is slightly upset, but what can he do. "Phew," he sighs. "Alright let me call my girl and have her come up and get this money," he says as he grabs his phone from his pocket and starts to dial. Just as he's dialing, an incoming call interrupts him. "Yeah?" he answers.

Yo!" Latif shouts. "I just left the barbershop, getting my haircut. I'm on my way home to wash my hair and change clothes," he adds as he talks in riddles, just in case any unwanted listeners are on the phone.

"Alright bet," Dre says wondering how things went. "I'll call you when I get local," he says as he hangs up the phone. He stands there in deep concentration for a few seconds in somewhat of a trance.

"Primo!" Chico shouts. Is everything ok?" he asks with concern.

"Y…yeah," Dre replies. Now it will be, he thinks to himself. The man at the barbershop is the Mayor's one and only co-defendant. After hearing Tony express to him how valuable the man is in this case, Dre took it upon himself to get the man out of the way. Dre just hopes that the orders have been completed. If he knows Latif and Mu-Mit, he's sure they've done nothing less than what he instructed them to do. They will never under-do anything. They live for murder. They are known to over-do everything. The absence of the man at trial should help the Mayor tremendously. All is well, should end well.

"Brrrrr!" Latif chirps imitating the sound a pigeon makes. "Brrrrrrrr! What happened to that boy? He was talking shit, we put a clapping into that boy!" he sings along with rappers "The Clipse" who blare through the speakers.

Mu-Mit pulls into the carwash on South Orange Avenue and Ninth Street. Instead of pulling inside, he parks close to the building and gets out. He pops the trunk open, snatching a set of license plates and a screwdriver. He quickly places the plates onto the vehicle. After that, he immediately snatches the temporary tag from the back window. He then proceeds into the carwash.

This vehicle belongs to Enterprise Car Rental. Dre's sole purpose in renting it was only to make the hit. They substituted the plates for a fake temp tag, just in case someone saw them at the barbershop. They will never be able link them back to the vehicle.

When Dre gave them the instructions to handle the man, neither Latif nor Mu-Mit hesitated. They have been waiting impatiently for Dre to let them loose. They both feel like two wild animals being trapped in a cage, with leashes on their necks. Dre doesn't realize how much damage he's doing by holding them back like this. When he finally lets them go, they will explode with no control. They're paid weekly salaries of $2,500.00 apiece. Dre figures that by paying them and keeping them full, they'll be alright, but what he doesn't realize is, it's not really about the money for them. They just live for murder.

As they cruise through the carwash, Latif continues to sing along. "Brrrrrrrrr! What happened to that boy?"

What happened to him? He got caught slipping. It wasn't hard for them to locate the man. The streets talk. Tony gave Dre the man's name without even realizing that he had done so. Dre turned the name over to Latif and Mu-Mit. They did their homework by beating down the streets. They got a little information from this source and a little from that source, and in a matter of two days they had enough information to track him down. All their leads led to the man's barbershop which he has been working in ever since he's been out on bail. Now without him present at trial, they have no one to flip on the Mayor.

"Sucker ass nigga!" Latif shouts. "You should have seen the look in his sucker ass eyes!" It felt good, hearing that hammer blast. I ain't heard it in a while. I almost forgot what it sound like," he laughs. "It felt like my very first time having sex," he laughs. "Like a girl getting her cherry busted," he whispers. "I'm ready to go again," he says sternly. "It's time! Dre bullshitting."

"No bullshit. I got a plan. Being that Dre doesn't want to move, we gone just have to do our own thing. Remove these mufuckers on our own without him knowing that we behind it. You with me?"

Latif nods his head up and down. "Yeah," he whispers. "Of course I'm with you," he mumbles.

"Good enough!" Mu-Mit says.

Latif proceeds to sing along with the CD. "Brrrrrrrr! What happened to that boy?"

///// CHAPTER 32 /////

Days Later

The Mayor sits back on the floor in the tight corner of his dorm. He secretly dials the numbers on his phone as he keeps his eyes on the gate to make sure no Marshals are creeping up on him. His phone rings as he eagerly awaits an answer. After the fourth ring, someone picks up. "Hello!" the man shouts with an agitated tone.

"Jacob?" the Mayor asks.

"Uh, may I ask who is calling?"

"Is this Jacob?" the Mayor asks with uncertainty.

"Yes. Who is calling?"

"The Mayor," he replies sternly.

"The Mayor? What Mayor?"

"Bloomberg, motherfucker! Stop talking crazy. The Mayor...from Newark."

Jacob finally recognizes his voice. Hey!" he shouts with joy. "Long time no hear from. When did you come home? How come you haven't been to see me yet?"

"Nah, Jake I ain't home yet," he says. "Soon though," he claims, while nodding his head up and down.

"So things are looking good?"

"Can't look better," he says trying to sound as confident as possible. In all reality though, he doesn't even believe his own statement. "Ay," he says attempting to change the subject. "I have not done anything special for my girls in a while. What kind of boyfriend would I be if I didn't do something special for the loves of my life," he says smiling from ear to ear. "I need something really special. You already know how I do," he says arrogantly.

Jacob is a jeweler from New York. The Mayor has spent hundreds of thousands with this man over the course of his career.

"Something special like what? You have anything in mind?"

"Nah, I don't know. You know I been gone for a minute. I don't know what's hot and what's not. I tell you what though...the jewelry that you have of mine, melt it all down and start from scratch. Make some pieces for my ladies."

"Melt it down?" Jacob asks with a high pitched tone. "That's a lot of jewelry to melt down. You sure about that?"

"Yeah, I'm sure. When have you ever known me to be unsure? Melt it all down."

When the Mayor was arrested he instructed Liu to take all of his jewelry over to the jeweler. His plan was to sell it all back to him if things got tight for him financially. In total, his jewelry package is worth well over $400,000.00.

"All of it!" he shouts. The chain, the bracelet, earrings and the ring. Melt it all down. The watches, you can sell them. I'm done with all that shit. I ain't got no use for it no more. When I come home, I'm doing shit differently. No more, diamond bezel watches and huge medallions. I'm doing plain faced, stainless steel Presidential Roleys, leather band Patty's and Franks. All that nigga jewelry, I'm done with it," he says arrogantly. "Melt it all down and make some earrings and necklaces. That's later on down the line though. Right now, I need something real fly. Something different," he whispers. "You know what? What's up with a pearl necklace set?"

"Pearls? It's funny that you ask about that. I just made some beautiful pieces for Mary J. The pearls are Kokichi Mikimoto from Japan. They're beautiful. When I say flawless, that's an understatement. Tell me what you want and I can make it happen."

"Ay man, I don't know. Whatever Mary J got done, make mine a step better," he says arrogantly.

"Ok, I'll take care of you. They come in several colors but white is the most valuable so I'll take it that's what you want. That's if I know you?" he teases. "White with rose overtone. 8.5 by 9 mm. Those on a 51 inch rope look awesome, trust me. Strung on triple stranded silk thread, incredible. Platinum clasp, to top it off."

"What is all that worth?"

"You know I take care of you. I'm only going to charge you my cost," he claims. "Let me get a round about estimate for you," he says as he presses the numbers on his calculator. "Ah, twenty grand for you. You can't beat that. I charged Mary $37,000.00 for the exact same piece."

"Alright. You know I need all the accessories to go with it. I can't half step with it," he says casually. "Earrings, bracelet, the whole shit."

"I got you," he claims. I have some gorgeous earrings, with a matching pendant. Trust me when I say beautiful. And the bracelet is out of this world."

"Ok, do you."

Jacob starts calculating. "Give me $6,000 for the bracelet. Ah, $2,250 for the earrings. The ring, beautiful…platinum setting. The diamonds are absolutely flawless. Total weight, about a carat. 3 grand is the best I can do for that. And the pendant, I'll throw in for free," he claims.

"What's the total damage on that?"

"Ah, one second, one second," he says as he calculates. "31,250…just round it off to $31,000."

"Listen, I need two of the identical sets."

"Oh, I forgot about your two wife situation," Jacob teases."

"Ay," he replies casually. "I only got $58,000 to play with. Shit tight. Fast money done slowed up," he says with a smile. He doesn't trust Jacob's price the least bit. In no way is he buying the whole, 'giving it to you at my price' shit. He's sure Jacob will make a hefty cut off this deal.

"58?" he asks slowly. "Boy, you drive a hard bargain, but how can I tell you no?" he asks. "Deal!"

"That's a bet. Now how long is it going to take you? I need the pieces delivered to them asap?"

"I got you. I'll call you when it's ready. You give me the addresses. It's that simple."

"Let me make a phone call and I'll have the paper on your counter before you close," he says arrogantly.

Meanwhile In Union

Dre walks into Tony's office. "What up?" he asks.

"Close the door behind you," Tony whispers.

Dre slams the door shut and makes his way over to Tony's desk where he seats himself.

Tony looks Dre in the eyes for a matter of seconds before speaking. The silence is killing Dre. "What's up?" he asks.

"I just got off of the phone, receiving the call of a lifetime."

"Oh yeah?" Dre asks.

"Yeah," he says nodding his head up and down. "Remember the kid, Thomas Howard, I told you about?"

"Who?" Dre asks, knowing exactly who Tony is speaking about. He was sure that the meeting was in reference to the murder.

"Thomas Howard," he repeats. "Your brother's co-defendant."

"Oh, what about him?" Dre asks stringing him along as if he doesn't already know.

"He will or can no longer be a problem to us. He was murdered a few days ago at his barbershop."

"Word?"

"Word," Tony agrees. "You know what that means right? With no co-defendants, I'm going to rip right through this case," he claims. "He has so much going in his favor, now. Too bad for the young boy, though. But what can I say? One man's misfortune, is another man's gain. Unfortunately that's how the ball bounces."

"Yeah, I guess you're right," Dre says as he admires the decision he made. He's never been the one for senseless murder but this murder, makes all the sense in the world. His baby brother's freedom is on the line. "I guess you're right," he repeats nodding his head up and down. "I guess you're right," he repeats to himself.

///// CHAPTER 33 /////

The Next Morning

Dusty cruises the town with no apparent destination, while his passenger pulls a blunt from his pocket and passes it over to Dusty. Just as soon as it touches his fingertips, he jams it between his lips and blazes it. The pungent odor fills the car immediately. Dusty takes the biggest pull ever. Instead of exhaling, he just lets the smoke marinate inside of his mouth for damn near a minute. He hogs the entire blunt, not sharing the least bit with his three passengers. This comes as no shock to them, which is why the passenger is already rolling another blunt.

As much as ILL Wheel nags Dusty about smoking these blunts, he just can't give them up. In the beginning, he would only smoke them once or twice a week. His habit is rapidly growing. It has increased from twice a week to four a day. He loves "Wet" so much that he doesn't even waste his time smoking plain marijuana. Regular marijuana doesn't come close to the feeling that he gets when he smokes the 'Wet'.

The euphoria is starting to kick in. Right now he's cruising at about ten miles an hour and not even realizing it. His eyes are spaced out, while he stares straight ahead in a trance. He can clearly hear the conversation that his boys are indulging in, but it seems so far away. The words that come out of their mouth seem to drag along. At this point his brain is cooking and he's loving every minute of it.

The blunt dangles from his mouth. He tightens his lips around it, pulling with all his might. He pulls so hard that his face almost caves in. He coughs from the huge intake of smoke, yet and still he continues to inhale as much as he can. The more he pulls the higher he gets. Just when he thinks he can't get any higher the PCP takes him a level higher. He takes a breather just to stop the car from spinning. His vision becomes blurry. He attempts to eliminate the dizziness, as he's shaking his head from side to side. The harder he shakes the faster things around him spin.

A few miles away

Dre sits at the table alone at IHOP, as he consumes the rest of his breakfast. He sits there discreetly as he listens to the three Newark Police Officers, who occupy the table next to him, laugh and joke like little children.

Dre's attention is drawn to the entrance of the parking lot, in which he can see clearly through the glass window. Lil Mama's Infiniti pulls into the lot slowly and cruises around until she reaches the middle of the lot. A male passenger hops out, carrying a shopping bag in his hand. He walks casually over to a Hummer H3, which sits in between two vans. He hops into the passenger's seat and the reverse signal lights up immediately. Lil Mama zips out of the parking lot as they're backing up. Seconds later, the Hummer H3 with the Massachusetts license plates exits the parking lot.

Dre feels a certain amount of confidence in believing that another successful deal has been completed. He looks to the table to his left. The police officers are laughing hysterically. They're making joke after joke, not even realizing that the joke is actually on them. A 400 brick sell has just been made right under their noses. A deal almost equivalent to their yearly salaries combined was made right before their eyes and they don't have a clue.

One officer busts out damn near in tears as he laughs at yet another one of their corny jokes. Dre looks at him smiling from ear to ear. Don't think I'm laughing with you, he thinks to himself. "I'm laughing at you," he smiles.

Many Hours Later

Thirteen hours and three blunts later, Dusty has reached an all time high. He's so high that he had to give up the wheel. He switched seats with his passenger several hours ago. It got to the point where he began hallucinating, seeing strange things before his eyes. Huge droplets of sweat covered his entire body. His throat passageway felt like it was closing up on him. Never in all his years of smoking has he ever felt like that. He's never been that scared in his life. Even with the many horrific side effects, he continued to smoke. He loved the euphoria so much that he was still willing to put himself through the torture.

The driver cruises along Lyons Avenue slowly. He's in search of ILL Wheel's Cherokee, hoping it's not here. He circles the block twice and still no sight of the vehicle. "He ain't home," the driver whispers.

"Yo?" Dusty mumbles with a groggy voice, as he attempts to lift his head up. Lifting his head is almost impossible, on the account that his head seems to weigh a ton. He cracks one eye open instead. "Where we at?" he mumbles, before his eye closes.

"Just rolling," the driver replies, but Dusty doesn't hear him. He's faded back into la-la land. "D!" the man shouts. "D!" he shouts again getting no response from Dusty. The man nudges Dusty with his elbow and still he gets no response.

The driver double-parks right in front of Dusty and ILL Wheels apartment building. He sneakily slides the keys from the key ring, while leaving the car key in the ignition. He passes the keys to the backseat passenger, who quietly exits the vehicle. The other man in the backseat follows closely behind as they make their way toward the building.

The driver cruises up the block and makes a U-Turn in the intersection. He parks the car in the very first vacant spot that he finds. This spot happens to be perfect. He can see the entrance of the building clearly from here.

After testing out every key on the ring, the men finally find the right one. Both of the men know the apartment well. They've been in here several times prior to this.

"I'll hit Wheel's room, you hit Dusty's," he instructs while pointing to his right. They both scatter in opposite directions. They search the rooms high and low as if they're on an Easter egg hunt.

In no time at all, the man appears in the doorway. "I got it. You got anything?"

"Nah, not yet," the man replies as he fumbles through many piles of dirty clothes, which cover the entire floor of the closet. "What you got, work?" the man asks as he turns around facing the man.

"Nah, money," he replies as he holds the shoe box high in the air.

"Bet, help me. I'm sure something in here," he says as he ransacks the closet.

The other man grabs hold of the dirty clothes hamper and turns it upside down. "Got it!" he thinks to himself as two plastic bags fall onto the floor. He quickly unties the first bag and to his glory he finds many bricks of dope. "Here we go!" he shouts as he opens the second bag. "Yep, we got the mother lode," he cheers as he sets his eyes on the stacks of money that lie in the bag. "Come on. Let's go," he says nervously.

////// CHAPTER 34 //////

7 a.m. the next morning

Dusty and ILL Wheel step out of the elevator side by side. Coincidentally, they just happen to have come home at the same time.

ILL Wheel is up bright and early as usual. His day begins at 5:30 in the morning because he has to drop his girlfriend off at work. At this moment he has a series of moves to make which total up to about fifty bricks.

Dusty, on the other hand, spent the night in his car. After his boys dropped themselves off, Dusty laid back in the driver's seat. The quick nod turned into a couple hours of sleep. Just by chance he happened to have awakened. He woke up in shock, not even realizing where he was or how he had gotten there. His memory of the prior day has been erased. He can't recall any part of the day, even if his life depended on it.

One thing that he is aware of, is his headache is excruciating. He's never felt this bad in his life. He's extremely dizzy. He's close to losing his balance with each step that he takes.

Dusty walks a few steps behind ILL Wheel. Just as ILL Wheel gets to the door, he shouts, "What the fuck!" He notices that there is no lock on the door. The entire cylinder is missing. He automatically looks to the floor where he finds it lying on the carpet. His heart pounds rapidly as he thinks of what may have happened. He pushes the door open and runs inside.

Dusty realizes what's going on and trots in behind him. ILL Wheel runs right into his room. The mess confirms the fact that someone has broken in. Please? I hope this ain't what I think it is, he says to himself as he's running to his closet. He opens the door and looks inside. Just by the way it looks; he realizes that his dope has been found. Just to confirm it, he digs through the clothes and his boxes that are all scattered around. He digs deep, hoping that maybe they left some behind by mistake.

It only takes a matter of seconds before he realizes that he's been cleaned out. His heart pounds even faster as he runs over toward his dirty clothes hamper. The fact that it's turned upside down tells him that the money is gone as well. Tears drop down his face instantly as he thinks of his entire savings gone. He drops to his knees, combing the area, hoping to find anything that they may have left behind. He crawls on his knees in heavy search, but as much as he hates to admit it, he realizes that the chances are none. "Shit!" he shouts as he collapses on the floor. Tears drip down his face rapidly.

Dusty gains enough composure to realize what has happened. He takes off in full stride in the direction of his room. He runs straight to his dresser drawer. Before he gets there, he sees that all the drawers have been pulled out and thrown on the floor. He quickly realizes that his hard earned stash of $32,000.00 is no longer here.

"Yo!" ILL Wheel shouts from the entrance of the room. "Who the fuck you brought here?"

Dusty turns around in shock. "What?" he asks in a baffled manner.

"You heard me! Who the fuck you brought here? Nobody knows where the fuck we live!" he shouts with confidence.

Dusty stands there in a blur. He wears the dumbest look on his face. "I ain't bring nobody here," he lies. His mind begins to wonder, but he attempts to keep the confident look on his face. The faces of each and every person that he's brought here pops up in his mind. He's brought so many people here, that he would never be able to pinpoint who could be behind this. ILL Wheel has always warned him about bringing people here but he's never listened. He's brought dudes here and a few of his female friends. "I ain't never bring nobody here!" he lies once again.

Dusty doesn't have the slightest clue that he's been had. He doesn't realize that his blunt was specially laced just for him. They laced the blunt with the intent of getting him delirious so they could break into the apartment. He was so high last night that he would never ever be able to solve this issue.

ILL Wheel stands there in silence for a quick second as he entertains the thought that maybe Dusty set this entire caper up. Nah, he thinks to himself. Maybe so? If he isn't the culprit, then who is, he asks himself. He can't imagine who it could be, but what he does know is, they've made the come up of a lifetime. They have gotten away with his own $77,000.00 in cash, $40,000.00 of Dre's money, and close to 70 bricks of dope. "They got every fucking thing!" ILL Wheel cries. "$40,000 of his money, 70 bricks, and $77,000 of my own money!" he cries with tears running down his face. "It's your fucking fault!"

Of all the things ILL Wheel just mentioned, the only thing that sticks out in his mind is, $77,000 of my own money. "Damn," he sighs silently as he realizes how much less of a stash he had. "It ain't my fucking fault!" Dusty shouts back defensively. "They took all mines too. $70,000 of mine too," he lies.

ILL Wheel quickly thinks of the $60,000 tab he has with Dre. He doesn't have one dime to contribute to it. "Damn!" he shouts. Them niggas gone kill me, he thinks to himself. "Somebody gone pay for this shit! This ain't going down like that! I swear on everything I love, somebody gone pay!" he claims. But who, he asks himself.

///// CHAPTER 35 /////

Mu-Mit cruises along West Market Street, while Latif occupies the passenger's seat. In the backseat, there sits a close friend of Mu-Mit's, who goes by the name Candy Kev. Actually, he's closer than a friend. He's more like a little brother to Mu-Mit. Mu-Mit practically raised him. Mu-Mit's younger brother and him were the best of friends before Mu-Mit's brother died in a stolen car crash over two decades ago.

Mu-Mit and Latif listen quietly as he speaks. "I hear what ya'll saying, but one crew taking over the whole town...I just don't see that happening, word to mother!" he says with confidence. "That shit might have worked back in the day, but not today! Nah!" he shouts. "I don't think so. I'm 35 years old. Real talk, you know I been around. I done seen how ya'll, the older niggas done it. I witnessed how me and niggas from my era did it, and now I'm still here to see how these young niggas doing it. Ya'll want to know the difference? Niggas from ya'll era vibed off of intimidation. Acting crazy and niggas respecting them just because. Never really had to do nothing, but just because they thought you would, niggas wouldn't step out of line. Don't get me wrong, there were a few real mufuckers like yourselves who really put it down, but for the most part, the majority of the mufuckers was living off of their reputation. That shit spilled over into my era as well. On the whole a bunch of punk mufuckers hiding behind money. This era is a whole different story! These young niggas ain't fronting! They don't care about nothing! They don't love nothing, fear nothing or respect nothing. These niggas don't even love they mama, so how you expect them to love anything else? They don't give a fuck about a nigga reputation. In fact if you got a rep, they'll test you even faster. They want to prove to everybody that respect you, that you're not worthy of the respect. Look at how many niggas we know that got killed as soon as they got home...Cashmere for instance. Look, he came home on that 'back in the day' bullshit and the Mayor got his ass up outta here."

"For the record," Mu-Mit interrupts. "The Mayor didn't do that. That wasn't his work."

"Nah? You sure? That's the word on the street."

"You know you can't believe everything you hear on the street. Just trust me when I tell you, he had nothing to do with that."

"Well, if he didn't who did?" he asks.

"Lil Bruh, that's a whole nother khutbah right there. Anyway, what was you saying?"

"Well, like I was saying...you know what I mean. Them young niggas been hearing about the old heads all they life. They get the word that he home and they start to feel threatened. They automatically assume that he coming home on that 'back in the day' bullshit. So what do they do? They peel his cap back before he even gets established."

"Ay man, you kind of contradicting yourself," Latif interrupts. You thirty mother-fucking five! You an old head to them teen-age boys. You double their age. You said you did a six year bid and you just coming home. I'm sure they heard how you put it down."

"Ay baby, my case is rare. These young mufuckers took a liking to me and most importantly, they don't feel threatened by me. When I first came home I had a little friction with them until they realized that I wasn't on that take over shit. In fact, I copped work off of them. I even took a couple of bricks on consignment, just to make them think I needed them to help me get right. That made them feel comfortable. I would cop a couple of bricks from them here and there. Not enough to make them think I had some real paper. If they thought my cheese was up, that would have gave them reason to feel threatened. Once they became comfortable with me, I started doing me slowly but surely. You know, I know everybody who somebody, so I can easily get my hands on that exclusive dope that nobody can't get their hands on. They saw how valuable I was to the team, so they opened their arms for me. I ain't no dummy though. I know they think they using me, but fuck it, I'm eating! I get the work and give it to them for the same price as I get it. Every now and then if I get some shit that I got a little room with, I'll add a quarter to the price here and there," he admits. "They comfortable with me now. They think I'm one of them. You heard what my boy Jay-Z said? I dumb down to double my dollars," he sings a verse from rapper Jay-Z. "You get it?" he asks. "Truthfully, I'm a Salvatore Ferragamo shoe, Armani suit wearing, Bentley GT driving nigga, but I gotta dumb my game down just to make them feel like I'm one of them. Look at me, Omavi Jeans, Nike ACG boots. That ain't me! I'm almost 40 years old! You know what I'm driving these days? A got damn Pontiac Grand Prix. I ain't never drove an American car," he laughs. "It may sound funny, but guess what? I'm getting hell a money while other niggas my age getting pushed. They got the wrong mentality. You gotta dumb down to double your dollars. Even the broads I fuck with. My wife is from Canada. Persian broad who makes six figures a year in the real estate game. I imported her ass here," he laughs. "I'll never let them know that. They will think that I think I'm better than them, so you know what I do? I even let them hook me up with a couple of them little dirty hood rat bitches they fucking with," he smiles.

"I understand the whole dumb down process, but if you play dumb too long, eventually you'll really become dumb!" Latif shouts.

"I don't plan on being here that long," he says sarcastically.

"Man, let me tell you like this," Mu-Mit says. "I ain't got time for the mind games," he whispers. "I'mma do me! And anybody get in the way of that, got a problem! Yeah, I got a rep, but I don't hide behind it. I'm forty-six mufucking years old. I been busting my gun for over thirty years now. I started doing this shit when I was 14 years old. I was busting my gun back then and I still bust my gun now. I dare a mufucker to step out of pocket," he says furiously. "Ain't nothing change, but the gray in my beard," he says as he rubs his hand over his thick course beard.

"To me my way and to you yours," Candy Kev sings. "Hold up, slow down right here," he says as they near the Exxon Gas Station on Central Avenue and West Market. "Paper man!" he shouts from the back window. The Star

Ledger salesman runs up the yellow line thinking that someone wants to purchase a newspaper.

As the man gets closer to the car he recognizes Candy Kev's face. "Candy Man, what's up?" the raggedy looking man asks.

"Here, check this out for me!" he demands as he passes the packet of 'After Party' to him that Mu-Mit just gave him. "Chirp me and let me know what it is."

"Bet!" the man shouts as he walks away with joy.

30 Minutes Later

As the three of them sit in Nubians eating their breakfast, Candy Kev's chirp sounds off. "Yo?" he shouts while lowering the volume. "What it do? What the business is?" he asks in a playful manner.

"That's a ten all day," the man replies.

"Nuff said," Kev replies as he tucks his phone into his pocket. "It is what it is," he says looking Mu-Mit directly in the eyes. "It's a go. I already told you, I'm good for 300 bricks a week at a minimum. It's on you. I'm ready!"

///// CHAPTER 36 /////

"Court is now in session!" the bailiff shouts.

Hearing those words almost frighten Miranda to death. Where is the fucking lawyer, she asks herself. She's just meeting Tony and can't stand him already. His negligence makes her believe that he cares nothing about her freedom. She often asks herself where her father found him. Stupid ass, she thinks to herself.

Suddenly the doors swing open wildly and an overly confident, cocky Tony Austin walks swiftly into the courtroom. His aura is so different from the last time that he was here. The judge embarrassed him so badly the last time that he was forced to do something that he hasn't done in years. Today, he's actually wearing a suit.

He steps up the aisle with a confident swagger. His face displays more arrogance than his walk.

A burst of relief fills Miranda's heart. The judge's face shows hatred as he sets eyes on Tony and Tony loves it. He pops the buttons of his pin-striped charcoal grey Zegna suit jacket, exposing his soft pink custom fit shirt and his suspenders. His slightly oversized multi-colored bow tie adds tremendous flavor to his outfit.

"Mr. Austin," the judge says accompanied by a head nod.

"Good morning, your honor," he replies loud and clear. "Please excuse me for my tardiness?" he begs.

"Counsel, now that's more like it," the judge says wearing a phony smile on his face as he looks Tony up and down. Jealousy fills his heart. He wishes his suits looked that good on him. His Napoleon complex kicks in as it always does. Oh how he wishes he were about 6 inches taller. He figures at that height he could be the man that he always wanted to be. "Dressed to impress, huh?" he asks as the rage sets on his face.

Tony can sense the hate and loves every second of it. He smiles slightly. No, dressed for success, he says to himself as his smile transforms into a stone cold stare.

Meanwhile in the Bronx

Dre sits behind the steering wheel of his Cherokee, while Chico hops into the passenger's seat. Dre has a clear view of the entire block from where he's parked. In the middle of the block there sits Lil Mama's Infiniti. An old Spanish woman walks away from the car carrying a laundry bag. The bag consists of two thousand bricks of 'Death Certificate'. Dre changed the stamp just as they requested. Lil Mama dashes out of the parking space and speeds up the block.

"Here," Chico says as he hands the bag of money over to Dre. "155 thousand," he whispers. "Primo, please promise me you won't give anyone else our name?" he asks.

"Chico, baby, I don't believe you. I know the rules to this shit. I respect bitness," he says mispronouncing the word intentionally. "Before I do bad bitness I won't do no bitness. You got my word on that."

"Good. Let me get over here and let the lady in. I'll call you in about three days," he says as he exits the vehicle. Dre pulls off casually.

As he's driving he gets a sudden burst of anxiety that fills his gut. He has to meet with the 'After Party' connect in less than one hour.

Just as he jumps onto the ramp of the highway, he picks up his phone. He's calling ILL Wheel to tell him to have the money ready when he gets there. He doesn't have anytime to waste.

"Hello?" ILL Wheel answers.

"Yeah. You around? Time to tighten up," he whispers into the phone.

ILL Wheel hesitates before speaking. He's been dreading this phone call. He doesn't have a clue of what he's going to tell Dre. He owes him close to $60,000 and doesn't have a penny to contribute to it. "Yeah," he mumbles. "I'm around."

"Alright. I'll hit you when I get local. I'm thirty minutes away," he says before hanging up. A queasy feeling fills his gut. He just realized how loose he's been with his lips lately. He's been doing more talking on the phone this week alone, than he's done in years. He realizes that he's getting comfortable and he needs to be mindful before it's too late.

"Damn!" ILL Wheel blurts out. He wonders what the outcome of this is going to be. "How can I tell this man I don't have his money," he says talking to himself. "Should I duck him? Nah, then I'm sure he'll have me killed. Damn!"

///// CHAPTER 37 /////

In Fort Dix

The Mayor paces back and forth up the sideline of the basketball court. He's never been so nervous in his life. "Come on ref!" he shouts furiously to the inmate who is the acting official of this game. "You babying that motherfucker. That was a bullshit foul! Put some panties on him!" the Mayor shouts to the man on the opposite side of the court. "Sorry motherfucker!" he shouts furiously as the man goes to the foul line.

The Mayor is highly competitive. He hates to lose at anything and has always been like that. Today, he's losing big. His team is down by 10 points. He looks at the clock and figures that he has hope. It's the last quarter with six minutes left.

The Mayor's anger would make you think that it's a championship game, but it's not. To the average inmate, the stakes may seem high, but to a man of his status they're playing for peanuts. Actually it's not peanuts they're playing for. They're playing for soup and tuna. The winning team gets 50 cases of Oodles of Noodles and fifty cans of Tuna.

The Mayor put up the stakes for his team, while the inmate from Detroit put up the stakes for the opposite team. The inmate from Detroit and the Mayor are quiet rivals. They both secretly hate each other. They both had about the same status on the streets. On the inside, they both have about the same amount of followers.

His name is Ronald, but he calls himself Ronald Trump. He has just as much ego as the Mayor. No room is big enough for the two of them to be in at the same time. They hate everything about each other. They look at each other and see an egotistical, obnoxious individual. What they don't realize is they are damn near a mirror reflection of each other.

"Make that 25 shrimp flavor and 25 chicken flavor!" Ronald Trump says in a deep southern accent. "I got my boys on a special diet. No meat! Ooh, and the foul shot is good!" he shouts. "This gone be a fucking blow out! Want to up the stakes? A couple loaves of potato bread? My boys love that shit," he teases.

The Mayor tries to ignore him but it's killing him. He's a poor sport. He's always been a sore loser. "Come on, Action Jackson," he says to his point guard who is making his way down the court. "Come on, make it count," he says desperately. "You know that appeal you been talking about? Win this game and my attorney will be on it first thing in the morning."

"Ooh, low blow," Ronald Trump sighs. "Aw man, I don't believe you. You bigger than that. You the Mayor. You'd put a man's freedom on the line for a bullshit ball game? That was desperate!" he laughs. "We supposed to be bigger than that. Me, I would give him ten stacks toward his appeal just because I know him. I'm like that!" he shouts arrogantly.

"Whatever, nigga! You always talking that big boy shit.

"I talk the talk cause I walked the walk," Ronald Trump claims. "Nigga I speak the truth. I got thousands of niggas that will vouch for me too. Ask somebody about me. My money as long as train smoke. I already told you what I'm worth. I put mines on the table. What you worth? You ashamed to tell? You scared the people will think less of you, once they find out that you all hype?"

"Nah, I don't know what I'm worth. You heard what my boy Don King said, right? If you can count your money, you ain't got no money."

"Nigga whatever! You ain't got no real dough. I done tricked off more than you done made in your lifetime."

"Think so?" the Mayor smiles arrogantly. "I guarantee you, every dollar you got, I got four to match it. Nigga how much you worth? I'm talking about cold cash. Not a half a million in cars, a million dollar house. I'm talking stacks of green backs. Get your bank book and I'll get my bank books," he says putting emphasis on the plural tense. Let's make a bet! Winner take all? If I don't match you four dollars for every dollar you got, you can take everything. It's only money to me!" The Mayor stands there quietly for a matter of seconds before speaking again. "Oh, you quiet now? I thought so. Money talks and bullshit walks! Put your money where your mouth is or shut up and play ball!" the Mayor shouts in a playful manner. "You hear that, right Action? He got ten for you, he claims. Everybody heard him, right?" he asks. "Come on ya'll," the Mayor claps his hands together. "Let's make it happen!"

Just as the point guard crosses over the half court line, three members of the opposing team swarm him, giving him no room to breathe.

"Bust they ass!" the Mayor shouts with confidence. "None of them can hold you. You see they got the whole force on you!" he shouts. He's seen his point guard under this type of pressure many times before. Action Jackson's basketball game isn't only respected in prison, but it's respected all across the land, from the Rucker to Denmark. Instead of wasting his talent here, he should actually be on somebody's NBA team. He would have been, if he could have kept himself out of trouble. Two weeks after he got drafted to the NBA, he got caught up in a federal investigation, which landed him life in prison. That's how the ball bounces!

Action Jackson fakes to the left and pivots to the right, bouncing the ball behind his back as he blows pass the first man as if he isn't even standing there. He then exerts a crucial crossover, which causes the next player to fall to his knees.

"Yeah, yeah, baby!" the Mayor shouts as Action Jackson drives straight to the middle of the court, bouncing the ball hard and violent. Just a little pass the foul line, he leaps into the air like a superhero. He's going for the dunk. He soars in the air over all of his opponents.

Suddenly, the ball slips out of his hands as he descends. All the men on the court run over to retrieve the ball, not paying any attention to Action Jackson. Everyone on the sideline is watching in awe, not knowing what is going on.

"What the?" the Mayor asks himself as Action Jackson collapses face first onto the floor. His body flips flops lifelessly as it lands on the floor. The Mayor quickly takes off in flight.

He leans over, grabbing him by the arm, attempting to lift him up, but to no avail. The Mayor tugs harder and harder. "Yo!" the Mayor shouts. The sound of his voice brings everyone to the court. They surround the Mayor and Action Jackson.

The marshals notice the commotion and run over. "Back up, back up! What's going on?"

"He just fell out," the Mayor says nervously.

"Back away from him!" the marshal says bending over close to the motionless man. He checks for a pulse. "Call the nurse!" he shouts. "He's not breathing!"

Everyone stands there baffled, not having a clue of what happened.

"Everybody back up!" the marshal says as the nurse comes running in, pushing a stretcher.

In just a matter of seconds the marshals have lifted his body onto the stretcher. Everyone watches in confusion as they rush the man out of the gym, leaving everyone in suspense.

///// CHAPTER 38 /////

Mu-Mit sits on the hood of his car while Latif sits on the trunk. Tension is on both of their faces. ILL Wheel paces back and forth, while talking on his telephone. He isn't talking about anything of importance. He's just using his conversation as a reason to be away from them. He also doesn't trust the two of them. If they decide to kill him, his girl will hear the shots. At least then, he won't be left here to die without her knowing his whereabouts.

Dre was pressed for time after spending way too much time in traffic, so he decided to send them to pick the money up. ILL Wheel had no clue they would be coming so that threw his plan off totally. He had already somewhat planned out how he was going to break the news to Dre. When Latif and Mu-Mit showed up, his strategy was disrupted.

ILL Wheel takes a sneak peek over at the two of them, who are getting more and more impatient by the second. He's never trusted either of them. He's always gotten the feeling that they don't like him. He's sure they were always looking for a reason to move on him, but he's never given them a reason to. Now he's sure that, $60,000 is all the reason in the world. Suddenly a light bulb brightens up his mind. Maybe, they broke into his apartment just to have a reason to move on him. I wonder? Damn, $60,000 he thinks to himself. He hopes Dre will understand, but he really doubts it. He is well aware that $60,000 is a lot of money.

ILL Wheel has witnessed how ruthless Latif and Mu-Mit are. He's sure that they won't hesitate to murder him if Dre gives them the word. Something tells him to snatch his .40 caliber from his waist and go for what he knows. Neither of them is expecting him to move which will help him get it off. Nah, I can't, he tells himself. That will just create a bigger problem for me. He's sure if he does that, Dre and the Mayor will send more goons out for him. He's totally baffled. He paces back and forth, just waiting to die.

Suddenly, the black Cherokee creeps pass them, parking directly in front of Mu-Mit's car. Both Latif and Mu-Mit make their way over to his vehicle.

Here we go, ILL Wheel says to himself as he sneakily grabs hold of his gun, underneath his shirt. I refuse to let them just kill me, he says to himself. Fuck that, he thinks to himself. Somebody going with me, he tells himself as he brings the phone closer to his ear. "Hello?" he says into the phone, making sure his girl is still on the phone to hear any shots that may be fired.

"Yo!" Latif shouts to ILL Wheel. "Big Bruh want you."

"ILL Wheel's heart bangs through his chest. "Lemme call you back if I can," he says sarcastically. "I'm about to go over to talk to my man," he whispers.

"Alright, call me right back," she demands as ILL Wheel hangs up on her.

He tightens up the grip on his gun. It's all or nothing, he says to himself. As he gets closer to the truck, Mu-Mit passes him on his way to the Cadillac. The stone cold look reassures ILL Wheel that it's about to go down. ILL Wheel stops short at the passenger's door where Latif stands, looking him directly in the eyes.

"Get in," Dre says casually.

Get in, ILL Wheel repeats to himself. Oh, hell no. It ain't gone be that easy, he says in his mind. He has taken enough guys on that ride to make him know better than to get in the car with him. He knows that is a definite no-no. If ya'll gone kill me, ya'll gone do it right here on the street. I ain't going nowhere with ya'll, he says to himself. He takes two steps back with fear. "Yo," he whispers. "I know you probably don't believe me, but it's true."

"Hold, hold, hold up," Dre says in a calm manner. "First and foremost why would you assume that I don't believe you?" he asks. I believe you. This the game. Shit happens. I believe it can happen. They just don't believe that it has happened," he says pointing to Latif who stares into ILL Wheel's eyes coldly.

"True story, I don't have a clue who could have done this. We don't bring nobody, but ya'll here," he pleads.

"So, you think this may be an inside job? Is that what you're saying?" Dre asks in a confusing manner. "You think one of us done it?"

"Nah, I ain't saying nothing like that. I'm just saying nobody don't know where we rest, like that."

"Where the boy Dusty at?" Latif asks.

"Upstairs...sleeping," ILL Wheel whispers.

Latif snickers. "Let me get this right...mufuckers break into the spot and take 70 bricks and 40 cash of Big Bruhs, almost 80 of your own, and 70 of his and he's able to sleep? He must don't know the pressure ya'll under right now," he laughs. "He sleeping," he smirks. "Got you all on front street alone to explain. The work was given to both of ya'll which makes both of ya'll responsible for it. He doesn't even give a fuck enough to come down with you," he says sarcastically. "For all he know, you could be laying here dead as a mufucking door knob right now." Latif peeks his head inside the jeep. He shakes his head from side to side. "Huh," he sighs. "Your call, Big Bruh," he whispers.

Damn, ILL Wheel says to himself. He didn't look at it like that, but now that Latif has brought it to his attention, it does look rather strange on Dusty's part. Is he behind this, he asks himself. Nah, I don't think he would do that. You never know with him getting high like he does. He might be going bad, ILL Wheel thinks to himself. "I didn't wake him up. He didn't know ya'll was here. If he knew he would have came down with me," ILL Wheel says in Dusty's defense. "Listen," he says looking Dre in the eyes. "I swear on everything, I wouldn't play no games with ya'll. Not for nothing...I mean, I ain't no punk or nothing, but I seen how ya'll roll. You think I would put myself in a situation where I got to go to war with ya'll?"

"Wouldn't be a war," Latif blurts out confidently.

ILL Wheel continues to speak, totally ignoring Latif. "I'll never play with your paper. My big Homie hooked us up. I wouldn't shit on his name like that. Ahmir could have easily walked away from here, leaving us stinking. He didn't have to introduce us to you. I will never fuck up his name. I know you probably don't want to fuck with me no more but somehow I'll get that paper back to you. Somehow...that's on everything! I don't give a fuck if I have to go on a robbing spree, laying the whole town down. You gone get yours back. I promise you that."

Dre picks up his phone and starts dialing, while ILL Wheel stands there in confusion.

"Just give me a little time and I'll fix this. I promise," ILL Wheel says.

"Enough said," Dre interrupts his pleading. "I'll give you the benefit of the doubt. I wanna believe that you wouldn't bust a move for a punk ass sixty cent?" he says looking ILL Wheel in the eyes. "I'll do one better than giving you a little time to get it right. Lil Mama on her way. She got the work for you. Give me all the profit you make until you pay off the tab. Fair enough?"

ILL Wheel does the calculations in is head quickly. Damn, he thinks to himself. He's going to have to sell 1500 bricks in order to pay this debt off. Doing 300 bricks a week, they'll be working for 5 weeks for free. He's sure that will be rough, but it's better than losing his life.

"Fair enough?" Dre asks again.

"Fair enough," ILL Wheel confirms.

"Pssst," Latif sucks his teeth as he walks away from the jeep.

ILL Wheel watches Latif carefully.

"Yo, she on her way, alright?" Dre shouts out, interrupting ILL Wheels thoughts.

"I'm out!" he yells as he pulls out of the parking space. "Yo, La, call me!"

Latif walks away, ignoring him. ILL Wheel analyzes the situation. He predicted it to be worse than it actually turned out. He just knew his life was over and here it is Dre didn't even blink at the loss.

Mu-Mit and Latif pass ILL Wheel as they cruise up the block. Neither of them acknowledges him. They continue to look straight ahead as if he isn't there. Their presence makes him feel uneasy. He's sure that they were eager to move on him. Dre was able to put them on hold this time, but what is going to happen the next time they find a reason to move out, he wonders. "I have to do something to these two old niggas before they do something to me," he says aloud as he dials his girls number just to let her know that he made it out of the situation safe and sound. For now?

///// CHAPTER 39 /////

One Week Later

The Mayor sits in the center of the day room along with thirty other inmates. As they're watching the television, a commercial featuring NBA player, Lebron James comes on.

"You see that kid," the Mayor whispers to the man who sits right next to him. "I look at him and I see a lot of myself. Two ghetto niggas who come from nothing, but manage to make something out of themselves. I gotta respect him cause like me, he changed his own destiny. There's only one difference though...he's worth a couple a million dollars for bouncing a ball up and down the court. Me, I'm worth a couple million dollars and I never bounced a ball in my life," he says sternly. "Ask yourself, who really balling?" he says arrogantly.

"Blackhead!" the marshal shouts, interrupting his heart to heart moment. The Mayor looks over in his direction. "Someone is here to speak with you."

"Speak with me?" he asks. Who, he mumbles under his breath. The Mayor already has it figured out. Someone hear to speak with him can't mean any good. He's been locked up for several years now and every time that he's heard that, bad news has followed.

He follows the marshal up the corridor. "Who is it?" he asks the marshal. "What is it about?"

"I don't know. They just sent me to get you," he replies as he pushes the door open.

The Mayor's questions are answered when he's greeted by his least favorite people in the world. In the room sits Federal Agents Dumber and Dumbest.

"Blackhead...excuse me. I mean, Mayor. Come in and have a seat," Dumber says as he pulls the empty chair closer to him. "How have you been?"

The Mayor doesn't reply. Aw boy, he thinks to himself. Here we go with this shit again. He's sick and tired of these random meetings with them. In all the years that he's been in custody, he would figure that they would have given up already. They just don't seem to get it. They continuously try to break him down. They want that connect so bad.

"Sit right here," Dumber says, while tapping the back of the seat.

"Hmphh," the Mayor sighs as he sits down slowly.

"Why are you like that with us?" Dumbest asks with a cheesy grin on his face. "In all the years that we've known each other, you would think that we would be a little closer. We consider you like family," he smiles. "You, on the other hand, get upset when you see us. Jeez," he sighs. "For crying out loud."

"Mayor, Mayor, Mayor," Dumber says in a low whisper before sitting quietly.

The Mayor is well aware of what he's doing. He's trying to create more tension between them. The Mayor decides to break the ice. How is Stevens doing?" he asks, referring to Federal Agent Dumb.

His question catches both of them by surprise. Dumber displays a shocked look on his face. "Not too good, but he has come a long way though," he says looking completely sympathetic.

The Mayor shakes his head from side to side. "I'm sorry to hear that," he says staring at the floor. He looks up into Dumber's eyes. "I was hoping he would have croaked already," he says staring the agent right dead in the eyes.

The looks on their faces right now are priceless. They can't believe what he's said. The nerve of him. He gloats inside. He feels like he finally got even with them. When his mom was dying, instead of showing him a little compassion, they tried to use his mother's situation to make him roll over on the connect. He adds insult to injury by smirking at them.

Dumbest changes the subject. "You do know what you're here for, don't you, wise guy?"

"I'm sure I do," the Mayor says figuring they are about to start their routine bargaining and pleading, hoping that he'll turn the connect over.

Dumber drops a brick of the 'After Party' on the table. A lump forms in the Mayor's throat. Oh shit, he thinks to himself. He tries to remain cool and calm, but at this point he realizes that he has fucked up big time.

"Do you know what this is?" Dumber asks.

The Mayor shakes his head negatively. "Not at all. What is it?"

"Look closer," he suggests as he grabs the brick of dope and shoves it in the Mayor's face.

"Yo!" he shouts moving his head back away from the dope.

"Yo, what?" Dumber says as he stands up. He hates the Mayor so much that he wishes he would even act like he wanted to get aggressive so he would have a reason to give him the beating of a lifetime.

The Mayor can sense this as well. He knows there's no way possible that he can win against them being who they are, so he just calms down and puts a smirk on his face.

"Back at it, huh?" Dumber asks.

"Back at what?" the Mayor asks nonchalantly.

"Don't play stupid," Dumbest snaps. "You are well aware of what's going on!"

"I'm clueless," the Mayor lies.

"Well in that case, let me give you a clue then," Dumber snaps. "Dumb fucker! Last week a man from your basketball team falls out and dies on the basketball court. They shake his cell down and what is found? 200 bags of heroin, that's what!" Oh shit, the Mayor thinks to himself. Damn, he mumbles under his breath, but he still manages to keep a nonchalant look on his face. "A completely healthy man just falls out and dies?" Dumber asks. "His family requests an autopsy and what is found? An abundance of heroin," he laughs.

"So what does all this have to do with me?" the Mayor asks.

"Uhhmm, I don't know," Dumber says looking away. "Why would we bring him here?" he asks his partner.

"Uh, I dunno...maybe cause it's his heroin," he says sarcastically.

"My heroin?" he smirks. "Ya'll crazy. A thousand dope dealers are housed in this facility and ya'll point the finger at me. You gotta be kidding," he laughs.

"No, I'm afraid not. We are not kidding. This is not a jokey-joke," Dumber says with venom bleeding from his eyes. "So is it yours?"

"You serious?" the Mayor asks, further pissing the man off.

"Serious is an understatement. 200 bags of your heroin found in a federal institution and another murder for you. Ask yourself how serious it is. As if you don't already have enough trouble on your hands."

"My hands? That ain't my dope," he says sternly.

"Well if it ain't yours, then whose is it?" Dumbest asks.

"That's what you get paid $40,000 a year to figure out," the Mayor says sarcastically.

"Try $150,000 a year, fucking asshole," Dumber replies.

Damn, the Mayor sighs to himself. He has to wait all year for $150,000? I can't imagine living like that. Sheez, no wonder they're so uptight, he mumbles to himself. "Forty thousand...a hundred and fifty thousand...same shit," he whispers throwing his hands in the air palm up.

He now has both of the agents' blood boiling.

"So, is there anything you would like to tell us?" Dumbest asks.

The Mayor maintains his composure. He refuses to say anything to incriminate himself. He's sure that there is no way that they can put this on him, but he still doesn't trust it. He knows how the Feds operate. He's seen them flip guys' words around, making innocent men look guilty. He has to outsmart them, but how he wonders. His eyes set on the blank pad and ink pen that sits in the center of the table. He quickly grabs hold of it and begins scribbling on it.

They watch him in confusion. "So, what do you have to say?" Dumber questions.

He finally finishes scribbling. He slams the pen down and pushes the pad toward Dumber who curiously grabs it and starts reading.

It reads: I wish to make no statements at this time. 6:04 p.m., July, 2007. It's signed D. Blackhead. Two lines down a phone number is printed. The name under the number is Tony Austin Attorney At Law.

Dumber smiles after reading the note.

"I don't wanna talk. Holler at my attorney," the Mayor says arrogantly.

Dumber snatches the paper from the pad and rips it into tiny pieces over the Mayor's head. The pieces of paper fall onto his face like snowflakes. "Fuck you and your asshole of an attorney. You have a lot of faith in that nigga of a lawyer that you have. One thing that you will soon learn is that your nigga attorney is a mere peon when it comes to us," he says sternly. "I can show you better than I can tell you. Watch me!"

///// CHAPTER 40 /////

Mu-Mit and Latif sit parked on Orange Street as Candy Kev walks toward them cautiously. He hops in the car. "What's good!" he yells loudly.

"It's all good," Mu replies.

"La, what up?" Kev asks.

"Ay man, you already know. How the young boys say it? It's gwap season," he says smiling from ear to ear.

"Yo, La, hand that to him," Mu requests.

Latif grabs the bag from underneath the seat and passes it back to Kev.

"I know we agreed on 300, but shit moving crazy," Mu says. "We can't keep enough of this shit. Niggas coming through, a hundred here and two hundred there," he lies. "That's only 200."

"That's cool," Kev replies. "This shouldn't take no longer than about four days, word to mother. If you call me tomorrow night, I'll probably have about half the money for you." Candy Kev quickly does his calculations. Mu-Mit and Latif are giving him the work for $210.00 a brick as opposed to the normal $220.00 they normally charge. They lowered their price for him to give him an incentive to get with them. He claims that he's currently getting his work for $200.00 a brick, but he would meet them at $210.00. Getting the work at $210.00 gives him room to make anywhere from a $20.00 to $40.00 profit per brick on the wholesale side and $240.00 profit on the breakdown. "What that come up to...$42,000? Yeah, I'll have at least 15 of that for you by tomorrow night," he claims.

"Ay, don't worry about it," Mu says casually. "Just hit me when you're done. You know I ain't about to stalk you. You're a brother to me. I know you straight up."

"Word to mother," he agrees. "Lemme, go ahead. I'll hit you in a couple of days!" he shouts as he exits the vehicle.

"Yo, cruise through Baghdad," Latif suggests. "Let's see what's taking the young boy so long."

Minutes Later they're riding up Baghdad and although the boy's car is parked at the corner they don't see a sign of him. Just as they reach the middle of the block, they see a huge Ford Customized van pulling over. This catches both of their attention. The passenger's door opens wide and the young boy hops out and runs straight through the alley the exact same way he does when they drop off work to him. Although the van has dark tinted windows they can still see inside due to the sunlight which peeks in.

They're both shocked to see who is behind the wheel. "Look at the fag ass nigga, Parlay," Mu-Mit says.

"Damn sure is," Latif replies. "No wonder it's taking the young boy so long. Parlay trying to cut in the middle."

Parlay sits there with a dumb look on his face as if he's been busted. He gives them a head nod because he's sure they've seen him. Neither of them reply. They just stare at him with stone cold eyes. Parlay cruises off and they pull over waiting for the young boy to come out of the alley.

Minutes later, he jogs out onto the block. He walks past the car as if he doesn't see them. "Yo," Latif calls.

He spins around suddenly. "Oh, what up?" he says with a fake grin on his face. "I ain't even see ya'll out here," he lies.

"What's going on? We been waiting for your call? Something wrong?" Latif asks.

"Nah," he replies as he walks toward the car.

"Something gotta be wrong. You getting it from somewhere else and we didn't even get ours yet."

"Oh that? Nah, man. He front me that. That ain't got nothing to do with ya'lls. I can't turn down no free work," he claims.

"Ay man, I feel you, but we trying to form something here. What can we do to eliminate him out of our picture? What he front you?"

"A hundred," he whispers.

"Enough said. We can do that for you. Matter of fact, I can have that to you asap. If that's the case, will you cut him out?"

"Absolutely," he replies.

"That's what it is then," Latif says casually.

////// CHAPTER 41 //////

In Fort Dix

"Now, I'm craving your body, is this real?" the man sings the tune of Earth
Wind and Fire's 'The Reasons'. "Temperatures rising, I don't want to feel.
I'm in the wrong place to be real. Woahh, and I'm longing to love you just for
a night. Kissing and hugging and holding you tight. Please let me love you
with all my might?" he whines. "The reasons! The reasons that we here!
The reasons that we fear our feelings a-won't disappear. Ohhhh yeah! Ba-ba-
ba-ba-ba-ba-ba-ba-ba-ba-ba-ba-ba-ba-ba-baaaa. Ohhh ah," he sighs. "Ooh and
the love game has been played. And our illusions were just a parade. And all
the reasons start to fade," he synchronizes. "After all the reasons why. All
the reasons were a lie!" he shouts as he hits the high note. "Can't find the
reason," he sings while lowering his voice. "Why I love ya."

The sound of a man's beautiful voice echoes throughout the prison. A
voice this beautiful should have been signed to Motown Records. Instead, it
has a federal number assigned to it. The owner of the voice is trapped here
doing federal life. He's been incarcerated since the late seventies after getting
convicted for robbing banks from New York to North Carolina. The fast life
interrupted the man's dreams of becoming a world renowned singer. Instead
of doing concerts all over the world, he does mini-concerts in the halls of this
prison. On a world tour, he probably could earn $100,000 a show. In here, he
just earns a little extra commissary from the prisoners, who request songs
from him.

The Mayor sponsors him regularly. Hearing him sing these old songs
takes him back in the day when he was a little child, listening to his father
play the same songs over and over on Saturday mornings. These songs bring
back so many memories; bad ones as well as good ones. At that time he and
his family were barely making ends meet. That's the bad memory. The good
part was he was free.

He has gotten accustomed to falling asleep to the man's vocals. He can't
get a wink of sleep without him. Tonight, the man is greatly needed. Tonight
is one of the loneliest nights that he's had since the beginning of his bid. He
truly misses being in the presence of his two women. He would give every
dollar he has just to be home in his bed right now.

He's gotten used to being incarcerated. At first, he prepared himself to
finish his life off in prison, but after hooking up with Tony and listening to
him tell him over and over how he's going to get him freed, he has developed
hope. Watching Tony rip through his cases made him believe in Tony. Having
hope is good, but it also can be a bad thing because hope only builds anxiety
for him.

The Mayor bangs his head on the wall with frustration. Damn, I gotta
get the fuck outta here," he mumbles to himself. "Old School!" he yells
interrupting the singer, who is now flowing.

"Mayor, what's up?"

"Let me get a little Olivia by the Whispers."

"Hmm, hmm, hmm," he clears his throat. "La, la, la, la, la" he blurts out, exercising his voice. "What will your kin folks say?" he begins to blow. "Olivia the slave! It must be breaking their hearts in two. Listen close, they're calling you," he whispers. "Olivia the slave," he blows. "Got distracted on her way… to grandmother's house," he sings as he raises the volume of his beautiful voice. "A wolf in lamb's clothing came. Blew her mind and changed her ways and now she's lost and turned out," he whines. He sings and sings until he not only puts the Mayor to sleep but he also sings himself to sleep as well.
Two Hours Later

The Mayor and Benderas are awakened by the startling noise of five marshals in their cell. "Blackhead, Benderas, get up!" the marshal shouts. They both awaken groggily not having a clue of what is going on. "Both of you out of the cell!"

Benderas gets off the bottom bunk slowly. The marshal gets aggravated with him and yanks him by the arm, pulling him out of the cell. "Come on, come on, let's go!"

"Yo, yo, ease up," the Mayor demands totally resenting how they're handling the old man. "What the fuck is all this about?" he asks knowing exactly what's going on. He's sure that they're shaking his cell down in search of the dope that they believe is his. Never in a million years will they even find a grain of heroin in here, let alone a brick. The Mayor learned his lesson when it comes to resting your head where the work is. If he would have known better years ago, he wouldn't be in the position that he's in right now.

Both the Mayor and Benderas stand outside of the cell as the marshals literally tear the cell apart.

Twenty minutes later they finally realize that there is nothing in the cell. "It's clean except for this," the marshal says sounding extremely disappointed. He holds the Mayor's cell phone high in the air.

Damn, the Mayor sighs to himself. He's sure they're going to make a big deal over the phone. He'll take a cell phone charge over a dope charge any day. The phone is his least worry. He'll have another one of those by tomorrow, once he gives the word to his favorite marshal in the world. "Of course it's clean," the Mayor replies. "What did you expect to find in here?" he asks trying to look and sound as innocent as possible. "Can somebody tell me what this is all about?"

The marshals ignore him as if he hasn't said a word. "Benderas back inside. "Blackhead, let's go!

"Huh? Let's go where?"

"You heard the man," a voice says from afar.

The Mayor looks to his left where the voice came from and his stomach turns when he sees who it is. Dumber and Dumbest are strutting up the corridor.

"Let's go!" Dumbest yells.

The Mayor's mind begins to race. He's baffled at this point, but he still manages to keep the look of confidence that he always displays.

"Hurry, hurry. Let's go!" Dumber shouts to him.

The marshals surround the Mayor as they escort him away from the cell. He peeks back at Benderas who is shaking his head from side to side with despair. The Mayor walks away clueless as to where they're taking him.

Dumbest yanks him by the arm, pulling him close to him. He whispers in his ear. "I told you to watch me. Are you watching?"

///// CHAPTER 42 /////

Parlay sits in his van parked on a side street. Sitting in his passenger's seat is one of the most dangerous old heads in the town. His birth name is Vernon Jones, but he's earned the name 'Tippy-Toe'. That name derives from how sneaky he is. He's known to sneak up on his prey and put them to rest. He's played on damn near every major league team in this town. His position has always been murder. He's done hits for all the bosses dating back to the late seventies.

"Yeah, man, I got a problem," Parlay admits. "Well it ain't a problem yet, but if I don't handle it now, I can see it will become one."

"Give it to me. I take on all problems," Tippy-Toe replies.

"It's two mufuckers getting in my way. Everywhere I turn, they there. Every time I look up, there they go. You know how you can sense when a mufucker ain't feeling you? Well every time I bump into them I get that feeling."

"So, what you saying young fella?"

"I'm saying I got a quarter for both of them. 12, 500 apiece."

Tippy-Toe nods his head up and down. "Sounds like a plan. You got info on them? Anything? Who are they? Young boys?"

"Nah," Parlay hesitates before saying anymore. "Old heads."

"Yeah? Who? I know them?"

"I'm sure you know them. Latif and Mu-Mit."

"Latif and Mu-Mit," he repeats aloud. "Lester Lyle and Larry Brown," he whispers. "Yeah, I know them very well. Ask me do I give two shits about either of them? Not at all. You know me. I move for the dollar. Fucking Larry Brown gave himself the name Mu-Mit," he laughs. "One who brings death? Who the fuck is he to give himself a name like that? That's like a mufucker giving himself the name crazy, or killer? You don't give yourself those types of names. Names like that are not given they are earned. I earned my fucking name!" he says with rage. "I never really been too fond of the boy Latif. He greasier than a Florida fish sandwich. I look at him and can tell he ain't real. He faker than a three dollar bill. Anyway, I never approved of how he moves. He moves like a skeezer, jumping around from bed to bed. No loyalty to nobody. I never trust them kind of guys. And Mu-Mit, a cat offered me fifty grand to off him back in the day. The shit never went through though because the cat that offered me the bread got pinched by the Feds before we could even seal the deal. Apparently Mu-Mit had been extorting his crew and shit? I ain't too fond of either of them. They move around from team to team. Either you gone be with the Yankees or you gone be with the Mets. Whoever is winning, that's who they want to play with. Me, I'm the total opposite. I don't play for no team. I'm a freelancer. I'm no friend or loved one to anyone. All money is green to me. I move for the dollar."

"So, do you want the job or not?"

"And you know this. I never turn down a dollar. Consider it done."

//// CHAPTER 43 ////

Dusty cruises the town all alone, just puffing. He pulls up to the red light. As he's sitting there, he takes a huge pull. Suddenly out of nowhere he gets the irresistible urge to run the light. He slams his foot on the gas pedal and takes off, zooming through the intersection. The car that is creeping through the intersection just misses him by a small fraction. Dusty zooms up Clinton Avenue doing 90 miles an hour, taking another pull of the smoke every block and a half. On his face he wears the goofiest smile. His eyes are stretched wide open. "Oh shit, oh shit," he laughs goofily as he speeds up the block. He's now doing 110 miles an hour. He zips through yet another intersection, almost causing a three car accident. He laughs hysterically as he sees cars swerving in order to get out of his way.

A group of people are crossing the street and when they hear his car roaring up the block they hurry to get out of his way. He speeds recklessly up the block. As he gets closer to the people he steers the car in their direction instead of steering away from them. Just as he's about to smack into them, he swerves just barely missing them. He laughs satanically. He's cracking himself up.

On the sidewalk he sees two men walking slowly down the block. In a matter of seconds, he's hopped onto the sidewalk, speeding toward them. They dash off of the sidewalk onto the street to get out of his way. In an attempt to hop off of the sidewalk, he scrapes the entire right side of his car against the brick building. He tears his mirror off completely. As he dips into the intersection a car cuts off his path. The man accelerates to get out of his path, but Dusty swerves in his direction. He strikes the back of the car slightly. He smiles devilishly. As he's speeding up the block, he takes another pull followed by another and another.

Meanwhile In Yazoo, Mississippi

All eyes are on the Mayor as he walks through the mess hall. He just arrived here early this morning. He still can't believe that he's all the way in Mississippi. Once they told him that he was being shipped out, his pride wouldn't allow him to even ask them where he was being shipped to. The longer the plane ride went on the more curious he became. Two and a half hours later, he arrived here in Yazoo, Mississippi; a place that he never even knew existed. A part of him is quite baffled at the fact that he's so far away from home in foreign land. The other part of him realizes that jail is jail all across the country.

Never did he expect to be shipped out of Fort Dix, but they definitely had another plan for him. He was sure they couldn't ship him out just because they assumed the dope was his. At first he thought the whole shit was a game, but now he sees how serious it is. He now realizes that he may wear that charge. He's not sure of the seriousness of this matter, but he's sure he will, once his lawyer comes to see him.

Tony was furious when the Mayor told him. After hearing the Mayor's story, Tony hung the phone up on him. The Mayor called him back over and over with no reply. Finally, he started calling the office and Mocha answered, telling him that Tony refuses to accept his calls at this time. Hearing that pissed the Mayor off gravely.

The Mayor struts confidently up the aisle, holding his tray with both hands. It's hard for him to believe that he's actually in a mess hall. He hasn't stepped foot in one in years. He's never eaten prison food. Today he has to on the account that he's starving.

As he sits down, he thinks of how good he had it at Fort Dix. To think, he has to start all over again disgusts him. He looks down at his tray at the piles of mess. This is a long way from Filet Mignon. "Angghh," he sighs as he actually thinks of putting it in his mouth. "This bullshit," he says to himself. He sticks his fork in a pile of stiff potatoes, shifting it around. "I can't eat this shit," he says with his mouth but the growling of his stomach changes his mind. He lifts the fork to his mouth slowly.

"Lil Bruh!" a voice shouts from afar. The Mayor turns slowly to see where the voice is coming from. Across the room, a man stands up with his hands high in the air. The Mayor squints his eyes in an attempt to see who it is.

"Lil Bruh!" he shouts again, attracting a great deal of attention. The man starts to make his way toward the Mayor. As he gets closer the Mayor finally realizes who he is. The Mayor's eyes brighten up with joy at the sight of a familiar face. Seeing someone from Newark eases his homesickness.

"Lil Bruh, what up?" the man shouts in a very excited manner. He's just as excited to see someone from home.

""Bas, what's the deal?"

"What the fuck you doing all the way down here, Lil Bruh?" he asks with a big smile on his face. "Where you got shipped from?"

"The Dix. How long you been down here?"

"Almost two years! They shipped me from Otisville. They thought they was hurting me," he laughs. I told them…I'll go anywhere ya'll want me to go as long as ya'll paying for it. Shit!" Bas shouts as he takes a seat side by side with the Mayor. "You just left the Dix?" he asks in a high pitched voice. You can see in his eyes how genuinely happy he is to see the Mayor. His voice is also full of excitement. "Hey, what's up with Old Man Rafiq? How about Gary Saleem?" he asks, not giving the Mayor time to answer the first question. "Twin still down there? How about Big Ak from Dayton?"

The Mayor laughs to himself. Same old Bas, he says to himself. He's always as hyper as a heart attack. "Yeah, he still down there. They all chilling. Just doing that time, trying to get home," he says casually.

Bas snatches the Mayor's tray away from him. "I can't let you eat that, Lil Bruh," he smiles. "I want for my brother what I want for myself," he snickers. "I got whatever. Don't worry about nothing. This us down here. They love me. I got all things. You know how it goes."

The Mayor nods his head up and down. Maybe this ain't gone be that bad after all, he thinks to himself. One thing he knows about Bas is he's gone be alright wherever he is. "Man, I didn't expect to see nobody down here that I knew."

139

"Remember this, Lil Bruh, no matter where you go in the world, there's always gone be a Newark nigga there. And trust me, nine times out of ten, if he a real mufucker he runs the joint. It's how we bred, Lil Bruh," he laughs hysterically. "Yo, where you at? Let me see if I can make some moves to get you moved in with me. Don't worry, Lil Bruh, I got you. Go ahead and put ya feet up, nigga."

The Mayor sighs with relief. Bas is like a breath of fresh air. The Mayor is happy to know that he doesn't have to start from scratch. He can just get in where he fits in until he's balanced enough to stand on his own two feet.
Back in Newark/ Brick City

Dusty has completely lost his mind. He's pulled over on Ninth Avenue, which is one of his stopping grounds. Everyone stares at him in awe. They have never witnessed anything like this before. Dusty stands in the middle of the street ass naked. The cars swerve to miss him, yet and still he runs toward them trying to make them hit him.

Spectators stand on the sideline as he puts on a show. He's stripped himself of all his clothes and is running around like a maniac. Instead of trying to help him, they just stand there in laughter. It's not a puzzle. They know exactly what Dusty's problem is. He's tripping off of the "Wet." The blunt they gave him before they broke into the apartment, messed him up totally. Their intentions were not to mess him up like this though.

Finally, they figure that they've seen enough. "Come on, let's get him," one boy says to the crowd of men. He and another boy run towards the street. Dusty sees them and takes off laughing like a hyena.

Despite his swiftness, they manage to trap him off in an alleyway. He starts to cry loud and hard. Please don't kill me," he begs while lying on the ground covering his head with his hands.

"D, you bugging."

"Don't kill me!" he screams at the top of his lungs. "Please!"

"Yo, call Wheel," the boy demands.

The boy hits ILL Wheel on the chirp.

"Yo, what's good?" ILL Wheel asks.

"Yo, where you at? Your boy, D, tripping off the 'Dip'. You better hurry up and come get him, asap!"

"Where ya'll at?"

"My hood," he replies. Before he can even hang up, police sirens sound off from every direction. Someone must have called the cops due to all of the commotion.

"Please don't kill me?" Dusty cries.

Dusty's cries of murder makes them nervous. They fear the police may believe him. They take off in opposite directions, leaving Dusty laying there screaming his head off.

Dusty sees the police running toward him and he attempts to get away, but they draw their guns and tackle him to the ground. "Help me, please! Somebody help me!" he screams like a lunatic. They ignore his cries and continues to drag him to the car where they toss him into the backseat and take him away. "Help me!" he cries. "Please!"

///// CHAPTER 44 /////

Mu-Mit and Latif cruise through Baghdad in search of the young boy. They have not heard from him in 4 days, ever since they dropped the 100 bricks on him. This isn't like him. They both get the feeling that something isn't right, but they can't quite put a finger on it.

"Slow down," Latif demands. "There go Jessie right there. Pull up on him?" Before they can even pull up to him, he comes walking toward the car. "Jess, what up?" Latif shouts from a few feet away.

"Shit. Ya'll back in shape yet?"

"Back in shape? We ain't never been out of shape."

"Nah?" Jessie asks with a look of confusion on his face.

"Where my lil man at?" Latif asks.

"He just left a few minutes ago."

"Ya'll ain't been having no work?" Latif asks.

"Yeah, we got work."

"What ya'll got?"

"Welcome to Baghdad."

"Welcome to Baghdad? What the fuck is that?"

"It's new. We had it for a couple of days now. It's good too. I mean it ain't no 'After Party' but it sells. I asked him when the 'After Party' was coming back and he said ya'll sold out and was waiting for the re-up."

"That's what he said? We ain't never gotta re-up. This shit is unlimited. That's bullshit! We got plenty. He must have fucked up something," Latif whispers as he starts to dial the boy's phone number. Latif gets angrier as he hears that the phone is no longer in service. "Something ain't right," he whispers. "Jess, when the young boy comes back through, tell him that it's imperative that he calls me. It's life or death," he says sternly. "His!"

Meanwhile in Miami

Miranda gets called out to visit unexpectedly. She can't figure out who could be coming to see her. The only person that would be coming all the way to Florida to see her, would have to be her lawyer and he didn't tell her he was coming, so she doubts that it's him.

Maybe something has come up, she thinks to herself as she steps into the visiting hall. Nervousness fills her heart. I hope it's not bad news, she utters to herself. She steps into the room cautiously. She peeks around for his face, but she doesn't see him in sight. All of a sudden a familiar voice echoes throughout the room.

"Randy!" the deep voice sounds off.

Miranda can recognize that voice from anywhere. She turns around slowly only to see the shock of a lifetime. Paralysis takes over her entire body when she locks eyes with Sha-Rock's best friend, Big Skip. She tries to move, but she can't. Fear has her legs weighed down. How did he find me here, she asks herself.

"Come here!" he shouts with a half a smile on his face. "I fly for almost three hours to visit you and you don't even want to come holler at a nigga?" he teases. Finally she gets it together. She steps toward him slowly. He meets her halfway with his arms wide open. "Give me a hug girl. Look at you. You looking good," he smiles, as he backs away from her.

He takes a seat and she sits across from him. Tears begin to well up in her eyes. She parts her mouth to speak, but Skip interrupts her before the words can leave her mouth.

"I know…how did I find you here, right?" he asks with a smile on his face. She nods her head up and down without saying a word.

"Ya'll case was big up North. It was all over the news on TV and in the newspapers. Watching my boah, Killer Cal going out in a blaze, as I always knew he would…killed me. One thing I must admit, ya'll definitely made history," he whispers. "It wasn't hard to find you. You're a celebrity," he smiles. "I got my little girl to Google your name and viola…I'm here," he smirks. "I told that hard head boy. You know him, he wouldn't listen. All he kept saying is, 'he has it all figured out'. He said, it ain't gone be no repercussions, cause we catching niggas slipping," he says mimicking Sha-Rock. "And look who got caught slipping. My best boah," he says with tears in his eyes. "That shit messed me up. And you in this fucked up situation," he says with sympathy. "All he had to do was wait for me like I asked. That's all he had to do. Randy, how the fuck did ya'll get caught up in all this? What the fuck happened?"

"What didn't happen?" she whispers. Tears drip down her pretty face as she begins to tell her version of the story. The lump that forms in her throat prevents her from talking.

Big Skip looks at her with eyes of stone. "Randy, I raised that boah. I taught him everything he knew. You know my motto. Take no prisoners and leave no witnesses. That's how I trained him. One thing I know for sure is, he would never leave a witness. Something about this isn't making sense. I can't put this puzzle together. You know why? Cause you're the missing piece. Tell me something," he says sternly.

Miranda sits there full of fear. All the things Skip is saying are true. She's heard Sha-Rock say that a million times. She wonders if Skip has it all figured out. "Skip, I don't know how, but it bit him on the ass," she lies.

Skip stares her square in the eyes. "So, Tony Cochran is on the case, huh?" How the fuck does he know all of this, she asks herself.

"The newspaper told it all," he says as if he's reading her mind. "I got my subscription to the Miami Herald," he smiles. "Hopefully, the lawyer works his magic and gets you out of this mess. Then me and you can have a formal sit down in private without all these extra ears around. I know if we put both of our minds together, we can get to the bottom of this. It shouldn't be that hard for us to come up with a culprit. Now should it?" She shrugs her shoulders in fear. Tears drip down her face.

"Randy, stop crying," he says with compassion. He grips her hand as he stands up slowly. "I love you," he says loud and clear. "I just love my boah, Sha-Rock more," he whispers before walking away from the table. He leaves Miranda sitting there with her head buried in the palms of her hands, weeping like a baby. For an entire year she's been praying for her freedom. They say be careful what you pray for. Right now, she's about ready to reverse her prayers.

///// CHAPTER 45 /////

In Yazoo, Mississippi

The Mayor peeks around nervously with the cell phone held close to his ear. Thanks to his man Bas, he already has a cell phone and all of the necessities that he needs to make him feel comfortable and at home. He's calling his attorney for the 100th time, but as usual he's not answering. The Mayor is now furious. He dials the phone once again.

In South Orange, New Jersey

Tony sits in the leather recliner in Rafael's Custom Shoe Shop. "Ralphie," Tony says with a Cuban cigar dangling from his mouth. "I won't need this until months from now. That will give you ample enough time to make it right. You know how I want these, right?" he asks the owner as he's on his knees tracing the outline of Tony's feet onto the cardboard. "No rubber sole, Ralphie. Three quarter, tie ups. This skin should look real good, right?" he asks as he holds the huge sheet of chocolate brown elephant skin in the air. Make the blazer, three-button with the vents on the side."

"Tony, Tony," the owner says with a heavy Armenian accent . "Please?" he begs. "I have been dealing with you for years. Don't you trust me by now? I know how you like everything," he smiles.

"My bad, Ralphie. You know I'm a perfectionist," he says. The ringing of his cell phone interrupts his apology. He stares at the number. He quickly realizes that it must be the Mayor. He didn't start receiving calls from this number until the Mayor got shipped away. He presses no, sending the Mayor right to his answering service.

"Oh, that's how he wanna play?" the Mayor utters under his breath. "He don't wanna answer my calls? Who the fuck does he think he is? I made him and I can break him. He don't wanna answer my calls, but I bet you I know somebody calls that he will answer. He wanna play? Let's play."

Meanwhile in the Bricks

ILL Wheel sits at Dusty's bedside. Tears fall from his eyes as he listens to Dusty talk.

"Yeah, I got a call from the NBA Commissioner this morning," he claims as he stares straight ahead with his eyes spaced out. He's wearing no facial expression whatsoever. "They said I have to make my mind up cause being a rapper is going against my contract. They say I can't do both. They said I have to let them know if I'm going to rap or play ball. I probably just ghostwrite. You know I ghost wrote Lil Wayne's whole album, right?"

"What the fuck are you talking about?" ILL Wheel asks furiously.

"Matter of fact, can I see your cell phone? Pharell supposed to be ready with my beat. If he keeps bullshitting, I'm going to have to call Swiss Beats up. He dying to work with me. Yo, this morning when I left the house, Keish·

was bugging, pulling on my clothes and acting crazy," he smiles still staring straight ahead.

"Keisha who?" ILL Wheel asks without a clue.

"Keisha, Keisha, mufucker. My girl Keisha. Keisha Cole. She bugging cause I had to break the news to her. I ain't ready for no relationship. I'm too young for that shit. Plus with two careers, I ain't got no time for her. Money over bitches," he smiles. "She found Alicia Keys' phone number in my phone. That shit broke her heart. I told her the truth. Me and Alicia always gone have a thing for each other. I was her first. I'm always gone be able to get that," he smiles as he turns his head. He stares ILL Wheel square in the eyes. "Answer the phone. That's probably Fifty Cent. He's supposed to call me today. He wants to sign me to G Unit. Never mind, let it ring. I want to see what Dr. Dre wants to do first. I rather be with Aftermath any day over G Unit. What you think?"

I think they definitely got you in the right place, ILL Wheel thinks to himself.

After the police took Dusty away, he only performed worse. No matter how much they warned and threatened him, they could not control him. After record checking him for warrants and him coming up clean, instead of giving him petty charges like indecent exposure and so forth, they decided to take him to the psychiatric ward. It was plainly clear to everyone that he needed psychiatric help.

The doctor informed ILL Wheel that his breakdown is the results of the PCP. He also stated that at this point it's impossible to determine if he'll be like this forever. He said in some cases the person bounces back partially and in other cases they never return back to a normal state.

ILL Wheel looks at Dusty in this state and he cries at the thought that he may have lost the best friend that he knows and loves.

/////// CHAPTER 46 ///////

On Baghdad

The young boy pulls up and double-parks in the middle of the street as Jessie runs over to the car. Jessie leans in the vehicle, grabbing hold of the sleeve of five bricks of 'Welcome to Baghdad.'

"Ay, Latif just came through," Jessie informs. "He said tell you to call him."

The kid brushes Jessie's statement off by waving his hand. "Yeah alright," he says arrogantly. "Yo, chirp me when you get down to the last 'breezie' (brick)," he says changing the subject totally. He peels off recklessly.

Jessie hates to be in the middle of this. He can already see where this is going. He linked them together thinking of the money that could be made. Now that he thinks of the situation, he can't believe that he even got himself involved in this mess. He should have known better because he's never known the young boys to do good business. He knows one thing for sure. Latif and Mu-Mit will never take a loss like this. Another thing he knows is that he's never seen these young boys back down from anyone. This can easily turn out to be one big massacre.

Meanwhile a few Miles Away

Mu-Mit and Latif stand in front of Iberia's Restaurant talking with Sha from Jersey City.

"Yeah man we waited and waited for your call forever," Mu-Mit says. "After that incident, I called and called. I didn't know what the fuck happened to you. I started thinking the worse. I figured you might have got caught up in the mix. I thought you got pinched."

"Aw nah," Sha replies. "After the murder, shit went sour. Shooting after shooting took place. The projects got so hot that they put the big Police Mobile Unit right in the middle of the courts. Nobody couldn't get a dime out there," he sighs.

"You wasn't involved in none of that shit was you?"

"Hell no! They don't have a clue. His crew got the word that some Bloods murdered him. So they retaliated against the Bloods. It was all out war from there. Like 3 Bloods got murdered. Then two of his boys got murdered but like six more got wounded. Man, it was a blood bath, right dead in the middle of the projects. Shit was crazy! The mobile unit just left two days ago. Later for that shit. I want to forget all about that," he smiles. "I came to talk to ya'll about the samples ya'll gave me. Ya'll still got that?"

"Definitely," Mu replies.

"Yo, that shit was fire. Is it still the same?"

"Absolutely."

"Well, we need to put that in motion. Asap!"

"Hey, we right here. You ain't said nothing," Mu-Mit smiles. "Let's make it happen."

"What's the best price ya'll can give it to me for?"

"I mean, as I said before, we getting it at 180. We rocking it at 220."

"Damn," he sighs. "Ain't no way in the world I can do nothing with that. I can't cop at 220. I serve my niggas at that same price. Check, I do about 60 a day on the ground and about three or four hundred bricks a week on the wholesale side. I move all throughout the town. Overall, I'm good for about 800 bricks a week."

800, both Latif and Mu-Mit say to themselves as they think of the profit they can make off of him alone.

"Well tell us what's good for you and we'll let you know if we can swing it," says Mu.

"Come on Mu? I can't name the price on ya'll work."

"Give me a second, alright?" Mu asks. "La, let me speak to you over here, real quick." They both step a few feet away and whisper back and forth with each other. After a few minutes of that they walk back over to Sha.

"We just kicked it and we came up with a number that you should be able to do something with," says Mu. "I know you said you getting it at 185. There's no way in the world we can match that and only make 5 dollars. If you can meet us at 195 me and my man will split the fifteen dollars. We're really killing ourselves doing that but if you move like you said you move we'll get ours in the long haul."

"195? I mean, ten more dollars is way more than I care to pay, but if that's what it takes to make this deal happen, I have no choice. I guess the work is worth it," he whispers. "You do still have the same shit right?"

"The same shit, Bruh," Mu replies with a trace of agitation in his voice.

"The way me and my connect work is like whatever I cop, he fronts me the same on consignment. Like if I cop 300 bricks, he front me 300 bricks, feel me?"

"No question. I'm saying though, what do you plan on copping the first time around?" Mu asks.

"I need like 250 right now."

Damn more consignment, Mu thinks to himself. He quickly calculates the money that they already have out on consignment. Candy Kev owes for 200 bricks. The young boy owes for 100 bricks. In total that's $64,000. Of the $64,000 only $10,000 is actually their money. The larger portion belongs to Dre. Which means if anything is to happen, they will be in the hole for $54,000. Mu-Mit doesn't think anything should go wrong, but he still has to cover their asses. Dre will put anything in their hands with no questions asked. Mu just wants to make sure that he makes the right decisions and not over play his hand. "Check it out. Right now we got a lot of work out on consignment. Like 200 grand," Mu exaggerates. "We can't spread ourselves too thin, understand? I mean after we collect all the dough and start all over, that's a different story. We'll be more than willing to give you whatever you want. Right now we're in a position to put 100 on top of the 250 you cop. How that sound?"

"Ah," he sighs. "It sounds like this deal ain't beneficial for me at all. I wanna work with ya'll, but ya'll gotta work with me. I'm a big nigga. You know how I do. You can't spoon feed me. If we gone work together ya'll gotta give me room to breathe so I can do me. I'm already taking a ten dollar price cut as it is. It might don't sound like a lot, but at 800 bricks I lose at the minimum $8,000. Then to cut down my workload, I'm losing all around the board. I mean if you cutting down my profit margin, it makes sense to increase the work load so I can make up for it at the end," he says with a look of disgust on his face.

Mu-Mit and Latif stand there in silence. Oh how they both would hate to blow this deal. This will be their best connection so far. They look at each other and communicate with their eyes. Latif's look confirms Mu-Mit's thoughts. "I feel you," Mu replies. "We definitely want this to happen. I guess we can put the 250 on it."

"Alright, good looking out," Sha mumbles.

"So, when will you be ready to move?"

"I'm ready as we speak. All you gotta do is tell me when and where and we can make it happen."

"Ok, that's what it is," Mu replies. "I'll give you a call in about I say, two hours? Alright? How that sound?"

"Sounds like a plan," Sha says. "I'll get with ya'll later, then."

"Most definitely," Mu whispers as he shakes Sha's hand.

Mu and Latif proceed to Mu's car and they pull off. As they're riding in silence they're both thinking of how their plan is coming together. It may have been a little rocky in the beginning, but things are definitely working themselves out. After making a few of the right connections, they've managed to make a fairly decent plate for themselves. They do share the same fear though. They're both worried about the $123,000 consignment tab that they'll have out in the streets after this move. Out of the $123,000 only $14,500 is actually theirs, which means if anybody messes up they're in the hole dearly.

The reality sets in. The young boy from Baghdad pops up in both of their minds. "Let's swing back through Baghdad," Latif suggests.

"You took the words right out of my mouth," Mu replies.

"If that young boy fucked up the paper, his ass is out," Latif threatens.

"Definitely!" Mu agrees.

///// CHAPTER 47 /////

In Montclair, New Jersey

Dre's former girlfriend stands in the kitchen. In one hand she holds the cordless phone and in the other she holds Dre's Nextel bill. She's been busy calling numbers randomly, trying to get in contact with girls that Dre may be dealing with.

"One, two, three, four, five, six," she counts. "Damn, twenty, twenty-one, twenty-two. Damn," she says as her eyes scroll down the page. Seeing the same number so many times has alerted her. "Twenty-six times in one day," she says aloud. "I know this is a bitch." She immediately starts to dial the number.

The receiver picks up on the first ring. "Hello?"

"Yeah!" the woman shouts hastily. "Who this?"

"Who is this? You called my phone," the young voice says.

"Well, if I didn't find your number on my man's phone bill, I wouldn't be calling you." Little does the woman know, this relationship is purely platonic. This is Lil Mama on the phone. "Do you know Dre?"

"Yeah...and?"

"Yeah and...my ass. How do you know him?"

"Listen, you got this all wrong. Take this up with Dre. I ain't the bitch to worry about. Please leave me out of all this?"

"Leave you out of it?" she barks. "Bitch you put yourself in all of this. I'm his wife! Did he tell you about me?"

Lil Mama snickers. "I never asked," she laughs. "Listen, I have way too much to do besides going back and forth with you. I have to go now. I'm hanging up. You have a good day, ok? Bye!" she says before hanging up in the woman's ear.

"Bitch, you better stay away from him!" she shouts. It's too bad that the girl has already hung up on her.

In Manhattan, New York

Dre sits at the cozy table in Cipriani's Restaurant in the Soho section. Sitting directly across from him is one of the most adorable women he's ever set eyes on. Her blonde wet and wavy hairdo looks good up against her high yellow skin. Her beautiful hazel eyes make the picture complete.

This is Dre's actual first date since he's been home. He really doesn't want to be here now. If it wasn't for Tony's persistence he wouldn't be here. Tony made this arrangement without Dre's consent. The woman is a high profile attorney out of Washington D.C. She and Tony work together from time to time. She saw Dre with Tony once and stated to Tony how she just has to have him.

Dre stares into her eyes, admiring her beauty. Not only is she beautiful. She's intellectual and highly motivated as well. She has all of the qualities that he told himself he would be looking for once he gets his act together.

Dre made a promise to himself that he will not get involved with love until he's financially stable. He truly believes that love only gets in the way of making money. He also refuses to fall in love while he's living an illegal life. He learned his lesson with that. Hearing all the stories while he was locked up about how his girl was running around with different guys made his bid a nightmare. He made a promise to himself then; never again would he get caught up like that. He swears that as long as he is on the streets, he will never fall in love. That way if he ends up in prison again, he can do his time with no attachments. He made an observation while incarcerated. All the single dudes laid back and did their time with ease while the married dudes or dudes with girlfriends did their bids on the phones arguing and stressing themselves out for their entire bids.

"I can't believe that the women in New Jersey are allowing you to be single," the woman says while flirting with her eyes. "They must be slacking. You wouldn't last a day out here in D.C."

Dre smiles. "No one is allowing me."

"I know, I know. But what's the problem with you? Why don't you have someone?"

"Problem? There's no problem. I'm just not ready for that right now. Right now, my primary concern is getting me together. I'm not looking to get into anything right now."

"So, basically you're just looking for a little ass from time to time? You can tell me the truth. I mean if you're looking for a one night stand you can tell me. It's cool. Keep it real. Shit, for all you know I could be looking for the same," she says with a sexy smile.

Dre returns the smile. Wow, he thinks to himself. "Didn't I just tell you, I'm not looking for anything?"

"I bet you won't turn down ass though? Now would you?"

"It all depends on how much headache comes with that ass," he smiles. "But nah, for real though…ass ain't that serious for me these days. I've had more than my share of ass. I've had in country ass and out of the country ass. If I don't get another piece of ass for the rest of my life, I'm good," he says confidently.

"That's because you have never had ass like this," she smiles before sipping on the Merlot.

Dre is shocked to hear this conversation coming out of her mouth. He's blaming it all on the wine. He humors her by playing along with her. "Trust me…ass is ass," he smiles.

"I beg to differ," she says licking her lips afterwards. "I agree with you to a certain extent. Some ass is only ass. Then other ass is to die for," she smiles.

"To die for? I just told you that I have had all types of ass and I have yet to find some that is worth dying for? I truly doubt it Miss," he says with a devilish grin on his face.

"Are you challenging me? Don't forget I'm an attorney. I love challenges. If you're so sure about that, how about a little bet?" she asks with her eyes half closed. The wine is really settling in now. "Please make it worth my while though?"

"What are you willing to lose?" he asks confidently.

"No, the question is what are you willing to lose? No money. I need something that means something to you. I've listened to you and what I hear is a bunch of bullshit about you getting you right. I can see right through the bullshit. You're scared to fall in love again. Somewhere down the line, you've given your heart to the wrong woman and she broke it into wittle, wittle pieces," she says mimicking a baby. "Now you guard your heart like Fort Knox. Poor baby," she says with a devilish look on her face. Dre smiles, but deep down inside he knows she's right. He wonders how she heard all of that in his conversation. "Put your heart on the line? I bet you one night with me will change your mind. You will never say ass is ass again as long as you live. There is power in this pussy. Trust me, I know how to use it. If I'm right you have to give me your heart and give me the chance to prove to you that all women aren't here to hurt you. If you're right, if when you wake up in the morning, you still feel that ass is ass, you can leave. No strings attached. Never call me again in life. We'll both act like it never ever happened. How does that sound?"

Dre's phone rings before he gets the chance to answer her. He sees that it's the house number. Something tells him to ignore it, but he knows if he doesn't answer she'll just continue to call over and over. "Hold on, one second, please?" he says to the woman. "Hello?" he answers the phone.

"Where you at motherfucker?"

"What?" he asks, trying hard to remain calm.

"Who the fuck number is 390-4242?" she asks.

He automatically realizes that this is Lil Mama's number. How the fuck did she get hold of that number, he thinks to himself. "Let me call you right back?"

"Fuck that. Don't hang up motherfucker! I'm on my way to her house, right now!" she shouts into the phone loudly. She can be heard all the way across the table. The woman sits there trying to act as if everything is normal.

Shit, Dre thinks to himself. This garbage can ass bitch, he thinks to himself. He can't believe that his past is haunting him. A mistake he made over 20 years ago is still tearing his life apart. How can I pull this off, he asks himself. I need to get this dissolved. If she goes to Lil Mama's house, she'll draw attention to the girl. I can't let that happen. If I leave now, I'll blow the opportunity of a lifetime. Damn, he sighs to himself. "I'll be right there," he says with massive attitude. He hangs the phone up furiously. "Listen, I'm sorry about that."

"Don't worry about it. I see you're having a bit of a situation. Handle your business. My offer still remains. You give me the rain date?" she says sexily.

"All done?" the waiter asks.

"Yes," she replies as she pulls her American Express Black Card from her purse.

"I got it," Dre says digging into his pocket for the cash.

She looks at the $385.00 bill. Yeah right. On your salary, she says to herself. She assumes that as Tony's paralegal this bill is his entire week's pay. The tip alone will cause you to eat cold cuts for lunch for the rest of the week, she says to herself. "I can't let you pay for this. I got this one. I don't need your money. I got my own. I only need your heart," she says leaving Dre speechless.

///// CHAPTER 48 /////

The Mayor and his attorney sit face to face directly across from one another. This is the first time that they've spoken since their incident. The Mayor is extremely pissed with Tony, but little does he know that Tony is even more pissed with him. "I been calling you for days," the Mayor says, staring Tony in the eyes. Disgust covers his face.

"I know," Tony replies very casually.

"And, that's it?" the Mayor asks sarcastically. He truly expected Tony to at least make an excuse of why he hasn't returned his calls. "No reason why you haven't returned my calls? I've spent hundreds of thousands with you and it has really come to the point that you answer my calls whenever you feel like it?"

"Listen, we're both adults here. You know perfectly well why I didn't answer your calls. Let's not play this game. I'm this close to getting your black ass freed," he says as he holds a tiny space in between his index finger and his thumb. "Now they fixed your ass. They got you all the way out here in West Bubble Fuck," he whispers sternly. "How could you make a dumb ass move like that?"

"Hold up, hold up? Without even asking me if it was mine? You already convicting me? You worse than these crackers. How you just gone attack me like that? Who side are you on?"

"I'm attacking you? No, you're attacking yourself with your own arrogance. You're your own worst enemy. A little humility goes a long way. You should try it?"

"Arrogance? Humility? Look who talking? Mr. come to court whenever the fuck I feel like it."

Tony snickers at him, which pisses the Mayor off even more. Venom bleeds from his eyes. "Take a look at the stupid shit you got yourself involved in. I bust my ass until the wee hours of the night trying to find an opening in your case and just when everything starts to go in our favor, you create another situation for yourself. Why?"

The Mayor realizes that Tony is absolutely correct, but his arrogance won't allow him to admit it. He sits there looking like a stubborn, spoiled child. "Why not?"

"Why not?" Tony laughs. "I can give you a hundred reasons why you should not. The first one on my list being, so you don't spend the rest of your fucking life in prison. "Why not?" he repeats sarcastically.

The Mayor realizes that his question was a stupid one yet and still his ego is on the defense. "Seems like to me, you're more worried about my freedom than I am," he says arrogantly.

"Yeah, it does seem like that. Doesn't it? For some strange reason I thought we were equally concerned. I wonder where I could have gotten that idea from? Do you think it I could have gotten that idea from you the way you begged me to get your freedom back when we first met? If I knew you had as little concern as you do I would have never taken the case."

That statement cuts through the Mayor's pride like a sharp knife. He's so pissed right now. "You didn't have to take the case. I could have found any attorney to defend me. Let's keep it real, this relationship was built around cash money. You and me both know that you're initial attraction to me was the green. This is your livelihood. This is how you eat. Don't act like you did this for me as a favor. Listen. There are thousands of lawyers who would have taken my case."

"Oh, just like the lawyer you had before me, who almost had you spend the rest of your life here?" Tony smiles devilishly.

Another stab to the heart. "And guess what? I still would have been alright. I'm gone do me wherever I'm at. Trust and believe that. I ain't gotta tell you that. You already know. Whether on the street or in the pen, I'm the same nigga. I live better in prison than most niggas live on the outside. I eat, fuck and still get money," he whispers. "I'm good. It don't matter to me either way."

Tony slams his briefcase shut. He stares at the Mayor as he stands up. "I wish I would have known this years ago. I wouldn't have put so much energy into it," he whispers. "If you like it, then I love it," he smiles a phony grin. "If you're good with the situation then I have no choice, but to be good with it. It's your life. Good day!" he shouts as he spins around and walks away.

The Mayor sits there with a foolish look on his face. It takes him less than two seconds to realize how simple he just sounded. Truly he wants to call Tony back to apologize, but his huge ego would never allow that. Damn, what can I say, he asks himself as Tony gets close to the door. He's one second too late. Tony disappears out of his sight. Fuck him, he thinks to himself. Who the fuck he think he is, he asks himself as he sits there furiously.

///// CHAPTER 49 /////

On Baghdad

Jessie runs up to the young boy's car and hops right in. The young boy just missed Latif and Mu-Mit. Is he a few seconds too late or is he just on time?

Jessie could sense how aggravated they both are with the situation. Latif finally revealed that the young boy owes them for 100 bricks and an additional 25 that he agreed on selling for them. His total equals approximately $31,000.00.

Jessie knows Latif well and he's heard so much about Mu-Mit. One thing that Jessie knows for sure is he's heard of cases where both of them have murdered for little or nothing. He's sure that 30 grand is more than enough reason for them to go on a rampage.

Jessie just hopes that he can get in between this and stop the situation before it gets ugly. "Ay, you just missed Latif by a few minutes. He said make sure you call him," Jessie says as he hands the young boy a sloppy stack of money.

"Man, fuck Latif!" the boy shouts furiously. "That's a wrap!"

Damn, Jessie thinks to himself. It's obvious that the young boy doesn't know what he's up against. "What happened with ya'll? I thought shit was going good?"

"It was," the boy replies innocently. "Then they tried to play me on some straight sucker ass shit. They tried to stunt me like I'm a son! They tried to run that slick ass old head game on me. Giving me bricks, trying to get me to bring everything back like I'm working for them or some shit!" he shouts. "They tried to be slick, now they ain't getting shit back. They got fucking swindled. You might as well tell them they can chalk that up as a loss. They can take it how they want to take it, but you better warn them. Tell them to stop coming through here like they looking for me before they get something they don't want!"

"Come on," Jessie begs, hoping that he can talk some sense into his head. He doesn't want to see this happen.

"Ay man, I already got my mind made up. It is what it is!"

Meanwhile A Few Miles Away

Mu-Mit cruises through the town. Both him and Latif are riding in silence, but so many thoughts are ripping through their minds. The $31,000 tab is priority right now. They both feel highly disrespected. He hasn't called back by the assigned time that they set amongst themselves. Now they both agree that he's too late. His phone call can't save him. His time is up. There's nothing that anyone can say to prevent them from moving on him.

Mu-Mit's phone rings, interrupting their thoughts. "Yes?" Mu answers rather politely. "Alright, bet! I'll hit you. Peace!" he shouts before hanging the phone up.

Latif stares him in the eyes. "What up?" he whispers.

"That was Dre," he says with despair. "He said it's time to tighten up. He's getting with the people later and wanted to know how much we got toward that tab."

"So, let's tighten up then," Latif says sternly. "He putting pressure on us, so it's time we put a little pressure on the kid. We been more than patient with him. Time is up. Either we get our money or everybody suffers, bottom line!"

///// CHAPTER 50 /////

In Yazoo, Mississippi

A host of inmates fill the day room. The Mayor and Bas have an announcement to make and they're just waiting for the perfect time to make it. They don't want to miss anyone. Everyone's presence is greatly needed.

Bas looks at the Mayor and gives him a head nod to signal that it's time for the announcement. The Mayor returns the head nod. Bas stands up confidently. "Let me get everybody's attention for a second," he says loud and clear while shutting the television off. "First and foremost, I want to introduce my brother to everyone. I just want everyone to be familiar with who he is. He just got shipped here from Fort Dix. Any cosmetics or food that you can spare is greatly appreciated," Bas says as he winks at the Mayor. "I would like to formally invite every one of ya'll to a party that I'm giving him at his request. It's called a PSI party. For those of you who have never been to a PSI party let me brief you on it. You don't have to bring a gift to a PSI party. All you have to do is bring your paperwork. Being that we all have to live together, Lil Bruh just wants to know exactly who he's living with. If you are who you say you are, you shouldn't have anything to hide. Look, I got mines right here," he says as he holds a sheet of paper in the air. "Look, Lil Bruh got his," he says as he points to the Mayor who is holding his paper in his lap.

The Mayor sits there arrogantly. The whole party is his idea. He does this in every jail that he's been in. This is necessary for him to know who is who before he begins to get acquainted. On the paperwork it will state if a guy has cooperated with the Feds in his case which will give a guy the label of a snitch. The Mayor can't stand the sight of a snitch.

"We'll give everyone enough time to get hold of their paperwork," Bas says. "I say we start the party at 7:30 sharp. Don't be late," he demands.

The Mayor looks around at all the men's' faces. He can clearly see which guys are confident in who they are and which ones are not. Each man knows exactly who he is and if he has ever cooperated, now is the time for everyone to know.

Meanwhile In New Jersey

Dre sits in Tony's office listening attentively to Tony speak.

"I can't get over that shit. I'm so close to cracking this case wide open and now this. I told you I need him clean!"

Dre listens without replying; although he dislikes how Tony is talking to him. His guilt makes him refrain from saying anything. He hated to give his brother the work for this reason, but his brother forced his hand. What was he supposed to do?

"Then I go there and the cocky fucker says I'm more concerned with his freedom than he is. Can you believe that shit? He tells me, he's good. He

155

eats, fucks and still gets more money on the inside than most guys get on the outside. Blew me away." Tony cracks a smile. Although he was very pissed at the time he's managed to get over it. He's learned not to take the Mayor seriously when he starts to talk off the wall. "I kindly got up and walked out on his ass. I left him right there with those stupid ass words still in his mouth. I'm telling you Dre…his arrogance is going to be the key to his demise."

"I tell him that all the time," Dre agrees. "On the real, I don't think he meant you any harm. It was his pride," Dre attempts to defend his baby brother.

"I know but he talked real dirty to me."

"Please man, let it go. Not only does he need you, he wouldn't choose another lawyer over you. He definitely respects your work."

"I can't tell! He told me any lawyer could have done what I've done for him. Do you know what his problem is, Dre? His money. He has so much of it that it makes him feel invincible. He feels that money can buy him out of any situation. Before you came back into the picture, his money was starting to get low. You should have seen him. The lower his money got, the more humble and down to earth he became. He was a total different dude. He was as humble as a kitten. You could actually hold a sensible conversation with him. Now, you can't sit in the same room as him," Tony laughs. "You have to step on a ladder just to be on his level. I don't know what to do with him," he laughs. Tony began pissed off with the Mayor, but his anger has managed to wear off. Tony finds him to be humorous at times. Tony cracks up at some of the things that come out of his mouth. "If I didn't have genuine love for him, I would have been stop representing him," Tony informs. "You're more concerned with my freedom than I am," he says mimicking the Mayor. He laughs hard, as he replays it in his head. "I wanted to crack his fucking head open," he chuckles. "I just gotta stay away from him for a minute. And you have to do the same. If you love him, you'll stay away from him. He can't afford anymore trouble. We're close to freeing him. I have his freedom in my hands. Don't make me drop the ball. Trust me, he's coming home. Just keep him clean."

"So, what about this new beef? Can it hurt him?" Dre asks.

"Hell no!" Tony snaps. "They have no proof that it's his. They're just trying to scare him into talking. They don't have anything on him. Just so happen, they were already in the process of shipping him away. That had nothing to do with it. You been in the FEDS. You know how they do. Diesel therapy," he sings. "Fly your ass all over the world for free," he laughs. "They just wanted him to think that he was being moved for that purpose. No need to worry about that. Just keep him clean!"

Back In Yazoo/ Hours Later

The party is officially over. The Mayor was happy to find out that everyone left the party with the official stamp of approval, which made the Mayor feel a little at ease.

The Mayor steps toward his bed where his bunkie lays back on the top bunk. He's actually the only man who didn't reveal his paperwork. That makes the Mayor very uncomfortable. He figures everyone should have been more than anxious to clear their name, unless of course they have something to hide.

The Mayor sits on the edge of his bed. He stares at the wall quietly. Tony comes to mind. The Mayor realizes that he went way too far the other day. He should have never said those words that he said. He could really see that he had pissed Tony off. For the first time ever, he feels like he should apologize. As easy as it may sound, it is extremely difficult for him to take a step like that. Should I, he asks himself as he tosses the idea around in his head.

The Mayor gets up and stands right by the bed. He stares at the inmate on the top bunk, who appears to be sleeping. "Yo," the Mayor says. "Yo," he repeats while nudging the man lightly.

The man awakens, groggy eyed. He peeks through his half closed eyes. "Oh, what up?"

"What happened baby? We had to have the party without you," he smiles. "We waited for you to show up but you never came back."

"Oh, I fell asleep. My fucking head is killing me," he sighs. "Sorry about that."

"Don't worry about it. It's alright. You can just show me the paperwork. I'll tell Big Bas that you're good and he'll tell the rest of them guys. You got the papers close by?"

The man sits up slowly. The Mayor can sense that something isn't right. The man hops off of the bunk and walks toward his locker, which sits a couple of feet away. He digs for a matter of seconds shuffling things around, while the Mayor watches over his shoulder. "Damn," he says. "It should be in here somewhere. I can't find it."

Whatever, the Mayor thinks to himself. He can see right through the bullshit. "Want me to look for it? I know you got a headache," the Mayor says, playing right along with the man.

"Nah, I'll get it. It should be right here," he says as he skims through a small stack of legal documents.

"Ho, ho, ho!" the Mayor shouts. "What's that right there?" Ain't that it?"

"Where?"

"Go back. Right there. That's it right there," the Mayor says anxiously.

"Damn, I didn't even see it," he claims as he pulls the sheet of paper away from the stack. He reads it over himself before passing it to the Mayor.

The Mayor reads the paper thoroughly before arriving to the moment of truth. The man stands up slowly. The Mayor looks to the bottom of the paper where he finds what he's looking for. He sees the code, 5k1.1, Departure for Substantial Assistance to the Government. In plain terms, he's a snitch. The Mayor looks the man square in the eyes. He doesn't need words because his eyes say it all.

The man starts rambling. "I was a kid man. I didn't know no better. They bamboozled me, man. They tricked me. I didn't know they was gonna flip everything around on me like that. They played games with my words. They flipped them all around. Trust me, I was a kid?" he pleads.

"I understand," the Mayor says nonchalantly. "It can happen." Of all the inmates for the Mayor to be bunkies with, they have him with a snitch. He can't believe it. He will never be able to feel comfortable with this man as his bunkie. He'll always have to be on his P's and Q's, living with the fear that the man may tell something on him. He could easily just say the wrong thing over the phone and the man will have something to tattle-tell. He can't and will not live in that type of fear. "When you leaving?" the Mayor asks.

"Huh?" the man asks with a confused look on his face.

"I said, when are you leaving? Ain't enough room for both of us in here. Sometimes I keep a dirty yard. I can't have you snooping around," he smiles a phony grin. "I ain't living with no snitch," he says with aggression.

"Come on man? That was over ten years ago. I told you they tricked me."

"If they tricked you once, they can trick you again. Once a snitch, always a snitch. All you gotta do is request a move. It's that simple."

"It ain't that simple," he whines. "What am I going to tell them my reason is?"

"I don't know. You'll come up with something," the Mayor says as he steps toward the man. Rage fills his eyes. "Tell them you fear for your life," he whispers.

///// CHAPTER 51 /////

Mu-Mit cruises through Baghdad slowly as he and Latif look around in search of the young boy. Him nor his car is in sight. The block is just full of customers buying dope.

As they get closer to the middle of the block, they spot Jessie who is right in the center of all the action. Him, a couple of other dope feigns and three young boys stand on the porch huddled up together pitching dope to the customers who run back and forth. Jessie is in the process of making a sale, when he hears Latif call out his name. He looks up and as soon as he spots Mu-Mit and Latif he takes a deep breath. Damn, he thinks to himself. Jessie loves Latif like a brother. Normally joy fills his heart whenever he sees him, but lately he hates the sight of him. He now feels a great deal of pressure when Latif is around. Huh?" he asks with his eyebrows raised high.

"Come here," Latif instructs as he lays back in the seat, just peeking at the scenery.

Jessie finally makes his way over to the car. He tucks his money in his pocket as he's leaning his head close to the window. "What up, La? What up, Mu?" he asks already knowing what's up. He's sure the next question will be pertaining to the young boy.

"Yo, he came through?" Latif asks.

I knew it, Jessie thinks to himself. "Damn," he mumbles under his breath. "A while ago."

"You told him to call me?" Latif asks.

"Y, yeah," he stutters.

"What he say?"

Jessie hates to lie to his man, but he refuses to tell him what the young boy really said. Jessie knows what type of problem that will create. "Nothing really," he whispers.

"Oh nothing," Latif says nodding his head up and down. "Ok. Dig, dick off. We'll give you time to clear the area. We gone spin around the block real quick. I'm about to lay everybody the fuck down," he says in a calm manner.

"Come on, La?" Jessie pleads. "You gone have me all up in the middle of some bullshit," he whines.

"Na, I ain't gone put you in the middle of it. That's why I'm telling you to step. Anyway, fuck these niggas. It ain't gone be nothing to be in the middle of," he says furiously. "Everybody out here pumping his work?"

Jessie stands there shaking his head from side to side. Fear is evident on his face. "Pssst," he sighs.

"Huh? Who all got his work?"

"Just me and the other dude with the blue hat on," Jessie mumbles.

"Too bad. Everybody gotta pay. We're about to circle the block. Go ahead and bounce now. Jess, leave," he whispers as Mu-Mit pulls off.

Mu-Mit circles the block slowly, trying to give Jessie ample time to clear the block. As they turn back onto the block, they both peek around.

Jessie has done as they instructed him to do. Just like a magician he has disappeared.

"You want to park around the corner and let me out so they don't see your car?" Latif asks.

"For what? Just like they know the young boy beat us, they gotta know that it's us. I'm pulling right up to the porch," he says as he snatches his .44 Magnum from his waist.

Latif grabs his .357 from his lap. "Pull right up on them."

Before Mu-Mit can stop, Latif forces the door open and flies out of the car with his gun aimed at the crowd. He catches everyone by surprise. They're all startled. One young boy looks as if he's about to take off running. "You move, I'll bang yo mufucking back out!" Latif threatens with aggression. "Everybody lay the fuck down! Now!"

Mu-Mit hops out of the car and stands there with the door wide open. He aims his gun at the crowd as well. He peeks around. His head swivels quickly, looking in every direction just in case there is someone lingering around that they have not seen.

"Everybody crawl into the fucking alleyway! Now!" he shouts as he walks toward them. At the sound of his voice, they begin crawling like little scared roaches. Once they're in the alley, he stands over them one by one, making them empty their pockets. He shoves the money into his pocket as they hand it to him. "Gimme the dope too," he says. After making his collections he stands up and backpedals away, still aiming his gun at the crowd. "Listen, I don't know what affiliation ya'll got with the kid Sway, but he just made it hard for everybody. Ain't nothing moving out this mufucker until we get paid. Tell 'em he done fucked up. This gone go on everyday until we get ours. Mu, get in the car," he says as he waves his gun at the crowd. Latif gives Mu-Mit time enough to get in before he hops in.

Latif hangs his gun out of the window as Mu-Mit is pulling off. "Dumb ass niggas!" Latif shouts as he plops back in the seat. "Operation Shutdown is now in effect! They not only made it hard for themselves, they just fucked it up for everybody in the town. We tried it Big Bruh's way and look what happened? It didn't work! Now we doing it our way. If you ain't moving with us, you ain't moving!" Latif says as Mu-Mit drives up the block.

///// CHAPTER 52 /////

Dre taps on the door of Tony's office. "Come in!" Tony shouts. Dre walks in carrying a briefcase in his hand. "Dre, what up?" Tony asks as he sits behind his desk, just brushing his hair vigorously. He continues to brush as he stares into the mirror that sits on his desk. Finally, he lays back in his chair, just rubbing his hand over his wavy hair.

"Here," Dre says, shoving the briefcase toward Tony. "That's two hundred thousand," Dre whispers.

"Oh, ok. I'm on my way out to deposit it within the next hour. I'm just waiting on a conference call."

"Cool. I'm gone for the day. I have a few things to handle. I'll just give you a call later on tonight."

"Ok, be safe," Tony whispers as he begins stroking his hair again.

Dre leaves out, and exits the building. He gets into his truck and cruises away. As he's driving, he can't help but to think of how good things are going for him. At this point, he has nothing to complain about. The last two weeks have been the best two weeks of his entire hustling career. He managed to score a profit of $400,000.00. All of his clients have stepped their game up to almost double the workload he started them off with. He's also made some new connections with a couple of dudes from out of town. He just recently added South Carolina and Virginia to his roster of states that the 'After Party' has eased into. Slowly but surely the 'After Party' is spreading out just as he hoped it would. His ultimate plan is to have the 'After Party' in every state. If there's a ghetto there, and people there want to get high, he plans to be their source to do so.

His phone rings, interrupting his thought process. He looks down and gets agitated when he sees the display has Cindy's name on it. He quickly realizes that he does have one thing to complain about. "Yeah?" he answers.

"Yeah. Where you at?"

"Huh?"

"Where are you?"

Get it through your head, we are not together, he says to himself. He hates to answer her when she questions him, but he just does so to keep the drama down. For the life of her, she just doesn't get it. As many times as he has told her that they're not a couple, she still carries on as if they are. He can't wait until his parole is over so he can cut all ties with her and end this nightmare. Until then, he has to play it cool. He knows that he has to keep her close because she's too dangerous to be on the opposite side. She knows this, which is why she acts the way she does. She knows that she has him by the balls. On many occasions she's threatened to call parole on him. Dre is sure she will. She's always been a vindictive girl and over the years it seems as if it has gotten worse. The fact that she knows he doesn't have the slightest interest in her, makes her that much more wicked. Dre knows that if she ever gets the feeling that she will lose him forever, she will make it where no woman could ever have him to herself. She's told him that more times than he can remember. With him knowing that, he's forced to change his attitude and at least act like things are alright between them. "Working, Cindy, working. Ay, look in my drawer. I left a couple of dollars in there for you. Go hit the mall or something," he says as he fakes a laugh. "Leave me alone," he says in a playful manner. "I'm working."

"Whatever," she laughs.

"Yo, I'll hit you when I'm done working."

"Alright," she replies.

"Later!" he shouts before hanging up. "Grimey ass bitch," he mumbles to himself. Money has always been her main concern. It never fails him. Money could always buy him out of any situation that they have ever had.

Twenty-five minutes later, Dre is cruising through Englewood, New Jersey. He cruises up the block and makes the quick right turn into the huge parking lot. He parks and hops out of his jeep.

He enters the office building. "Mr. Goldberg," he says to the security guard who sits at the desk.

"Fourth floor," he replies. "First door to your right."

"I know," Dre interrupts.

Dre enters the office and the secretary sends him to the back office.

"Andre," the old man shouts with a heavy accent. "How are you?"

"Good, good," Dre replies as he hands over the briefcase. "That's $250,000.00 in there. That's the paper we discussed last week. That should cover any possible mishap that I could get into. Bail money or whatever."

"Yep, this should do it."

This is Dre's newly appointed attorney. This man is a highly recommended attorney. Dre realizes that anything can happen any minute in this game; wherein he could spend the rest of his life behind bars. He's already spent half of his life incarcerated. He's sure with his criminal history, just catching a mere misdemeanor, will finish him for life. He has no one out here that he can trust, which is why he's forced to rely on this attorney. Unlike the Mayor, Dre doesn't trust Tony the least bit. He can see it now, they run into a problem and Tony runs off with all of their money. Never, he thinks to himself as he entertains the thought.

Furthermore, Dre has to be prepared for the worse. He hates to think like that, but it's the reality of the game. If anything goes down, he and his brother will be co-defendants. There is no possible way that Tony could represent both of them. If Dre doesn't prepare now, he could find himself in a situation where he's behind the wall searching for an attorney. Desperateness could cause him to make the wrong decision. Right now he's 100 percent sure that this is the best representation his money can buy. Hopefully, he'll never have to find out.

///// CHAPTER 53 /////

The Next Morning

It's 6 in the morning and Jessie has just stepped back on the block not even ten minutes ago. Latif informed him last night that the robbery landed them close to $7,000.00. Latif told Jessie that they're now $24,000.00 away from their goal and they're not going to stop until they get every penny that is owed to them. On top of that, they want interest. Jessie begged him to let him see if he could talk some sense into the young boy's head, but Latif refused. He said it's way too late for talking. Jessie just wishes he wasn't in the middle of all this.

Jessie stands on the corner just observing the block. Everything is flowing as usual, as if nothing ever happened out here yesterday. Jessie was hesitant to come back out here today, but he figured if he didn't he would put himself in a bad spot. If he hides out, he thinks they will assume that he has something to do with what happened.

Jessie pulls his phone from his pocket and hits the chirp button. He's calling the young boy. Yesterday, before Latif and Mu-Mit came through, he was in the process of waiting for a re-up of the work. Unfortunately, they disturbed his groove. Several times last night, he considered telling the boy that he was robbed yesterday, just so he could keep the money. Greed and his habit made him consider it, but honesty made him reject the act.

"Chirp! Yo!" the boy shouts loudly. "J, what up? Where you at?"

"Chirp! Baghdad," Jessie whispers. "Come through. I need to see you," he says as he grasps the stack of money that he holds in his pocket.

In less than five minutes, Jessie spots the boy's new Impala coming up the block. He steps toward the curb awaiting the boy's arrival. After the $30,000.00 come-up, he was able to buy himself a new car. He thanks Latif and Mu-Mit wholeheartedly for that. If it weren't for them, he wouldn't have been able to do so.

He slams on the brakes directly in front of Jessie and Jessie trots up to the car. "J, what it do, baby?" the young boy asks with a grin on his face.

Jessie leans his head in the car as he digs into his pocket to retrieve the money. "What up?" Jessie greets him.

"You," he replies as he waits for Jessie to give him the money.

"Here, that's $700.00, right there," he says as he hands the money over.

"Alright bet," the young boy says as he tries to sneakily grab hold of his nine millimeter.

Jessie spots the gun before he can get it off of his waist. His eyes stretch wide open. He wants to back away from the car, but fear has his feet glued to the ground.

The young boy points the gun at Jessie's head. He fires once. Pop! He misses, but Jessie feels the wind blow right pass his face. He finally manages to get enough movement to take a few steps away from the car. He backs away clumsily, almost tripping over his feet.

Pop! He fires once again. The bullet pierces through his shoulder blade, forcing Jessie backwards. He falls to the ground in a seated position. He uses his hand to balance himself so he can get up, but he has no strength in his left arm due to the wound. He collapses onto the ground falling towards his right side. Pop! Pop! Pop! Pop! The boy fires recklessly as Jessie covers himself as best as he can. Bullets bounce and ricochet in every direction, except for Jessie's direction. Pop! He fires once again before peeling off. Sccuuurrrr!

///// CHAPTER 54 /////

Two blocks Away from Red Hook Projects

Four men occupy the room of the abandoned apartment. Three of the men surround one man who is sitting on the edge of the window sill. Two of the men watch anxiously as the standing man loads the 'After Party' into the syringe. "Ready?" he asks the man who is sitting on the window sill.

"Yeah," he growls as he leans back against the window to prop himself. He then tilts his head to the right. The man grabs the sitting man and keeps his head in position by pressing his index finger on the man's chin. Just when he feels that he's secure, he presses the point of the loaded syringe into the man's neck. He slowly injects the dope into the thick vein that protrudes through his skin.

"Ahhh, yeah," he growls as the dope swims through his bloodstream. The other men watch with greed and jealousy as he appears to be enjoying the sensation.

Suddenly, the man's body begins to jolt uncontrollably. The needle bounces off of his neck and blood squirts like water from a water pistol.

"Ho, ho, ho!" the man shouts nervously while still holding the needle in his hand. The man falls backwards. His head bangs into the window causing it to shatter. His body trembles uncontrollably. "Oh shit!" the man shouts. The other two men back away in fear. They don't know what to do to help him. The man's body does flip flops like a fish does out of water. Finally, he lands on his back.

The man drops the syringe and snatches the handkerchief from his own neck. He ties the handkerchief around the man's neck attempting to stop the bleeding. Blood soaks through the cloth instantly. Suddenly the trembling of the man's body stops. He just lays there as still as can be while his eyes roll up in his head. The sight of this makes one of the men dash out of the apartment without warning.

"Come on, man, don't do this to me!" the man cries as he continues to apply pressure to stop the bleeding. Ay, go and get help!" he shouts. The man takes off into flight at the sound of his voice. "Please man, don't do this? Please?" he cries. "You can't die on me man! Don't do this!" he begs. The man's eyes finally close. He lies there with a peaceful look on his face.

"No, don't do this!" he shouts. "No!"

Yes, despite the man's begging and pleading he's done it. He has encountered death.

"No," he cries. No! Damn, man," he cries. He removes his hand from the man's neck and stands up slowly. He backs away from the corpse slowly. "Damn!" he shouts. The loaded syringe that lies on the floor calls his name. He quickly trots back over near the body. He bends over, grabbing the needle, before dashing out of the apartment, leaving the dead man alone to rest in peace.

////// CHAPTER 55 //////

"I don't believe this shit," Latif smiles devilishly. "I tell you one mufucking thing, they got the right one now. Don't they know I live for this shit?"

"If they don't, they will," Mu-Mit replies as he cruises down the block.

"That sucker ass nigga tried to take my man out of here. The nigga fucked with something I love. You touch one of mine, I gotta take 3 of yours. That's just how it goes. I felt fucked up seeing Jessie in pain like that. Felt like it was all my fault. Now it's all about the get-back."

Mu-Mit cruises up 11th avenue. As soon as they hit the intersection of 7th street and 11th Avenue, Latif snatches both of his guns from his waist. They're both fully loaded and ready for action. Mu-Mit snatches his .44 from his waist as well. As they're turning onto 8th street, they're surprised to see that the block is empty, except for a few dope feigns that are standing near the porch that they normally pitch from.

"Oh, they laying low now, huh?" Latif asks as he looks around. "I should just spray the whole block up! That'll let them know we ain't bullshitting with them!"

"Nah," Mu-Mit denies. "Them ain't nothing but dope feigns. Let em' live. Our beef ain't with them."

"You right," Latif agrees.

A raggedy looking dope feign sits on the porch across the street from the work house. Mu-Mit and Latif are so busy watching the porch that they're not even paying attention to the man. He secretly grabs his phone and hits the chirp button.

Ten seconds later a young boy dashes out of an alleyway on the same side of the street that Mu and Latif are on. His face is covered with a gray and white scarf, which is tied around his head and face like a Taliban. In his hands he grips an M-16.

"Oh shit!" Mu-Mit says at the sight of the man. He swerves onto the other side of the street trying to get away from him. He's caught them by total surprise, not giving neither of them time to fire. Their main concern is getting out of his way.

"Baghad, bitch!" the young boy says as he runs toward their car, spraying recklessly. Bbbdd, bbbdd, bddd, bdddd! The gun is full of so much power that he can barely hold it down. His body shivers from the impact, each time he mashes the trigger.

People start dispersing into every direction to get away from the machine gun toting boy. He can not handle the weapon the least bit. He shoots recklessly. Bullets soar into the air in every direction, giving Mu-Mit time to get away.

Mu-Mit increases his speed. He passes right by the boy. Instead of letting them get away, the young boy runs up the street behind them, still firing away. Bbbbddd, bbbddddd, bbbddddddddd!

Mu-Mit is leaning real low, barely able to see ahead of him. Over the top of the steering wheel, he sees the image of a man dash in front of him. He's wearing a Taliban scarf as well. He cuts off their path. Pop! Pop! Pop! He fires aiming directly at their windshield. Glass shatters and disperses everywhere. "Oh, shit!" Mu yells out.

"Run that mufucker over!" Latif shouts furiously. "Run him over!"

Mu-Mit steers the car toward the young boy. He backs away trying to get out of their way, but he never stops firing. Pop! Pop! Pop!

Latif hangs his arm out of the window, holding his gun over the roof of the Cadillac. Boom! Boom! Boom! He fires attempting to hit the young boy. He backs up in a tight alley and continues firing. Pop! Pop! Pop!

All of a sudden a huge force bangs into the back of the Cadillac and rocks the entire car. Another huge crash follows. Latif turns to look behind him and there he sees another young boy standing on a porch a few feet away, holding an automatic weapon. Boc! Boc! Boc!

The impact makes Mu-Mit lose control. He swerves uncontrollably until he's able to regain control. Latif then aims his gun at the young man on the porch. Boom! Boom! He fires just to keep the young boy away from him. "Mu, get the fuck out of here!" Latif shouts nervously.

As they're zipping up the block fireworks are popping off sounding like the war on Al-Qaeda. They finally get away from the gunmen. A few people stand huddled up at the corner of 12th avenue and 8th street, just looking at the action. As they approach the corner, Latif hangs his gun out of the window. He fires at the crowd. Boom! Boom! They scatter in attempt to get away from him.

Mu-Mit zooms up the block. They're both so enraged right now.

"I'mma kill these mufuckers!" Latif shouts furiously.

////// CHAPTER 56 //////

Red Hook Projects are always packed, but today the flow is at an all time high. Dope-feigns run in out. Pitchers stand at every entrance, meeting the dope-feigns. Heavy action flows throughout the entire area.

A group of four dope-feigns walk up to the stoop. Three young boys stand side by side. Each one of them has about six to ten customers huddled up around them.

"I'm looking for that 'After Party'," the man whispers to his group. You heard Sonny overdosed from that yesterday, right?" he asks.

"Nah, I ain't know that," one man replies.

"Yeah, it took him right outta here," he says.

"Who got that? I need that in my life!" the man shouts with joy. "Who got 'After Party'?" the man asks anxiously.

"I got it!" one boy shouts.

"Right here! Right here!" another shouts, trying to steal the sale.

"After Party, right here, Pop! How many you need?" another boy asks digging into his bag.

Meanwhile in Elizabeth, New Jersey

Dre and his boy Smooth from Red Hook Projects sit in the food court inside of Jersey Garden Mall. Smooth talks while Dre listens and eats at the same time.

"Here it go, right here," Smooth says, nodding his head toward the shopping bag that he holds in his hand.

"Slide it under the table," Dre whispers with a mouthful of food trapped in between his jaws.

"That's a buck, seventy ($170,000). What a nigga gotta do to get that price lowered?" Smooth asks with a smile on his face.

"We'll kick it," Dre smiles in return.

"Yeah, alright," he laughs. "Listen, let me tell you, that shit is on fire. A nigga died off that shit yesterday," Smooth whispers peeking around to make sure no one is listening.

"What?" Dre asks, hoping that he's heard wrong.

"A nigga died off that shit," he repeats. "Nigga, we catching bodies with this shit," he smiles. "Once the word spread, niggas started coming from everywhere for that shit. Imagine that, you would think they would stay away from it cause it killed a nigga. Instead it makes them want it more. I sold out as soon as everybody found out what he died from. "That's why I had to step it up. I'm about ready to flip everything," he says. Smooth normally buys three or four hundred bricks a week. This is the biggest score ever. Today he's stepped his flip up to 850 bricks. "Yo, whatever you do, don't serve nobody in Brooklyn shit. I'm the only nigga over there that got it and everybody want it. They gone have to go through me to get this shit. I want

$300 a brick, straight up. We about to eat. I'm low. I just got a call from my little man. He said he only got three bricks left."

Dre sits there nervously. Damn, he thinks to himself. That's two lives claimed by his dope. The human side of him feels sympathy for them, but the hustler in him can only think of dollar signs. The Feds quickly come to his mind. This can be dangerous for him. If the dope continues to claim lives, he's sure they will be out on the street trying to find out where it's coming from. His brother comes to mind. He hopes they don't try to attach his name to it being that they already believe that it was his dope that killed the man in Fort Dix. Worry fills Dre's gut. He loses his appetite as stress replaces his hunger. Damn, he thinks to himself.

///// CHAPTER 57 /////

Mu-Mit and Latif sit parked on Osborne Terrace in Newark. Today they're riding in a rented Chevy Trailblazer, being that the Caddy was put out of commission. Mu-Mit had to put it in the body shop for body work. When him and Latif saw the size of the bullet holes that were in the car, all they could do was thank God that they were not hit. The average guys would be ready to fall back from the beef after the incident, but not these two. Being in the middle of that drama only excited them more. Now that they know what they're up against, they're forced to come up with another strategy. They realize that it's almost impossible to go through Baghdad to retaliate. Now they have to do the next best thing.

"You sure this where he live?" Latif asks.

"Yeah, I helped him move here about a month ago," Jessie explains.

"So, what about our boy?" Mu asks. "You don't know where he rest?"

"Not at all," Jessie replies.

"Damn!" Latif shouts furiously. "I want this so bad that I can taste it! You don't know where none of the other ones live?"

"Nope," he mumbles.

"It's alright," Mu-Mit replies. "We'll walk 'em down. Get them one by one. When they look up, we gone be right there," he smiles.

"Where this mufucker at?" Latif asks hastily. "What time you say he come out?"

"He the first one on the block every morning and the last to leave. He open up like 5 on the dot."

"What time is it?" Latif asks.

"Four twenty," Mu-Mit answers.

Just as soon as the words leave Mu-Mit's mouth, the door of the raggedy house cracks open.

"Uh, oh," Latif sighs. A young boy walks out of the house. He rubs his eyes to remove the sleep from them. "That's him?" Latif asks.

"Yep," Jessie replies. He hates to even be a part of this act. Of all the dudes from the block, Jessie is closer to this one than any other. Jessie has nicknamed him, 'Baghdad's Finest'. He's the fairest one of them all. It's too bad that he's getting caught up in it all, but Jesse realizes that this is how the game is played.

"Yeah, baby!" Latif shouts, clapping his hands with excitement. The man trots down the steps without a clue. "Mu, as soon as he steps onto the street, just go! Now!" Latif shouts.

The man is crossing the street. As he's approaching the yellow line in the street, Mu-Mit mashes the gas pedal full force. The boy double takes at the car which is speeding toward him. He jogs quickly toward his car attempting to get out of the way of the reckless driver. What he doesn't realize is the reckless driver is coming for him. He reaches for the handle of his car door. Mu-Mit slams on the brakes just short of him, as he's about to step foot into his vehicle. The slamming of the brakes startles him. He turns around abruptly. "Boom! Latif fires from close range, hitting him in the abdomen. Boom! He fires again, ripping through his chest. He gasps for air as the slug cuts off his oxygen. He tumbles face first onto the asphalt. Latif goes to work. He raises up from his seat, hanging out of the passenger's window. He begins dumping. Boom! Boom! Boom! The boy's body bounces high off of the ground after every shot. "You little bastard," Latif shouts. Boom!

"Come on, that's it," Mu-Mit says bringing Latif back to reality. "Let's go!" Sccuurrr! He peels off quickly, leaving a trail of burned rubber and a bloody corpse.

"One down and a million of them little bastards to go," Latif says.

///// CHAPTER 58 /////

Parlay sits behind the steering wheel of his customized van. "Here," he says as he hands the man in the passenger seat a bag filled with dope. "That's 250 bricks," Parlay says.

"Alright, good looking," the man replies.

Parlay fronts the man 250 bricks at a time. The average guy wouldn't front this man anything because they fear they may not get their money back. On the streets of Newark, this man is somewhat of a beast. He has a crew that moves at his command, with no questions asked. He's ruled his housing complex with an iron fist for over ten years now. In the past ten years, his crew has been responsible for a great percentage of the city's murder rate, which is why he has nicknamed his crew the 'Trauma Unit'.

Although many may label this crew as bad guys, that's very untrue. His crew may consist of a group of bad guys, but he's the total opposite. He doesn't use his strength for senseless robbery or extortion, unlike other rulers who lead a crew of this magnitude. Of all the men that make up his team, he's the most sensible one. His crew is a bunch of wild young boys that have been under his command since they were 12 and 13 years old. They love him wholeheartedly and are completely loyal to him. In their eyes he can do no wrong. He's raised them from teens, taking better care of them than their own parents have. His top priority is getting money and the only way he will ever step out of character is if someone gets in the way of that.

This man and Parlay have a good business relationship. Parlay bears witness that this man doesn't pay back because he has to. He pays back because he wants to. If he were to ever decide that he didn't want to pay back, there is nothing Parlay would be able to do. There's not one man that Parlay knows who will go up against the 'Trauma Unit'.

The man looks at Parlay and notices stress all over his face. "What's the deal?" he asks. "You ain't looking like yourself. Something wrong? You got stress written all over your face."

"Yeah?" he asks looking rather shocked. He looks in the mirror and sees exactly what the man is talking about. He leans back in his seat. "Yeah, I'm going through a little something, something," he admits. "But it's about to be over with real soon. I ran into a little situation, but I got it situated already."

"You sure? If anything I can do to help you, you know I'm here," he claims. "What is it though, anyway?"

Parlay hesitates to reply. "Trauma, it's cool," Parlay smiles a phony grin.

"Talk to me," Trauma demands.

"Nah, it was just a little situation with some old mufuckers who just came home."

Trauma's eyes brighten up. "What they on that bullshit?"

"Something like that. Niggas stepped to me on some extortion type shit. Basically, trying to force me to buy dope from them."

"Oh, on that old head back in the day bullshit. Mufuckers don't know, it's a new day," he laughs. "Who are they?"

"Some mufucker named Mu-Mit and he got a hype man named Latif. You know them?"

"Never heard of them."

"I already got the whole scoop on them. They ain't nothing but puppets for the Mayor."

"The Mayor? Aw man," he sighs. "He off his bullshit again?" he asks as he shakes his head from side to side. "So, he trying to run shit from the prison, huh? That nigga crazy," Trauma laughs.

"Really, his older brother handling shit out here for him."

"Damn, how you know all that?"

"Ay, you know the streets talk. I know everything. They even said that the Mayor nigga's lawyer is really the plug. Everything supposed to be coming from him."

"Word?"

"Hey," he says shrugging his shoulders. "That's what they say."

"How the dope? Is it any good? What's the name of it?"

"The After Party. I heard it's fire. It's making a little noise in a few spots."

"The After Party?" Trauma asks with agitation in his voice. A nigga from my hood told me he just ran into a new plug and that's where he got right now. He said he met some Poppy over there in the Bronx. Lying ass nigga! Yo, that shit fire, too," he says nodding his head up and down. "So, he must be with them mufuckers, huh?"

"Must be. The word on the streets is they plan on taking over the whole Newark."

"Please," Trauma laughs. "Imagine that? Man, I wish them mufuckers come my way with that goofy ass shit!"

"Nah, you ain't even gotta think about that shit. I got my man on that right now. Them mufuckers outta here. I put a quarter up for the both of them. Them niggas history!"

"A quarter? Nigga I'm right here. I'll do it for free! You know I can make it happen. Just say the word and I'll press the button!"

"The word," Parlay says with a devilish grin on his face.

///// CHAPTER 59 /////

In Miami

"Listen, Miranda, in order for me to get through this case, you have to keep it totally real with me. That way, I'll know just what we're up against. You can't have me in the dark. Take the blindfold off of my eyes, please? What is it? How did this thing go down? I need all the details."

Miranda takes a deep breath while pouting like a baby.

"Miranda, do you want to spend the rest of your life behind bars?"

She shakes her head from side to side. "No," she whispers. Although she wants to be freed, she's still afraid to open up to him. She's never told anyone the details of the situation because she's afraid to do so. She's not sure if she can trust Tony with that information.

"I didn't think so. What's the deal? Talk to me?" Tony can sense the fact that she's scared to open up to him. "Miranda, I'm your attorney. You have to trust me. I'm on your side."

She peeks around nervously. She then pauses for a few seconds before speaking. "It all started when we came down here to visit my mother's gravesite for her birthday."

Five minutes later and she's done telling the details of her entire stay in Miami. She told everything from start to finish, including the details of the horrifying murder. Reenacting the situation has brought tears to her eyes.

Tony looks at her with an absolute blank look on his face. "Can I ask you one question?"

"Yes," she mumbles.

"Why didn't you tell? Anyone else, whether it was male or female would have told just to free themselves. After all, you didn't pull the trigger."

"But I created the atmosphere. Anyway, I just couldn't make myself tell. I felt like I was just as guilty."

"Indeed you were, but again, you didn't pull the trigger. Which means, you are not the murderer. Which means you shouldn't be charged with murder." Tony can't believe that he actually just said that. He's totally against snitching. In fact, he won't even represent a snitch. On two different occasions, he was hired by clients who he later found out had snitched. He immediately removed himself from the case. In this situation, he can't help but wonder why she didn't. The fact that she didn't just makes him respect her even more. "So, are you still in contact with your ex?"

How could I be, she says to herself. She shakes her head from side to side. She's told Tony everything except for that one little detail. For the life of her, she will never tell anyone that. "No," she whispers.

"So, let me get this right. You take the wrap for the scum-bag and he leaves you out to dry, right? Typical," Tony laughs. Miranda sobs harder at the very thought of that. "Don't cry," he says attempting to comfort her. "We're going to get you out of this situation. I promise."

///// CHAPTER 60 /////

ILL Wheel and Dusty sit in the living room of their new apartment. After the burglary, Dre instructed ILL Wheel to relocate for security purposes. He told them this time it was only a break-in. Next time it could be a home invasion with a double homicide.

Today is Dusty's third day out of the hospital and instead of getting better, he's actually gotten worse off. He barely talks but when he does it's about nothing. He just rambles on and on.

ILL Wheel is forced to keep Dusty with him throughout the day because he's afraid that he may get into major trouble if he's left alone. The whole ordeal has been stressful for ILL Wheel but what can he do? Dusty is a friend in need. He'll never turn his back on him even though Dusty brought all this upon himself. This all could have been avoided if Dusty would have just listened to ILL Wheel about smoking the 'Wet.'

The bell rings and ILL Wheel dashes to the door and opens it.

"Ay Wheel," Lil Mama greets as she steps inside.

"What up?" he replies.

She makes her way over to the couch and takes a seat right next to Dusty. As she's sitting, she passes the shopping bag over to ILL Wheel. "Hey, D," she greets.

Dusty doesn't respond to her. He doesn't look her way not once. He continues to look straight ahead. Not only does he not realize that she's here, he doesn't even know that he's here. He stares at the wall ahead of him with his head tilted slightly. On his face, he wears the same cheesy grin that he wears the majority of the day. It's almost like the grin is glued on his face. Every couple of minutes, he'll mumble a few words to himself only loud enough for him to hear. ILL Wheel doesn't have a clue of what he says, but whatever it is must be hilarious because he falls into laughter afterwards. ILL Wheel hopes and prays that Dusty comes back, but by the looks of it, he seriously doubts it.

ILL Wheel passes Lil Mama a shopping bag filled with money. "That's $65,000," he whispers. "54 for the last shit and 11 toward my tab."

ILL Wheel has been paying Dre back a little at a time just as Dre instructed him to. It's rough on his lifestyle because he has no money for himself. He'd rather struggle a little than to lose his life though. He can't wait to finish off his debt so things can go back to normal.

He has to work so much harder being that Dusty is no longer a part of the action. With Dusty no longer working, ILL Wheel is forced to take care of him. ILL Wheel definitely has a full plate; a huge debt, babysitting and taking care of a grown man, watching out for the law, and any wolves that may be plotting against him. Can he handle it all? Or will he lose his mind just as Dusty has?

///// CHAPTER 61 /////

Dre awakens from a good night's sleep. He rolls over and is greeted by the disturbing sight of Cindy sleeping. He shakes his head with aggravation. Just as his morning is about to be spoiled, he remembers what today is and all of a sudden, his morning brightens up.

Today is a very special day and he's not even going to allow Cindy to mess it up for him. This is the very first birthday that he's been home for in 15 years. This calls for a huge celebration, but Dre being the modest guy that he is, will not make a big deal of his birthday. However, he does plan to observe it in his own way.

Today he will not do any work of any sort. No score of any magnitude will make him budge today. He plans to just lay back and count his blessings. Throughout his many years of incarceration, he's ran into many guys that are never coming home, which makes him realize that him getting a second shot is a blessing.

He will spend his entire day in the Big Apple. He already has it all planned out, with reservations and all. He plans to start his day by eating breakfast alone, at the Trump Plaza Hotel. Next, he plans to hit the New York Men's Racquet Ball Club in Manhattan, where he will get a manicure, a pedicure, a facial and for the remaining time, he will just lounge around in the sauna. That should last until lunch time. He plans to have a light lunch, alone again, at his favorite Japanese Thai Restaurant, 'Tao'. He plans to spend the rest of the afternoon doing something that he's never done, but has always dreamed of doing. He will actually take the time out to go to Carnegie Hall to see Michael Franks perform. His last meal will be eaten at the Russian Tea Room. By that time, he figures he will be full and quite fatigued from his busy day. He plans to finish his night off at a nice little Swedish Massage Parlor that Tony recommended. He's going to hire three beautiful, tall, blonde haired women to take turns massaging his body and hopefully his special day will end with a happy ending.

He rushes into the bathroom. He's very anxious to start his day. As the steaming hot water awakens his body, his telephone rings. He fumbles along the sink trying to locate it. Finally he grabs hold of it. He has his eyes closed to prevent the soapy lather from going into them.

"Hello?" he answers, wondering who it is.

"Dre!" Tony shouts. "Listen, I need you to hurry up and come into the office! Something major just came up and we need to handle this asap!"

Dre hesitates before replying. "Tone, I wasn't coming in, today," he whispers. "Today is my birthday. I have plans."

"Cancel them," he replies with no consideration. "This is serious! I need you at the office in one hour, exactly," he says before hanging the phone up in Dre's ear.

Dre can't help but wonder what the urgency is all about. The only thing that comes to mind is his brother. He wonders what type of dilemma he's gotten himself into now.

One Hour Later

Dre sits in Tony's office alone. All the rushing Tony did and he's not even here yet. The longer he takes to come, the more curious Dre becomes.

Tony busts through the door. "You ready? Let's go!" he says as he rushes out of the door. Dre follows close behind as Tony gallops down the hall.

"What's the problem?" Dre asks.

"A terrible emergency," he whispers as they step into the elevator. Tony's phone rings. "Yes?" he answers.

Dre impatiently waits to hear the details, but Tony continues to babble on the phone. Anxiety rips through his gut.

They exit the building quickly. Dre has to trot just to keep up with Tony. Tony finally stops about 100 feet away from the door. "Hold on, one second?" he begs, covering the phone with his hand. "Ay, do me a favor? Drive, while I tend to this call?" he asks, tossing the keys to Dre.

Dre catches the keys in mid-air. He takes a few steps toward Tony's assigned parking space. Tony's car is not in the spot. Instead, there's a snow white, convertible Bentley, GTC parked there. The black top makes the bone white leather interior look just that much creamier. A temporary tag is plastered to the back window.

Dre looks at Tony. Tony smiles from ear to ear. "Happy birthday, motherfucker!" he smiles.

Dre stands there with a look of confusion on his face.

"Here!" Tony shouts while handing him the phone.

Dre slowly reaches for the phone. "Hello?" he answers.

"Happy Born Day, nigga!" the Mayor yells into the phone. "How you like her?"

Dre's face frowns up with frustration. He looks at the beautiful vehicle and realizes that what sits before his eyes is $200,000.00 worth of heat. He knows that this car will bring him nothing but unwanted attention. "Thanks but no thanks," he whispers into the phone.

"What?" the Mayor asks.

"Thanks but no thanks," he repeats. "That's your life, not mines," he says before handing the phone over to Tony.

Tony senses the fury on Dre's face, which causes his smile to vanish from his own face. "Call me later," he says to the Mayor.

"So, what part did you play in all of this?" Dre asks furiously. "Is this what your little emergency was all about? Do you think I have time to play foolish games with ya'll?"

"Dre, hold up, listen? Your brother wanted badly for you to have this car for your birthday. He asked me to make it happen. I didn't think it would be a problem."

"You didn't think it would be a problem? I just come home from doing 15 years of my life in the FEDS and you don't think me driving around in the same ghetto that I caught my charges in, with a $200,000 car is a problem?

177

Both of ya'll got the game fucked up! What type of idiots are ya'll?" he ask as he tosses the keys back to Tony. He walks toward his Cherokee, leaving Tony standing there with a dumbfounded look on his face.

"Dre, what am I supposed to do with it?"

"You can crash it into a brick wall for all I care!" he shouts, while hopping into his jeep.

He cruises off slowly. They have managed to ruin his special day. He can't believe that they would put his freedom in jeopardy like that. How could they be so ignorant, he asks himself. Suddenly, realization sets in. Dre is sure that his little brother would never put him in harm's way intentionally. Dre realizes the Mayor just doesn't get it. He's used to living a lavish lifestyle and he can no longer live that way. He can no longer drive high line cars so by buying the car for Dre he can somewhat live his life through Dre. Dre understands his reasoning, but he totally opposes it.

Now, Tony on the other hand, Dre can't understand him. As a criminal attorney, he should be telling Dre to stay out of the light instead of coaching him into being flashy and flamboyant. Dre feels Tony should know what type of trouble that can bring. Maybe, that's what he wants, Dre thinks to himself. After all, he is an attorney. He doesn't make money unless guys get caught up. Maybe he's hoping I get pinched again so he can make thousands of dollars taxing me like he taxes my brother? Maybe he wants to get me out of the way, so he can continue robbing my brother blind? I'm not sure, but I think he has an ulterior motive? One thing for sure, I will never let him or anyone else send me back to prison. "That's my word!" he says aloud.

///// CHAPTER 62 /////

Many Hours Later

Cindy listens to Dre's phone ring consecutively until the answering machine comes on for the eightieth time. She hasn't heard from him since he left the house this morning. In fact no one has heard from him. Tony was the last one to see him. After the slight disagreement they had this morning about the Mayor's birthday present to him, he hasn't picked up his phone not once.

Just as Cindy is about to leave yet another message, a voice states that the mailbox is full. "Motherfucker!' she shouts aloud. She dials once again and this time the phone doesn't even ring. "Oh, now he's going to turn his phone off, huh?" she asks herself. She's now furious. She's quite sure that he's spending his birthday with another woman. She just wonders who it is and where they are. Damn, she says to herself. This is unlike him. Maybe he's gotten into trouble? She dials the phone once again, hoping desperately for an answer.

Meanwhile In Washington D.C.

The constant ringing of the phone finally stops. For the past few hours the phone has been ringing back to back non-stop. The chirping of the phone lets him know that his battery is officially dead. He hasn't answered the phone once since this morning. After the incident with Tony, he was so furious that he didn't want to be bothered with anyone. That was until Angelique called him asking what day he wanted to cash in that rain check. That was all the talking she had to do in order to get him to take the long drive to D.C.

They spent the duration of the afternoon and most of the night just touring the city and enjoying each other's company. All the while, she could barely wait to get her hands on him and it showed in her behavior. Not even ten minutes in the house and they're at it already. The heavy make out session has both of them hot and sweaty. Intense foreplay has both of them stark naked, rolling around like two teenage kids. They grind and kiss passionately. The sound of Angelique moaning and Dre's heavy breathing fill the air.

Dre rolls off of the bed and lands onto his feet. His toes sink into the thick, soft plush carpet. He snatches Angelique from the bed as if she's a rag doll. He flips her upside down and holds her in the air by her waist. Her soft skin is dripping wet, making her rather slippery. Their bodies cling together like saran wrap. She wraps her legs tightly around his neck as he begins licking her middle like an ice cream cone. Her body quivers after every stroke of his stiffened tongue. The more he licks the wetter she becomes. The sensation is melting her away.

She wraps her lips tightly around his shaft. The feeling forces him to thrust in and out of her mouth slowly. She sucks as he licks. The heat from her mouth sends hot flashes throughout his body. Their rhythm is somewhat magical as they maneuver their bodies gracefully. She winds her hips slowly, teasing him by giving him a little taste, before moving herself away from him. He tightens the grip on her waist to prevent her from moving. Once he has her trapped, he feasts on her, while slowly sliding himself into her mouth. The feeling makes his legs wobble after each stroke. He picks up his pace. He strokes harder and harder. She grabs hold of his ankles with fear of falling out of his grip. The sound of slurping echoes through the room.

The intensity becomes way too much. Dre's knees buckle and they both collapse onto the floor. Angelique laughs hysterically. "Uuhhmm," she snarls as she formulates her body into a crawling position. "Come get it Daddy?" she begs.

Dre crawls directly behind her. They grind with their bodies glued together. Dre plants soft, wet kisses up and down her spine. She arches her back to meet his lips. The touch of his lips sends a tingling sensation throughout her entire body. She begins ramming her self against him with massive force. The impact is enough to knock him to the ground. He balances himself by backing up, planting one foot on the floor. He rests one hand on his knee as he smacks her rear with his other hand. He smacks her again and again. Her rear claps like thunder. He sits back enjoying the view and the sensation. The more excited he gets the harder he smacks. The harder he smacks, the hornier she becomes. He smacks her cheeks over and over until her yellow ass is cherry red, with the bruises of his hand imprint all over it. "Yes," she sighs as she crashes into his body forcefully. He slows her down by grabbing her waist tighter and digs deeper. She gasps for air as he fills her insides totally.

After a few gentle strokes she lies flat on the floor and Dre collapses on top of her. She lies there with her legs spread apart, as still as she can be. She desperately awaits his entrance. He teases her before entering her. The anticipation is driving her crazy. She winds her hips in a circular motion. He drops all his weight on her, pinning her to the floor. The closeness of their bodies makes it impossible for her to move even the slightest bit. The feeling of dominance is enjoyable to her. It causes her to get hornier and hornier. Her body trembles, signaling to Dre that she's almost there. He pounds harder to help her reach her goal. The pounding becomes way too much. She gets onto her knees and attempts to crawl away from him. He crawls behind her, trying to catch up with her. Finally, he has her trapped. She's trapped herself in the corner. Dre grabs hold of her tiny waist and starts to pound all over again.

"Right there," she mumbles.

He applies pressure onto her back pinning her to the floor. In the same motion, he lifts her ass in the air. He begins to deep stroke her passionately while she moans and groans. He backs up, standing onto his feet. He grabs hold of her ankles, and places her into a head stance. Her back is pinned against the wall, as he grabs hold of her ankles. He holds her ankles, tight at his waist side. He stands there holding her legs in the air as if her body is a wheel barrel. He pulls her legs, while digging deeply into her middle until she screams at the top of her lungs.

"Get it daddy! Get it!" she shouts.

Instead of continuing, Dre lets her legs go and backs away from her. Angelique looks over her shoulder wondering why he's stopped. He snatches her by her arm, pulling her onto her feet. He backs himself against the wall, pulling her toward him.

They kiss passionately as she wraps her arms around his neck. She jumps into his arms, and straddles her legs around his waist. He instantly thrusts himself inside of her. He palm grips her firm rear, digging deep into her skin with his fingertips. Their bodies crash into the wall violently. The loud thumping sounds as if the walls are caving in.

"Fuck me," she whispers in his ear before nibbling away at it. He follows her demand and begins pounding away with rapid speed and powerful force. Her screaming pierces through the air waves, breaking the sound barrier. He pounds and pounds until she trembles like a leaf. He grabs her waist tighter, almost squeezing the little life she has left out of her.

Aghh," he grunts before they slide down the wall slowly. Their bodies are still glued together. Dre falls asleep before they make their landing. Angelique buries her head deep into his chest. She falls asleep right behind him.

It's a beautiful sight to see as they lie on the floor as peaceful and serene as can be. Snoring can be heard from many miles away. Sweet dreams.

///// CHAPTER 63 /////

2 a.m.

Latif tip-toes through the pitch black alley. He grips a semi-automatic handgun in the palms of each of his hands. As much as he hates automatic handguns he's forced to use them tonight. He knows exactly what he's up against. There is no way he can fight this war with only six shots. He picks up his pace with hope of reaching the end of the alley. He peeks around attentively before hopping the small fence which separates the two backyards. His heartbeat doubles the normal pace as he sets his eyes on the little bit of streetlight that's coming from the block ahead of him. Midway through the alley he begins to tip-toe even more quietly. As he gets closer to his destination, he can now hear loud talking and laughing. The closer he gets the louder and more clearly the voices sound. From the sounds of it there are male and females out there. His heart beats faster and harder. He scales the wall of the abandoned house so his shadow isn't visible.

He stands a few feet away from the entrance of the alley. He pulls his ski-mask snug over his face. The loud sound of talking lets him know that he's caught them with their pants down. Now, he says to himself before dashing out of the alley. As soon as he steps foot onto the cement he begins firing at the crowded porch. Boc! Boc! Boc! Boc!

Screaming echoes throughout the block as everyone attempts to get away from him. The sound of glass breaking sounds off as their liquor bottles fall to the ground. Two young girls flee from the porch. Latif's reflex makes him aim at the girls with the intent of firing, but he spares them and lets them escape. He aims at the porch. Boc! Boc! Boc! He fires consecutively. Bodies fall and this excites him more. He fires away with both guns simultaneously. Boc! Boc! Pop! Pop! Boc! Pop! Pop! Boc!

Mu-Mit speeds up the block. He slams on the brakes as he reaches Latif. One man attempts to jump off of the porch, but Latif aims right for his back. Boc! Boc! He fires.

"Aghh!" the boy screams as he falls onto the ground.

Latif backpedals toward the truck, still firing. Boc! Boc! He hops into the truck and fires two more shots at the porch, even though there is not a single person moving. Either he's killed everyone or they have enough sense to play dead.

Mu-Mit speeds off with the door still wide open. Latif rips three more shots just for the sake of it. Pop! Pop! Pop! The sound of gunfire excites him. "Pussies!" Latif shouts as he pulls the door shut.

Police sirens echo throughout the neighborhood causing Mu-Mit to increase his speed.

"Shut em' down!" Latif shouts furiously. "Now what? Huh?" he asks, looking in Mu-Mit's direction. "Baghdad what?"

///// CHAPTER 64 /////

The Next Morning/ 7:15 a.m.

Dre tip-toes to the door as Angelique lays on the bed ass naked. Three back to back episodes of Dre's energy draining love making put Angelique out for the count. She lays nestled in a fetal position, sleeping like a baby.

He opens the door quietly to avoid waking her up. He manages to close the door behind him without her missing one z.

Meanwhile in East Orange

Cindy paces back and forth through the apartment. She hasn't gotten one wink of sleep all night. At this point she's more furious than she is tired. All types of evil thoughts run through her mind. The lonely night has given her more than enough time to come up with hundreds of ways to repay him. She's sure that he's spent the night in the comfort of another woman. The thought of that drives her insane. All she could visualize in her mind is Dre and some woman making passionate love. Little does she know they shared more dirty sex than actual love-making.

She dials his phone once again with hopes of him answering it. Her hopes are shot down once his answering machine comes on. She becomes even more furious at the sound of his voice.

The ringing of her doorbell interrupts her thoughts. She stomps over to the door and snatches it open without peeking through the peephole. "What?" she barks hastily.

The sight of two white men at the doorstep catches her off guard. She quickly switches up the tone of her voice. "Yes? May I help you?"

"Yes, you can," one man says in a polite manner. "We're looking for Andre Blackhead? This is his place of residence, right?"

Cindy pauses before replying. Who the hell is this, she asks herself. What do they want?

"Does he or does he not live here?"

"Uh, yes," she stutters.

"I'm his parole officer. Is he home?"

Parole, she thinks to herself. Oh you wanna play a bitch out, she laughs to herself. Now look. You played yourself out. Payback is a bitch, she smiles on the inside. "No, he isn't home."

"May we come in?" he asks, already taking the initiative to creep pass her.

"Sure, come right on in," she smiles devilishly. "Come right on in."

Six Hours Later

Dre steps into his office and takes a seat at his desk. He's quite exhausted from the long drive. He lays his head back with his eyes closed, trying to meditate. As soon as his eyes close thoughts of last night with Angelique occupy his mind. He replays scene after scene over and over.

A tapping on the door sounds off. "Dre!" Tony shouts.

"Psst," Dre sighs. "Come in!"

Tony walks in slowly. Just the sight of Tony pisses Dre off. "Where have you been?" Tony asks hastily.

Dre is shocked at his question. Tony has never questioned him. "Huh?"

"Where you been? Everyone was worried about you."

"Everyone like who?"

"Everyone like me, and Cindy. I called you, but the phone kept going to your voice mail."

"My battery died," he mumbles. "Why ya'll looking for me like that? Anyway I told you I wasn't coming in."

"I know but after Cindy kept calling me, I got alarmed. I thought something may have happened to you. She seemed to be worried to death about you."

"That bitch ain't worried about nothing. I ain't thinking about her ass. She wasn't worried about me when I did those 15 years," he says sarcastically. "And she shouldn't be worried about me now."

"Well you need to start thinking about her, especially while she holds your future in her hands," he whispers. "Parole went to the house today."

"Parole? Oh shit, he thinks to himself.

"Yeah. I don't know what the hell she told them, but when they got here they had a bunch of questions. You're playing a dangerous game. I don't know what the situation is with you and her, but you need to straighten it out."

"There's nothing to straighten out. We haven't been together since I went down. She left me the beginning of the bid. I only got paroled to her house because I had nowhere else to go. I have no feelings for her whatsoever. No sexual attraction, nothing."

"Does she know that?"

"Yeah, I tell her all the time, over and over, but it seems as if she isn't listening!"

"I don't know? It's your situation. You have to correct it or it's going to haunt you. She assumes that you were with a woman. You know what they say about a woman that is scorned? With that in mind, you don't know what type of bullshit she fed them."

"What did you tell them?"

"I told them that I sent you to Hudson County to walk a client into a precinct to turn himself in. They had no choice but to bite on it, but I'm sure the thoughts were still lingering in their heads. You're going to need to be on point because I'm sure they're going to be on your ass from here on out."

Dre shakes his head from side to side. He's sure Tony is absolutely correct. Knowing what type of person Cindy is, he can't imagine what type of nonsense she could have told them. Damn, he thinks to himself. Things are going smoothly for him. The last thing he needs right now is a parole violation. "Damn, now would be the perfect time for me to bring the Bentley out, huh?" he asks sarcastically.

"Dre, I apologize. I wasn't thinking logically. That was a bad decision on my behalf. It's just that your brother wanted so badly for you to have it."

"What's the matter with him?"

"Dre you gotta realize one thing. He has an addiction and unfortunately prison can't help him. He's addicted to the flamboyant lifestyle. He said it best when he told me he lives better in prison than most guys live on the outside. He has the movement to do pretty much whatever he wants to do. He's not content with just making the money. His real enjoyment comes when he spends it. Right now, he can't drive expensive cars and wear precious jewelry and that probably makes him sick to his stomach. He probably feels dead and worthless, so what does he do? He tries to live his life through his loved ones. You should see the gifts he buys for those girls. They get new cars every six months," he sighs. They get monthly allowances of $20,000.00 apiece. That's $240,000.00 a year for nothing. All they have to do is be there to answer every one of his phone calls and never miss a visit and in return they live the lives of attorneys and physicians. "That is low end attorneys, of course," he says arrogantly with a slight smirk on his face. It's pathetic but what can I say? At the end of the day, it's his money. He has it bad. Look," he says as he extends his arm to show Dre his watch.

"What about it?" Dre asks as he stares at the rather boring looking watch.

"This was my birthday present from him last year. From the looks of it, nothing spectacular, right? No diamonds, plain old reptile band. If you had to guess, how much it cost, what would you say?"

"I don't know," Dre says shrugging his shoulders. "Maybe a couple of hundred?"

Tony snickers. "Wrong my friend…try $124,000.00. It's a Daniel Roth Limited Edition. The jeweler came here to the office and hand delivered it personally. I tried to talk your brother into taking it back, but he refused and told me that I'm insulting him by denying his birthday present to me. It's an addiction. He can't help it."

"Well, I'm sorry but I can't let his addiction drag me into a situation, bottom line."

"I feel you 100 percent."

The intercom sounds off. "Dre," Mocha shouts. "You have a call on line one," she whispers. Dre presses the button. "Hello?"

"You spent the night with your little bitch, huh?"

"Cindy, what did you tell the people?" Dre asks in the most pleasant voice that he can. He tries hard to cover up his anger.

"I hope that bitch was worth it!" she says before banging the phone in his ear.

Dre looks at Tony with a sympathetic look on his face. "This bitch gone get me sent back to prison. You gotta help me."

///// CHAPTER 65 /////

ILL Wheel cruises the block attentively in search of his Homie, 'Shotgun'. As he's cruising the block he sees a set of high beams flashing in front of him. He slows down as he approaches the jeep.

The dark tinted windows of the white Grand Prix rolls down slowly. ILL Wheel pulls over close to the curb once he recognizes the driver. The passenger hops out of the car and quickly crosses the street coming toward ILL Wheel's car.

He hops in and they quickly do their signature handshake. "Shotgun, what it do? What the bitness is?" asks ILL Wheel. "What up?"

"Big backing," Shotgun replies.

"What's good with you?" ILL Wheel asks as he pulls a bag from underneath the seat. He hands over the bag which consists of thirty bricks of 'After Party.' As he's waiting for the money, he peeks through his driver's side mirror to make sure no police are in the area. "Ay, what up with your little brother?" he asks as he turns his face toward the passenger. He gets the shock of a lifetime when his eyes look into the barrel of the chrome .40 caliber handgun. "Ho!" ILL Wheel says with a baffled but stern expression on his face. "Don't play like that," he smiles a cheesy grin.

"Playing? I ain't playing. You already know what it is!" he says aggressively as he rests the gun against ILL Wheel's right temple.

ILL Wheel looks in the boy's eyes to try and determine if he's serious or if this is a joke that he's playing on him. The blank expression on his face makes it hard to tell. Suddenly he bites down on his bottom lip, making ILL Wheel sense that he may be serious. Nah, he can't be, ILL Wheel says to himself. They've known each other for years. No way in the world would he do something like this? His eyes become stone cold. "What's banging Blood?"

"My 40 if you don't do what the fuck I say!" He pats ILL Wheel's waist and quickly locates ILL Wheel's gun.

ILL watches as he snatches the gun from his waist. This reassures him that this is not a game that he's playing. He truly can't believe that this is happening. He actually got caught slipping. He never saw the need in drawing his gun when dealing with his Homies. Why would he?

Another man jumps out of the backseat of the Grand Prix and runs over to ILL Wheel's jeep. He hops into the backseat directly behind ILL Wheel. Before he's even seated, the passenger hands ILL Wheel's gun over to him.

ILL Wheel wonders why the man has gotten into the jeep. They already have the dope. He's expecting them to leave but instead, "Let's go!" the passenger demands while poking ILL Wheel in the neck with the gun.

"Where?" ILL Wheel asks.

"Take us to the fucking work!" he shouts angrily.

"Come on Blood?" ILL Wheel pleads. "You know this ain't right. You already got the dope, let's just dead the whole situation?"

"Dead the situation, my ass! Nigga you ain't right! The word came from my Homie that the Hood you banging ain't official. Your big homie, Young Cash, he ain't real right, cause his big Homie wasn't real right!"

ILL Wheel listens attentively as he tells him that Ice was never an official Blood which means that he never had the authority to bring Ahmir in and give him the status that he did. All this boils down to the fact that all these years they've been repping something that they're not. They're not even considered to be Bloods. ILL Wheel can't believe his ears.

"Ay man, I didn't know. I thought he was official. Come on man? How can I fix this on my end?"

"By taking us to the work. Let's go!"

ILL Wheel still sits there in a baffled state, until he feels a powerful force bang into the back of his head. The man in the backseat has struck ILL Wheel with the butt of the gun. "Drive motherfucker, drive!" he shouts before striking ILL Wheel twice more.

This catches him by surprise. He attempts to shake the dizziness away. Just as his vision begins to clear up, he gets struck again. "Alright, alright," he slurs.

"Alright my ass!" Shotgun shouts. "Let's go!"

ILL Wheel pulls off slowly and off they go.

Meanwhile a Few Miles Away

Mu-Mit and Latif have changed cars again. After their episode they knew that it was time to switch up. They got the word from the street that the incident only claimed one life, but it left another boy in critical condition. Two others were seriously wounded as well. They still didn't get the guy they really wanted, but they still consider it a job well done.

At this moment they're on their way through Baghdad again. They refuse to let them breathe. They realize when dealing with these young boys the only way they will win are if they're persistent.

"Yo, don't go up 11th Avenue," Latif suggests. "Let's come down from 12th Avenue," he says. He figures by switching it up, they may have a better chance of catching them off guard.

Mu-Mit cruises down 9th street in the black Dodge Charger rental. Although it's broad daylight they're not concerned the least bit. They have their ski masks ready and the false temporary tag is waving in the window, which means it's impossible for anything to lead back to Mu-Mit's wife, who has rented this car for him. Dre has someone who rents cars for them when it's time to do dirty work, but Mu-Mit didn't want to tell Dre because he was afraid Dre would try and stop the beef altogether. They are sure that everyone who is aware of this beef will know that it's them, but no one will be able to prove it.

Mu-Mit is so anxious to get this over with. He feels like it's going on way too long. Deep down inside he feels that Latif doesn't handle situations properly at times. He's sure if he had made the move the other night, there would have been more lives claimed. As much as he hates it, he's forced to sit on the sideline and watch due to the fact that they don't have a driver. Several times Mu-Mit has been tempted to put Latif behind the wheel, but he doesn't trust him. Although he claims he can drive, Mu-Mit has never seen him behind the wheel of a car in all the years that he's known him.

"I ain't sparing nobody!" Latif shouts. If they in the way they getting it. Fuck that! Everybody out here know what's going on, so if they still coming out here, then fuck 'em!" he shouts while looking at Mu-Mit for his approval.

"I'm with you Bruh," he whispers.

As they cruise along 12th Avenue they peek around at the many people that are in the area. "Slow down a little," Latif says. "Let me see if he up here. You never know? Nah, I don't see him."

Mu-Mit makes the left turn down 8th Street. Both of their mouths drop to the floor when they see what's before them. In the middle of the block there sits a huge mobile police unit parked on the sidewalk.

"Oh shit," Latif says. "We done shut these mufuckers down," he says flattering himself, but deep down inside he knows that isn't really the case. Anytime a series of shootings take place the unit sets up. This particular situation has set off three shootings and Latif has no clue how many took place out here before this event. Little does he know, this unit should have set up a long, long time ago. "We ain't eating, ain't nobody eating!" he says. He appreciates the fact that they can't get money, but there's a bigger problem now. Now that the block will be safeguarded by police all day and night, no one will be out here. With no knowledge of any of their whereabouts, it will be extremely difficult to find them.

Mu-Mit drives down the empty block as casual as he can. He's never seen the block this lonely before. There's not a soul standing around anywhere.

"Now look! Nobody ain't getting no money!" Latif shouts. "Young dumb mufuckers!"

Mu-Mit shakes his head from side to side. "Ain't no telling how long this shit gone be out here. They normally set up for months."

"How the fuck we gone catch these little bastards then?" Latif asks.

"Don't worry. We'll catch up with them. Just gotta have patience and I'm sure they'll walk right into our hands. Trust me."

In Bloomfield

ILL Wheel sits in the corner of his bedroom, hog tied with duct tape covering his mouth. He's in shock. He still can't believe this is actually happening. Bigger than that, a part of him feels like a sucker for the fact that he actually brought them to his house. The gangster side of him feels like a sucker, while the rational side of him tells him that he was in a no win situation. He could have refused to bring them here and they would have killed him already or he could lead them to what they want and there's a chance that they may let him live. Or will they?

One boy sits on the edge of ILL Wheel's bed while the other two ransack the apartment. The boy aims his gun at ILL Wheel while staring down the barrel with one eye closed. ILL Wheel looks at him with hate in his eyes. He realizes that he's trying to intimidate him right now. ILL Wheel is very familiar with this crew and one thing for sure they are all wild and reckless. None of them have any respect for life. He hopes and prays that they spare his life. If they do, they'll never live to brag about this situation, for sure. He's sure the chances of them sparing him are slim because just like he knows them, they know him and what he's about. Just like he knows how reckless they are, they should know how wild his crew can get. He's sure with them knowing that, they're going to kill him in here in fear of his retaliation.

Both of the other men appear at the doorway. "We out!" one man shouts while holding a bag in his hand.

Damn, ILL Wheel sighs to himself as he looks at the bag which contains 165 bricks of dope. In the other hand the man holds another bag that's filled with money. ILL wants to die right now at the thought of taking another loss, but if he dies he will never get the chance to repay them for disrespecting him like this. Shit, he says to himself as he thinks of the money that he will owe Dre after this. That is if they allow him to live. He's sure Dre will never believe this. Just when he halfway paid his debt and now this?

The man who is sitting on the bed stands up slowly. ILL Wheel's heart pumps with fear. The moment of truth has arrived. This is the time that he's been dreading throughout this entire ordeal.

They huddle up talking to each other and as hard as ILL Wheel strains to hear them, he can't. He's sure they're talking about killing him.
"Fuck that!" one boy says loud enough for ILL Wheel to hear him.

ILL Wheel tries to read his lips as he mumbles the rest. What is he saying, he asks himself.

"Nah, nah," the boy says aggressively.

The man that is talking is the one that ILL Wheel doesn't know at all. He's never even seen him around. Of the three, he only knows one of them. The other one, he's seen around, but he doesn't know him personally. Shotgun and the other man appear to be debating back and forth. ILL Wheel figures that they're debating if they should kill him or not. ILL Wheel watches closely as Shotgun whispers while moving his hands aggressively.

They all make their way toward ILL Wheel. He swallows the lump that forms in his throat. He's never been this afraid in his life. It seems as if it's taking them forever to get over to him. "Please God," he prays silently. "Please don't let them kill me," he begs.

Finally they're here. The man bends over close to ILL Wheel. ILL Wheel looks in his eyes. He wonders what's next.

The man draws back and begins pistol whipping ILL Wheel abusively. The blood gushes from his head in more places than can be counted. The pain is excruciating, but the fear that he may lose his life makes him overlook it. His hands and feet are tied together which makes it impossible for him to protect himself. He tries to tuck his head close to his chest and use his shoulders to block the blows, but even that doesn't work. The man draws back high and slams the gun into ILL Wheel's skull. You can hear the cracking from the other room. From the looks of it, he's trying to pistol whip him to death.

Minutes later, ILL Wheel lies on his back half conscious. He can barely see through his swollen eyes. He peeks one eye open and thick blood globs drips into his eye.

He feels someone standing over him. "Nigga, we spared you," the voice says. As delirious as ILL Wheel may be, he still recognizes Shotgun's voice. "We were ordered to murder you. You lucky. Don't let me catch you nowhere around here again cause next time, I'm gone do what was supposed to be done. Niggas want you dead. I'm the reason, they gone let you live today. The next time I won't be able to save you. Take it from me…get low. And your man, Ahmir, Young Cash, let him know that it's over for him too. He got a shoot on sight out on him. Every Blood everywhere want ya'll right now. I heard that he down south right now, but even that can't save him. Anywhere the homies at, he ain't gone be safe there. Both of ya'll food!" he barks as he stands up. He then gives his cohorts a head nod and they start to make their way to the door. Before Shotgun walks away he lifts his leg high in the air and kicks ILL Wheel in the head with all his might. The sound resembles the sound of a watermelon splattering onto cement. It actually sounds worse than it feels because ILL Wheel is so out of it that he's numb to anything that can be done to him.

The three boys run out and slam the door behind them, leaving ILL Wheel lying there barely conscious.

///// CHAPTER 66 /////

In Jersey City

It's bright and early Saturday Morning. The three small children have been up watching cartoons on their raggedy little television set for a couple of hours now. They're now ready for their breakfast. The seven year old little girl leads her 4 year old sister and two year old brother toward their mother's room. They have to step high over all the clothes that cover the floors.

Getting through all of this debris is as adventurous as mountain climbing. The odor of the house is stomach turning. The house smells so bad that it blocks out the odor of the toddler's dirty diaper. He's been wearing this soiled pamper since 10 o'clock last night and still it can't compare to the rotten smell that fills this house.

They climb over the junk and debris desperately, resembling a scene from the 'Little Rascals'. Finally, they get to their mother's door. The three of them stand side by side.

"Knock on the door," the seven year old tells the four year old, as she backs away from the door. She hides in the hallway. Her mother hates when they awaken her. On several occasions she has snatched the door open and smacked whichever child she could get her hands on first. The older girl has enough sense not to be anywhere near that door when it opens. "Go ahead," she says as she pushes her sister towards the door.

She taps it a few times lightly. She too is afraid of the outcome. "Mommy?" she whispers. She taps a little harder. "Ma," she says just a little bit louder.

The three of them stand there expecting the door to open any minute. They're all in running position, so when she comes out they can take off. Whoever gets caught will probably get the beating of a lifetime.

After standing at the door, knocking and yelling for minutes, the older girl decides to go in. She grabs the doorknob and pushes the door open slowly. She peeks through one eye, not knowing what to expect. The last time she pushed the door open, she witnessed a strange man on top of her mother naked, while her mother screamed at the top of her lungs. It broke the little girl's heart. She hates her mother for that, but little does she know, that is how they were able to eat dinner that particular night.

She peeks over at the bed and is shocked to see that her mom isn't there. She pushes the door open and the baby dashes right inside. The two girls follow the baby's lead.

"Owww!" the four year old screams at the horrific sight.

"Mommy!" the seven year old screams at the top of her lungs.

Their screams make the baby cry as well. The three of them stand there crying and screaming hysterically as they look at their mother who is lying on the floor in a pool of blood. In her arm, there's a syringe jammed deep into her vein. The dried up blood stains her entire arm. Right next to her, there's a small empty packet of dope. The stamp reads: 'After Party.'

Meanwhile in East Orange

Dre quickly gathers all of his clothes, dumping them into a huge garbage bag. He rushes even though he's sure that he has plenty of time. He just gave Cindy $2,000.00 to go over to Eighth Street in Manhattan. She begged him for the money to go shoe shopping. He had to play it cool just so he could make his move.

She swore to him that she didn't tell parole anything, but he still doesn't trust her. It was difficult for him to play it off like everything was ok, but now it's over. He's gone.

Tony has found Dre an apartment. Now he can live in peace, without worrying what types of revengeful tactics she will try next.

Dre throws one bag over his shoulder and holds the other one in his hand. He trots to the door and opens it. He stands there with his foot holding the door open. He quickly tosses the house keys onto the kitchen table, before stepping out of the door. The door slams shut behind him. "Bye bitch," he mumbles as he walks down the stairs. It's over. Or is it?

///// CHAPTER 67 /////

In Essex County Jail

A middle aged inmate sits at the table playing cards. He's surrounded by three young Bloods. The middle-aged man has just been shipped to this building and he's already established himself. He moves around comfortably as if he's been here for years. All the young guys seem to have a liking for him. They not only accept him, they also seem to respect him. They've done research on him and found out that he's here awaiting trial for a triple homicide. Just hearing of his credentials makes them respect his gangster. He's already gotten a few offers from them about joining forces with them. They've asked him over and over. They say he's the perfect candidate.

As perfect the candidate as he may be, he can never join sides with them. Not only would joining a gang go against everything he believes in, it would also defeat the purpose of him being here.

"Game!" he shouts. "It's over for ya'll" he laughs. I mean that literally, he mumbles to himself. He slams the cards down on the table as he stands up smiling from ear to ear.

He walks to his cell, where he lays back on his bunk. He peeks around nervously before pulling his cell phone out. He begins to dial.

In Yazoo, Mississippi

The Mayor lays back in his cell. He and his new bunkie have been reminiscing about Newark for hours. His old bunkie did just what the Mayor instructed. He got himself moved in fear of losing his life.

"Aw man," Bas laughs. "That was back in me and Jamad's Land Cruiser days," he says as he thinks of the good times he's had. The Mayor feels his phone vibrate. "Hold up," he says as he picks his phone up. He looks at the phone and realizes who it is instantly. "Yo, what up?" he whispers.

In Essex County

"Big Bruh, it's all good. Everything is going as planned.

In Yazoo

"That's what it is," the Mayor says. "Peace," he whispers before hanging the phone up in his ear.

The man's sole purpose in being shipped to that particular building was for murder. The middle aged man is on the Mayor's payroll. The Mayor instructed Emily, the Warden to ship the man there. The Mayor has sent order for him to murder the young kid who he had the altercation with while he was there. He promised the kid that he would repay him and now the time has come. The Mayor knows just how the man works. Once he makes the kid comfortable enough around him, he will make his move. He'll rock him to sleep. I told him that he was fucking with a nigga over his head, he thinks to himself. He should have listened.

///// CHAPTER 68 /////

ILL Wheel stands in the center of his bedroom. After being stuck here for hours with no possible way of getting loose, Dusty finally came home.

ILL Wheel is furious. He feels so disrespected right now. He can't believe that they had the nerve to violate him the way they did. His face is badly bruised and swollen, but the good thing is that he's alive. He realizes that is truly a blessing. "They got that off, but now it's my turn! They should have killed me while they had the chance!" he says with rage as he dials numbers on his phone.

In Baltimore, Maryland

The raunchiest porno DVD ever made plays loudly on the 50 inch plasma screen which sets on the wall. The young man sits laid back in his seat with his feet elevated on the desk before him. He presses rewind on the remote and watches closely as his favorite scene replays. "Damn," he mumbles in a perverted voice. His cell phone rings. He presses pause, not wanting to miss a single second of the action.

He looks down at the number which is foreign to him. "Hello?" he answers. He recognizes the voice instantly. "ILL motherfucking Wheel, what up?" Ahmir asks with a wide smile on his face. He's so happy to hear from one of his best friends. He hasn't heard from either of them in months.

He listens attentively as ILL Wheel tells every little detail of the problem he encountered. "Word? He said what?" he asks with a high pitched tone. "Say no more!" he shouts before he hangs the phone up.

He paces back and forth around his office. He laughs demonically. "I'm food," he mumbles. "Picture that! It's over for me? Nah, it ain't over until I say it's over."

///// CHAPTER 69 /////

Mu-Mit pulls out of the parking space as smoothly as he can. Latif watches up ahead of them as Jay limps slowly toward his Mercedes. By the way that he drags himself along, Latif can tell that he's exhausted.

Both Latif and Mu-Mit are exhausted as well. They have been sitting out here for hours waiting for him. They were told before that he normally leaves the projects before 11 P.M. every night. Tonight marks the second night that they know of, that the case was different. Last night they spent the night in their car waiting for him and he never left. They figured he must have a little girl who lives somewhere in the projects and he must have spent the night with her. The night before last, when he came to his car where they were waiting, it wasn't even 10:30. Everything was perfect except for the fact that he wasn't alone. Apparently, he and his crew were on their way out somewhere. They pulled off five cars deep. Latif wanted to go for it, but Mu-Mit recognized the problem that it could cause. In his mind he knew there was no way they would be able to get out of the hole if they would have blasted one shot. Being that they were on their way stepping out, Mu-Mit was sure they were strapped. They don't want a wide open shoot-out. They only want to hit their target and keep it moving.

Tonight is perfect. He's all alone, just like they need him to be.

"Now!" Latif says sternly as Jay steps onto the asphalt. Mu-Mit steps on the accelerator, trying hard not to burn out, so that Jay will not hear them coming. "Go, go!" Latif shouts, hoping to catch up with him before he gets into the car.

They're easing up on him. Mu-Mit slams on the brakes just as Jay is grabbing hold of his door handle. He turns around immediately. The first thing he sees is a huge .357 magnum aimed at him. He ducks, while fumbling for his own gun. He's way too late. Boom! Latif fires. The slug crashes into his abdomen like a hot ball of fire.

As he grabs hold of his gun, he sees Latif's face. He's sure he knows the face, but he can't figure out from where. He slowly pulls his gun from his waistband, but Latif is a few seconds ahead of him. Boom! Boom! Latif fires again, aiming straight for the man's head. The impact smashes into his face, but he doesn't feel the slightest bit of pain. He's already out for the count. The first bullet pierces his brain and kills him instantly. He falls face first lifelessly. His body splatters onto the asphalt.

Latif extends his arm out of the window and fires two more shots at his head. Boom! Boom!

"That's it. Let's go!" Mu-Mit shouts.

Mu-Mit pulls off abruptly, forcing Latif to fall back into his seat.

"Hold up!" Latif shouts. Mu-Mit slams on the brakes. Latif tosses a red bandana out of the window. It lands on the dead man's back. The red rag will make police think that this murder is gang related. This way the murder can never lead back to them. Mu-Mit pulls off and races up Broad Street with no headlights on. He makes the first right and zooms up the block. After making the quick left, he turns the headlights on and pumps his brakes to slow the car down. He peeks through his mirrors continuously to make sure no one is tailing them.

Latif lays back in his seat, holding the blazing hot gun in his hand. The smell of gunsmoke fills the car. The job was just as easy as they both expected it to be.

"Now look at 'em," Latif teases. "We tried to get with 'em but, nah," he says sarcastically. "So we had to get at 'em!"

///// CHAPTER 70 /////

Dre stands on the balcony of his Hoboken Condominium, just staring peacefully into Manhattan. Tony got this spot for him. This luxurious apartment is a long way from Cindy's small two bedroom apartment. It's fully loaded with all the amenities that a man of Dre's stature should have, a jacuzzi, two bedrooms, three bathrooms, granite countertops, marble floors, swimming pool, tennis courts and a gym.

As Dre stands there watching the waves of the water roll peacefully, his phone rings. He looks down at the display and sees Cindy's name bright and clear. His stomach turns at the sight of her name. It's been a couple of days now since he last spoke to her. The last time they spoke, she begged him to come back, but he refused. She told him that she felt as if he just used her until he got on his feet. That made him feel so guilty that he got Tony to mail her a check for $10,000.00. He figured that would cover her rent for at least nine months. He admitted to her that he has no feelings for her whatsoever and what they once shared was over a long time ago. He stated to her that they could never be an item ever again. She cried hysterically after hearing that, but the fact still remains. Dre presses no on his phone. Deep down inside he's sure that he hasn't heard the last from her.

In Washington D.C.

Angelique sits at her desk in her lavish office. Ever since her and Dre's rendezvous, she hasn't been able to get him out of her mind. She feels so foolish about the entire situation. She can't believe she played herself the way that she did. She's never acted on impulse like that before. What makes it even worse is the fact that he hasn't called her since. That makes her feel worthless and degraded. At the end of the day, she set the rules and all she can do is abide by them. She's never been played like this, which is why it's so difficult for her to accept. The situation plays on her pride and self esteem. Usually men fall at her feet. The fact that Dre is paying no attention to her makes her want him even more. All these years she's believed that she had the power of the pussy. Dre now makes her feel that her pussy is powerless.

Right now she holds her phone in her hand. "Hell no," she tells herself as she thinks of calling him. Oh how badly she just wants to hear his voice. Before she knows it, she's already in the process of dialing. She presses *67 to block out her number. Her heart races as the phone rings.

Meanwhile in Hoboken

"Pssst," Dre sighs as his phone rings again. "She just don't get it," he says aloud. He assumes that this is Cindy calling him again. He looks down at the display and it reads, caller unknown. "Does she think I'm going to fall for that one?" he says aloud before pressing no, sending her to his answering service.

Damn, he must know it's me, Angelique thinks to herself as she listens to his answering service. She refuses to leave a message and belittle herself any further. She hangs the phone up sadly. I guess he's right, 'ass is ass'.

///// CHAPTER 71 /////

Trauma sits in the driver's seat of his rented Envoy. In the passenger's seat there sits Candy Kev. The back seat is occupied by two members of the Trauma Unit. They've been riding around headed nowhere for the past two hours.

Trauma cruises up the pitch black block. The empty block feels so deserted. The presence of the creepy cemetery to the left of them makes the scenery look quite spooky.

Trauma pulls over and parks in the middle of the block. Candy Kev looks around, wondering why they're parking on the dark block.

Trauma turns the radio off and leans his head back onto the headrest. The truck is now very quiet. Candy Kev begins to feel rather uneasy, yet he tries to remain cool and calm.

Trauma pulls his nine millimeter from his waist and lays it on his lap. Candy Kev now becomes quite frightened. He tries to act as if he isn't, but his face tells it all. The tension in the air is thick. He feels like his life is in danger, but why, he asks himself. He hasn't crossed them in any way. Things have been going smoothly between them for years. They've never had any issues once they've gotten to know each other. They have accepted him as a member of the crew. What the fuck could all this be about, he asks himself.

The sound of a bullet being slammed into the chamber of a semi-automatic gun echoes throughout the truck. The sound comes from the seat behind him. His heart is racing, but he still remains as calm as he can. The same sound repeats itself, but this time it comes from the seat behind the driver's seat.

Something ain't right, he tells himself. His gut tells him to push the door open and try and make a run for it. I'll never make it, he says to himself. He then considers the fact that maybe this isn't about him. If he runs and that's not the case, he'll never be able to hear the end of this. He'll be the laughing stock and none of them will ever respect him again. "What up?" he mumbles while slowly turning his head toward Trauma.

Trauma grabs hold of his gun, while staring straight ahead. He grips the gun tightly, while resting it on the top of the steering wheel. "You tell me," he replies, still looking straight ahead.

"I don't know," he mumbles. "Shit just don't feel right," Candy Kev admits.

"Nah?" Trauma asks. "You don't know what's going on?"

"N, nah," he whispers.

"Think hard." Trauma pauses before speaking again. "You don't have nothing you want to tell me? Let me give you a hint. Something you told me wasn't true."

Candy Kev thinks hard. He wonders what Trauma could be talking about. "Ay man, I don't know what you're talking about. Ya'll my peoples. I keep it real with ya'll."

"Oh yeah? So where you say you got that 'After Party' from again? Some poppies in the Bronx, right?" he asks as he turns his head facing Candy Kev. "You do keep it real, right?"

All this over that, Candy Kev thinks to himself as he sits there quietly. He's not quite understanding this entire ordeal.

"Let me show you how real you been keeping it with us. That dope coming from the Mayor. His brother giving it to some old head mufuckers and they running around the streets with it."

Damn, Candy Kev thinks to himself. He's hit the nail on the head. He definitely knows everything.

"Word on the streets is they're going to take over the town and they're using you as the puppet."

"Nah, Trauma it ain't like that," he pleads.

"Wait, there's more. They're using you to get close to me so they can bump me off and take over our set," he lies.

"What? Who told you that? Hell no! Nothing like that didn't come up," he claims.

"Sure it did," Trauma says as he taps his gun against the steering wheel.

"Ay man, I swear to ya'll that nobody ain't gone make me go against ya'll. Ya'll like family to me, word to mother! Ya'll been good to me ever since I came home. Please don't let nobody make ya'll think no shit like that," he begs.

"So you saying that ain't true?"

"Hell no, it ain't true!"

"Well, they playing on you then. That's their plan. They just didn't tell you. They got you all up in the Nestle Crunch."

Candy Kev sits there quietly. I can't believe that Mu would put me in a situation like this, he says to himself.

"Kev, I don't trust you," says Trauma. "I don't feel comfortable around you. A part of me believes that you're setting me up."

"Man, I swear to God, I won't do no shit like that. I ain't got nothing to do with that shit. The niggas came to me with the work. It was good so I took it. I figured we could all capitalize off of it. I had ya'll in mind to. You know I ain't no selfish nigga. I came to you with it first. I offered it to you at the same number I got it for. I wanted all of us to eat," he babbles. "True indeed, I lied about where I got it from, but you know how it goes. If everybody knows your plug, the plug ain't worth nothing. If that's their plan, then I didn't know shit about it. I swear on my mother."

"I don't believe you."

"Come on, Trauma? I ain't bullshitting you."

"How much of that dope you done moved already?"

"I don't know…about 1,000 bricks."

Trauma nods his head up and down. "They gave you a thousand at once?"

"Nah, like 250 at a time."

"How many you got left right now?"

"I just got some new shit yesterday. I got about 175 left right now. After I finish that, I'm done with it. I swear! On the real, if you want me to give that back, I will. Fuck that! I ain't trying to be in the middle of this shit!"

"I hear you. I want to believe you, but if something happens to me it's my own fault. Especially being that I already got the word that they coming for me. Now, I gotta get them first. The only way I'll let you live is if you bring them to me. I dunno, maybe call them for a 1,000 brick sale or something and when they get there, we will be waiting for them." He sits quietly for a second. "I'm not sure yet. I'll put something together."

Candy Kev listens closely. He can't believe that he's mixed up in all of this. He's seen Mu-Mit in action several times and knows that he's a beast. On the other hand, he's also seen Trauma and his unit at work too. Damn, he thinks to himself.

"For the time being, that 175 you got, we need that. How fast can you get that to us?"

Candy Kev can't believe his ears. He looks at Trauma with a blank look on his face. Are they going to rob me?

"How fast?" Trauma asks anxiously.

I have to try and stall them off, he tells himself. "I can't get hold of it right now," he lies.

"No problem. It's cool. We'll just get together, tomorrow bright and early. We'll come by the house up there in Union."

Oh shit, Candy Kev thinks to himself. How the hell do they know where I rest? Candy Kev has never taken any of them to his house. He can't help but wonder how Trauma knows this.

"By that time, I'll have it all figured out...how you can bring them to us. Now get out," he instructs.

"Huh?" Candy Kev asks as he looks around at the dark block.

"You heard me. Get out before I change my mind and leave you here, stinkin'."

Candy Kev grabs hold of the door handle. They're sparing his life. He has to hurry before he changes his mind.

"Hold up," Trauma says as Candy Kev steps foot onto the ground. "Take this," he says as he passes his gun over to Kev. He stares at the gun with a blank look on his face. "Take it," Trauma says as he pushes it closer to Kev. "Just in case you go against our plan, you'll be able to protect yourself. You already know how we do. We gone be on your ass," he mumbles.

"Trauma man, go ahead? I ain't taking that," he says as he closes the door.

"Alright," Trauma says as he pulls off slowly. As he cruises up the block, he peeks through his rearview mirror where he sees Candy Kev trotting up the block. Trauma is sure that he's embedded enough fear in him to make him do anything that he needs him to do.

///// CHAPTER 72 /////

Tony lays back in his enormous California King size bed. The black satin sheets rise up and down in a constant motion. Tony grabs a handful of the slippery material, while leaning his head back against the headboard. He moans with ecstasy. Just as the feeling gets even better to him, his mind becomes occupied with other thoughts. Miranda's case has been on his mind day and night. He can't help it. He just has to crack this case. He has a plan. He just hopes and prays that it works.

A sudden jolt makes Tony look down to the center of the bed. Mocha lifts her head up. She tosses the sheets to the side irately. Anger fills her eyes. "What…am I down here for the hell of it?" she asks in a sassy manner. "What, I don't do it for you no more? I can't get it up?"

"Mo, please. It's not you. It's me."

"Oh, no you didn't hit me with the, it's not you, it's me, bullshit," she says furiously swaying her head from side to side.

"Mo, I promise you," he pleads. He lays his head back banging it into the headboard. "It's work. My mind is on it day and night."

"Psst," she sucks her teeth with frustration. "Well you know how the saying goes? All work and no play makes Tony a dull boy," she says looking down at the shriveled piece of manhood that she holds in her hand. She relieves him from her grip and crawls out of the bed. She walks away, stomping hard. Her huge firm rear shifts hard with every step. Her tall 4-inch stilettos bang loudly across the hardwood floors.

Tony is sure that it's the job that has his mind occupied. He watches her walking away and the beautiful sight reassures him of that. There she is completely nude except for her bright yellow shoes, which happens to be Tony's favorite pair. The lemon colored shoes up against her ebony complexion is a turn on for him. The way she walks some may call it 'stank,' but Tony considers it sexy. He just loves the way her ass bounces with each step. "Wife!" he calls out to her.

She spins around hastily. Her huge breast swing freely. Her silver dollar sized nipples are so hard they could break through cement.

He just enjoys her beauty for a few seconds. Little specs of glitter are plastered against her chocolate skin causing highlights to bounce around the room with her every move. Her flat tummy exposes her sexy detailed six pack. Her tiny waist flows right into her broad hips. Her thick luscious thighs are enough to make a man drool over himself. She stands there resembling an African sculpture. "I swear to you, it's my work. It's not you. Look at you. I still find you as attractive and sexy as I did the very first time I laid eyes on you. You're my gorgeous, African queen."

"Nigga, whatever," she says as she spins around and stomps away. "Tell that bullshit to the judge!" she shouts from the hall.

///// CHAPTER 73 /////

Mu-Mit leads the way as Latif follows him out of Amin's Halal Chinese restaurant. They're both hungry, but exhausted from the long day. They've been riding since early this morning putting things into perspective.

Mu-Mit throws his hood on to protect his bald head from the heavy flow of rain. Latif puts his bag of food on top of his head to do the same. They both jog to the car. In just seconds they're both soak n wet.

Latif gets in the car first. Just as Mu-Mit is about to get in, he sees a shadow over his shoulder. He turns around quickly, with his finger on the trigger of the gun which he grips inside of his pocket.

"Mu-Mit what up?" the man says.

Mu-Mit and the man stand face to face. The fact that the man was able to sneak up on him makes him slightly uneasy. Mu-Mit is familiar with the man yet and still he exposes his gun just to let him know that he's prepared. Truthfully, he knows that he was caught totally off guard, but he will never admit it to anyone. "Tippy, what up?"

Latif hops out of the car, standing at the door. His gun is drawn as well. "Mu, what up?" he asks sensing a slight bit of tension. He stares coldly at the man who stands before Mu-Mit.

The man sees the discomfort on both of their faces. "Hold up," Tippy-Toe says. "I come in peace."

Mu-Mit still grips his gun tightly. He doesn't trust Tippy-Toe the least bit. He doesn't know who he could have gotten in contact with. Anyone that knows him knows that he's a hit man who will honor any contract.

"I want to rap to you," he says.

"Rap then," Mu-Mit replies quickly.

"Can I get in the car out of the rain?" he asks.

Mu-Mit doesn't even consider his request. He doesn't even trust him on the same block as him, let alone in his car. "Let's go over here," Mu-Mit says pointing to the pre-school right next to the Chinese restaurant. "My car filthy," he says letting him know that they're riding dirty, just in case he has other intentions.

Tippy-Toe walks sneakily onto the sidewalk. It must just be his nature. He almost glides when he walks, making no noise at all. He peeks from side to side glancing at his surroundings. His aura makes both Mu-Mit and Latif want to off him just because.

They stand under the canopy side by side. Latif runs over and stands on the opposite side of Tippy-Toe. They have him squeezed tightly in between them giving him no room to maneuver. You may want to call it a murder sandwich that they have him in. If he even budges slightly he can say goodbye to his life. Both of them have their fingers on their triggers.

"You was close to losing your life," Mu-Mit says further defending the fact that he got caught slipping. "You better stop that sneaking around shit."

"I can't help it," he replies. "That's my name," he says with a cheesy grin as he shifts his eyes from side to side peeking around cautiously.

Mu-Mit looks around on the sneak tip trying to figure out where he could have come from. It seems as if he just popped out of nowhere.

"I been looking all over for you," Tippy-Toe claims.

"What for?" Mu-Mit asks arrogantly.

Tippy-Toe pauses briefly. "Ya'll names buzzing throughout the town."

"All good, I hope," Mu-Mit says with a devilish grin.

"A lot of shit going down in the town and ya'll names popping up in the middle of it all. To make a long story, short, somebody put a price on ya'll heads. I was offered 25 grand to pluck both of ya'll."

"Oh yeah?" Mu-Mit asks while nodding his head up and down in a cocky manner.

"Yeah. Niggas saying ya'll running around trying to muscle ya'll way in. That's how the shit came to me."

"So you gone take the money?" Mu-Mit asks while staring square in his eyes.

"Come on Mu man?" he says in a high pitched voice. "You always on that bullshit," he whines."

"I'm just asking. I need to know. Twenty five stacks is a lot of trap."

"I mean, it's fair for a square, but nothing to destroy a friendship over."

"So, how about it was a hundred grand?" Mu asks. "Would you have went for it?"

"Mu, knock it off. Ain't no amount of money worth destroying a friendship."

"Tip, you knock it off. We both know that me and you ain't never been friends. I mean we ain't never had no friction, but we ain't never been friends either."

"Man, later for all that," Latif interrupts. "What is it?" he asks anxiously as if he's ready to move out on Tippy-Toe. "What you want?" he turns to face Tippy-Toe. "What brings you here? You said all that to say what?"

Tippy-Toe pauses before speaking. "Dig man, I like what ya'll doing. I respect the whole movement. I came here to ask ya'll what I can do to be a part of this? I'll do whatever it takes."

"Ay man, no disrespect, but we ain't never played on the same team. I'm 46 mufucking years old. Ain't no need to start no new shit."

"Come on, Mu, I'm willing to do anything," he claims.

Mu-Mit looks over to Latif and they lock eyes for a few seconds before Mu-Mit looks at Tippy-Toe. "Anything?"

"Anything," Tippy-Toe confirms.

///// CHAPTER 74 /////

The Next Morning

Tony awakens bright and early. He rolls over, reaching for Mocha, but all he feels is a cold pillow. With both eyes still closed, he feels around for her, but she isn't there. His mind quickly replays last night's scene. He quickly remembers that she never came back to bed. She must have slept in the guest room, as she always does when she can't get her way. "Mo!" he calls. He pauses a few seconds before he calls again. "Wife!"

Today is a big day. He's flying out to Miami in less than three hours. He wonders how this day will turn out. He hopes and prays for the better.

He lays back in his bed. He looks to his right at the huge transparent glass walk-in-closet. From where he is, he can view his entire wardrobe. All his shoes are lined up along the floor. Over 100 suits are hung up on the rack of the right wall, color coded. His shirts fill up the entire left wall. The middle rack is full of his casual wear while the top shelf holds his hat collection.

He lies there mentally putting his outfit together as he does every day when Mocha steps into the room. She's completely naked, still dripping wet from her shower. She steps hurriedly into her own glass closet, where she immediately starts picking her clothes off of the rack. "Good morning to you too!" he shouts.

Four Hours Later

Tony is in the prosecutor's office in Miami. Sitting close by his side is Angelique. She knows how stressful this case has been for Tony. Although she's here for his support, her bigger purpose in being here is because she thought that maybe Dre would have come along as well.

They sit there quietly awaiting the prosecutor's arrival. Angelique breaks the silence. "So, what's up with your little employee?"

"He's cool. You haven't heard from him?"

Before she can answer him, the door opens and the prosecutor walks in rapidly. "Good day," he mumbles.

"Good afternoon," Tony and Angelique shout out simultaneously.

"Folks, we have to make this snappy. I have to be in court in thirty minutes," the prosecutor says.

"What I have to say will only take five," Tony replies.

"I'm listening."

"I have a proposition or more of a request, I should say."

The prosecutor sits there reading a stack of papers that he holds in his hands. From the looks of it, he's not paying Tony the least bit of attention. "Go ahead, don't mind me. I'm listening. Be mindful that I have to be in court in 28 minutes," he says as he looks down at his watch.

Here we go, Tony says to himself as he winks at Angelique. "My client, Miranda Benderas is not the murderer. I think everyone is well aware of that. All the evidence points to her boyfriend and we all know this. I've spoken to her and informed her that there is no way she can walk away a winner in this situation. She in return told me that she never told because she feared for her life. Obviously she's witnessed him commit some gruesome crimes and she is extremely fearful of him. She got hooked up with him when she was just a child. Their relationship was always an abusive one. She tried to get out of it on many occasions, but he wouldn't allow her to leave him. He would threaten her life and even the life of her mother when she was alive. There was a period where he was incarcerated for approximately three years. During that time, she chased her dream of modeling. She's quite good at it, I must add. She's been on a few sitcoms and a few prominent runways. Her boyfriend returns home from prison and interrupts her career because of his own jealousy and insecurities. He threatened to kill her if she didn't stop her modeling. Their reason for coming to Miami was to visit her mother's gravesite on her birthday. While staying at her godfather's house, apparently the godfather had some company over and my client and her boyfriend witnessed a drug deal going down. That sparked a thought in her boyfriend's criminal mind. It was then that he came up with the idea to rob the godfather. She tried hard to talk him out of it, but his mind was set. She resisted until her own life was threatened. She informs me that his plan was to only rob her godfather. Murder didn't come into play until the man refused to turn over his possessions."

"Twenty three minutes, I have to be in court," the prosecutor says without looking up from his papers.

"She's ready to cooperate," Tony whispers. Just saying this leaves a sour taste in his mouth. The prosecutor looks up. Tony has finally gotten his attention. "On one condition," he says with his index finger high in the air.

"What is that? If I may ask?"

"You have to grant her the witness protection program. She fears if she testifies against him, she'll be killed. She's stated to me that the only way she will even consider that, is if she can relocate. The tri-state area is out. Philadelphia is out and so is Miami. What do you think?"

The prosecutor pauses for a brief second. Tony's heart races as well as Angelique's. They're hoping that he bites for the bait. Finally he speaks. "I think I'm leaving for court now," he says as he stands up. He begins walking toward the door. "Leave your number with the receptionist and I'll give you a call. Good day!" he shouts as he leaves them in the room alone. They sit there more baffled now than they were before they got here.

"All we can do is wait for the decision," Tony says with a sympathetic look on his face. "That is her only hope. The ball is in his court."

///// CHAPTER 75 /////

An 18-wheeler tractor trailer flies up the New Jersey Turnpike doing 92 miles an hour in the fast lane. The huge tractor bounces with every bump. All of a sudden, the driver loses control and the tractor swerves into the middle lane uncontrollably. For some reason traffic is piling up, back to back in both lanes. Each car has less than a car's length in between the next one. This makes it impossible for the driver of the Infiniti in the next lane to move in either direction. The tractor crashes into the Infiniti viciously. The trailer latches onto the roof of the Infiniti and drags it up the highway.

The driver of the tractor tries desperately to stop, but the weight of the cargo he's carrying makes it impossible to stop on the dime like that. The Infiniti, which is still hooked onto the tractor, is forced into a Lincoln Navigator. Now both vehicles soar up the highway at top speed until they smash into into a small Toyota. The snake-like chain of vehicles zip recklessly up the Turnpike.

The driver of a convertible Jaguar sees the string of vehicles coming behind him. "Oh shit!" he shouts nervously to his passenger. He steps on the accelerator harder and manages to zip out of the way and dips into the next lane in a nick of time. Thick smoke fills the air as the driver slams on the brakes of the trailer. Burning rubber can be smelled from miles away. The sudden stop makes the trailer swing out of control fiercely. The cabin of the truck heads straight for the cement divider that separates the highway and crashes into it brutally. The driver of the tractor is ejected from his seat and thrown through the windshield. The trailer pins the Navigator, the Infiniti and the Toyota against the divider, crushing the cars completely. The small Toyota goes up in flames instantly.

The driver of the trailer lands on his back on the opposite side of the highway. Miraculously he's able to stand on his two feet. He wobbles dizzily and disoriented. A Ford Expedition comes at him full speed. The driver tries hard to swerve around the man, but it's impossible. He hits the man, knocking him flat on his back before rolling over him like a rag doll. Two minutes later, a young rookie State Trooper arrives on the scene. He jumps out of his car and runs toward the scene of the accident. The smell of burning flesh fills the air. He damn near faints at the sight which lies before his eyes. Never in his young life has he seen anything this horrific. He calls for the rescue squad, screaming hysterically.

Fire men and the rescue squad had to cut four dead bodies from the vehicles. The driver of the tractor is dead as well. The Trooper figures that the driver must have dozed off from lack of sleep and lost control of the truck.

He climbs into the truck to gather the information he needs in order to contact the owner. As he's getting in something strange catches his attention. A packet of heroin lies on the seat. The Trooper picks it up and can't help but to see that it's empty. The Trooper flips the bag over in the palm of his hand and reads the print. The words 'After Party' is stamped boldly across the packet. He shakes his head with misery. "One bag of dope claims five lives. It's a shame," he mumbles to himself.

Yes, the driver nodded off. Was it from lack of sleep? No, it was from the bag of 'After Party' that he bought from Philadelphia an hour and a half ago.

///// CHAPTER 76 /////

The milky white convertible Jaguar XK zips through McDonald's parking lot hastily. The baby blue top is peeled back, exposing the creamy leather interior.

"Stunting like my daddy! I be stunting like my daddy! I'm a young stunner!" the driver sings along with rapper Lil Wayne. "Can't see lil niggas cause the money in the way," he shouts at the top of his lungs. "If you ain't gone ride fly then you might as well hate!" he shouts with an arrogant look on his face. "It ain't my birthday but I got my name on the cake!" he shouts bopping from side to side. The music is busting through the speakers exploding into the air. Everyone looks and stares as he passes them. "Believe dat and if your man wanna play and I'mma fuck around and put the boy brains on the gate. Hey! Pick 'em up? Fuck 'em let 'em lay. Where I'm from you see a dead body everyday!" He bops his head up and down psychotically. "Make a song about me, I'm throwing shots back at 'em," he says as he holds his hand in the air waving it around like he's shooting a gun. "Bitch I'm the boss!" he shouts as he zips into the parking space. "Stunting like my daddy! Stunting like my daddy! I'm a young stunner! When I was 16 I bought my first Mercedes Benz. I must have fucked a thousand bitches and her girlfriends," he sings with a confident smile on his face. "How you want it? Show me my opponent! Show me my opponent," he repeats before turning the music down.

The passenger leans back low in his seat with a look of disgust on his face. Being here brings back memories that he would rather not relive.

The driver pops the door open. "Bookkeeper you going in?" Ahmir asks as he hops out of the car.

"Nah," he answers quickly. "I'd rather not," he says as his mind replays his days of being out here in 0 degree weather, begging and conning people out of their hard earned money. He looks at himself back then and looks at himself now. He definitely realizes how far he's come. He blames it all on Young Cash for giving him a second shot. Thanks to him he's been able to turn his life around. He's been clean now for several months and doesn't have the slightest urge to get high. He has his own apartment down in Baltimore and he even has a little piece of car to get around in. That is a long way from sleeping on the street here in Newark.

Young Cash stands next to his car, just enjoying the scenery. He didn't realize how much he misses this place until now. He stands there taking sniff after sniff of the polluted air. "Aghh," he sighs. "Bookkeeper, I miss this shit!"

"Young Cash, this shit depressing as hell," the Bookkeeper whispers.

The loud sound of an engine roaring steals Ahmir's attention. He looks to the entrance where he sees a red Cherokee coming toward him. The driver cuts the wheel swerving right around Ahmir. He parks side by side with Ahmir's car. The driver hops out cheerfully. "Young Cash!" ILL Wheel shouts.

"ILL motherfucking Wheel," Ahmir sings as they greet each other with a tight thug hug.

"Got damn, you riding boy," he says as he steps closer to the Jaguar. He examines it carefully.

"Go ahead man," Ahmir says modestly, blushing from ear to ear. "It's the minimum," he says arrogantly. "Shit," he sighs.

"She looking good as hell!"

"Why wouldn't she? She $92, 000.00.," he says arrogantly. "This shit was almost a pancake. A motherfucking dumb ass truck driver must have fell his dumb ass to sleep behind the wheel on the turnpike. He just missed me by an inch. I heard on the radio that he killed 4 motherfuckers and his stupid ass self," he says with no compassion. "Lucky, I still got the wheel," he says as he acts as if he's steering a car.

"Motherfucker, you never had the wheel," ILL Wheel teases.

"Nigga, whatever. I'm here ain't I?" he asks. "I will smoke yo ass! That's the SRT, right?" he asks as he looks to the back of the jeep.

"Why wouldn't it be?" ILL Wheel asks arrogantly.

"Good, I won't feel like I took advantage of you once I beat on you!" he smiles. "Later for that shit right now, though. We can race for keeps later. Right now that shit neither here nor there," he says as the look on his face turns stone cold. "What's the deal? Tell me how that shit went down."

ILL Wheel quickly begins telling all the details of his episode. "They pistol whipped me and the whole shit," he says before Ahmir interrupts him.

"Hold up, I can't take no more. I gotta let this shit out. Me and you don't even supposed to be here having this conversation. I supposed to be standing over your grave right now," he says with rage. "If that was me, I would have died in that car. I would have never took them to my crib. Fuck that! Nigga, kill me right here," he says in a cocky manner. "Now go ahead…finish your story."

///// CHAPTER 77 /////

In Ivy Hill

It's 12 noon and Mu-Mit sits parked in the rented Ford 500. He lays back in the driver's seat, alone in the car while Latif sits on a stoop close by. Latif holds the Newark Star-Ledger over his lap, staring at the same pages that he's been looking at for the past 30 minutes. In no way is he reading the paper. He actually has his eyes on the doorway of the Coliseum Gym which sits across from him.

Their purpose of being here is stalking their prey. Three whole days of tailing the man has given them all the information they need to not only abduct him, but to rob him of all his goods as well. They have his daily routine down to a science. They've managed to follow him from morning to night without him noticing them. The distinguished color of his car stands out like a sore thumb. The Root Beer colored car can be spotted from ten miles away.

Every morning he starts his day off by working out at this gym, where they have been sitting parked behind his convertible Lexus for almost two hours now. If their timing is correct, he should be on his way out of the door within the next five minutes.

Their timing is perfect. Not even three minutes later and Doughboy is dragging himself out of the building lazily. He looks extremely fatigued. His nylon work out suit is drenched with sweat.

Latif looks over to Mu-Mit and gives him a head nod. Mu-Mit ducks down in his seat so he can't be seen. Latif peeks around to see what the scenery looks like. There are a few people in the area, but he's sure he can work around them.

Doughboy steps onto the sidewalk with his head hanging low. He's still huffing and puffing from his workout. He looks over at Latif barely paying attention to him. Just as he passes, Latif stands up and trots behind him. He hears the footsteps but Latif is already too close for comfort.

Latif jams his pistol deep into the fatty part of Doughboy's lower back. He turns his head suddenly, standing face to face with Latif. Doughboy recognizes Latif's face instantly. "Keep moving, fat boy," he whispers as he pokes him even harder. Doughboy attempts to put up a little resistance by pulling away. "I swear to God, if I have to chase yo fat ass," he says biting on his bottom lip. Doughboy takes the threat seriously. He immediately stops resisting. He looks around with hope that someone is watching all of this, but everyone seems to be busy going on with whatever it is that they're doing. "Let's go, let's go," Latif says nudging Doughboy. "Any funny business, I'll blow your whole back out," he says as they walk side by side. Doughboy is so scared for his life that he just walks along with no resistance at all.

As they're approaching the car, Mu-Mit pops the back door open for Latif. "Get the fuck in," Latif demands as he forces Doughboy into the backseat. He realizes the seriousness of this matter and again he attempts to put up a little fight. Latif grabs him by the back of his collar tightly, wrapping it around his neck. His circulation is cut off causing him to choke. Latif then pushes him into the car and slides right next to him. Mu-Mit pulls off casually, as he looks around making sure no one is paying attention to them.

Latif knows the only way this caper will go smoothly is if he pumps fear into Doughboy from the very beginning, letting him know that they have no time for games. He draws his gun hand high in the air before crashing the pistol into Doughboy's skull.

"Aghh," he cries. "Alright, alright. You got it," he whines.

"Shut up, fat stinking bitch!" Latif shouts as he bangs him in the skull again.

Doughboy covers his head with his hands to protect himself from the blows. As his hands block the back of his head, Latif slams the gun into his face with all of his might, hitting him right between his eyes. Everything becomes blurry before stars appear before his eyes.

Latif then grabs him by the back of the neck, forcing his head between his legs. His fat makes it quite difficult, but Latif manages to do it. "Lay down!" he shouts. Doughboy lays down as instructed to prevent from getting hit again. Latif jams his big body down between the backseat and the back of the driver's seat. He lays there in the extremely uncomfortable position. He barely has enough room to breathe.

"What up now, you fat bitch?" Latif asks as he thinks back to the day when Doughboy disrespected him. "Talk slick now!" he shouts as he bangs the gun onto his head once again. "What happened to all that slick ass talk? Huh?" he ask as he strikes him again.

"Aghh, come on man?" he cries.

"Come on, what?" Latif asks as he bangs him in the head again. "Popping all that shit," he teases. "Showing off for them sucker ass niggas. Now look? All you had to do was go with the plan but naw. Now look at you. I should shoot you in your fucking head right now."

"Nah man, come on," he cries. "Whatever you want, you got it."

"Shut the fuck up!" Latif shouts.

In less than ten minutes, they're pulling up to the destination. Mu-Mit peeks around cautiously before pulling into the narrow driveway. Latif grabs hold of Doughboy's keys which are laying on the seat next to him. He grabs him by the collar, lifting his head up. He jams the gun into Doughboy's mouth. This where it's at, right?"

Doughboy looks up with fear. He wonders how they know to bring him here. "Right?" Latif asks more aggressively. He sticks the gun further into Doughboy's mouth until he gags. "Am I right?" Doughboy nods his head up and down. "Who in there?" Doughboy shakes his head from side to side. "You lying to me? If you lying to me, I'll blow your fucking brains out. Listen to me. We gone walk in here and you gone take us to the dope. I ain't got time for games with you. You got five seconds to get that dope in my hands or I'm flipping yo fat ass," he says angrily. "What key is it?" he asks as he holds the key ring in the air. Doughboy quickly points the key out and Latif hands it over to Mu-Mit.

They enter the apartment cautiously. Just like Doughboy stated, there is not a soul in the apartment. "Where the dope, fat ass?" Latif asks before striking him with the gun again.

"Aghh," he sighs. "The bathroom," he says as he leads the way. Once they're inside, he points to the ceiling.

"The ceiling?" Latif asks. "Mu, hit the ceiling."

Mu-Mit steps onto the sink and presses around on the ceiling until he reaches the correct square. He lifts the block and sticks his hand inside, fumbling around until he locates a bag. "Got it," he says with joy. He drags the bag down and hands it over to Latif while he continues to look around for more to no avail. "That's it," he says as he hops off of the sink.

Latif unzips the bag and looks at the piles and piles of bricks of dope. Doughboy stands there in total fear. He's sure that his clock is about to be punched. At this point he realizes that he has nothing to lose. He knows how this game goes. There is no way in the world that they're going to let him live. With him knowing this he decides to take his destiny into his own hands. He looks at the huge revolver and suddenly he gets the motivation to make his move.

Doughboy snatches away from Latif with all of his might. All in one motion, Doughboy smacks Latif's gun hand, with his left hand, while throwing a wild bolo at Latif's head with his right hand.

The gun falls onto the floor before the punch lands on Latif's chin. Latif stumbles backwards from the blow. He lands onto the sink in a sitting position. Doughboy dives onto the gun. Nervousness fills Latif's heart as Doughboy sits up on his knees with the gun in his hand.

"Boom! Boom! Boom! Mu-Mit fires while standing directly over Doughboy. All three shots rip through his skull before he collapses onto his face. The gun falls from his grip as his hand hits the floor. Latif grabs hold of the gun and grips it tightly in his hand. Whew," he sighs to himself. He digs into his pocket and retrieves a red bandana which he drops onto Doughboy's body. He spins around quickly and takes off at top speed. They exit the apartment and off they go.

///// CHAPTER 78 /////

Dre sits in his cozy little office just looking out of the window when Tony walks in. "Dre, I'm in the middle of a meeting with a long time client of mine, who I would like to introduce you to."

Dre listens as he pays close attention to the look on Tony's face. He looks as if he's uncomfortable. Dre can sense that he wants to say something, but he doesn't know exactly how to word it. Tony taps a pencil against the window sill, while not even looking in Dre's direction.

"Who is he?" Dre asks. "Introduce him to me for what?" he asks making Tony even more uncomfortable.

Tony hesitates before replying. "I may be out of bounds for this, but still I'm going to do it. I'd rather let him talk to you if you don't mind?"

"What is it dealing with?" Dre asks curiously.

Just meet him and hear him out, ok?"

Dre throws his hands in the air, shrugging his shoulders. "Alright," he mumbles.

Tony leads Dre into his office. Dre steps into the office, wondering what he should expect. Finally, they all stand in the center of Tony's spacious office. "Doesn't look like a FED, Dre says to himself expecting the worse.

"Dre, this is Imamu. Imamu, this is Dre," Tony says. They shake hands coldly.

Dre looks him up and down, starting with his shiny bald head and going down to his silky bright disco shirt. His eyes then go down to his slim fit, super tight jeans. Finally, his eyes set onto the man's Louis Vuitton flip flops, which expose his newly polished toe nails. His finger nails are manicured as well. Dre gets the impression that he's either an extreme metro sexual or he's straight out gay. Dre tries hard to look him in his eyes, in attempt to read him, but it's difficult due to the fact that they're hidden behind pitch-black Cartier shades.

"What's up?" he asks with a deep African accent.

Dre replies by a head nod.

"First let me say that all of this is completely off of the record," Tony says. "Never ever have I done this before. I benefit nothing from this meeting. I've made the introduction. While you two discuss this matter, I will step out of the room. I don't want to hear details. I don't want to know anything. This is the last that I will ever hear of this. I'm done…out of it. Anything that takes place is between you two, ok?" Dre is baffled at the entire matter. He stares at Tony wondering what all this is about. Imamu nods his head up and down, letting him know that he understands. "Now, I will step out of the room and leave you two alone," Tony says as he exits the office.

Imamu and Dre stand face to face with about three feet in between them. Imamu takes off his shades and stares Dre square in the eyes. "Let me start off by saying that Tony and I have known each other for three years now. He is not just my attorney. I like to think of him as a friend. I trust him with my life. I know he always has my best interest at heart. With that type of relationship, at times I tend to talk to him on a more personal level. I told him a problem that I'm having and he said he may have someone who can help me. Needless to say, he brought you here."

"Problem being?" Dre asks nonchalantly.

"I have a situation. A multi-million dollar network running smoothly for years up until three months ago. A problem here, a problem there, now the bottom has fallen out."

"Huh?" Dre asks.

"In plain terms, I'm in need of material desperately and can't seem to find what I need."

Dre doesn't like the sound of this. He knows exactly where this is going. He doesn't believe that Tony brought him in here for this. Who the fuck is this, he asks himself. What type of bullshit is Tony on, he further asks himself. "Your network consists of?" Dre asks as if he doesn't have a clue of what the man is talking about.

"Heroin," he mumbles.

Dre stares at him coldly. "Huh?"

"Please hear me out?" he begs. "I know this may be awkward for you, but I promise you, this is no bullshit. As I told you, I've known Tony for years. He will vouch for me. If you can't help me please just point me in the right direction? My business is suffering."

"Let me get this right? A multi-million dollar operation and you're suffering? How?"

"No connection. I've been searching high and low with no success. I ran into a few guys, but they don't have the magnitude to supply me. If you can help me there are millions of dollars to be made. I'm telling you pounds and pounds," he claims.

"Can't help you," Dre says as he spins around, turning his back on the man. He walks away from him quickly.

"Please, wait?" Imamu begs. "Don't be alarmed. I know what you think. Look, no wires," he says as he unbuttons his shirt exposing his bare, boney chest. "Look, my ID," he says as he digs into his back pocket for his wallet. "I'm good. Tony will give you my history. I'm as clean as a whistle. I have never had a problem with the law in my life, trust me?"

"Stop it," Dre says. "I don't doubt your credibility. I just can't help you. I don't know where to begin," he lies.

"Please, just point me in the right direction?"

"Point you in the right direction?" Dre asks. "You go that way," he says while pointing toward the window. "And I'm going this way," he says pointing to the door as he walks away. "I'm out! Nice meeting you."

"Wait. Please?" he begs as Dre slams the door behind himself.

///// CHAPTER 79 /////

Mu-Mit and Latif sit in the car while Candy Kev hops into the backseat. "What up?" he says in a low whisper. "Here," he says as he passes the money to Latif. "That's fifty-two thousand and five hundred." He exhales slowly. He's pissed to no end. Of the $52,500.00, $34,650.00 actually came from his own savings. Trauma did exactly what he said he would do. He came to Kev's house bright and early that next morning to get hold of the 175 bricks of dope.

Candy Kev turned the dope over with no hesitation. The last thing he needs is a problem with Trauma and his unit. Just to think things were going fine with him until they stepped into the picture. He knew he should have never gotten involved with them.

He refuses to tell Mu-Mit what happened. He's sure Mu-Mit will go to bat for him against Trauma, but he'd just rather pay the money and forget that any of this ever happened. He's very sure that Trauma will never allow that though. He told Kev that as soon as he comes up with a plan on how they're going to bring them in he'll tell him. He also said until then things are good between them. He claims that there are no hard feelings, but Candy Kev doesn't trust them. He plans to stay out of sight for a second just to let this whole situation blow over.

He feels quite guilty knowing that someone is coming for Mu-Mit and he's not making him aware. Mu-Mit has taken care of him since he was a kid. He practically raised Candy Kev.

As a teenager Kev had no problems because everyone thought he was actually Mu-Mit's younger brother. In fact, Mu-Mit is the one who not only introduced him to Islam, but he gave him his Shahada as well. He gives credit to Mu-Mit for opening his eyes and showing him the light. A part of him wants to tell Mu-Mit, but the other part tells him to stay out of it.

"We waiting for the new shit to come in as we speak," Mu-Mit says. "I'll give you a call as soon as I get it in my hands, alright?"

"Nah, just hold up for a minute. I'm breaking out of town for a few days," he lies. "My lady tripping on that I don't spend no time with her shit, so I'm flying out to Vegas for a few days."

"Oh, ok. When are you leaving?"

"I'm flying out in the morning. I'll just hit you as soon as I get back," he says as he opens the door and steps out of the car.

"Cool, I'm here. Go enjoy yourself."

"No doubt. As Salaamu Alaikum!" he shouts as he slams the door.

"Wa Alaikum As Salaam wa Rahmatullahi," Mu-Mit returns the greeting of peace. "I love you Lil Bruh!" Mu-Mit shouts.

Hearing that makes Candy Kev's stomach turn. "I love you too," he mumbles.

Meanwhile a Few Miles Away

Ahmir and ILL Wheel sit side by side on the plush suede love seat while

Dusty sits directly across from them in the center of the couch. Ahmir and ILL Wheel listen carefully to the older man speak.

Suddenly a frown appears on the man's face. He turns looking towards Dusty. "Youngblood, did I say something funny?" he asks firmly. "Every time, I look out the corner of my eye, I see him making faces. He laughing at me like I'm Bernie Mac or some motherfucking body!" he says staring straight at Dusty. Venom bleeds from his eyes. He's good and ready to jump over there and ring Dusty's neck.

"Nah, nah, Unck," Ahmir interrupts. "Don't mind him. He ain't here. His mind ain't right," he whispers.

"Ok, let me know something then. I don't play no motherfucking games like that. Making faces behind my back and shit," he says staring coldly at Dusty for a few seconds before turning away, rolling his eyes with rage. "As I was saying before I was so rudely interrupted," he says looking back at Dusty.

Dusty sits there with the dumbest smile on his face. He hasn't even blinked an eye at Eddie Price. Only God knows what is on his mind at this point.

To see Dusty in this condition broke Ahmir's heart. Dusty recognized Ahmir, but he still acknowledged him rather bland, which made Ahmir feel terrible. ILL Wheel told Ahmir not to take it personal, but he can't help it. ILL Wheel also told him that he goes days without hearing Dusty say a word. Ahmir hasn't even seen the worse of his behavior. He's only seen him with the stupid look on his face, but remaining quiet. He has yet to hear some of the foolish things that come out of his mouth.

"This is the Ak-47, Assault Rifle," Eddie Price says. "This clip holds 30 rounds. It has a sighting range of 800 feet and a killing range of 1500 feet. Which means it can kill farther than you can see."

Ahmir sits back quietly. One thing that he's learned about Eddie Price is that he hates for people to talk when he's talking. He nods his head up and down just to let Eddie know that he hears him. Hearing all the measurements and so forth are boring him to death. He isn't worried about the distance because his plan is to hit everything up close.

"You said you want to clear up a block right?"

"Exactly," Ahmir replies.

"Well this baby here shouldn't leave nothing standing, trees, cars, poles, nothing and nobody. Of course it ain't just about the weapon. The man standing behind the weapon counts for everything in the world. If you can't work this big motherfucker, it's useless to you. With me behind this ain't nothing getting away," he says getting slightly excited. The look in his eyes is fierce.

Ahmir smiles. "Unck, you a cold dude, man."

"Cold? You ain't seen cold," he says with a straight face. "I killed bitches and babies in the Vietnam War," he says with his face frowned up. "What the fuck you think I care about killing a raggedy ass nigga?" he asks as he stares into Ahmir's eyes. His lips quiver uncontrollably. The look in his eyes makes Ahmir and ILL Wheel a little nervous. "All I'm saying is if you want to invest in some expertise, I'm here. After all, you like family to me. You Slim grandbaby. I can't let nothing happen to you. Days before Slim passed, he told me if anything ever happened to him, he would need me to watch after you. I think the Old Man knew his time was coming."

Hearing Slim's name almost brings tears to Ahmir's eyes. He still hasn't gotten over the fact of how Slim died. Every time he hears his name he feels as guilty as he did the day they found him dead. Ahmir thinks back to what Slim told him once. He said any man in the hood who is referred to by his first and last name is normally a legendary man. He said it's an honor to be identified by both names. Eddie Price, he says to himself. It amazes Ahmir how both Slim and Eddie Price refer to each other as being legendary. They have mutual respect for each other.

"I would be more than happy to eliminate any problem you have," Eddie Price offers.

"I'm good," Ahmir replies.

"Why get your hands dirty when you don't have to?" Eddie asks. "You got way too much going for you, Neph. You made it out. Not too many guys can say that."

"Thanks but no thanks. This personal," Ahmir whispers. "How much for this?"

"For anybody else, two thousand. For you Neph..give me fifteen hundred."

Ahmir grabs hold of the rifle and examines it thoroughly. He smiles inside. "Every time, I think I made it out, they keep calling me back," he sings in a low whisper. "I'll take it."

//// CHAPTER 80 /////

Tippy-Toe sits in the passenger's seat of the black Magnum. Sitting behind the steering wheel is Parlay. They watch closely as Mu-Mit walks out of the Hess service station's convenience store on Lyon's Avenue.

"Two stupid mufuckers," Tippy-Toe mumbles. "Fucking Pinky and the Brain," he says as he watches Mu-Mit hop into the car. "That's the Brain. He so fucking smart that he's stupid."

Parlay sits there quietly. He can't wait until all this is over with. They've been a pain in his ass ever since they stepped onto the scene. Soon that pain should be relieved.

"Now," Tippy-Toe says. "Don't tail 'eem too close," he says as he snatches his .38 revolver from his waist and lays it on his lap.

Parlay allows four cars to pass him before he pulls out of the parking space. He starts to creep up the block. He keeps his eyes focused on the Ford 500.

They tail him for approximately ten minutes before Mu-Mit finally pulls over and parks on Coit Street.

"Wait for him to start backing into the parking space," Tippy-Toe says slowly. Just as the car is backing in, Tippy speaks again. "Now!" he shouts. "Box him in," he says as he grasps his gun tightly.

Parlay's adrenaline is pumping. He steps on the accelerator and in a matter of seconds they have Mu-Mit trapped in the parking space.

Tippy-Toe rises up in his seat, leaning toward the window, but for some reason his left hand extends toward Parlay. "Don't move!" he says as he places the gun onto Parlay's temple. "I'll blow your brains out," he threatens. He slams the car into the parking position.

Parlay sits there in total shock. His mouth is wide open. He can't believe that he's been played like this. Through his peripheral, he sees Latif come trotting out of a small house to the right.

Mu-Mit walks quickly to the back door of the Magnum. He grips his gun tightly. He doesn't trust Tippy-Toe the least bit. Mu-Mit is still not sure if Tippy is setting them up for the kill which is why he put his plan together the way he did. He made sure that him and Latif were not in the car at the same time when they pulled up on him, so it would be impossible to spray the car up and get both of them.

Mu-Mit hops into the backseat and Latif hops in seconds after. They both draw their guns before they're seated.

"Drive," Tippy-Toe says as he takes the gun away from Parlay's head and jams it against his rib cage. To your van!" Parlay's mind races a mile a minute as he peeks through his rearview mirror and sees them with their guns drawn. "Drive motherfucker!"

Parlay fretfully puts the car into drive and cruises up the block slowly, wondering how he can get out of this situation. What should he do? Should he refuse? Hopefully, he'll ride by a police car and he can run into them head on. Should he try and make a run for it at the next traffic light? Thoughts run through his mind back to back, but none of them seem to make sense at this time. The end results to all of them are murder.

"Where he park the van?" Mu-Mit asks.

"On Frelinghuysen." Tippy-Toe reeled Parlay in perfectly. The car that they're riding in was rented by Parlay for Tippy-Toe so he would have a way to move around until he got the drop on them. He stated to him that it would be impossible for him to track them down without a car.

Just a few hours ago, Tippy-Toe called Parlay and they met up. At that time, Parlay was on his way coming back to Newark from Elizabeth. He told Parlay that he just saw Mu-Mit going into the Doll House, Go-Go Bar. He told Parlay in order to catch him right, he will need a driver. Parlay offered to get someone for the job, but Tippy-Toe told him they had no time to wait. Furthermore, he trusts no one. They had to hurry and get back to Irvington right away before he left. Parlay hated to do it, but he parked his van right there and hopped on in. Needless to say, he fell for it. That was the dumbest mistake that he could have ever made.

"Step on it," Tippy-Toe shouts. He's getting the feeling that Parlay is creeping purposely.

Approximately 12 minutes pass and they're cruising along Frelinghuysen Avenue. Just a few blocks short of Seth Boyden, Mu-Mit spots Parlay's van. "Park behind your van," Mu-Mit instructs. Parlay does exactly as he's told without hesitation.   "Where the keys?" Tippy-Toe asks as he starts fumbling through Parlay's pockets until he retrieves them. "Here," he says as he hands them over to Mu-Mit.

Mu-Mit hands them to Latif. "Go and check it out," he whispers. "Passenger side," he adds. Latif peeks around before jumping out and running over to the passenger's side of the van. As he steps onto the sidewalk, he draws his gun, just in case all of this is a set-up.

Mu-Mit sits in the backseat with his gun aimed at the back of the passenger's seat. If Tippy-Toe makes the slightest move he'll get the shock of a lifetime.

Latif opens the door of the van and waves his gun around, as he peeks around inside. He steps cautiously inside and finds the van to be completely empty. He dashes out and runs to the back of the van. He quickly waves Mu-Mit on.

"Go ahead," Mu-Mit says still aiming his gun at the back of the seat. "Leave the keys in the ignition."

Tippy-Toe jumps out and runs over to the driver's side where Parlay sits. He drags Parlay from behind the steering wheel. Mu-Mit waits until they're a few feet away before he hops out. He follows close behind with his gun underneath his shirt, yet it is still aimed at Tippy-Toe.

Tippy-Toe throws Parlay inside the van and hops in behind him. Latif hops in and Mu-Mit follows close behind. Mu closes the door behind him. As he stands there he gets a strange feeling in his gut. He second guesses the idea of both him and Latif being inside the van at the same time. All of this can easily be Tippy-Toe's set-up to attain the $25,000 that is on their heads. Maybe

Tippy-Toe will have someone come and trap them off while they're in the van and try and kill both of them. He gets paranoid. He watches through the tinted windows carefully. If that happens, he's sure this will turn into a blood bath. "Latif, lock them doors."

Tippy-Toe slams Parlay onto the driver's seat. He places the gun on his temple again. "Bust the box open!"

Parlay can't believe his ears. How does he know about the stash box? "Huh?" he asks with a blank look on his face.

"You wanna play stupid? Huh?" he asks aggressively. "Bust the motherfucking stash box open!"

The word on the street is Parlay works right from the van. Rumor has it that there is no stash house, All his work is in his stash box. Someone passed that information off to Tippy. He passed it on to Mu-Mit and Latif and the rest is history.

"I don't know what you talking about," Parlay says nervously. Just as he says it, the 400 bricks of dope that he has in his box occupies his mind. He wonders if they can tell that he's lying. He refuses to let them take his dope.

"You watch the windows," Mu-Mit tells Latif. They quickly switch positions. Latif watches the rearview mirror and the side mirrors constantly, while Mu-Mit stands behind Tippy-Toe. He has himself centered in between Parlay and Tippy-Toe just in case things start looking funny he will already be in position. He stands there fully prepared with his gun in his hand ready for action.

"Oh, you don't know what I'm talking about?" Tippy-Toe asks. Boom! His .38 revolver sounds off, leaving a ringing in all of their ears.

"Owwwww!" Parlay screams as the hot steel rips through his lap. He looks down trying to see where he's been hit. He can't tell because the burning sensation rips from his abdomen down to his knees. Suddenly, a pounding force rips through his lap before his muscles contract. He sits there in shock.

"Now do you know what I'm talking about?" he asks sarcastically. "Now bust the motherfucking box open!"

This changes Parlay's mind. Now he realizes that this is not a game. He quickly reevaluates the situation and realizes that no amount of dope is more valuable than his life. "I need the keys," he screams in a high pitched tone.

"Here," Latif says as he passes the keys over to him.

Mu-Mit looks down at Parlay's lap. An excessive amount of blood has soaked his jeans up already. He now believes that Tippy-Toe is being straight up.

Parlay starts the van up quickly. He then presses a few buttons nervously. "There ya'll go," he says as he points to the right side of the dashboard. They all sit there awaiting the box to pop out, but instead there's nothing.

"You playing with me?" Tippy-Toe asks while gritting down on his teeth. He aims the gun at Parlay's head.

"No, no!" he screams. "Hold up, please? I don't know what happened," he says as he fumbles with the buttons once again. He's as nervous as can be. He looks at the dashboard again and in seconds the entire right side of the dashboard pops out like magic.

Boom! Boom! The .44 Magnum sounds off loudly. Tippy-Toe tumbles over and falls face first into Parlay's bloody lap. Mu-Mit blasted him from behind. He never trusted Tippy-Toe from the very start, but he needed him to bring Parlay to him. It was like killing two birds with one stone. Tippy-Toe never knew that Mu-Mit was well aware of the fifty grand contract that Tippy-Toe was offered back in the day. Someone very dear to Mu-Mit told him as a warning. He would have stepped to Tippy-Toe a long time ago. The right time just never revealed itself. Mu-Mit knows the only reason Tippy-Toe didn't come for him is because the kid who put the money up got pinched before any money actually got put on the table. One thing Mu knows for sure is that if he was willing to move once, he'll definitely try to move again. Now he no longer has to worry about him moving again in life. Mu-Mit kicks Tippy-Toe's gun to the back of the van.

Parlay sits there frozen stiff. The dead man lying on his lap has him at a loss for words. He just sits there with his teeth chattering nervously.

"La, get the work!" Mu-Mit instructs. Latif quickly unloads the contents of the stash box into a garbage bag that he pulled from his own pocket. "And this the mufucker you hired to come after me?" Mu-Mit asks angrily. "Look at him!" Mu-Mit says as he grips Parlay by the back of the neck and forces him over the body. His face is pressed against Tippy-Toe's bloody head. The smell of the fresh blood makes Parlay queasy. "Look at him!" he repeats. He snatches him up by the neck and places his gun in Parlay's mouth. He slowly squeezes the trigger. As he's doing so, his mind takes him back to the day when they ran into Parlay on the street. "Sa'laikum, Mu!" he can clearly hear Parlay say. He bites down on his lip, shaking his head from side to side. Latif looks at him, wondering why the gun has yet to sound off. "I can't do it," Mu-Mit whispers. "He Muslim."

"So, and?" Latif asks with a clueless look on his face.

Mu-Mit replies by shaking his head no. "His blood is sacred," he whispers.

Latif steps over, aiming his gun at Parlay. Boom! Boom! Boom! He fires. Parlay's head slams into the driver's side window loudly.

Mu-Mit exits the van first, while Latif follows close behind. Mu-Mit runs straight to the driver's seat of the Magnum. Latif pulls a blue bandana from his pocket and tosses it onto the bodies before slamming the door. Police will find this flag and think that this murder is in retaliation of the two murders that they committed when he left red flags on the bodies. This will bring heat to all the gang members, leaving them in the clear.

"Call it a gang war," he laughs to himself as he runs toward the Magnum.

///// CHAPTER 81 /////

Tony walks into Dre's office. Dre looks up at his entrance. He's wearing a saddened face. "Dre, I know what you said but please? The other day you wouldn't hear me out, so please just listen to me?"

"Tony, listen, I can't help the man."

"Dre, you listen, please? Trust me this is one deal that you can't afford not to make. If you turn your back on it you will hate yourself forever. This has been my client for years. This guy is the real deal. He's been begging me to plug him into someone. I would never do this for anyone in the world. The only reason that I'm willing to get in the middle of this is because I trust the both of you. He's so desperate that he offered me $250,000.00 just to link the two of you together.

"250, Dre says to himself. "Tony, a dude of that magnitude doesn't just lose his plug. He's too valuable. No one will cut him off unless of course there's a reason that we don't know about," he says with his eye brows raised high. "I don't trust him. All this shit could easily be a set up for the both of us. I'm telling you, I don't think he right."

"Right? The boy is sparkling clean. He's never had a problem with the law in his entire life."

"Well, if that's the case how are you his attorney? He had to get pinched doing something?"

"Actually, I never represented him. I represented his uncle, but he paid for everything. At that time, I didn't know him from a can a paint. I taxed him, one hundred grand for the case."

"What was it a murder rap?"

"Nah, drugs. One whole year we were in contact, which is how we got tight."

"I still don't understand how a dude of that stature doesn't have a plug."

"Let me tell you why. His connection is afraid to deal with them at this point."

"Ok, now you talking...see! Why is he afraid?"

"Hold up and I'll tell you. The connect thinks that Imamu is hot."

"I told you something ain't right about him. He's probably right too. He probably is hot."

"Dre, he's one hundred percent wrong. Listen, his uncle was on his way back to Florida with 10 kilos of pure heroin, and was pulled over on the Turnpike. His bail was set at five million dollars."

"And he made it?"

"No, it took me ten months to get him a bail reduction. Finally, I got it down to two and a half million. Imamu put the money up and he was released. He was at court on time once every month for almost a year. Just a few months ago we were at court and things started going against us. No matter what I tried, it just wouldn't go in our favor. The Federal Prosecutor put in the motion to remand him right then. You know me, I have the gift of gab," he says arrogantly. "I started running my mouth and talked the judge out of it. The very next court date, needless to say, I was standing there alone…no uncle."

"He jumped a 2.5 million dollar bail?"

"Sure did. Imamu got a package put together for him and he fled the country, straight to Africa. Imamu had been trying to contact his connection for months until they changed numbers and locations on him. They seem to think that it's impossible for him to have made a bail like that. They think he told. Dre, listen to me, he's clean. I can show you the paperwork on him. Who do you think I am? I will never turn you onto a rat."

"Tony, you wouldn't know a rat if he crawled over your face," Dre says with a smile, but deep down inside he truly believes that. Dre believes that Tony doesn't have the eye to pick up on things like this. He feels the streets develop that sense for you. He would never expect an attorney to be able to sense something like that. One thing for sure though, the numbers that Tony are throwing around have definitely sparked Dre's curiosity. "What is it that he's trying to do?"

"He said he wants to get a kilo or two just to test it out?"

"You have a lot of faith in him, right?"

"Total faith."

"Ok,then, I'll get the two keys if you serve them to him? How about that?"

"Dre, I'm an attorney. You're asking me to go against everything to make a dope sell? How does that sound?"

"What, are you scared to lose your license to practice law? If you are so sure about him, you shouldn't be worried at all. If you aren't willing to take the gamble on your man, then why should I?"

"You're a dope dealer. Your business is selling dope. Am I afraid to lose my license over a dope sell? Hell yeah, which is why I don't sell dope. I practice law," he says sarcastically. "I see that this conversation is going nowhere so I'll just go to my office and tell him no deal. Sorry to bother you," he says as he walks toward the door.

"Wait," Dre says. Tony turns around quickly. "I'll do it. I'm doing this for you, not him. Tone, if this deal bites me on the ass, I want you to know that it's all your fault and you should feel fucked up for the rest of your life."

"Dre, I vouch for this man totally. I would never do anything to jam you up."

"I hear you. Send him in. Anyway, I would hate to be the cause of you losing that $250,000 score if I don't make the deal," Dre says with a smirk on his face.

Tony's look becomes stone cold. Dre has just pissed him off. "Dre, who the fuck do you think I am? I listened to you on several occasions while you assassinate my character as if I'm a gold digging whore. I don't know how you see me, and I really don't care as long as you respect me in my presence," he says sternly. "I don't need handouts. I earn mine. No one has ever given me anything. I come from the trenches just like you. I paid my own way through college and law school. I wasn't born with a silver spoon in my mouth. I came up the ladder of success on my own with no help from my little brother," he says sarcastically. "I wasn't fortunate enough to always be on the winning team, but I guarantee you one thing. I've led a couple of teams to the championships." Dre takes this extra personal. He knows just what Tony means by that. "What is that suppose to mean?" Tony pauses before replying. "It means that I'm tired of you attacking me and I would appreciate it if you never do it again. At the end of the day, I'm a man just like you. I don't disrespect you and you are not going to disrespect me. I would never take a dime for introducing you and him. Not one cent. I told you, I'm not a dope dealer. I'm an attorney. I make mines practicing law." Dre sees the anger in his face. "You right. I apologize." Tony walks away slowly with no response. "I'll send him in," he says before closing the door behind him.

Imamu walks in moments later. He steps over to Dre's desk, extending his hand to greet him. Dre stands up. "First of all, let me say thank you." Dre looks in the man's eyes and attempts to study him. He just wants to feel his vibe to see if he can trust him or not. "So, what are you trying to do?" Dre asks as he sits down behind his desk.

"I would like to do a small test run just to find out how much the material can withstand. I don't know, maybe three or four?"

Wow, Dre says to himself. He wonders how much Imamu is willing to pay. That can be expensive. "You know, I'm just a little man," Dre says trying to throw Imamu off. "I can get hold of a few bags here and there but four kilos is a lot. That can be quite expensive. I don't even know if my people have that type of capacity," he says purposely downplaying his situation just in case Imamu is not right.

"Really, price doesn't matter at all at this point. I'm not a haggler. Your price is your price. What is it going to cost me?"

"What are you willing to pay?"

"Whatever price you set."

Dre realizes that this can go on forever. Imamu is definitely on top of his game. Dre decides to go on and jump out there. "What were you paying?" He can't believe that he just asked such a personal question.

"Seventy thousand a kilo."

"I'm at seventy-five."

"Seventy-five it is. What are you working with?"

"What do you mean?"

"I mean, what type? I've always worked with Mexican Mud. Is that what you have or China White?"

"China White of course." His eyes light up with joy. "Good! When can we put this in motion? I can have 300,000 right here in less than an hour."

"No, I need two days at least. And we will not meet here. I don't want to violate the man's place of business. I'll give you a call and give you all the instructions, ok?"

"Ok," he agrees. "What you say goes. You're the man."

///// CHAPTER 82 /////

Ahmir and ILL Wheel were cruising through the town in search of any of the men that violated ILL Wheel. They rode through the block several times this morning, but the block has been quite dead. Just by chance as they were cruising along South Orange Avenue, ILL Wheel spotted a familiar car. The car belongs to Shotgun's younger brother. The car is double-parked on the corner of Salem in front of the Halal breakfast spot. They have been waiting patiently for the boy to come out of the restaurant. ILL Wheel hates to get him involved because they have always been cool, but his brother crossed the line.

"There he go," ILL Wheel says with his heart beating rapidly. Ahmir steps on the gas pedal as hard as he can. The jeep's engine growls with speed. Sccuuuuurr! The tires screech as Ahmir slams on the brakes. He turns the wheel to the right, just missing the boy's Chevy Impala by inches. The young man stands trapped in between his own car and ILL Wheel's car.

He stands there in total surprise not knowing what to do. He's frozen stiff. The female passenger watches closely, not knowing what to expect. ILL Wheel jumps out waving his .45 automatic in the air.

"Wheel, what up?" the boy asks frantically.

"Nigga, you already know what's up! Your brother said, I'm food. Tell him he should have ate me. Boc, boc, boc! He fires away, aiming all below the belt. The series of shots knock him off of his feet. People run away from the scene, screaming hysterically. The man lies there on the ground, squirming around, attempting to get up, but ILL Wheel starts firing again. Boc, boc, boc!

His zone is broken when he hears the female passenger screaming at the top of her lungs. He hops into the passenger's seat of his car. As he's slamming the door, he looks down at the boy who happens to be rolling around in agony. "Tell your brother, I'm on his ass!"

Meanwhile Several Miles Away

Mu-Mit sits in the driver's seat while Latif sits in the backseat. Mu-Mit's man, from Jersey City is in the passenger's seat. They sit parked on Ferry Street. They chose this street to make the deal because so much is happening on the busy street that no one should be paying attention to them.

They're in the middle of their biggest score ever. The man hands Mu-Mit $117,000.00 for 600 bricks. They cut their price by $25.00 for him. Even with only a $15.00 profit margin, they still score $4,500.00 apiece.

"Listen, this shit on fire! I can't keep this shit. The whole fucking town blowing up my phone," he says in an excited manner. "Yo, put another five hundred to the side for me. I should be done with this in about 2 or 3 days."

Mu-Mit hands him the dope. He's smiling from ear to ear at the man's reaction to the dope. "Like that?"

"Like that! This that shit right here. I don't know what happened and how the news spread that fast, but everybody want this shit!" His phone rings, interrupting him. He looks down at the display. "I'm out, that's a 150 brick sale, right there!" he shouts while pushing the door open. "I'll hit you," he says as he slams the door shut.

He walks quickly to his car and speeds off. "Damn!" Mu-Mit shouts. "He left so fucking fast, that I didn't even get the chance to ask him about that other dope. That's probably a good thing though. It's too close for comfort. We fuck around and put that dope out and those murders link right back to us. Fuck that! We gotta move that shit somehow though. That's money just sitting."

They're in a strange situation. They have close to 650 bricks of dope and nowhere to move it. They scored 220 bricks from Doughboy and they scored 416 bricks and $20,000 in cash from Parlay. That equals $139,920 in dope. That is if they wholesale it. The $20,000 in cash makes this a $160,000 vick. This will go down in history as their biggest sting ever. That is if they can find someone to unload the dope onto.

"Salaam!" Latif blurts out. "I'll call him and see if he will take us down to Asbury with him. I figure if we split the profit with him, he should do it with no problem. He was talking that bullshit but I'm sure he ain't gone turn down $40,000 for doing nothing."

"Call him!"

///// CHAPTER 83 /////

Two Days Later

Yesterday Trauma received the shocking news of Parlay's death. There are many rumors spreading throughout the street but the most widespread of them all is Parlay was selling bricks to a Crip and he robbed and killed him. The town may have bought that, but Trauma begs to differ.

Trauma did research on the man who was found with Parlay and learned that he has always been a paid hit man. Trauma clearly remembers Parlay telling him that he had someone on the job to murder the two old heads. Trauma feels that it's safe to assume that the man had to be who he was referring to. How they ended up getting murdered, he has yet to figure that out, but he's sure he will get to the bottom of it.

At this time he has given his squad the official S.O.S (Shoot on Sight) for the two old heads, wherever they are found.

Trauma rings Candy Kev's bell. Candy Kev peeks through the peek hole and as much as he hates to answer it, he does anyway. "Trauma, what up?" he asks timidly.

"Them old head niggas, you know. They just murdered my man," Trauma says with tear filled eyes.

"Yeah?"Candy Kev asks. Uh oh, he says to himself. He knows exactly what this means.

"Yeah! That's war! It all boils down to you telling me everything you know about them or I'm putting you on ice," he says sternly.

"I don't know shit about them. I was just getting dope from them."

"Well, I don't know what you gone do, but I'll be back in two days and you better have something for me or I'm letting the unit loose on you!" he shouts as he walks down the steps. "You hear me?" he asks while looking over his shoulder.

"Come on Trauma?" Candy Kev replies while nodding his head up and down. Damn, he sighs to himself. What the fuck have I gotten myself into? "I got you," he whispers.

Meanwhile in Asbury, New Jersey

Mu-Mit and Latif sit in Salaam's living room of his shabby little apartment, watching television. Today makes their second day down here. Latif was absolutely right. Salaam accepted the offer without a second thought. He added a clause in their agreement though. The only way he would agree was if they abided by his terms. His terms being; after they move the dope, they have to help him move in on the dudes that he's had his eyes on. They were forced to agree.

Salaam's phone rings. "Yello?" he answers. "Ah hah. Yeah, alright! Later!" he says before hanging up the phone. "That's my lil man, Divine. You know, from yesterday. He said they like it. He wants 30. I told you they buy anything down here."

Yesterday was a slow day for them. Salaam passed out a few samples here and there, but all they were actually able to sell was seven bricks. Today has been a little better though. First thing this morning, Salaam got a call for a 20 brick sell and now this call for 30. That's about 60 bricks down and 576 more to go.

"I didn't really plan to be down here penny pinching," Mu-Mit admits. "I was hoping to find one mufucker or two at the most to take all this shit off of our hands."

"Yeah, at this rate, we gone be down here for about two months."

"Don't worry ya'll," Salaam says. "It's slow money, but it's sure money. The real dough gone come when we start laying these pussies down," he says as his bad eye twitches. "It's all good! Help them get their money right. Stack it up and we gone come and take it all," he laughs satanically. "It's the American way!"

//// CHAPTER 84 ////

6:30 P.M in Union, New Jersey

Dre is at the office later than he's ever stayed. He stands at the window of his office, looking out into the parking lot. His undivided attention is on the Dodge Neon which is parked in the center of the parking lot. To the naked eye the car appears to be just an ordinary car. No one would ever suspect this car to be loaded with 8.5 pounds of uncut China White, heroin.

Dre made this order specifically for Imamu. The material cost Dre $180,000. In return, he made $300,000, which scored him a profit of $120,000.

Dre got the money from Imamu yesterday just to safeguard the deal. This is the first deal that he required the money up front. His decision was made for safety purposes only. Dre figures the less contact they have during the deal, the better. With him having a lack of trust for Imamu, he felt that this method would make him feel a little more at ease with the situation.

Dre's phone rings. He picks up on the first ring, but the caller hangs up on him. Dre knows that the caller is Imamu. He instructed Imamu to call him as he's entering the parking lot. His heart races as he stares at the Range Rover Sport which is creeping through the entrance. He watches closely to make sure that Imamu is alone as he promised he would be. Imamu stated that he had someone to pick the work up for him to eliminate any risk of him actually getting into trouble. Dre understands exactly what he means, but he declined. Dre told him the only way they have a deal is if he picks the dope up himself. Dre barely trusts him; let alone a third party.

Imamu pulls up and parks directly next to the Dodge Neon. He hops out casually and gets right into the car. After sitting for a few minutes, he gets out carrying a cardboard box in his hands. He dumps the box into his backseat before getting into his truck. Dre watches him pull out of the parking space. "Damn," he sighs. "I hope he is who he says he is?"

Meanwhile in Roselle, New Jersey

Cindy cruises along the quiet block. She reads the address from the paper that she holds on her lap and realizes that she's close to her destination. "Bingo!" she shouts as she approaches the house that matches the address.

She double-parks while peeking around in search of Dre's jeep, which she hopes to find out here. She thinks that this is where Dre may be living now since he's left her house. Her assumption is based on an address being matched to the phone number that she obtained from his phone bill. In her heart, she truly believes that he left her to be with the young girl that she had the phone confrontation with.

She looks up and down the block and she sees no sign of Dre's jeep. She's sure if he lives here, he should be home already. When they lived together, he was home after work everyday routinely at 5:15 and didn't move until the next morning. The car that is parked in the driveway of this particular house catches her attention. She starts to wonder if this car could possibly belong to the girl.

She picks up her cell phone and calls her good friend. "Hey Cindy?" the woman answers.

"What's up girl? You at work?"

"Not yet. I'm working the 7 to 3 shift tonight. I'll be there in a half hour."

"Good," Cindy says. "Do me a favor? I have a plate that I need you to check out for me." Cindy's friend is a police dispatcher. How convenient?

"Ok, what is it?"

Cindy stares at the plates and starts to read the numbers from it. "Sxc33t," she recites. "The make of the car is a white, four door Infiniti, G35. Let me know who that car is issued to, please?"

"No problem. Will do. I'll call you as soon as I get in."

"Please do," she says as she hangs the phone up. She smiles devilishly as she pulls off. Stupid motherfucker, she laughs to herself. Chasing behind that young ass bitch, she says to herself. She hopes and prays that this is her answer. "We gone see who get the last laugh," she smiles.

///// CHAPTER 85 /////

The young dope dealers stand huddled up on the abandoned porch as the customers swarm them in abundance. "911!" one boy shouts.

"Dirty Money!" another shouts.

"Training Day!" a boy shouts from the alley.

Many different stamps of dope are being sold from this stoop, but one reigns over all. "After Party, After Party!" the boy shouts with confidence. He already has a line of seven customers standing in front of him as is. Once the other customers hear that name, they switch their direction and step into the 'After Party' line.

'After Party' is having a tremendous effect on this block. Not only has it created major dope flow, but it has created a great deal of envy amongst the dealers as well. It's difficult to sell anything outside of 'After Party.' The smart thing for them to do would be to pool their money together and make 'After Party' the only dope sold out here. That way everyone would be able to eat. The only problem with that is not everyone can get their hands on it and the guys who can refuse to share the connect with the other dealers. Some may call it selfish, but others who know and respect the game, call it competition.

The tension has become thick out here over the past few days. There were always traces of 'After Party' out here. It was normally sold in inconsistent spurts. They would have it out here in the morning and sell out before the night came in. Or sometimes they would have it out here one day, but not the next day. The inconsistency made it possible for the other dealers to make a few dollars here and there in between the 'After Party' downtime. They've never had enough 'After Party' to make any real noise out here, but they've always had enough to keep the customers coming back with hope that there is some left. That was until a few short days ago. Then out of nowhere the dealers have been able to maintain a consistent supply of 'After Party.' This has increased the trafficking tremendously.

"After Party, After Party!" the young boy shouts arrogantly as the rest of the dealers look at him with extreme jealousy in their eyes.

Scccuuurrr! The Cherokee Sport stops short in the middle of the street, stealing everyone's attention. Everyone stops dead in their tracks. The passenger door flies wide open and a man with a white t-shirt tied around his face hops out aggressively. The weapon that he holds in his hand instills massive fear into everyone instantly. They assume that a robbery is about to go down. Everyone scatters into different directions.

The t-shirt bandit steps closer to the porch grasping the assault rifle with both hands. Deep down inside he fears the power of this gun. He closes his eyes and squeezes the trigger, not knowing what to expect. D, d,d,d,d,d,d,d,doom!" he fires as the gun sends a tingling vibration throughout his entire body. He opens his eyes only to see people scattering in every direction.

Boc, boc, boc! A man fires a few shots from the crowded porch. He isn't necessarily trying to hit anything. His only purpose is distracting the gunmen long enough for him to get out of the way. He hops off of the porch and takes off up the block full speed.

The gunman aims the rifle at him and fires. D,d,d,d,d,d,d,d,d,doom! Bullets soar in the air, in every direction except for the direction of the man who is fleeing the scene. The gunman spins the rifle around and aims at the porch once again. D,d,d,d,d,d,d,d,d,doom! The sound of glass shattering and holes being ripped into the aluminum siding on the houses sounds off loudly. "Aghhhhh," a few people scream simultaneously before tumbling over onto their faces. Some fall from being wounded while others fall over their own feet in a desperate attempt to get out of the way. The gunman fires again. Click! Click! His magazine is empty in a matter of seconds.

One man hears this and decides to take off. He runs across the street cutting right in front of the Cherokee. The gunman recognizes his face instantly. Damn, he says to himself, wishing he had more ammunition. The man runs straight for the alley. The driver of the Cherokee extends his gun gripping hand from the window. He aims as accurate as he can. He makes sure not to move a half an inch. He holds his breath knowing that can even make him lose his target. A red light shines on the back of the man's jacket. Boc, boc, boc! The impact of the bullet knocks the man off of his feet. He falls on his face but fear lifts him back onto his feet. He grabs hold of his back as he jogs lamely through the alley. Boc, boc, boc, boc! The driver fires rapidly, hitting nothing. The man has managed to get out of sight. "Come on!" he smiles.

The passenger hops in and the driver speeds off, leaving the hideous scene. The passenger unravels the t-shirt from his face. "You saw them mufuckers dropping?" ILL Wheel brags. He's breathing hard and fast from excitement.

"Did I?" Ahmir agrees. "Unck was right. This big, goofy ass gun will put everything down," he smiles as he speeds up the block.

"Yo, that pussy got away!"

"Who?" Ahmir asks.

"Shotgun. That was him that broke through the alley."

"He ain't get away. I put the beam on his ass!" Ahmir shouts. "I hit him, flipped his ass but he got back up and limped away. I still got my aim," he brags.

"He got away though!" ILL Wheel realizes that as long as Shotgun is alive, he's dangerous. "Damn! We gotta finish that nigga off."

///// CHAPTER 86 /////

In Miami

Tony just arrived here a few short minutes ago. He sits face to face with Miranda. She sits there with high hopes of hearing some good news come out of Tony's mouth.

"Miranda, I think I have something? I'm not sure if you're going to like what I'm about to say but hey, what the hell? I see this as the only way out. I spoke with the prosecutor and he's already gotten back to me. He's agreed to my proposal which means the ball is now in your court. You hold the key. Your future is in your hands now. You can either, get another shot at life or you can spend the rest of your life as a prisoner. It's a one shot deal. Here goes the ten million dollar question. Hear me out?"

Miranda sits there as nervous as can be. Tony's stalling is killing her. What could it be, she asks herself.

"So, are you ready?" he asks. "Do you want freedom or do you want to die here in Miami?"

"Mr. Austin, please? Just get on with it," she says hastily.

"Here it is…I've spoken with the prosecutor as I said before. He's willing to spare you and lessen your charge on one condition?"

"Which is?"

Tony hesitates before answering her. He assumes that he already knows how she will react when she hears this. He's definitely not expecting a good response from her. "Turn over the murderer. You gotta give him up."

"Snitch?" she asks with sarcasm. "All this time you've spent on the case? All the money that my father spent and snitching is the only answer you can come up with? I didn't need an attorney for that. I could have been done that. My public defender made that offer to me and he didn't cost anyone a dime!"

"Miranda, please? You have no option. It's either that or spend your life in prison. They have your back against the wall. You could dig Johnny Cochran out of the ground and not even he could get you out of this situation. The state of Florida refuses to let the case go without someone being convicted, bottom line." Miranda sits there with her lips puckered up, pouting like a little child. "It's just that simple. Trust me, I'm against snitching, but in this case it's different. Look at it. You're willing to do life for a scum bag that left you on the front line all alone. What type of man would allow his woman to do life for a crime that he committed? Huh?" he asks hastily. "Answer me, damnit! What kind of man would do that? Do you honestly think he loved you? Let me answer that for you. Hell no! He didn't give two fucks about you or you wouldn't be in this situation. If he truly loved you, not only would he not let you do time for him, he would have never put you in a situation like this from the start. He didn't love you nor did he respect you. Miranda, he used you. He probably never loved you. You may have easily been a jump-off to him."

She believes all his prior statements may have some validity except the last one. She knows that she was never his jump-off and back in the day she would have defended herself, but today she feels she has no room to do so. After spending these years in jail, she sometimes wonders was she his jump-off.

"You were nothing but a pretty fool to him." Tony realizes that he's pouring it on extra thick. He's showing no compassion for her feelings. It's all a part of his trap. He has to break her down in order to get her to give in. He realizes how stubborn she is so he knows that he has his work cut out for him. He can tell that he's getting through to her by the water that is building up in her eyes. She's getting weak, he thinks to himself. Now it's time to go in for the kill. "How could you be so foolish? I understand your morals, your loyalty and your code of honor. I think you're hiding behind some bullshit! You may think you're playing by the rules, right? That's cool when you're dealing with people who play by the same rules. Miranda, you can't be loyal to someone who doesn't know what loyalty is. Do you think he displayed loyalty to you in this situation?"

She shakes her head from side to side as tears pour from her eyes.

Round 2, he thinks to himself. Last round he attacked her brutally. This round he plans on boxing her strategically. That is unless she counters. Ding, ding, he sounds the bell off in his mind. "Miranda, your life is over. You're not even 30 years old. You've never been married. You've never given birth and you never will in here. There's so much out there for you, but you'll never know. You know why? Because of your foolish pride. The reality is you are going to die here. I've talked the prosecutor into putting you into a witness protection program far away from here. You can go anywhere in this world and use that beauty to your advantage. There are modeling agencies all over the world. I'll help you set your career up, if you need me to."

Miranda listens attentively. Everything sounds so good and simple except the main factor. There is no one to tell on. Sha-Rock is dead. She weeps harder at the thought of that.

"Miranda, you have another shot at life. Take it! All you have to do is give him up."

"I can't," she cries.

"Why, Miranda?"

"He's dead," she whispers.

Tony's stare melts her down completely. She now cries loud and hard with no shame or pride. He realizes that his silence is making her cry even harder, yet and still he does it purposely. "I know," he whispers as he peeks around cautiously.

This catches Miranda by total surprise. He knows. How? "Huh?"

"I said, I know. I've done my homework. You wouldn't help me so I had to go behind your back. Your father told me everything that he knew about him. I then hired a private investigator to track him down. It was then that I found out that he had been murdered."

Miranda begins to get uneasy. She wonders how much he really knows. She's so uncomfortable now that she can't even look him in the eyes. She keeps her eyes on the table to avoid looking at him.

"I know he's dead. You know he's dead. But they don't know he's dead. They'll never be able to prove that we knew. You never told me his name and I'll swear to that on a stack of a hundred Bibles. That's the God's honest truth. You were incarcerated in Miami, hundreds of miles away. You have no contact on the outside. You've never had a visit from anyone. How could you possibly know? Don't answer that question, although I would love to know how you knew this," he smiles. "I thought I had one up on you. I actually thought I was bringing you some news." He stops smiling. "Let's play it all the way out? Sign the papers for the witness protection program. Give them his name and you've done your part. You don't know his whereabouts. You give them his last address and from there it's their job to bring him into custody. During trial you get on the stand and tell them how he forced you into this situation. You tell them how much of a maniac he is. Present tense," he adds. "Miranda, you can do it. You're an actress remember? I saw you on 'The Wire.' Tell them how afraid you are and that's why you took so long to cooperate. Tell them you'd rather die in prison than to live in fear of being killed by him. Then you beg them to send you far away from here. Dress it up real nice. What are they going to do? Dig his body up so he can defend himself? Scum bag," he says with no compassion for the dead. "He's not here. Whatever you say he did, he did it. Technically, you're not snitching. Nothing that you can say will change his situation. His shit is over. Give the dead man up. You in or are you out?"

///// CHAPTER 87 /////

Two Days Later

Mu-Mit and Latif sit at the end of the coffee table counting stacks of money. Both of them have mounds of money sitting in front of them. Mu-Mit finishes counting first. He lays back in the recliner, while stretching his cramped fingers. He waits patiently for Latif to finish.

Latif slaps the last stack onto the coffee table. "Done," he whispers.

"What you come up with?" Mu-Mit asks.

"$23,000," Latif replies. "What about you?"

"$27,600," Mu-Mit replies.

Salaam stares at the money like a greedy dog. It's been quite some time since he's seen this amount of money up close. That is if he's ever seen this amount. Mu-Mit catches him staring and turns quickly facing him. "Not a bad day," he says. "How many we move today?"

"230," Mu-Mit replies.

"See, I told ya'll," he brags. "It ain't gone take that long. Man, today was a damn good day," he says already calculating his profit.

"It most definitely was a good day. Three individual sales made up the 230 bricks that were moved. Only one kid was a repeat buyer and that's the kid that copped the 30 bricks two days back to back. Today he bought another 30. Another buyer bought 80 and the last and final buyer purchased 150 bricks. Yesterday was not a bad day either. They moved a total of 80 bricks yesterday morning before 11a.m., but didn't sell one single brick thereafter for the rest of the day.

These past three days have been the best three days of Salaam's life. They give him a profit of $10.00 off of every brick they move. They lied to him, saying that they're getting the dope from their connect for $190.00 a brick. To make him feel appreciated they told him that they're splitting $30.00 into three ways. They couldn't tell him the truth that all the dope they have is profit because they didn't pay a dime for it. He's happy anyway. He's never imagined making this much money for doing absolutely nothing at all. The first day he couldn't believe he actually made a profit of $570.00. Just when he thought it couldn't get any better it did when Mu-Mit handed him $800.00 on the second day.

"La, give me three of those stacks you got over there," Mu-Mit says. Latif pushes the three piles closer to Mu-Mit. "Jake, here," Mu-Mit says as he gives Salaam two stacks and three hundred dollar bills. Mu-Mit shoves another $2,300.00 to Latif as a front. "La, this yours," he says as he dumps the rest of the money into a waste basket bag. "Shit," he sighs. "And this the connect money," he lies to throw Salaam off.

Salaam's mouth waters just looking at the money. Just to think last week this time he was damn near starving. He's been penniless for months. Had it not been for his girlfriend, he would have been living on the streets. He's fallen in love with the dope game. Now he sees why they tried so hard to persuade him into all of this. "I have to admit, I finally see the big picture," he says. "I mean, I always knew mufuckers get rich off that shit. I just didn't know a dumb fuck like me could get rich," he smiles.

"I tried to tell you," Latif interrupts. "The dope game a mufucker. Mufuckers could say what they want, but the dope game gives a mufucker hope. It's the only game that I know of that you could be dead broke today and filthy rich tomorrow. But you gotta be in it to win it!" Latif shouts.

"How many more we got left?" Salaam asks trying to figure out how much more money he can expect.

"About two hundred and sixty something bricks," he replies.

Salaam quickly multiplies the number of bricks by 10, which comes to a little short of $3,000.00 for himself. He does the multiplication in record breaking time and comes up with the answer. It's funny. Here you have a dude who was always at the bottom of his class in math, but right now he can add, subtract, multiply or divide any number without a calculator, or pen and paper. "Yo, when all this is said and done, nigga take me to the Caddy dealer," he laughs. "I been on these bad feet of mine for way too motherfucking long!"

As Mu-Mit is stacking his money into a plastic bag, his phone rings. He looks at the display. It's Candy Kev. "As Salaamu Alaikum, Believer! What's going on with you?"

"Wa Alaikum As Salaam," he whispers. "Same shit," he adds. "I was just calling you to let you know that I'm back in town. I'm on your clock now. How long will it take you to get to me?"

"Aw man, I'm O.T. right now. I should be back your way in about figure, two days," he says as he estimates the time that he thinks it will take to finish up down here.

"Two days," he repeats. "That's the soonest that you can get here?"

"Yeah, I'm afraid so."

"Well, I guess, I have to wait, huh? Just hit me when you touch. I'm here!"

"Definitely," Mu-Mit replies. As Salaamu Alaikum!"

"Wa Alaikum As Salaam," he whispers.

Back In Union, N.J.

Candy Kev hangs up the phone slowly. He attempts to move his head to the right, but the nine millimeter on his right temple makes it hard to do so. "He said he's out of town and he'll be back in two days," he whispers.

"Ok, two days it is," Trauma says from the front passenger's seat. "Don't go disappearing nowhere. We need you. Go on and get out of here," Trauma demands.

Candy Kev gets out with no hesitation. He closes the door and makes his way toward his porch. Shit, he sighs to himself. I gotta get myself outtta this situation.

///// CHAPTER 88 /////

The Oldsmobile sits parked on the quiet block. Loud music rips through the speakers. The smell of marijuana and 151 fills the air. Four young men sit quietly as they sip and smoke the minutes away. On the floor of the passenger's side sits a brown paper bag that has three more bottles of 151, better known as murder juice. They also have multi bags of weed. That's more than enough to keep their minds occupied for quite a while.

Sitting directly across the street there is an old Buick Century. Inside of the vehicle there are four more young men who are doing the very exact same thing, just sipping and smoking away. Only difference being their smoke of choice is not just plain marijuana and their beverage of choice is not 151. The marijuana dipped in PCP, 'Wet' and the drinking of codeine syrup 'Lean' can only end in one thing and that's murder. To take them to the next level, they've added another drug to their diet. The Zanex sticks which happens to be a downer as well, makes them lean and nod more than the codeine syrup. The codeine syrup along with the Zanex sticks is nicknamed 'Pancakes and Syrup.' This combination leaves them walking around like zombies.

Between the men in both cars they have enough ammunition to fight off a police force. The weapons range from Desert Eagles to Nine Millimeters to .40 calibers to Macs. In total they have over 400 rounds. As said before, enough ammo to fight off a police force, but that isn't the purpose. Their purpose in being here is to get ILL Wheel. They've been waiting for him to come home for hours now and they have no plans on leaving until they get him.

The men are nodding their heads up and down slowly, totally off the beat of the loud music. The PCP has stolen their rhythm, leaving them like zombies. The driver lowers the volume. "I can't believe that little bitch boy!" Shotgun shouts. "He always been a dud! Motherfucker actually had the nerve to come at me. Me!" he repeats. "I know that fag ass nigga don't think he gone shoot me and live to talk about it. I know he gone wish he murdered me," he says as he slowly shifts his body to the side with massive discomfort. The shot to his back was a mere flesh wound. The bullet went in his back and out of his shoulder without hitting anything vital. "Sss, agghh," he sighs as he changes his seating position. The longer he sits in one place, the more agitated the wound gets. "That nigga gone pay for that shit! I'm putting his ass on ice. He gotta come home sooner or later. We ain't going nowhere!"

They may as well roll some more blunts and pour another round because this can take a while. True indeed ILL Wheel has to come home sooner or later. Unfortunately for them this is no longer his home. The day after the home invasion, ILL Wheel packed his belongings into storage and they've been staying at hotels ever since.

///// CHAPTER 89 /////

Dre sits alone at the small table at Ruby Tuesday's on Route 22. His purpose for being here is not only for lunch, but he's here to meet the 'After Party' connect as well. He's made a very special order of 7 kilos.

The order is for Imamu. Imamu breezed through the work in record breaking time. Yesterday he came to the office and dropped a whopping $525,000 onto Dre. At $30,000 profit per kilo, Dre will score $210,000. Just to think, Dre almost passed up a great opportunity. He still feels uneasy with dealing with Imamu but the reward somewhat blinds him. He just hopes and prays that Imamu is on the up and up because if he isn't, he knows exactly what the consequences will be.

"Yes, can I have a Chicken Caesar Salad, and a Coke with lemon, please?" he orders as he sits there waiting the connects arrival.

Meanwhile in Asbury

"Slow down, right here," Salaam instructs Mu-Mit. "That house, right there to the left. That's a gold mine, right there," he barks. "One of the biggest niggas in this town. A boy who go by the name Everlasting, that's one of his stash houses, right there. This gone be the easiest sting in the world. The mufucker who spot this is, he ain't nothing but a working class kid. He innocent. The only thing he guilty of is holding the key to our happiness. This gone be like taking candy from a baby. Imagine the biggest bank in the world being guarded by a security guard without a gun?"

"That easy?" Latif asks. "It can't be. Then why would the boy trust everything here?"

"Because he thinks no one knows."

"How do you know?" Mu-Mit asks.

"Easy...my little stepdaughter used to hang out with the young kid. She never talked to me about the situation, but she told her momma a few things that caught my attention. I was ready to ease my way in through her without her even knowing it, but I said nah. That would have been fucked up. I didn't want anything to lead back to her, understand?"

"Definitely," Mu-Mit replies. "What you think this one worth?"

"Aw man, ain't no telling, Bruh. A great deal of the paper that floats through this town ends up in his hands. He got the yay (coke) game on lock!"

"Oh yeah?" Latif interrupts.

"Yeah," Salaam whispers. "Go ahead. Make a right at the corner."

Mu-Mit cruises along the block and does exactly what Salaam said to do. Both Mu-Mit and Latif sit there with the same thing on their mind. They wonder how much they can score from this. What Salaam calls money may not even be worth it to them. They can only hope that the vick is equal or of more value than what they already have going. Until now, neither of them were considering moving out like this although they agreed that they would. They were hoping that he would see how much money there is to be made in the dope game and maybe he would forget all about the robberies that he wanted to commit. They see a bright future ahead of them here in Asbury. Just as Salaam told them, there is major money to be made here. Yesterday they breezed through another 120 bricks and they've already sold 50 today. At this time they are only left with 94 bricks, which they're hoping to sell before the day is over with.

This is the best week they've ever had since they've been in the dope game. They both realize how much of a goldmine they've landed on. They have taken into consideration the fact that they managed to move close to 700 bricks of mediocre dope. They can't imagine how much 'After Party' they can sell down here, but they're sure to find out. There is less than a day's work of dope left which means it's time for them to re-up. Now they're about to slide their dope in. Only one problem though; they have to handle their end of the agreement in order to move on.

Both Latif and Mu-Mit have been stick-up kids all of their lives. The dope game is totally new to them. Now that they have had a taste of this life, they're both hooked. They could never see themselves having the patience to actually network and build a team to move product. Now that they have had a slight bit of success with it, neither of them actually have the drive or motivation to go back to their old hustle. At this point they're ready to get this on and over with just so they can get back to moving their dope.

"Slow down, right here," Salaam says. "See the yellow house, right there?" he asks as he points to his right. "That's another goldmine! A boy by the name of Born Wisdom. This is his spot. We gone hit the jackpot in here, too. It's gone be simple in and out."

"Young boy?" Mu-Mit asks.

"Ah, mid thirties. He riding around here in a brand new Mercedes and a Range Rover. His wife got a Mercedes too. The boy loaded! He straight pussy though. The fag ass nigga won't lick a stamp. Ain't gone kill nothing and ain't gone let nothing die. I got it all mapped out. All you gotta do is say the word and we in there like swimwear," he sings.

Latif and Mu-Mit both know this is the only way he's going to let them do their thing in peace. Therefore, they have to get this out of the way for him first.

"What up?" Salaam asks.

"Let's make it happen," Mu-Mit whispers. He looks over at Latif and the nodding of his head reassures him that he's ready as well.

"That's all you had to say. Tonight's the night!"

Back in Union

Dre sits at the table as confusion fills his mind. It's been almost two hours and the connect still hasn't arrived. He's starting to feel paranoid like people are watching him. He's been at the table way too long. He's had appetizers, his lunch and dessert and still no sign of the connect. He hands the check along with the money to the waitress, while dialing the connect's number for the twentieth time. He has yet to get an answer from them. This is very unlike them. The phone rings for the tenth time before the generic answering service comes on. He hangs the phone up. Confusion covers his face. He wonders what has happened. Did they get knocked off on their way here to me, he asks himself. That is the only answer he can come up with. A part of him wants to leave, but he's not sure if he should. Maybe they got caught up in traffic, he wonders. If he leaves, they will get here and he'll be gone. Dre realizes that a few lousy minutes can cost a man his freedom. Maybe, I should wait another half hour, he debates with himself. Nah, if they come, they'll call me.

He gets up and walks out of the restaurant. Before stepping out, he peeks around cautiously to make sure the coast is clear. He walks slowly to his truck. He walks right past the truck while peeking around. He's not sure if he should get in just yet. Maybe the people are somewhere around waiting for him to get in the truck. The cash that sits inside his truck is more than enough evidence needed to drag him into a situation.

He walks around the parking lot as casual as he can. He watches his surroundings closely. Once he gets into the truck, he hops in and zips out of the lot. As he cruises along Route 22, his mind races with all kinds of thoughts and none of them are good. What could have happened to the connect? He has not a clue.

///// CHAPTER 90 /////

Later that Night

Latif presses the doorbell and impatiently awaits an answer, while standing on the dark porch. Salaam and Mu-Mit stand on opposite sides of the doorway. Both of their faces are covered by ski masks.

Latif's heart beat speeds up, when he hears footsteps approaching from behind the door. He gives them a head nod to let them know that someone is coming. Finally the moment of truth has arrived. The door swings open slightly. The man stands there with a puzzled look on his face.

"Hey, Tanya here?" Latif asks.

"Who?" the man asks while looking even more perplexed.

"Tanya? I think this the house."

"Tanya? I don't think," he manages to utter from his lips before he's snatched out of the doorway by his collar. He stumbles forward. Mu-Mit swings his gun high and then mashes it into the center of the boy's forehead. The man wobbles dizzily. Mu-Mit pushes him inside while Salaam and Latif follow close behind. Once inside the hallway, both of them draw their guns. Latif quickly pulls his mask out of his pocket and pulls it snug over his face.

Mu-Mit yanks the man by his collar with one hand while he holds his gun to the back of the man's head with his other hand. Mu-Mit's grip is so tight on the man's collar that he's cutting off the man's circulation of air. Mu-Mit lifts him slightly in the air, causing the man to walk on his toes. "Nice and easy. You hear me?" he whispers in the man's ear, with his lips almost glued to the man's earlobes. "Who here with you?"

They have been sitting parked out here for hours just watching the house. They were here watching when the man got in from work. Salaam wanted to follow him in then but Mu-Mit refused because it wasn't quite dark enough at the time. No one has come neither in nor out of the house while they were sitting out here. The only way that someone is here with him is if they were already inside when he got there.

"Nobody, nobody," he mumbles nervously. This has caught him totally off guard. Never in a million years did he ever expect something like this to happen.

Latif pulls a roll of duct tape from his pocket and snatches a piece from the roll as he's catching up with Mu-Mit. He quickly smacks a slab of the tape over the young man's mouth.

Latif and Salaam enter the apartment first, with their guns waving. As soon as they're inside they cautiously breeze through the small apartment room by room checking for anyone who may be inside.

Mu-Mit slams the man onto the living room floor furiously. He rolls the man over onto his stomach, while pressing the gun against the back of his head. He mashes his knee onto the center of the man's back just to keep him pinned to the floor. Latif runs back into the room. He tosses the rope to Mu-Mit who unravels it and begins the process by first wrapping it tightly around the man's left wrist. The rope is so tight that it's cutting through his skin. He then snatches his right arm, abusively, damn near ripping it out of the socket as he's tying both hands together behind his back. Mu-Mit stands up and snatches the man onto his feet using the rope.

"Aghh," he whines.

"Listen, I'm only going to ask you this one time and one time only," he informs. "Take me to the work," he whispers harshly. The man starts to walk toward the closet without hesitation. Salaam and Latif watch with anticipation.

When the man gets to his closet he stops and gives Mu-Mit a head nod signaling to him that this is the location. Mu-Mit then gives his cohorts a head nod. They snatch the door open and their eyes are greeted by a huge walk in closet which is as neat as can be inside. Mu-Mit forces the man into the closet. Where is it?" he whispers. The man steps halfway through the closet and stops. He lifts his head up, nodding toward the top shelf. Latif and Salaam are busy ransacking the closet doing their own search. "Right here, right here, somebody," Mu-Mit says while pointing in the direction.

Salaam's thieving eye quickly locates two sneaker boxes standing on top of each other. He anxiously grabs them and snatches them open one by one. "Yep," he mumbles. "Got it!" He extends the open boxes toward Mu-Mit for his approval. Mu-Mit digs inside and finds two kilos of cocaine lying in each box.

"Where the rest at?" Mu-Mit barks scaring the life out of the man. He tightens up his grip on the boy's scrawny neck. The man struggles to shake his head from side to side. His eyes show fear and sincerity. "Don't waste my fucking time," Mu-Mit whispers while grinding his top and bottom teeth together. "Don't let me look through this apartment and find more. Don't make me do it," he threatens with rage in his eyes. The boy continuously shakes his head from side to side negatively as the tears pour from his eyes. Mu-Mit looks over to Latif. "Here get him. Let me look around the joint."

Mu-Mit nor Latif were really up to this at first, but once they got here they got into a zone. Mu-Mit doesn't know the going rate for cocaine right now, but he does imagine they have at least $100,000 more to divide up now. Seeing the four kilos of coke makes them think there can be more somewhere in here and if it is, he's sure he can find it. Latif grabs hold of the man by snatching him by the rope. Mu-Mit and Salaam search throughout the apartment like detectives.

Minutes later they all stand in the bedroom, while the man lays there face down on the floor. "Let's go!" Mu-Mit shouts.

Salaam takes off toward the door first. Mu-Mit makes it there in second place. As Mu-Mit is about to exit the apartment, he realizes that he doesn't feel Latif behind him. He turns around quickly, only to see Latif drawing his gun. He stands over the man as he aims the cannon at the man's head.

"Yo!" Mu-Mit shouts. Latif turns around quickly at the sound of Mu-Mit's voice. Mu-Mit shakes his head from side to side. "Nah!" Latif stands there in confusion, while Mu-Mit continuously shakes his head negatively. "Let's go!" Latif still hasn't moved a muscle. "It's over!"

Latif finally starts to step toward Mu-Mit. Salaam has already approached the door. "Let me pop his top?" Latif begs.

"Nah, let's go," Mu-Mit replies still shaking his head negatively. "The young boy innocent."

Seconds later, they all exit the apartment leaving the young man happy to be alive. They walk casually to their car. They hop in and pull off nonchalantly, drawing no attention to themselves.

"Didn't I tell ya'll, it was gone be easy?" Salaam shouts with joy. "Like taking candy from a baby! One down and many more to go. We gone drain this town dry!"

///// CHAPTER 91 /////

2:20 A.M.

Ahmir sits parked on Tremont Avenue in East Orange. From where he's parked he can see the entrance of the Tremont Lounge clearly. ILL Wheel informed Ahmir that this is Shotgun and his crew's Friday night hangout. They can be found in here every Friday night faithfully.

Ahmir sits in the driver's seat of the stolen Cherokee. The passenger's seat is empty. You may ask where is ILL Wheel? Three car lengths in front of the Cherokee there sits the Buick Century. Sitting on the curb in between the Century and a Maxima there sits ILL Wheel.

The bar is a few minutes away from closing, which means any minute now someone will be heading out to the car to retrieve the guns. ILL Wheel hasn't hung out with Shotgun and his crew on a regular basis, but he has been out with them enough times to see how they operate.

At the closing of the bar, Shotgun sends one of his flunkies out to get the guns, so that when him and the rest of his crew exit, they won't step out naked and blind. They start so much trouble when in the bars and clubs that they're sure people are dying to get even with them. That is why they're always prepared.

ILL Wheel watches the door and sees a few people stepping out in spurts, which lets him know that show time is near. His heart races at the very thought of what is about to take place.

Finally, he spots a familiar face. Damn, he sighs to himself as the individual gets closer. The fact of who it is almost makes him want to stop the attack. He really doesn't want to go through with it. "Shit," he sighs as the individual gets closer. ILL Wheel grips his gun tightly even though his heart is telling him not to go through with it.

Fuck it, he says to himself. He thinks of the situation they put him in. He didn't start this beef. They initiated it, he tells himself in order to make himself go through with it. As the individual steps within two feet of the car, the alarm sounds off and the lights illuminate the area. ILL Wheel's eyes brighten up like a deer does when they are greeted by headlights on a highway. Instead of freezing up as they do, he stands to his feet. As much as he hates to do this, he has no choice because the spotlight is already on him. He charges his prey like a raging bull.

The individual backs up with total fear. Boc! ILL Wheel fires at the individual's head, realizing that his face has already been seen, which means this individual can always testify against him. The individual falls backwards onto the ground and ILL Wheel fires three more shots. Boc! Boc! Boc! He doesn't miss a shot.

He quickly takes off into flight toward the Cherokee, where Ahmir sits watching the entire act as it plays like a movie. The lifeless girl lays there as stiff as a board.

ILL Wheel hops into the jeep. His face shows sympathy. Ahmir looks around only to see crowds of people swarming the front door trying to see where the shots have come from. He makes a quick U-turn and speeds up the block in the opposite direction.

"Damn!" ILL Wheel shouts. "Why the fuck they had to send her out?" he asks sadly. As much as he hated to do it, he had no other choice. If it were the other way around, she would have done the same thing.

The girl he just murdered goes by the name of Charlie Baltimore. Her red hair and her skin tone makes her resemble 'Charlie Baltimore' the rapper, which is why her peers have given her that nickname. To the naked eye she may appear a pretty, petite, innocent and sweet piece of red-bone eye candy. In reality ILL Wheels knows that her beauty is a decoy. She and her crew use her look of innocence to blind ignorant guys who don't know her. Shotgun and his crew have used her to reel in bait on more than enough occasions. She's also known to bust her own gun as well.

"I don't believe this shit! I just shot a bitch! Why the fuck they had to send her out there?"

"Who is she?" Ahmir asks.

"Charlie Baltimore."

"Who is she? One of their bitches?" Ahmir asks as he's driving along Central Avenue. He peeks through his mirrors consistently, to make sure that police are nowhere near them.

"Nah, she Dog," ILL Wheel replies.

"Oh, fuck her then!" Ahmir shouts with no compassion. His eyes are stretched wide open. "That's what it is then! If she a bitch and she banging, then she can get it too!"

Ahmir makes the right turn onto Ninth Avenue. Midway through the block, he pulls over and parks. They peek around cautiously before hopping out. They run across the street to the Audi station wagon that sits parked there. ILL Wheel stashed the car here a couple of hours ago, so they would have another vehicle to move around in after the episode.

ILL Wheel hops into the driver's seat and Ahmir gets into the passenger's seat. ILL Wheel pulls off, leaving the jeep deserted. As he's cruising along Ninth Avenue his mind is going in many directions. At this point he's sure that he's just declared war. He doesn't exactly know what the outcome will be, but he does know things can get hectic. Shotgun loves that girl like a sister. In fact, they all have special feelings for her. ILL Wheel can't imagine what type of feelings this will spark for them. He's actually touched something they all love. This may have been one of the worse mistakes that he could have ever made. It's way too late now. Ain't no turning back.

///// CHAPTER 92 /////

Saturday Morning 9 A.M.

A greatly disappointed Dre steps out of his office. Tony just called him into his office. Dre is more confused now than he was the other day. Not only has the connect not answered or returned his calls, but the number is now out of service. Dre assumes the worse has happened. He's almost sure that they've been knocked off. This is the only answer that he can come up with for them not to return his calls. He's getting nervous now because his own supply is getting low as well. Not knowing the situation is driving him crazy.

Dre approaches Tony's office door. Tony told him that he has a call waiting for him. Dre is sure that is Imamu trying to get in touch with him. Dre steps through the door and Tony hands him the phone.

In Yazoo, Mississippi

The Mayor lays back on his bed peeking around cautiously as he holds the cell phone close to his ear.

"Hello?" Dre says slowly.

"Yo? What up?" the Mayor asks.

Dre is shocked to hear his brother's voice in the place of Imamu's. His heart starts to beat fast and hard instantly. Just hearing his brother's voice makes him nervous. He hates to think that his brother's phone may be tapped. He doesn't want them to be linked together by anything, but their blood relationship, which is why they have agreed to always communicate through a third party. "What up?" Dre asks.

"Shit," the Mayor mumbles. "How about you? You alright?"

"Yeah," Dre replies with a slight bit of sarcasm in his voice.

"You sure?"

"Positive," Dre replies.

"You sure everything good?"

"Yeah," Dre replies with agitation in his voice. "Why wouldn't it be?" Oh, Dre thinks to himself. He realizes that maybe his brother knows something. "What's the deal though? How is life treating you?"

"Ah, life is good! You don't sound too happy to hear from me though. Why? You ain't heard from me in a couple of days, right?"

Dre quickly realizes where his brother is going with this conversation. He's talking in code, referring to the connect. "Nah, you haven't called. I didn't know what was going on with you. I was getting worried. It ain't like you not to call."

"Nah, I'm good. I just didn't like your last conversation. I know you my big brother and all, but you have to watch how you talk to people. I know you don't mean no harm, but to another person things may sound quite intimidating. Especially when you been talking one way then out of the blue you just switch up like that. That could hurt people's feelings and they don't know if they can trust you."

Trust me, Dre thinks to himself. Oh, I think I got it.

"You will have people scared to be around you. You always had a way of lashing out with your tongue, feel me?"

"Yeah, I feel you," Dre replies. "I try to be mindful, but sometimes I can't control my temper. Shit just be happening. It's not always my fault. Mufuckers be coming at me with all types of shit. What I'm supposed to do…back down?"

"Nah, I feel you. You know lately it seems like you got two sides to you. You be talking one way, then out of nowhere you just up and switch the conversation. A mufucker might think you crazy and stop fucking with you all together. Especially how loud you be talking."

Dre has it all figured out. The connect is scared to deal with him because out of nowhere he's started ordering kilos of heroin now. They're accustomed to him buying the kilos and letting them do the chemistry for him. He assumes that they're not sure if he's setting them up. Dre breaks down his brother's last statement. How loud he talks has to mean the quantity he asked for. He does realize that asking for four kilos and then seven more in a matter of days on top of his normal order, can be quite alarming for anyone. "Listen, mufuckers gone have to get used to the tone of my voice!" Dre shouts as if he's furious. "I'm gone talk louder and louder until I get my point across!" he shouts blasting the volume of his voice. "Feel me? What I'm supposed to do, sit there quietly like a church mouse? Huh? I'm good! Don't worry about me!"

"I ain't worried. I'm just saying people can get the wrong idea. Later for that though. What's up with my niece? I ain't seen her in a minute. I know she growing up fast," he chuckles. "I would love to see her. Tell her to come see me next visit."

The Mayor doesn't even have a niece. Dre realizes that his brother has switched the topic and is now referring to their messenger. "Yeah, she thinks she's grown. I need you to try and talk some sense into her head. She's driving me crazy. I'll tell her that you want her to come and check you out. I'm on my way back to work. Your boy, Tony is standing here cracking the whip," he smiles. "He's working the kid like a slave. Later Lil Bruh. Love you!"

"Love you too," the Mayor mumbles.

Tony stands there in complete confusion. He has no clue what the entire conversation was about. He chalks it up as a big brother, little brother spat.

Thirty Minutes Later

Dre's phone rings while he's sitting at his desk. An unfamiliar number pops up on the display. "Hello?"

The connect's voice rips through the phone, putting a smile on Dre's face. The voice sounds like music to Dre's ears. It was just as he figured. They contacted his brother just to make sure everything is on the up and up. He understands them totally. Safety is priority. He also believes that they wanted to make sure that the Mayor is well aware of what unsuspected moves Dre has been making. Dre loves and respects the loyalty that they show his brother. He wonders how they developed such a tight bond. He assumes the Mayor must have made them billions before he went in because in the short period that he's been in the picture, he's sure that he's already made them a few millions. Still, they will go over his head, treating him like he's a peon.

"Ok, tomorrow," he says with a smile. "Yep, same place," he says before hanging up the phone. "Once again it's on," he sings with a cheesy grin on his face. "Mo money, mo money, mo money."

///// CHAPTER 93 /////

The Bookkeeper drives Ahmir's Jaguar, while he rides in the passenger's seat. Frustration covers the Bookkeeper's face as he's talking to Ahmir. "I knew this shit was going to happen. That is the reason why I didn't want to come up in the first place. It's not for me. I don't give two shits about this place. The only thing that this town does for me is bring back bad memories," he claims. "I knew you couldn't handle it. This town will suck you dry. It's a trap. I know so many people that have moved far away from here to better themselves. They go out to west bubble fuck and really make something of themselves. For some strange reason everybody ends up coming back. I can't understand it. Not me, I ain't never coming back to this shit!" he says with certainty. "Look at it. You said we were coming here for no more than three days. It's been way more than three days already. I knew you was bullshitting when you told me that."

"I wasn't bullshitting you," Ahmir replies. "This shit just taking longer than I thought. My man here alone. I can't leave him like that."

"Don't leave him like that. Take him with you. Young Cash, this ain't yo life no more. Get it through your head. Busting guns, gang banging, and drug dealing…that ain't you no more."

"Bookkeeper," Ahmir says, as he's about to start his defense, but he's interrupted.

"Rasheed," he corrects him. Ever since he's gotten his act together, he refuses to let Ahmir call him Bookkeeper. He constantly tells him that the Bookkeeper was a drug addict, con man and he wishes to close that chapter of his life.

"My bad…Rasheed, true indeed, that ain't my life no more, but I'm still the same dude. The only thing that has changed about me is my eating habits. You know how the saying goes, you can take the nigga out the ghetto, but you can't take the ghetto out of the nigga."

"Young Cash, take a step back and look at your life. How much would you say you make about a day, down at the spot? About $10,000?"

"$10,000?" Ahmir replies sarcastically. He smiles arrogantly. "We make $10,000 during breakfast and another $20,000 the rest of the day."

"Ok, you're making $30,000 a day legal bread. You ain't got the law or the stick up man on your back. As long as ya'll pay the taxes you good. That's a great situation. You got the condo on the harbor. Got you a brand new Jag and the SS Chevy pick-up truck, right? You got yourself a good clean girl who happens to be 6 months pregnant with your baby. You got a lot going for you, right? Now will be the perfect time for you to go to jail for the rest of your life," he says with sarcasm.

"Yo man, don't jinx me like that!"

"Me jinx you? I ain't jinxing you. You jinxing yourself. You the one ready to put all you got on the line, not me," he says with a smile. "Yeah, I know how the saying goes, but you take that same nigga out the ghetto and put him in prison for the rest of his life and I guarantee you he wishes he could do it all over again. I bet you he would do it all differently!"

Ahmir drops his arrogant defense mechanism long enough to hear the Bookkeeper out. Everything that he's said makes all the sense in the world just as it always does. "I feel you," he admits. "I just can't leave them like this. They need me. I can't turn my back on them. They never left me alone to defend myself and I can't do it to them. Let me just clear the air and I'm out. I promise."

The Bookkeeper stops at the corner of Fifth Street, a few feet away from the highway. He hits the button for his flashers to start flashing. Ahmir digs into his pocket, retrieving a small stack of 100 dollar bills. He peels off two of them and passes them over to the Bookkeeper. "Here."

"What's that for?"

"Gas and toll."

The Book Keeper smiles. "I'm good. I got gas and toll money."

Ahmir opens the door and slides out of the vehicle. "Just a couple more days and I'll be there. I'll catch a flight, train, or something. That's my word!" he says as he slams the door.

"I hear you," the Bookkeeper says while looking in the mirror, rubbing his hands over his thick and wavy hair.

Ahmir starts walking away from the vehicle in the direction of the rented Dodge Magnum that is directly behind them. ILL Wheel has followed him here to see the Bookkeeper off to Baltimore.

"Young Cash!" he calls.

Ahmir stops in his tracks at the sound of his voice. "Huh?" he asks kneeling down in order to see the Bookkeeper's face.

"Just in case you never make it back to Baltimore is there anything in particular you want me to tell your lady? What would you like me to tell your child in the event that he or she never gets to meet you?"

Hearing that breaks Ahmir's heart. Low blow, he thinks to himself. He knows the Bookkeeper said that with the intentions of making him think of the worse case scenario. Tears damn near fall from his eyes at the thought of his child growing up without a father. He knows how rough it was for him and his brother and wouldn't wish that situation on anyone. He turns around quickly to avoid from letting the Bookkeeper see him shed a tear. As he's walking away, he hears the sound of his tires squealing, as they grip the pavement. He looks over his shoulder and watches the Bookkeeper speed off into the distance. Hopefully this won't be their last time together.

///// CHAPTER 94 /////

In Roselle, N.J.

Cindy's heart drops down to her panties as she lays eyes upon the young beautiful woman who exits the house. Just seeing how beautiful the young girl is, makes Cindy jealous enough to want to jump out of the car and beat the girl to death.

The youthful glow of her skin glistens from afar. Deep dimples set in her fluffy cheeks, giving her a look of innocence. Her silky Doobie lays straight down to the center of her back. A huge ghetto booty explodes from her tiny waist. Her tight fitting Juicy Couture sweat suit is so tight that it looks painted on. Cindy quickly observes her shoe game and gets more agitated when she finds Chanel wedge heel sandals on her feet, instead of sneakers like she expected. On one shoulder she carries a huge leather Chanel bag. The bag incites more anger within her. The bag is worth $2,700.00 and Cindy knows this because she has the bag, one size under that one. That makes her more furious. In the other hand, the girl carries a small Gucci shopping bag. The girl trots from her porch to her car. Her ass claps like an audience, as she stomps to her car. "Eeeel," Cindy sighs with jealousy. "Little funky looking bitch."

The report that Cindy got from her good friend was just as she figured. She found out that the car belongs to a 20 year old which was quite shocking to her. She could tell by the sassiness of the girl's voice that she was young, but she didn't expect her to be half of Dre's age. She's actually young enough to be his daughter.

Cindy looks at a sheet of paper that lies on her passenger's seat. It has all of Lil Mama's information on it; from her date of birth to her government name. It also has the date that the car was registered, which happens to be two months after Dre came home. What a coincidence.

Lil Mama backs out of her driveway and speeds up the block. Cindy lets her get a half a block away before she pulls out of the parking space and follows the girl's lead. She's in desperate hope of the girl leading her to Dre. She can't wait to see the look on his face. She knew that his reason for leaving was due to another woman and now she can't wait to blow this up in his face.

"Sneaky bastard," Cindy says aloud.

Many minutes later, Cindy speeds up Route 22 West recklessly, trying hard not to lose sight of the white Infiniti which is flying up the highway, zipping in and out of traffic. Finally the car soars to the right into the ShopRite parking lot. Cindy peeks her head around the cars trying to keep her eyes glued to the girl's car. She smacks her right blinker on and zips into the right lane without even looking to see if the lane is clear. "Honk," the horn sounds off as she cuts off the car in the lane, just missing it by inches. "Fuck you!" she shouts angrily, as she sticks her middle finger up at the driver behind her.

She speeds into the lot peeking around in search of the vehicle. She quickly locates it in the far corner of the parking lot. The Infiniti is pulling into a tiny parking space. Cindy pulls into the first empty spot she sees.

Cindy is parked and out of her car before the Infiniti is even parked. Before Cindy even realizes it, she's making her way across the parking lot. Just when she gets within fifty feet of the Infiniti, the driver's side door pops open. The young woman hops out of the vehicle, still lugging the Gucci bag in her hand.

"Excuse me!" Cindy yells, but the girl continues stepping along. Cindy assumes that she must not have heard her. "Excuse me!" she shouts a little louder. The girl looks in Cindy's direction, but does not recognize her so she continues to step around her car. "Ayanna!" Cindy shouts just as the girl steps toward the passenger's side of the big body Impala that sits parked. She stops short in her tracks, staring hard at Cindy trying to figure out who she is and how she knows her name. By this time Cindy is only a few feet away from her. The girl opens the door and sticks one leg inside the car. "One minute?" Cindy yells. The girl hurries to get inside the car, but Cindy corners her before she can do so.

"Wrong person," the young girl lies, trying to throw Cindy off.

"Bitch, I got the right person!" Cindy snaps.

"What?"

"You heard me bitch! Talk slick now, bitch!"

"Yo, come on!" the driver screams.

"No, wait!" Cindy yells. "You was talking real slick on the phone. Now run your motherfucking mouth. We face to face now bitch! Where the fuck Dre at?"

Now the girl realizes who this woman is. "Listen, I told you, you got the wrong bitch," she says as she slams the door in Cindy's face. Cindy lifts her leg high in the air and kicks the window with all of her might in attempt to kick the window out.

The driver drops the gear into reverse and backs up speedily. He peeks around nervously, hoping that no one is paying attention to the episode that she's creating.

Lil Mama watches through the window as Cindy bends over picking up a brick. They assume that she's about to attempt to hit the car, so the driver speeds up frantically. Instead Cindy runs in the direction of the Infiniti.

"Hold up, let me the fuck out!" Lil Mama demands. "She bout to hit my car." Just as the words leave her mouth the brick crashes into the back window, shattering it. "Stop this fucking car!"

"You crazy?" the driver ask as he speeds closer to the exit of the parking lot. The driver is Dre's man, Peanut from Philadelphia. "We got 500 bricks of dope and hell-a- cash in this mufucker and you want me to stop? Police come in here and we both going the fuck to jail. Fuck that car! Dre can afford to buy you another one!" he shouts as he speeds out of the lot.

Lil Mama is furious. All she can envision is that crazy woman vandalizing her car in totality. She picks up her phone and dials Dre immediately.

He picks up her call on the first ring. "Hello?"

"You better tame your bitch!" she shouts with rage. "That stupid bitch just bust my fucking windows out!"

"Slow down, slow down! Who you talking about?"

"Your stupid ass girl!"

"Where you at?"

"We just left the ShopRite, me and Peanut! We had to leave my car in the parking lot. She started wilding the fuck out. Ran up on me talking some bullshit. You better tell her something!"

Dre is shocked with what he's hearing. "Ya'll alright, right?"

"Yeah, we alright, but she fucked my car up," she cries.

"Fuck the car," Dre says in a calm manner. "Get Peanut to drop you off at your sister's house. I'll pick you up from there. We'll go and pick up the car together. I'll hit you back. Let me call and straighten out this dumb ass bitch," he says before hanging up. He quickly dials Cindy's phone number.

Cindy sees his phone number and just listens to it ring. "I knew you would call me now," she says aloud as she cruises down Route 22 East. The phone stops ringing, but it starts up again instantly. Cindy decides to answer it this time. "What motherfucker?" she asks sarcastically.

"What the fuck is wrong with you?" he asks.

"What the fuck is wrong with me? What the fuck is wrong with me?" she repeats. "You, what's wrong with me. You called to take up for your little bitch, huh?" she asks mockingly. "Eeel, you fucking with that little dirty ass young bitch?" she laughs. "Creeping around behind your back! Ah hah," she teases. "Meeting her boyfriend," she laughs harder. "You left me for her and she playing your stupid ass. That's what the fuck you get!"

Dre listens to her say what she believes to be true, knowing that she's totally wrong. Although she's wrong, he has to take it on the chin. It's not like he can tell her what their deal really is. That would be all the fuel she would need to start a real fire. "You miserable ass bitch!"

That statement hits her where it hurts. "Miserable?" she asks with sarcasm in her voice. "Yeah, I'm miserable, but guess what?" She pauses for a few seconds. "Misery loves company!" She hangs the phone up in his ear.

"Hello? Hello? Dumb ass bitch!"

///// CHAPTER 95 /////

Mu-Mit and Latif sit parked on Ferry Street. They just got back into town a few hours ago. They left Salaam back in Asbury to hold the fort down while they came up here to re-up. They have no plans on staying here any longer than they have to. In all reality, there is no real reason for them to be here. Their movement is limited except for Candy Kev and Mu-Mit's man Sha from Jersey City, who happens to be sitting in the backseat right now.

"Listen, I got 300 bricks for you. I'm about to bounce back out of town. That should hold you for a few days until I get back," he whispers. "What's up with that coke?"

"Ah man, streets dry as a desert. It's a drought going on. Everybody trying to
get hold of that shit. Shit been dry for months. Every now and then a few keys come in here and there but they don't last. By the time a mufucker try to re-up, it's already over with." Perfect, Latif and Mu-Mit think to themselves. "If a cat has some powder right now he could get rich."

"Yeah?" Mu-Mit asks.

"Definitely.

Mu-Mit's mind is racing a thousand miles an hour. "What the numbers looking like?"

"Aw man, prices up there. I know cats who paying $23,000 a joint. That's wholesale. They selling shit for like 28, 29, 30 a gram."

"Yeah?" Mu-Mit asks, not believing what he's hearing. He looks over at Latif who is nodding his head up and down. "Dig," Mu-Mit whispers. "I just ran into a couple a joints. I got four altogether, but I have to hold two of them for my little brother," he says referring to Candy Kev. "Gimme $21,000 apiece for them and they yours. I gotta move them quick though. I need to get back outta town by tonight."

"Word!" he shouts in an excited manner. "Man, that's simple. I can move all four before it even get dark. I know one cat that will take how many you can get your hands on."

"I only got them 4 and 2 of them gotta go to my little brother."

"You turning down straight money? I can make a phone call and have those bought right now."

"Nah, I have to hold two of them. You can take the other two."

"Alright I'm about to call my man up right now. I can go back to J.C., pick up the bread and we can make it happen. How long will it take you to get your hands on them?"

"No time at all. I got them in my possession. All I gotta do is go and get them. I say, meet us back here in one hour? I'll bring you the two joints and the three hundred bricks."

"Bet. I'm gone hit my man up and go and get his paper and then I will get with ya'll. He bleeding. I'm gone hit him over the head for 25 and make a quick $8,000 profit off of him."

Mu-Mit laughs at his statement. He thinks he's saying something slick. Little does he know that all of the proceeds is profit to them. The work didn't cost them a dime, thanks to Salaam and they're going to make $84,000 off of it. That is $28,000 a piece for the three of them.

Salaam was afraid to let them out of his sight with the work. He didn't trust that they would bring his portion of the money back to him. No matter what they said, he was not trying to hear them leaving without him. Finally Mu-Mit came up with the idea that made Salaam feel at ease. In total, they left Salaam with 70 bricks, which equal almost $16,000 in cash. Mu-Mit explained to him that if they never came back he has the money right in hands. That, coupled with the fact that Mu-Mit left an additional $5,000 there, assured Salaam.

That made Salaam happy, but it disappointed both Latif and Mu-Mit gravely. They can't believe that he would take them through a song and dance like that after all of the paper they've given him this week. His greediness and ungratefulness made them lose a certain amount of respect for him.

"Alright, one hour!" Mu-Mit shouts. "If anything changes, call me."

"One hour!" the man says as he gets out of the car. "Ain't nothing gone change. That's money in the bank. My man starving for some coke right now!" he says before slamming the door shut.

Just as the door closes, Latif's phone rings. It's Salaam. "Phew," Latif sighs. "Yo?"

"Where ya'll at?"

"Where we said we was gone be," Latif replies hastily.

"Well, ya'll need to make ya'll way back down here. It's a wrap...done."

"Got you. I'll call you when we're leaving," he says before he hangs the phone up. "Salaam done."

Now they're both eager to get out of town at this moment. There's money to be made. They can't wait to see how Asbury reacts to the 'After Party.' An hour ago, they just ordered 1,000 bricks from Dre. 300 will go to Sha. 300 will go to Candy Kev and the last 400 they will take with them to Asbury.

"No soon as we handle this, we out," Mu-Mit claims. "Let me call my little brother one more time. Mufucker been calling me crazy all week. Now that we here, he ain't picking up," Mu-Mit says as he dials Candy Kev's phone number. Mu-Mit pulls off while listening to the phone ring over and over just as it's been doing the past ten times that he's called him. The answering service comes on and for the very first time he leaves a message. "As Salaamu Alaikum!" Mu-Mit says aggressively. "Listen, I been in town for hours now. I need to see you like yesterday. I ain't gone be here too much longer and ain't no telling when I will be back. I got something I'm sure you can use. Get at me, Insha Allah? As Salaamu Alaikum wa Rahmatullaahi wa barakaatu," he shouts giving the full greeting. He speaks Arabic so fluently. It's just too bad that he's wasting all those beautiful words on a conversation about drug dealing. "He bullshitting!" Mu-Mit shouts as he hangs the phone up.

In Union, N.J.

    Candy Kev just watched the phone ring, standing away from it as if it was the plague. His phone alerts him that Mu-Mit has left him a message. He quickly picks the phone up and listens attentively. He slams the phone shut. He's curious to find out what Mu-Mit has for him, but not curious enough to actually call him back. He wants no part of this, which is why he isn't answering Mu's calls. Trauma hasn't come by at all today which gave him a little peace. He hopes he stays away for a few more days. The longer he stays away the safer he feels. He's sure he's not going to stay away too long though. He'll be at the door soon and when he does, he's sure he will want some results. Candy Kev has held him off for as long as he possibly can. He's sure that next time he won't leave taking no for an answer.

Block Party 3 - Brick City Massacre

///// CHAPTER 96 /////

Later that Night

Mu-Mit and Latif sit back lounging in Salaam's apartment after a long, but very lucrative day. They have managed to move 150 bricks of the 'After Party' already in just a few short hours. They both realize that the flow should pick up drastically due to the fact that the 'After Party' is a better quality of dope. Keeping that in mind, they've raised their price. They refuse to sell the 'After Party' for the same price they just sold the 600 and something bricks of garbage they had. It just doesn't make sense, which is why the price is now $250.00 a brick. If they paid top dollar for the garbage they assume they will have no problem paying this price for the better quality. The price change doesn't benefit Salaam the least bit. He still only receives the same $10 profit. They managed to get away with that by telling Salaam that they have a better quality of work, but they had to pay more for it. He bought the story with no problem. Now they both will get $30.00 per brick as opposed to the $20.00 they normally make.

Earlier today, Mu-Mit's man from Jersey City hooked back up with them and gave them the $42,000 for the two kilos just as he promised that he would. Once they got back here to Asbury, Salaam had the money for the 70 bricks waiting for them.

Mu-Mit told him to keep the money from the dope and he gave him an additional $7,200.00. Mu-Mit told Salaam that they had to sell the four kilos at $17,000 a joint just to get rid of them quickly. That deception was all Latif's idea. Now Latif and Mu-Mit take $30,700.00 apiece, while Salaam only received $22,600. Mu-Mit broke Salaam off his profit off of the kilos, although he still has two left. That is thanks to Candy Kev, who Mu-Mit has still not been able to get in contact with. Judging by Salaam's reaction about them leaving with the work and not taking him along, Mu-Mit knew he wouldn't believe their story. He only gave him the money to avoid hearing his whining and complaining. He was so furious at how Salaam acted earlier. He never really got over it, so he was sure he couldn't listen to another word come out of his mouth. Giving him the money was an attempt to save him from doing something to Salaam that he may regret later. In addition to the $17,000.00, Mu-Mit also gave him another $700.00 for his cut off of the 70 bricks he sold.

Salaam comes back into the apartment, whistling a tune. "Hey, hey, hey!" he shouts as he walks right pass them and goes into the bathroom.

"Look at him," Mu-Mit says to Latif. "He's happier than a fag with a bag of dicks," Mu-Mit says furiously.

Salaam has been running in and out of the apartment since they've been back. He tells them that he's out networking, but they both know that he's not telling the truth. The only networking that he's doing is with the cocaine dealers who he purchases cocaine from to supply his habit. Each time he returns, he's higher and higher and the smell of burning cocaine fills the air from his clothes. Also an aroma seeps through his pores. The mixture of the chemicals creates a perfume type smell.

Although it's his money, the fact that he's blowing it on drugs to get high off of pisses them off immensely. They feel stupid splitting the money up with him knowing exactly what he's going to do with it. That makes them not want to give him another dime, but they'll never do that because at this point, they need him more than he knows it. Without him they will never be able to move their work here in Asbury. Their plan, at this point, is to use him to build some of their own connections and once they do so, they will kick him to the curb like the bad habit that he is.

Salaam walks back into the room, still whistling the same tune. At this point they're both getting angry at the sight of him. He stops whistling long enough to speak. His bad eye twitches rapidly as it always does when he's high. "Yo, I think I'm gone cop me a little ride tomorrow. What ya'll think?" he asks with his eye twitching uncontrollably. "A nigga need some wheels, you know?"

"I think, you need to fall the fuck back," Mu-Mit says rudely. "You ain't been had no wheels. Don't start no new shit. The minute you buy a car mufuckers gone swear you had something to do with that robbery. Don't be stupid. Use your fucking head."

Salaam doesn't say a word in reply. He just walks toward the door on his way out again. As soon as the door slams shut, Latif speaks. "We got to be the dumbest mufuckers on the planet. We splitting money up with an addict," he says with seriousness written all over his face. "We just gave a mufucking junkie over 23 motherfucking thousand dollars. Hmpph," he snickers.

Mu-Mit's phone rings. "Now this mufucker wanna call," Mu says to Latif. "This Candy Kev right here. "Salaamu Alaikum!"

"Wa Laikum Salaam," Candy Kev mumbles.

"Where you been, Ock? I was up there all day today. I tried to wait for you, but you wouldn't answer the fucking phone. I called you a hundred times."

Candy Kev totally ignores what Mu-Mit just said. "When you coming through?"

"I just got back down the way. Man, it all depends on how shit go down here. I got something real nice for you. Something real slick came through and you know I had you in mind. When I eat Ock, you gone eat! Allah says, 'you're not a true believer until you want for your brother what you want for yourself.' I gotta take care of the Muslims and you my lil brother so I have to look out for you."

Candy Kev doesn't reply to his statements once again. "So, when you coming through?" he asks again.

"Man, about two days or so. You gotta be around though. I be moving. I can't wait. I'll hit you when I'm on my way up there. Answer your fucking phone!"

"Alright, I'm here," he mumbles.

"As Salaamu Alaikum wa Rahmatullahi!" Mu-Mit says in closing.

"Wa Laikum As Salaam!" Candy Kev hangs up his phone. He looks to his left with a long saddened face. "He still wherever he at," he whispers to

Trauma. Candy Kev can see the frustration in Trauma's face.

"Man, fuck that!" the man says from the bottom of the stoop of Candy Kev's porch. "This nigga bullshitting!" he shouts with rage as he paces back and forth.

They're definitely ready to move on him. He can see it on all of their faces. They're patience with him has worn thin. He realizes that now would be the best time for him to say something to hold them off. But what, he asks himself. He's already given them every excuse that he can think of. "I ain't bullshitting," he mumbles. "It ain't me," he says loud and clear. "Ya'll heard the conversation."

Trauma looks at him with rage in his eyes. "That's it. Your time is running out. You don't get him to me in two days, you gone take the weight," Trauma says as he gives his squad a head nod, signaling for them to go to the car. They walk off and he follows a few steps behind them. "Two days, Kev. That's all you got left. Not another minute," he says in a calm manner. "Make it happen or else." As he's walking away, he spins around and points his finger at Kev. He makes believe that his hand is a gun. He presses the imaginary trigger. "See you in two days."

Al-Saadiq Banks

///// CHAPTER 97 /////

In Harlem, New York

A security guard makes his rounds opening the doors of the Central Park East 2 Elementary School. Any minute now, children will be lining up at the doors for breakfast. The guard gets to the door of the main entrance and unlocks the lock before unraveling the chain. He drapes the chain over his shoulders while pushing the door open. For some strange reason, the door barely budges. He pushes a little harder and it cracks open, but it won't move any further.

The guard backs up against the door and tries to force the door open. This time it doesn't move at all. He sticks his head through the opening and all that he can see is a dusty printed shirt, huddled up behind the door. He automatically recognizes the shirt. It's Rawl, the neighborhood homeless man. "Rawl!" the security guard shouts angrily. Rawl sleeps here every night. The only problem the guard has with him is when he's still here in the morning when it's time for the kids to come to school. "Rawl!" he shouts again, trying to push the door on him, hoping to wake him up.

The guard rushes to the side door and exits. He runs speedily to the main entrance. "Rawl!" he shouts. "Gotta get up! School about to open!" he says as he taps the man with his foot. His foot doesn't sink into the man's body. It sort of bounces off of it. He taps him again and the stiffness of the man's body alarms him. He nudges him a tad bit harder and notices that his body is as solid as steel. The guard's eyes are attracted to a trail of blood that dribbles down the three-step platform. He backs away in fear. At first he assumes that Rawl has been murdered until he notices the tip of a syringe lying underneath his body. This tells him Rawl must have overdosed. He backs away even further. He immediately pulls out his walkie talkie and radios 911.

There should be no surprise as to what the syringe was loaded with? One more victim is down for the count. And the winner is; 'After Party!'

At the Essex County Morgue

The man stands over the naked corpse. He can't help but look at the beautiful shape she has. She's curvy and full in all the right places. He assumes that she must have lived a hard life judging by her ran down looking face. The harder he squints, the more he can see that she's actually an attractive woman. She appears to be in her mid thirties.

Thick dirt covers the bottoms of her feet. Her lipstick is plastered onto her lips sloppily. A tacky wig covers her head. Tracks and needle marks cover her entire body from head to toe. Any place that you can imagine someone shooting dope, she's shot it there. She's even shot it in places that you can't imagine. Needle marks can be found from her neck on down to the lips of her vagina. The dark scabs are the easier ones to look at. It's the pink colored, open sores that are enough to make you puke.

The man places the 'Jane Doe' tag on her toe quickly to get her in the

259

freezer and out of his sight. Just as he loops the string around her crusty toe another man walks into the room.

"Unghh," he sighs. "Shit! What's her story?"

"Ah, a hooker," he replies.

"A hooker?" he asks. "Who the fuck would pay to hook that?"

"You'd be surprised. Don't get it twisted. Somebody fucked her or she wouldn't have had a job," he smiles.

"Uhm, I guess you right," the man replies. Who is she? What happened to her?"

"Ah, Jane Doe...overdose."

"No type of ID?" the man asks as he fumbles through her junky pocketbook. Not a single piece of ID is in sight, but what he does find is a half empty bag of the 'After Party.'

///// CHAPTER 98 /////

"So, that's $42,000 for the coke and you already know the price for the dope, right?" Mu-Mit asks as he pulls the bag from underneath his seat. He quickly passes it to Candy Kev.

"Absolutely," Candy Kev says in a low whisper as he prepares himself to get out of the backseat of the vehicle.

"Nigga, cheer the fuck up too!" Mu-Mit teases. "You look like you just lost your best friend," he says with a smile as he looks at Candy Kev through the rearview mirror.

Candy Kev cracks a cheesy grin as he opens the door. He exits the vehicle clutching his bag of goods tightly.

Mu-Mit and Latif ripped through the work quickly just as they predicted they would. A few people complained about the price at first, but once they got a whiff of the work, they bought it with no haggling whatsoever. They left early this morning, leaving not a single brick there. They scored a total of $100,000 in just two days. Mu-Mit and Latif split up a profit of $24,000, $12,000 apiece, while they only broke Salaam off with $4,000.00.

At this point he's lucky to get anything from them. They're sick and tired of him. The few hours away from him is like a week long vacation for them. It will be over soon though. An hour ago they met with Dre and gave him money for 700 bricks and they took another 500 from him. That should hold them for another three days, they figure.

Mu-Mit just gave Candy Kev the two kilos that he was holding for him plus 300 bricks of dope. Now that their business here is done, they'll go and retrieve the 500 bricks of theirs and they're headed back to Asbury.

"Sa Laikum!" Mu shouts as Candy Kev slams the door shut.

Mu-Mit peels off slowly, steering the car to the right in order to get into the center of the one way street. Suddenly a Chrysler comes up from his blind side, just missing the car by inches. "Ho!" Mu-Mit shouts with a surprised look on his face. Latif looks to his right with great surprise as the Chrysler rides side by side with them. The Chrysler swiftly takes the lead by a foot putting the back passenger and Latif damn near face to face. A hand, gripping a chrome semi-automatic handgun hangs out of the window. Bloc! Bloc! Bloc!

"Oh shit!" Latif shouts. "Go, go!" he shouts as he ducks his head low. Mu-Mit swerves to his left and mashes the gas pedal harder, but the Chrysler is glued to his side. Bloc! Bloc! Glass disperses everywhere as the bullet crashes into Latif's window. He closes his eyes and uses his forearm to protect his face from the glass. Bloc! Bloc! The back passenger window shatters into pieces.

Mu-Mit swerves from left to right tactically banging his car into the Chrysler in an attempt to run them off of the road. Gunshots echo loudly. Bullets ricochet in every direction due to the fact that the gunman can not get a clean shot at them.

Despite the pandemonium, Latif manages to grab hold of his pistol. While still ducking his head low, he extends his gun out of the window. Without looking, he squeezes, hoping to hit something or at least intimidate the gunman enough to back away so that they can get away. Boom! Boom! The loud sound of the cannon catches them by surprise instilling a bit of fear into the gunman. Latif notices that their gunfire has stop. This gives him enough time to get himself in position. He lifts his head up. Bloc! Bloc! Bloc! The gunman aims straight for Latif's head trying to take it off. He fires consecutively as they speed side by side. Latif leans his head back on the headrest and fires. Boom! He fires again, this time he's looking the man square in the eyes. All of a sudden something strange happens. The gun falls right out of the man's hand onto the ground as he ducks back into the car, shaking his arm up and down. His face shows signs of agony. Latif assumes that he must have been hit in the arm. Latif fires again. Boom! The car fades behind them a little. Latif hangs slightly out of the window and fires again. Boom! Just as he fires he sees the driver of the Chrysler extending his gun out of his window. Boc! Boc! Their back window shatters into tiny pieces. Fear of his aim gives Mu-Mit all the incentive to try and make a break for it while they still have a chance. The driver of the Chrysler attempts to catch up with Mu-Mit, but his Dodge Magnum has way too many horses up under the hood. He leaves them in the dust.

"What the fuck?" Latif blurts out. "Who the fuck was that?"

At this point the only word that comes to both of their minds is Baghdad. "Motherfuckers!"

In Asbury, New Jersey

Salaam hangs up his phone. He now makes a call to Latif's phone. He's been calling them back and forth getting no answer from either of them. He was expecting them back hours ago. He has three sales lined up waiting for them to get back. The sales are a total of 130 bricks.

Latif's answering service comes on and Salaam leaves another message. "Yo, hit me back! Let a nigga know something. I'm starting to get worried about ya'll two mufuckers!" he states. He hopes that they're alright. He needs them dearly at this point. He has hopes of getting rich and without them, his hopes are dead.

No soon as he hangs the phone up, he digs his hand inside of his pants pocket, and pulls out a glassine vial of crack. He then digs his hand inside of his left pocket, retrieving his stem. He immediately dumps two tiny pebbles of crack into his stem and quickly places the flame from his lighter onto the back of his stem. He watches the sizzling rock with deep admiration until his bad eye begins to water from blinking so much. The pungent odor of the burning cocaine actually smells better to him than the sweet fragrance musk oil. The vapors seep into his nostrils making him eager to smoke. He quickly places the hot stem into his mouth and takes a strong pull until his face caves in. Three, two, one...blast off!

Many hours later

Mu-Mit sits parked on Bergen Street, directly across from Pathmark. Mu-Mit's wife's SUV sits not even a foot away from the entrance of UMDNJ Hospital. From the angle that they're sitting, they have a clear view of the Chrysler which sits in the parking space of the emergency section.

After their gun battle, Mu-Mit had to get out of the damaged rental. Latif hoped they would be here, being that the man was struck. His hopes came to reality when they cruised pass and saw the car already sitting here. That was about three hours ago. They've been sitting here waiting patiently. One thing for sure, they have to come out sooner or later.

Less than thirty minutes later, three men exit the hospital, walking toward the Chrysler. "Showtime!" Latif shouts with joy. The man in the back is wearing a sling on his left arm.

Latif snatches his gun from his waist while Mu-Mit pulls his gun from underneath his seat. They anxiously hop out of the SUV. Mu-Mit runs to the left side of the entrance, with his back pinned up against the gate. Latif stands on the opposite side of the gate.

Vengeance pumps through their veins. The speed of their heartbeats pick up, as the vehicle backs up and pulls out of the parking space. They both stand there quietly as they peek around in search of not only police, but potential witnesses as well. To their satisfaction, the coast is clear.

The Chrysler creeps up the path. Latif nods his head up and down once the vehicle gets within 100 feet of them. They both stand as still as possible, hoping that no one sees them. The nose of the car passes the fence and Latif pops out first. Boom! Boom! He fires, shattering the driver's side window with his first shot.

Boom! Boom! Mu-Mit's gun sounds off seconds later, as he squeezes the trigger with force. He steps to the back of the car not only to stay clear of any shots that they may send back, but to stay clear of Latif's gunfire as well. Boom! Boom! Boom! Latif fires again. Boom! Boom! Mu-Mit fires. The back passenger's window caves in completely.

The Chrysler jerks uncontrollably as the driver mashes onto the gas pedal. The Chrysler soars across the street uncontrollably at top speed. Police sirens roar throughout the neighborhood, signaling Mu-Mit and Latif to make their get away. As they're running to their vehicle, they watch in awe as the Chrysler runs smack into the brick wall.

As Mu-Mit peels off, he watches a man hop out of the passenger's seat, stumbling away dizzily from the car. They both would love to get out and finish him off, but the sirens are now coming closer. Mu-Mit mashes the gas pedal and speeds away from the scene. Another clean get away.

///// CHAPTER 99 /////

Dre lays back in his recliner that sits right next to his balcony. From where he's seated, he can view the 72-inch television screen that sits on his wall, as well as watch the waves of the Hudson River roll vibrantly.

The calmness of the water brings tranquility to his somewhat hectic life. The game is starting to take toll on Dre. The more money he obtains, the more paranoid he becomes. At this point his stress level is at an all time high. He's making more money than he's ever imagined, but he doesn't have the time to enjoy it. Lack of time is not the only factor. His paranoia makes him want to crawl into a cave and hide. He trusts no one and at times he feels that everyone is out to set him up.

He gets a nervous feeling in his gut each time one of his clients calls his phone. He realizes that all it takes is one phone call to not only end his career, but to also finish his life as well.

Dre has always been a human stress ball, who worries about every little thing. Leave it up to him to find a downside to every situation. When things are bad, he worries. When things are going good, he worries how long that will last. At the moment, things happen to be going smoothly, but he's sure that can't last forever.

With all the stress that comes with this lifestyle, he now has an added situation to top it off. This situation with Cindy is quite nerve wrecking. He realizes that she is a scorned woman and there is no limit to what she will do to get even with him. He's told her over and over again that the young girl is not the reason that he doesn't want to be her. He admitted to her that any feelings that he had for her, he lost while he was incarcerated. He also told her that he could never get over the pain that she put him through. She listened to him, but she still refuses to believe his story. In her heart, she truly believes that she lost her man to the young girl.

Dre is afraid of what she may do, which is why him and Lil Mama have been searching high and low for a new apartment for her. They're also in the process of trading her Infiniti in. With a different car and a new location, Cindy should be harmless to them. At least he hopes so.

Dre stares over his balcony as the small yacht sails slowly. He quickly envisions himself, laid back on his own yacht. Years ago that seemed far fetched but today it feels a lot closer to reality. At the rapid rate that his empire is growing, he can actually see himself owning his own yacht. The question is, if he's in a position to do so, would he ever? Probably not. His low-key lifestyle would never allow him to make such a move.

As soon as the yacht passes, he turns his face to the television screen. What's on the screen grasps his undivided attention. Stacks and stacks of kilos sit on a table along with a wide range of handguns and machine guns. Drug Enforcement Agents swarm the room in the background as one agent stands on the podium speaking. Dre is eager to hear what the man is saying. He turns up the volume from his remote.

Just as the volume increases the screen flashes and the camera zooms in on a Bentley and several other high line cars. The camera then zooms in on a beautiful house. Dre squints his eyes trying to figure out why this house looks so familiar to him. Before he can determine why, several mug shots appear on the screen. Dre is mortified at the mug shot that's on the top of the screen. "Oh shit!" he says aloud. Casper's photo jumps at him from the screen. Dre listens attentively as the agent tells all the details of the multi-million dollar organization that has been interrupted earlier today. Damn, he thinks to himself. "The leader is still at large," the agent says. "We have reason to believe that he's escaped out of the country. "Che-Che," Dre says aloud. Correct they are. Apparently they know everything. Dre can't believe his eyes or his ears.

Wow, he says to himself. His mind quickly replays his short stay in Atlanta. He replays him and Casper's conversation. He's so happy that he didn't accept Casper's invitation. He would have been dragged right into their situation. A baffled look appears on his face as he thinks of the fact that he may be linked to Casper in someway. He wonders how long the investigation could have been going on. He wonders if Casper's phone was tapped. He can hear Casper's words to him clearly. Fear sets in as he considers the fact that they may have him on a wire tap. He bangs his head onto his recliner with worry.

"In New Jersey an epidemic of heroin hits the streets," a different newscaster says loud and clear. The words 'A Brick City Massacre' is the headline that is displayed on the screen. The killer heroin, titled 'After Party' has already claimed nearly a dozen lives." Dre opens his eyes at the sound of that. He's hoping that he's dreaming. "There have also been noted deaths in parts of Philadelphia, New York, Connecticut, Delaware and Baltimore. The killer heroin is soaring through the east coast like a plague," the newscaster adds.

Dre's life flashes before his very eyes. He sits there with his eyes and his mouth stretched wide open. Never in his wildest dreams did he ever expect to hear something like that. Hearing the words 'After Party' on national television frightens him tremendously. "Oh my God," he says slowly.

A commercial comes on and he still sits there with his eyes glued to the screen. He's frozen stiff. Two sets of letters come to his mind instantly; FBI and DEA. The both of them means big trouble for him. I done fucked up now, he thinks to himself.

Now what, he asks himself. He knows one thing for sure and that is after hearing this on national television the officials have no other alternative but to get to the bottom of this matter. Unfortunately for him, he's not at the bottom of this matter. He's at the very top of it.

He's stuck in between a rock and a hard place and doesn't have a clue as to what he should do at this point. This was never a part of his plan. Should he do the sensible thing and shut down his operation? He thinks of the shipment of work he just received yesterday. He could never call them back to come and take it back. That wouldn't be hustler like.

He has a total of 6,000 bricks of packaged dope. 3,000 bricks are 'After

Party' and 3,000 bricks of 'Death Certificate' for Chico and his brother. "Death Certificate," he says aloud as he thinks of the dope. Wow, what a coincidence. He also has 7 kilos that he ordered for Imamu. Imamu, he says to himself. Is it a coincidence? He wonders if Imamu was sent to him to set him up? Maybe Tony is in on it as well? Nah, he says to himself, trying to clear his thoughts. "I'm bugging." In total, he holds nearly two million dollars worth of the killer heroin as they have labeled it.

His phone rings, interrupting his thoughts. He's somewhat afraid to answer it. "Hello?" he says in a low whisper.

"Yo!" Zaid from Delaware shouts. "You saw the news?"

"Yeah," he replies sadly.

"Talking about advertisement! We bout to blow!" he shouts with joy.

Dre hangs up on him instantly. It's obvious that he doesn't realize the seriousness of this matter. Why would he, Dre asks himself. He's only a pawn in this game. The real weight rests on Dre's shoulders. At the worse case scenario, they'll use him to get who they really want and that's Dre. This makes Dre even more worried. Just to think that each call can be a set up. He knows that he can trust no one at this point.

His phone rings again. He looks down at the display. The 215 area code quite naturally makes him assume that his man Peanut from Philly has seen the news as well. As soon as that call stops ringing, a 203 area code comes in right behind it. Shortly thereafter a series of calls come in back to back until he finally shuts the power off.

He paces back and forth throughout the apartment frantically. He opens his bedroom closet. The many duffle bags that sit on the shelf start to become an even bigger problem for him. He knows better than to keep the money at his house and has been wondering what to do with it. For months he's been trying to find a place to keep his money, but he has no one that he trusts to hold it for him. He's sure that these bags of money are all the evidence they will need to bury him in prison. He figures there is no better time to clean house. Where can he dump the money? He has no clue.

All of his life, his main problem was not having enough money. Today, his problem is having way too much money. He never knew that problem could exist.

///// CHAPTER 100 /////

Mu-Mit sits in the driver's seat of his wife's SUV while Latif sits in the backseat. In the passenger's seat there sits Candy Kev. Never before did they ever feel the need to seat themselves like this while he was in the car until now. Not knowing the situation makes them have very little trust for Candy Kev at this time.

"Hold up, hold up…you losing me," Mu-Mit says. "How could that be? As soon as you jump out the car, the gun shots started ringing. When could they have robbed you?"

"They were two cars deep. While ya'll was going through that, two niggas ran up on me before I could get in the car."

"So, you saying this was a robbery?" Latif asks.

"Tell me how the fuck they knew to be waiting out here for us!" Mu-Mit shouts furiously.

"I don't know," Candy Kev mumbles, trying as hard as he can to sound sincere. Inside he knows how they knew because it was all a part of Trauma's plan. As much as Candy Kev hated to do it, he had no choice. It was either him or them and apparently he chose them. There is one thing that he isn't lying about. They did take all the work from him. Right now, he's more frightened than he's ever been. A part of him wants to believe that Mu-Mit will never kill him, but then again, he's known him to murder closer friends for less.

"100 motherfucking grand," Mu-Mit sighs as he thinks of the loss of profit. "Did you recognize any of them?" Candy Kev shakes his head from side to side. "Nah."

"Not one of them motherfuckers? Didn't none of them look familiar to you?"

"Ah ah," he mumbles. No one says a word. The silence is killing Candy Kev slowly. He's sure they don't believe his story because he would never believe it if it were told to him. He would be willing to give anything in the world to not be in this situation that he's in. Latif sits there in rage. He doesn't believe a word that's coming out of Candy Kev's mouth. He's just hoping that Mu-Mit gives him the word to blow his brains out. Truly he doesn't believe that is going to happen because he knows how Mu-Mit feels about Candy Kev. He's told him over and over how much love he has for him. "Man this some bullshit!" Latif blurts out furiously. "I ain't going with this shit!" The agitation can be heard in his voice. Mu-Mit looks back at Latif fearing what he may do next. He looks down at Latif's lap where he has his gun gripped tightly. They lock eyes. Through the eyes Latif is begging Mu-Mit to give him the word. Mu-Mit shakes his head negatively. Candy Kev sees this and feels a small sense of relief. He just hopes Mu-Mit's word is enough to keep Latif off of him.

"That's your word?" Mu-Mit whispers.

"Yeah, Wallahi," Candy Kev mumbles.

As much as Mu-Mit doesn't believe the story, hearing Candy Kev put his Wallahi on it, gives him no other choice. "Alright then…that's what it is then," he says looking out of his window. "Later!" he says sternly, giving Candy Kev the signal that their meeting is officially over.

Candy Kev is quite baffled right now. He doesn't know whether he should get out before he changes his mind or if he should stay a little longer to further convince them that he's telling the truth. He doesn't trust them the least bit. Deep down inside he believes that they're going to do him. He figures they may just be letting him slide for the time being. He realizes that these are old time gangsters, unlike Trauma and his unit. The Unit will commit murder at 2 o'clock in the afternoon in front of the world, but the old timers will never move out like that. They're known to calculate everything down to the second and plan everything smoothly in order to get away with it. They would rather let their prey walk into their hands instead of forcing the situation. They will catch their victim when he least expects it. To Candy Kev that is far more scarier to deal with. If he has to die he'd rather they just go ahead and get it over with. Living his life with the fear of getting murdered will drive him crazy.

Candy Kev closes the door slowly. He wonders if he should say something just to try and further clear his name. This is my last chance, he says to himself. He wants to say something, but he doesn't know exactly what he should say. "As Salaamu Alaikum!"

"Wa Alaikum," Mu-Mit replies rather coldly. He's purposely cut the greeting in half where it only means 'and the same to you.' This is disrespectful to a believing man because it is normally used when returning the greeting from a non-Muslim. Candy Kev hears and recognizes the fact that he didn't give him the entire greeting. This just enhances his fear even more.

Mu-Mit and Latif watch Candy Kev walk away. "Mu, no disrespect to your religion, but I think homeboy using that Muslim shit to fake you out," Latif says with hesitation. He's not sure how Mu-Mit is going to accept what he's saying. "He put his law heed on some bullshit," he says totally mispronouncing the word Wallahi. "That mufucker lying! He set us the fuck up. He ain't fooling me. Don't let that Muslim shit blurry your vision. You know right from wrong. Just like with the kid Parlay, you couldn't pull the trigger cause he Muslim. The same Muslim who paid a Christian $25,000.00 to murder yo ass. He ain't care nothing bout that Muslim shit."

"Ho, ho, hold up, La. You my main man, but that's enough of that Muslim shit. You can find a better way to refer to it than that. Can't you?"

Latif senses the sincerity in his voice and his eyes. He knows he has offended him. "My bad, Bruh, but I started off by saying, no disrespect to your religion. Real talk, that nigga lying. His whole story plastic as hell. I can see right through it. I know he like a little brother to you and you hate to believe that he put you in the nestle crunch, but it is what it is. I'm telling you, he behind this shit. Now whether we move on 'eem or not, it's your call. I know you got that issue with doing what needs to be done to Muslims. I ain't got that issue. I ain't Muslim. I'll put him to rest without a second thought. It's on you, right now?"

///// CHAPTER 101 /////

Crowds of teen-agers and young adults stand huddled up in packs in front of Perry's Funeral Home. RIP, Charlie Baltimore is plastered on the front of everyone's t-shirt. Red is obviously their favorite color because everyone is wearing something with some type of red in it. Some only have red stitched jeans while others are flaming hard with red bandanas tied around their heads, red wristbands, socks and sneakers. However it can not be disputed this is definitely a Blood affair.

Tears cover the majority of the peoples faces while rage covers others. All in all, Charlie Baltimore will definitely be missed. Being that she was the only girl in their bunch, she was like a mother figure to them. The way she catered to them and spoiled them made even the toughest ones yearn for her motherly love. She was everything all wrapped up in one package. She was a female who could kick it with them as if she was a dude, but she could also give them information from a female's perspective. She showed them the love that most of them grew up without, but on the flip side they could count on her to hold them down in any battle. The best part of all was the fact that if they caught her at the right moment she would give them the most memorable night of bedroom action that they have ever had. She's had sex with the most of them, never really thinking much of it. She thought and moved out like a dude. If she was out with one of the Homies late night and had enough drinks to have her hot and horny she would use one of them to relieve herself. The crazy thing about her is, she would come out the next day and act as if nothing had happened. She totally respected one-night stands. The dudes on the other hand, were the problem. Each of them hoped that she would commit herself to them. That could never happen because her love for women overpowered her desire for men, hands down.

Shotgun sits on the curb with his head hanging low. A few of the Homies stand around him passing a bottle of 151 around. Shotgun grabs hold of his beverage of choice and throws the 'Lean' down his throat. This is how he's been keeping his sanity through this situation. He hates to deal with the fact that Charlie Baltimore lost her life because of his actions. Anyone else would have charged it to the game but his conscience won't let him. He feels like he should have taken better care of their First Lady. There will definitely be repercussions to this. He will never be able to sleep until he's murdered her murderers.

Scccuuurrrr! The Audi wagon stops short, stealing everyone's attention. The passenger stands up with his head peeking out of the sunroof. He grips the machine gun tightly. Gun shots start ripping repeatedly. The crowd scuffles and hustles to get out of the way. Some are successful in doing so and others are not so lucky. The gunman empties his clip of 30 rounds and drops down into the passenger's seat quickly. "Go, go!" he shouts before snatching his ski mask off of his face. "Goofy ass niggas!" Ahmir shouts. "You seen them mufuckers dropping like flies?" he asks with great appreciation.

"Hell yeah," ILL Wheel replies with joy.

"I hope they got enough t-shirts to put all them faces on!"

///// CHAPTER 102 /////

Dre walks into his uncle's house in Piscataway, New Jersey. "Hey nephew! How are you?" the nerdy looking elderly man asks. This is Dre's father's brother. Of the bunch of seven rowdy boys, this is the only one who earned an honest living. The 'others earned money by way of drug dealing, bank robbery, pimping, or number running. Needless to say, he's the only one who has actually made something of himself.

All the others are dead except for the oldest and the youngest one. One is dying from AIDS in prison and the other one will just die in prison. They both were sentenced to life back in the eighties.

This man is just grateful to be here. He's made an honest living by doing carpentry. With very little money and a great deal of craftsmanship, he's managed to build this house from the ground up for him and his wife.

As a child Dre looked at the differences of their lives and back then he thought his family had it better than his uncle's family. His uncle's kids were less fortunate. They wore Dre's hand me downs that he passed over to them once his father bought him the latest of everything.

Now Dre looks at it differently. His father was murdered by the same Italians that he ran numbers for most of his adult life. His mom died from cancer, but he's sure her loneliness and depression had a great deal to do with her death as well. He's just coming home from doing over 15 years of his life in prison, while his younger brother is facing life in prison. Meanwhile Uncle Fred and his wife are living happily ever after. They have raised three children who all are college graduates. One boy is a doctor, the other is an architect and the girl is a principal at a high school.

As a child Dre teased all of them about their shabby clothes and they would cry as he laughed hysterically in their faces. Who is doing the laughing now, he asks himself. They say he who laughs last, laughs the hardest. Dre now understands the meaning of that saying.

"So, Neph, what brings you here? I'm surprised to see you. I ain't heard from you in over twenty years."

Dre laughs. "It hasn't been that long has it?" he asks, knowing damn well that it's probably been longer than that. "Luckily you still have the same number. I found it in my mother's jewelry box."

"I'm sorry to hear about your mom. Ya'll didn't even contact us and let us know nothing. That broke my heart. It felt like ya'll didn't think enough of us to let us come and pay our respects. We're family. We need to be tighter than we are."

"Yeah, definitely. I was locked up, Unck."

"Phew," he sighs. "Boy, you stay locked up. Every time I turn around you in and out of jail."

"Uncle Fred that ain't true. I don't be in and out. I only been arrested once in my life. I went in back in 93 and I just came out a few months ago."

"Damnit boy! I ain't know that. I thought you kept getting into trouble.

That's a long time. I hope all that time learned you? What are you doing with yourself?"

"I work. I'm at a lawyer's office."

"You a lawyer, now. Shit, I guess with all that time, you had plenty enough time to learn all about the law," he smiles.

"Nah, I'm just a paralegal."

"It's all the same to me. I'm just glad to hear that you turned your life around. Now, what's the problem you told me you have?"

Dre pauses before replying. He doesn't know how he's going to present this to his uncle. He's afraid of how he may react. He quickly comes up with the most sensible story that he can think of. Here it goes, he says to himself. He hopes his uncle bites on it. "Uncle Fred, I'm on my way on vacation in the Bahamas with my wife to be for two weeks, but I have a small problem."

Oh, that's why he's here, Uncle Fred thinks to himself. I can't believe the nerve of him. I ain't spoke to the boy in twenty years and he's here to ask me for money? I should have known that he had some reason for popping up here like that. No way, he thinks to himself. He quickly tries to come up with an excuse on why he doesn't have the money to lend him. "What is it, boy? What can I do for you?" he asks. Anything but money, he says to himself.

"Well, I live in one of the worst neighborhoods in Newark," he lies. "They already attempted to break in to my apartment twice. I got a couple of dollars stashed and I'm afraid to leave it there alone for two weeks. I need you to hold it here for me until I get back."

Ah, that's it, he says to himself. "No problem, boy. I thought you had yourself a real problem? Sure you can leave it here. Ain't nobody here, but me and Dorothy. It's safe here. Where is it?"

Dre slides the duffle bag closer to his uncle's feet. His uncle looks down at the bag without putting any real thought into it. "You can't keep all your life savings laying around the house like that. You gotta get yourself a bank account. If you want, I'll open one up for you. How much is in here?" he asks as he unzips the bag. He's expecting to see a couple of thousand dollars. His mouth drops to the floor. "What the?"

"Unck, hold up. Take it easy."

"Easy my ass! Boy I don't want nothing to do with that illegal activity. I'm a hard working, honest man. I ain't never broke the law in my life and I ain't gone start now. I ain't gone be dragged into your bullshit. I thought you said you changed your life around? You ain't made all that money as no faralegal," he says mispronouncing the word ignorantly. "You done robbed a bank?"

"Unck, cool out for a second, please? Just listen. I did change my life around. I'm clean. I already did my time. The 15 years I did was because of this money. I ain't gone lie to you. It is dirty money, but they can't do shit about it. They can't convict a man twice for the same crime. I already did my time. Just so happen, they never found my money," he continues to lie. "That ain't my fault. What was I supposed to do, tell them where the money was?" Dre is lying through his teeth, but he knows he has to in order to make his uncle believe that he's doing nothing wrong by holding the money. He has nowhere else to put this amount of money without worrying about someone fleeing the country on him. Uncle Fred is about as honest as they come.

"How much is it?" he asks curiously.

"One million," Dre whispers.

"One million? Boy, take this dirty money and get out of my house. I told you, I'm an honest, hard working, clean man and I ain't gone be a part of this. I ain't never been in jail in my life and I ain't going at no 65 years old…not for you or nobody else! Go now!"

Dre listens to him shout and waits for him to take a breath so he can slide a few words in. "I'll pay you $125,000.00 to hold it for me."

Uncle Fred sits quietly not believing his ears. The number 125 echoes in his ears over and over. He's never seen that amount of money in his entire life. This changes his tune. He shakes his head from side to side. "When you coming back?"

"2 weeks, Unck."

"2 weeks it is and not a day later. Don't whisper a word of this to your Aunt Dorothy. She'll have a fit." He pauses for a few seconds as he thinks of how he's going to be able to hide this much money from his wife. "I know," he blurts out. "I'll build a spot in the wall of the basement. I can hide it there. I can do that in one day if I get started early in the morning. I'll wait until her Bingo day."

Dre digs into the duffle bag and pulls a plastic bag from within. He hands the bag to his uncle as he zips the bag up. "Here you go. I'm paying you in advance. $125,000.00 for a days worth of work. Never made that much in a day before, now did you?"

Uncle Fred replies with a cheesy smile. "Never!"

Three Hours Later

Today has been a rather hectic day for Dre. After leaving his uncle's house, he went to his attorney's office in Englewood. He gave his attorney another $250,000.00 retainer. The lawyer accepted the money, but it made him wonder what type of trouble Dre is expecting to get into wherein he needs a half of a million dollars to get out of it. Apparently he has no clue of who Dre is. He doesn't know that Dre's real purpose for giving him the money is not because of his fear of getting into trouble. It's actually his fear of having so much money lying around.

He feels a little more at ease being that he's unloaded the greater portion of his savings, but he won't feel free until he's dumped it all. Where he will drop it, he doesn't have a clue.

The excessive amount of money, as much as it is, is actually the smaller of his problems right now. The killer dope occupies his mind every second. He can't wait to get rid of it all. That should not be a problem at all due to the heavy volume of phone calls that he's been getting. Everyone is trying to get hold of the 'After Party' after hearing the news. As scared as he is to move it, he has no choice. He's made a few connections today already. In order to get it out of his possession quickly, he's doubled up each client's work load. He realizes that he may not receive his money until three weeks from now, but at least he will be free of the dope. His main concern is seeing Imamu so he can get rid of the seven kilos. The rest he's sure he can move in no time.

Meanwhile in the Bronx

Dre's man Chico hops into the white Infiniti FX35. "Hello Mami," he says. "Beautiful day, right?"

Lil Mama doesn't say a word in response just as Dre has trained her to do. He tells her over and over to limit her conversation and interaction with the clients. He trusts her, but he does know that men can be slick and conniving. He figures the less conversation she has with them the smaller his chances are of them actually getting to know each other. He fears if they ever get comfortable with her, anything is liable to happen. Whether it be someone trying to date her or trying to get to know her to get more familiar with his operation, it's all hazardous. She hands the bag of work over to Chico. "That's 3,000 Death Certificate and 500 After Party."

"After Party?" he asks. He's quite surprised. They have not had 'After Party' in some time now.

"He told me to tell you that he needs your help. He has a big supply and he doesn't want it to go bad before he moves it. He just needs you to move the 500 for him."

Chico knows better than to believe what she's telling him. Everyone in the world knows that the 'After Party' stamp has been labeled as killer heroin and that is his reason for him trying to dump it off on Chico. Chico is sure that if he knows Dre as well as he believes he does, he's trying to get rid of the dope as fast as he can in fear that the Feds may be onto him. Little does Dre know, Chico has no problem taking the dope because he's sure that he can move it in no time. Ever since the news cast, his phone has been ringing off the hook with customers trying to get hold of it. Instead of people trying to stay away from it, it's now an even hotter commodity.

Dope addicts all over the East Coast are in search of the dope. Every dope feign believes the dope claimed those lives because those individuals could not handle it. They believe their systems must have been too weak for it. They each believe that the strength of that heroin will only result in tremendous pleasure for them.

///// CHAPTER 103 /////

The Next Day/ 9 A.M.

Tony waits in his office for Dre to arrive. Tony has an afternoon case at the Essex County Court House that he's begged Dre to come along with him. Out of pure boredom, Tony just wants Dre to accompany him. He plans to go out for breakfast and just kick it until it's time for him to be in court.

Dre walks in sluggishly. He looks rather strange carrying a briefcase in each hand. "What up, what up?" Dre is totally exhausted. He hasn't had a wink of sleep and it can be seen in his baggy eyes.

Dre drops the briefcases onto Tony's desk and pops the latches open on the first one. "This is Lil Bruh's money," he says referring to his brother's profit from the past couple of flips. "That's 300 grand," he adds.

Things have been moving smoothly. Late yesterday Imamu and he linked up and he gave him the work that he ordered. As nervous as Dre was to actually make the sale, it was a relief to get rid of the work. Now all he has left is about 1,500 bricks and he has completely shaken the dope. He may not collect all the money until weeks from now, but at least he has half the battle won.

"Ok, I can deposit this before we go to eat," Tony claims.

"Tone, I need a favor?" Dre whispers.

"What up?"

"Shit getting crazy," he mumbles. "I need to do something with this bread. I'm stuck like chuck. I don't have nobody that I trust to hold this paper for me. I need you to deposit mines somewhere too."

Tony shakes his head from side to side. "Dre, I wouldn't mind, but shit isn't looking good on my end. I have a few banks that I'm working with, but I'm spreading the deposits out as thin as I can. Come on. This shit is getting dangerous. God forbid anything ever happens and they open up my safe deposit boxes...I'll be in a world of trouble."

Dre shrugs his shoulders while nodding his head up and down. Despair sets on his face. "I feel you."

"How much you got there?"

"Half-a-m," he whispers.

"Dre, baby, $250,000 here, $300,000 there. That ain't no punk money. That's real paper. Let me ask you the same question I ask your brother over and over...when is enough? I've watched you make a few millions. How much do you need to obtain before you decide to throw in the towel? Or are you waiting for the FBI to throw the towel in for you? You're just coming home from a 15 year bid and you wanting to position yourself, I feel that. Now you are more than in position. What is it that you want? A lifetime bid? Look at your brother...my man. He's not even 30 years old yet. As we both know, he's multi. He has more money than he could ever spend in a lifetime. On top of that, there's a small chance that he may never be free to spend any of it. What does it all mean? You have to know when to roll and when to fold. It's obvious that neither of you know when to fold."

Dre listens attentively. Deep down inside he knows that Tony is right. He nods his head up and down to let Tony know that he somewhat agrees with his statements.

"Listen, don't think I'm completely in the dark. I know exactly what's going on. I saw the news and I know why you're trying to get rid of the money. You're scared because you think the Feds may be coming for you, right?"

"Yeah," he admits shamefully.

"Well, let me clear up for you any doubt that you may have in your mind. They are coming. No doubt about that. You can bet your very last dollar on that. Do you actually believe that you can continue to make millions under their noses without offending them? I'll give it to you, you're pretty smart and you move extremely cautious, but even that isn't enough to save you. This game is not new. You didn't invent it. There is no tactic that you can apply that has not already been tried. Those guys are trained professionals. When your number is called, they're coming for you and guess what? They are going to get you. I'm not wishing bad luck on you; it's just the name of the game. Let me tell you something. You're playing a game that no one can win. It's not designed for you to win. It's like playing Russian Roulette with 5 bullets in the chamber and they give you not 5 shots but an extra bonus shot. They're painting the illusion that they're giving you something by giving you an extra shot, but in all reality, it's impossible to make it to the end of the game. I see you slip and slide around here as slick as grease. Even that doesn't matter because the people you're dealing with know how big you're doing it. You're playing a game, that when you're doing it as big as you are, people will admire and talk about you. If they talk about you, they can be heard. If they can be heard they can be recorded. If they can be recorded, you can be monitored. How can you get away from it all? By stopping while you are ahead. The Feds don't come for what you're doing today. They come for what you did yesterday. By the time they come they already have enough evidence to bury you. Let's just say that up until now, they have nothing on you from the past couple of months. If you just stop today, they won't have anything on you in the months to come. It's that simple. I'm with ya'll, but I can't keep putting my shit in jeopardy like I've been doing," he whines.

Dre lowers his head with shame. All the things that Tony is saying make all the sense in the world. Dre realizes that the fast money has officially blurred his vision. When he came home he had a clear head and promised himself that all he wanted was just enough and he would walk away from it with no problem. Up until now, he has completely forgotten about his plans.

"I'm not one to preach to anyone. You're a grown ass man. It's your life, your story. You're the author of the book. Write it your way," Tony says with his eyebrows raised high. "I already read the beginning of your book, all the way up to the middle. Judging by how fast you're rolling, I can already predict the ending. That is, unless you're crafty enough to throw a twist in the end. Listen, while you have the chance, you have to invest your money into something that can generate you some real capital. I'm not talking about a clothing store or a barber shop either. I'm talking about something lucrative that can feed your family for generations to come. I'll find somewhere to stash this money, but this is it. I can't take a penny more. That's it. You better do something. You have to find your exit."

Meanwhile In Asbury, New Jersey

Mu-Mit and Latif have just walked into Salaam's house. Neither of them really wants to be here. They'd rather be back in Newark trying to get to the bottom of their situation. Neither of them will be able to rest until they find out who is behind the caper.

They're only here for two reasons. One is the abundance of dope that Dre unloaded on them. They normally get no more than 600 bricks from him at a time. Yesterday, he damn near forced them to take 1,200 bricks.

The second reason is, Salaam has been calling their phones back to back, all day and night. Once the news showed on television, everyone here in Asbury have been going crazy, trying to get hold of the dope. With Salaam being the exclusive 'After Party' distributor, his phone has been ringing off the hook. Each time he receives a call, he makes two more to them. He claims that he has 400 bricks sold as soon as they touch down. Now, they're going to find out how true that is.

Hours Later in Newark, N.J.

"Did you see the look on that prosecutor's face?" Tony asks with a huge smile on his face.

"Did I," Dre replies. "He was stuttering like a mufucker. You stumbled the shit outta him."

Tony presses the button on his remote to open the locks of his Bentley. "Man, that cracker hate the fuck outta me," Tony laughs as he grabs hold of the door handle. Before getting into the car, a slow moving Chevy Trailblazer catches Tony's attention as it passes them. Just as the SUV gets pass them, the driver makes an unanticipated turn, cutting directly in front of them. This startles both Tony and Dre. The black dark tinted window rolls down slowly. Neither of them knows what to expect. They're both expecting to see a familiar face pop up, but instead, Boc! Boc! Boc! The gunshots start ringing long before the window is completely down and before the gun can be seen.

Dre stands there in complete shock for a matter of approximately two seconds before he drops to his knees and crawls to the back of the car in attempt to get to safety. Boc! Boc! Boc! Dre hears the bullets ripping through the metal of Tony's car. Boc! Boc!

Sirens ring off in the air, making Dre feel a certain amount of safety. The Chevy peels off recklessly. Dre lifts his head up, peeking through the back window. He sees the Trailblazer exit the parking lot wildly. By chance just as they get a few feet away, a County Sherriff vehicle damn near rams into them.

Dre stands and watches as the Chevy zips in and out of traffic directly in the heart of downtown Newark. "Tone!" Dre shouts as he makes his way to the driver's side. Once he gets there, he's shocked at what lies before his eyes. Tony lies flat on his back, with blood covering the front of his shirt. He lays there as still as can be. The look on his face shows that he's in massive pain. "I'm hit," he gasps as he grabs hold of his chest.

A detective comes running over to them. "Call an ambulance!" Dre shouts nervously. "He's hit in the chest!" The sound of police sirens fills the air. They're zooming pass in groups of three cars at a time. Dre is as baffled as he can possibly be. He can't imagine who could have taken these shots at Tony and why.

Tony lays there calm and collective. "Aghh," he grunts. He keeps his breathing short to avoid the pain that occurs when he breathes regularly. "Who was that?" he whispers.

"I don't know but we gone find out," Dre whispers in reply. Two more unmarked police cars pull into the parking lot, surrounding Dre and Tony. "Breathe. Just breathe," Dre says with sympathy.

"People clear it up!" the County Officer shouts to the crowd of people that have gathered around. "Back it up!" he shouts as the sirens of the ambulances get closer.

"Relax, baby. Just relax. Breathe."

///// CHAPTER 104 /////

In Hoboken, New Jersey/ The Next Day

Dre cracks his door open and snatches the Newark Star-Ledger from the hallway floor. The headline on the front page jumps at him. He can't believe his eyes. He swallows the lump that fills his throat. With a headline like that he can imagine what type of craziness may be reported in this story. He sits on the window sill and begins reading.

Attorney Tony Austin aka 'Tony Cochran' was gunned down as he leaves the Essex County Court House. Tony Cochran is the attorney of the infamous Newark Kingpin known as the 'Mayor.' As Austin and ex kingpin, Andre Blackhead (who is the older brother of Newark's Kingpin known as the 'Mayor') attempted to enter Austin's 2005 Bentley GT; a Chevy Trailblazer approached them while a passenger began firing random shots at them.

County Officers, who happened to be patrolling the area, heard the shots and raced to the scene where they found the wounded Tony 'Cochran' lying on the ground with a gunshot wound to the chest.

The driver of the Chevy, Jamal Jenkins, 21, of Newark led the officers on a high speed chase through the busy streets of Downtown Newark. Heavy traffic congestion just short of Newark Penn Station caused Jenkins to panic. He then dashed onto the sidewalk in attempt to escape. This in turn gave the officers time to catch up with the Chevy. After crashing into a local bus Jenkins along with his two accomplices, Laron Mildred, 25 of Montclair and another unidentified man were forced to exit the vehicle and flee the scene.

Jenkins and Mildred are in custody while the third man still remains at large. It has been reported that Jenkins and Mildred belong to the notorious street gang 'The Trauma Unit.' The gang is noted as one of the most treacherous street gangs in Essex County. Their gang is based on heavy drug trafficking and murder. Officials have reason to believe that the third assailant may be the gang's leader, 31 year old Horace Jackson, known to the street as 'Trauma.'

Attorney Tony Austin a.k.a. Tony Cochran is in stable condition and was released from the hospital a few hours later. Ex-Kingpin, Blackhead, 40 was released after questioning. Blackhead was just released from federal prison a few months ago and claims to be working as a paralegal in Austin's firm.

The motive is still unknown.

This story infuriates Dre. This is definitely not a good look for him, his brother or Tony. He's sure that anyone who reads this article will automatically believe that there is some dirty dealing going on.

"Horace Jackson," Dre says to himself as he wonders if this is a name that he may know from somewhere. "Trauma Unit?" he asks aloud.
In Watchung, New Jersey

Tony lays in his bed just relaxing his aching body. "Sssss, aghh," he sighs. Although he's in a great deal of pain his condition isn't half as painful as he's portraying it to be. He loves all the extra attention that Mocha is giving him. She's spoiling him like a baby and he loves every second of it.

"Sit still baby," she whispers. "What you need? I'll get it for you."

"Nah, I'm alright. I'll get it myself," he says before sighing again. "I'm going to get some iced tea. I'm a little parched," he whines.

She jumps up from the bed and runs out of the room.

Tony laughs at the sight of that. In all the years that they have been together, she's never catered to him like this and because of that he plans to enjoy it for as long as he can. She returns shortly with not a glass of iced tea, but an entire pitcher. "Thanks wife," he whispers as he gloats inside.

Tony is in total suspense. He doesn't have a clue as to why he's been shot. At first he assumed that they were attempting to shoot Dre, but he swears that he doesn't know who the Trauma Unit is. He says that he has never even heard of them, let alone dealt with them.

"Babe, I hate to say I told you so, but I told you so," Mocha says as she hands him a glass of tea. "You have to draw the line. It's supposed to be business. You're getting way too involved. This right here is too much. You could have lost your life. Those are your clients, but you're treating them like friends."

Tony nods his head up and down. "I hear you, but all this is business. Me and my assistant were just finishing up a court case."

"Just cut your personal ties. I don't want you to get dragged into anymore of their situations. Did you read how that article was written? The wrong people could easily get the wrong idea and think that you have more than just attorney, client business with them."

"Mo, this is just a case of being at the wrong place at the wrong time. They wrote it like that intentionally to make the public think that," he claims. "Anybody with common sense can read that article and know that it's all bullshit."

In Newark, New Jersey

Federal Agents Dumber and Dumbest stand in the lobby of their Gateway building headquarters. Happiness covers their faces. Dumbest stands there smiling from ear to ear as he reads the article out aloud.

"They should have killed the black fucker," Dumber snarls.

"It's all coming together like a stew," Dumbest says with great joy. "Why would someone try to assassinate an attorney? Either one of two reasons. Either the attorney made a promise to a client that he could not deliver or maybe he's part of the whole 'After Party' network?" he says with a smile.

"You think?"

"I don't know, but it's only one way to find out?"

In Yazoo, Mississippi

The Mayor paces back and forth throughout his cell. He's highly frustrated at what he's heard, but he's also quite confused. The news traveled to Yazoo as if it's only around the corner. Only problem is, by the time the news got here it got twisted along the way. The Mayor doesn't know exactly what happened.

The first rumor he heard was Tony and Dre were murdered in a courtroom after Tony's client lost trial and was sentenced to life. Supposedly, the brother of the client murdered them. Later on, the Mayor received word that Dre was shot, but survived, but Tony died on the scene. The Mayor wasn't able to get a wink of sleep all night, believing that could have been true. Not only did he think his chances of freedom were erased, he also was heart broken due to the loss of his good friend.

This morning he found out the actual truth, which was the best news that he's heard in his entire life. He still is confused because he hasn't been able to get in touch with anyone who can better explain the situation to him. At this point, he doesn't know why this happened. All he's left with are a few of his own assumptions.

He listens to the phone ring. He never dials this number, but this is his last resort being that Tony and Dre's phones have been off. His heart pumps nervously as he finally gets an answer. "Hello?" he says anxiously. "Yo, what up?"

"Who this?" Latif asks hastily.

"The Mayor, nigga. What's good?"

"Aw man, Lil Bruh, I don't know. I'm about to get out there right now and get to the bottom of this shit."

"I'm sure somebody know something," the Mayor snaps.

"Trust me, we gone get to the bottom of it."

"Do that. Dig this though…True story, my brother and that attorney are the closest people to me in the whole wide world. Without the lawyer, any chance I have at freedom is shot. And my brother, without him, I'd rather not live. That $10,000 a month salary ya'll on? That's paid to ya'll to watch over them and make sure nothing happens to them. Yesterday they were touched, which means ya'll ain't doing ya'll job. Ya'll just taking $20,000 a month from me for doing nothing. I'm gone tell you like this and I want you to relay the message to Mu-Mit. For half the money I can get bigger and more dangerous wolves. If anything happens to those two, I won't hesitate to put a lesser dollar up to erase both of ya'll. Real talk!" he says before hanging the phone up in Latif's ear.

///// CHAPTER 105 /////

ILL Wheel sits low in the passenger's seat while Ahmir drives. Dusty sits in the back quietly, just staring into space as usual. They have been moving around extra carefully. They know one bad move can cost them their lives. They only have each other, unlike Shotgun and his squad who have enough men that they can afford to lose a couple. It's them against an army. They realize that the attacks that they've made are highly disrespectful. Murdering a girl was a violation in the very first place, but to attack again at her funeral is a total violation. They somewhat regret murdering Charlie Baltimore, but at the end of the day there is no turning back now. They've made their beds and now it's time to lay in them. They are sure if they ever get caught slipping, it's over, ball game!

ILL Wheel's phone rings. He looks down at the display. "Damn," he sighs.

"What?" Ahmir asks.

"Fucking Dre again," he replies.

"Answer the fucking phone! Fuck that."

ILL Wheel has been ignoring Dre's calls since the house robbery. He doesn't have a dime of the money that he owes Dre and he's sure Dre doesn't want to hear that. The last incident was close and to come right back with another issue, he's sure a big mess is bound to take place. "I can't answer it. I ain't got the man's money."

"Ay man, shit happens. This the game. Fuck that, answer the phone. You don't be ducking no fucking body! Gimme the phone. I'll answer it." ILL Wheel hands the phone over with no hesitation. Ahmir answers it just as Dre is about to hang up. "Yo?"

"Yeah? Who this?" Dre asks, not recognizing the voice.

"It is who it is," Ahmir replies in a playful voice.

"What? Who this?"

"Nigga who this?" Ahmir asks with a smirk on his face.

"Hello?"

"Yeah, nigga what?"

"Who the fuck is this?" Dre asks hastily.

"This be Young Cash, nigga! What up?"

"Young Cash, what up Daddy. How you been? How long you been up here?"

"Not long. I just slid into town about a week or so ago."

"Cool, cool. Where ILL Wheel? I been trying to contact him for a minute now."

"He right here. Man, mad shit been going down, ya know?"

"Tell me about it," he says with sarcasm in his voice. "Dig, I need to meet with ya'll. It's real important. At 5 on the dot, we need to get together. We'll meet at Ponderosa's in West Orange. You know where that's at?"

"Trills."

"Alright, see you there!" Dre says before hanging the phone up.

Meanwhile a Few Miles Away

Trauma stands on Candy Kev's porch standing face to face with Candy Kev. "You sure?" Trauma asks. "Listen, I hope for your sake, that you're not holding out on information?"

"Yo, Trauma, on everything. I already told you everything I know about them."

Trauma walks away, leaving Candy Kev with the words in his mouth. Kev is sick and tired of them now. Being in the middle of this has been a living nightmare. If he had somewhere to go, he would have left already. That's not as easy as it sounds with three kids and a wife. He can't just pick up and disappear like that. He's been contemplating, sending the wife and kids to her mother's house, while he lays low somewhere until all this blows over. If this wasn't his own home, it would be different. He could just pick and start over someplace where they couldn't find him, but that isn't the case. Now he's forced to figure out another plan.

Candy Kev watches as Trauma gets into his car. I gotta get the fuck outta here, he says to himself.

///// CHAPTER 106 /////

Ahmir sits in the middle of ILL Wheel and Dusty. They all sit across from Dre. They have just arrived here. Latif and Mu-Mit have not even gotten here yet.

"Niggas set me up. They ordered the bricks and when I get there to deliver, they were waiting for me three deep," ILL Wheel explains. "Put the slammer to my head and made me take them to the crib," he says with shame. Just telling this story makes him feel like less than a man. He's totally humiliated by this ordeal. "We get there and they pistol whip me and shit until I finally told them where the work was. Look," he says as he points to a scab under his left eye that has not totally healed yet. "I only told them so they could let me go and I could get my revenge," he claims.

"No, you told them to save your life," Dre says casually. "You did what was right. That don't make you a sucker. They had the drop on you. It can happen to anybody. How come you didn't come to me?"

"You know we just had the situation with the 60 cash, so I was like damn, I can't tell him this shit. He'll never believe me."

Dre nods his head up and down. "Listen man we a team. When shit like that go down, I need to know about it. You can't have us in the dark like that. I just had a situation as you already know. For all I know, that could all be tied in together. If I would have known about your situation, I would have been a little more on point, feel me? You know who did it? Man, we could have put Mu and La on that asap. It would have been handled already. Tell me who it is and it's a wrap?"

"Nah," ILL Wheel replies. "This is personal. They didn't disrespect Mu or La. They disrespected me. It's my problem and I have to deal with it. They violated me. Mu-Mit and Latif, they your wolves. I got my own," he says pointing to Ahmir. He looks over to Dusty, who sits there with a goofy smile on his face.

"Oh, so that's what brings you here?" Dre asks, while staring at Ahmir.

"My man got a situation that needs to be situated," he says nodding his head up and down arrogantly.

"What they get you for?" Dre asks.

"Like 170 bricks and the rest of what you gave me was in money. They got that too."

"Damn, they scored on you."

"I promise you they ain't gone live to brag about it," Ahmir says sarcastically. "And the money, I got you. The $54,000, that's nothing. When I go back to B-More, I'll scoop that up and bring it back to you. I don't want this situation to stop the groove my man has going. Just let us handle this shit and then he'll get back to work, deal?"

"Filthy ass bastards!" Dre shouts with rage. "I'm telling you man, let me put the boys on it? That's what Mu and La are here for. Their job is to clean up the dirty work, so we can have a clear path while getting this money. A mufucker get in the path, they have to move him out. It's that simple. Speaking of the devils," he says pointing at the door.

They step over to the table at a moderate pace. "Peace!" Mu-Mit shouts before seating himself.

Latif shakes hand by hand around the table. "What up ya'll?" he asks as his hand dangles in front of Dusty's face. Dusty looks right pass him, as if he isn't standing there. Aggression sets on Latif's face. He feels like Dusty is playing him. "You don't see my hand?"

"Yo," Ahmir calls. He shakes his head from side to side as he points to his temple. "It ain't there," he whispers.

Latif finally snatches his hand away and sits next to Dre. "What up, Big Bruh?"

"Short and brief," Dre says firmly. "Let me tell ya'll how the shit went down just to clear up any rumors that ya'll may have heard. No beef with nobody, no altercations, nothing. We walking to the car and the Trailblazer cuts in front of us and start banging. I don't have a clue of what that shit was about?"

Lil Mama steps up to the table. Dre invited her as well. He wants to make sure that everyone is aware of what's going on and are on the same page. He also figures any information that anyone may have can be brought to the table and then maybe he can find out what all this is about.

Lil Mama walks around the table and stops short directly across from Ahmir. He stares at her in awe, admiring her booty and her beauty. He has no clue of who she is and what her purpose could be, but he has no problem at all with her being here. She sits right next to Dre on the opposite side of Latif. "Hey," she whispers to Dre only, as she's seating herself.

"I never heard of these cats," Dre says. "Ya'll?" he asks as he looks at Latif and Mu-Mit.

"Never heard of them," Mu-Mit whispers.

"Nope," Latif denies. "Trauma Unit, never heard of 'em."

"Trauma Unit?" Ahmir questions. "Everybody know them. We went to school with Trauma's little cousin Jamal. He a couple of years older than us though. Trauma Unit took the shots at you?"

"Jamal?" Dre questions. "Jamal Jenkins."

"Yep," Ahmir replies.

"That's the nigga who pulled the trigger," Dre says. "I can't figure out what this shit could be about? Where they from?"

"Well, I don't know where they at now, cause I ain't been on the scene, but they move around in a few places, right Wheel?"

"Yeah, they deep as hell. They be a little bit of everywhere. Anywhere they can muscle their way into, they gone do it. They really from 16th Avenue."

"Where at on 16th Avenue?" Mu-Mit asks.

"18th Street."

"18th Street?" Mu-Mit repeats. Candy Kev comes to mind instantly. That is his location. Mu-Mit looks over to Latif. The look on Latif's face says I told you so. He rolls his eyes with disgust.

Dre senses the tension and gets the feeling that they know something. "So, what's the deal?"

Mu-Mit pauses before speaking. "Dig Bruh, I don't have a clue of who them cats is, but we be moving out with my little man from over that way. The other day we get into a small conflict as we serving him. Now all this shit starting to come together. How them mufuckers know to come at you is beyond me."

"Small conflict like what?" Dre asks. "Can't be that small. Them mufuckers took a shot at an attorney, broad daylight, downtown Newark at the Courthouse.

"Some small shit," he says downplaying the matter. "A robbery," he admits. "They didn't get shit though. The shit ended up going the opposite way," he lies.

"It's obvious that they don't know who they fucking with, but they are about to see real soon, though."

"Whether the conflict is big or small, it's still a conflict. Ya'll out here running around getting into situations and telling nobody," Dre says with rage. "Ya'll got everybody else in the dark, while ya'll out here on some selfish shit, like it's just about ya'll. We a fucking team. You running into situations with Blood niggas," he says pointing to ILL Wheel. "And ya'll with these mufuckers. Ya'll got me running around this mufucker with a blindfold over my eyes. Ya'll gotta bring that shit to the big table. God forbid somebody get murdered, I wouldn't have a clue of what the fuck going on. What else going on out there? He looks to Lil Mama. You got something you been holding out on?" he snaps.

She shakes her head negatively from side to side. "Not at all," she whispers.

"And ya'll with that dumb ass Blood shit," he says to ILL Wheel and Ahmir. Thought them was your fucking homies, now look," he snaps sarcastically. "They done flipped on you. Now what?"

Ahmir steps up, not giving ILL Wheel a chance to reply. "Oh, that's nothing. We got that under control. You ain't even got to worry about that."

"I do have to worry about it," Dre replies viciously. "Ya'll part of my fucking squad."

"What happened?" Latif asks.

"Fucking Bloods called him and placed an order."

"Hold up," Ahmir interrupts. "That wasn't for everybody. That was between us."

"Ain't no between us," Dre snaps. "What part of that ya'll don't fucking understand?" None of them have ever heard Dre speak in this tone. "They placed an order and when he came to deliver, they jumped in the fucking car and held him at gun point and made him take him to his house. They pistol whipped him and the whole shit," he adds. "Ya'll keeping secrets and shit, got Lil Mama riding around here blind as hell. If something happens to her because of ya'll bullshit, we gone have problems. That's my word."

Latif speaks trying to give Dre some time to calm down. "So, ya'll got the low down on the Blood niggas?"

"Man, we know everything about them. We jumped dead on that a couple of days later. That's nothing."

"You sure?" Latif asks.

"Positive. Let's just handle this Trauma Unit shit. We got that other shit."

Dre sits there quietly just observing the looks on all of their faces. "So, now what?" he asks while looking at Mu-Mit.

"Now that we know where the problem came from we can come up with a solution. We on that as soon as we leave here. It's simple, I'll get with my little man and he gone take us to the niggas, bottom line."

///// CHAPTER 107 /////

In Essex County Jail/ Two Days Later

The young man paces back and forth around his tiny cell. The new case he's just caught has him stressed out of his mind. He wonders what type of bail will be set for him. He's sure his bail will be sky high for attempted murder on an attorney, at the courthouse. He prays that they even give him a bail, with that type of charge.

He sits down on the edge of the bottom bunk and buries his face in between his legs. The sound of footsteps approaching him causes him to look up. To his surprise, there stands a stranger directly over him. His defense mechanism kicks in, alerting him that there's a problem. He attempts to stand up, but he's struck on the chin by a wild haymaker. He collapses onto the floor. Two other men rush into the cell quickly, while a third man stands at the gate on guard.

The man scuffles, trying to get onto his feet. As he's tussling around, he ends up on the bottom, face down. The opposing man has him pinned to the floor with no way for him to escape. The man on the floor fights for his life. Either he doesn't value his life or he just doesn't have enough fight in him because he is definitely losing the battle. He tosses around flipping and flopping like a fish does when it's out of water.

The man that's standing to the right grasps a ice-pick in his hand. He draws back high in the air before driving the point into the man's neck.

"Owww," the man screams, before his mouth is muffled by the hands of the man who rides his back. The man bucks up and down like a wild bull, yet the man continues to stay on top of him. Not even two seconds later, another ice-pick is plunged into his kidney. All his squirming eases up as the agony of the pain slows his fighting down. The man notices that they have stolen the fight from him. He hops off of his back and retrieves his own ice-pick. The three of them kneel over him and go to work like butchers. They poke and carve the man like a piece of beef, while blood gushes from everywhere.

Seconds later, the men walk out of the cell casually as if nothing has happened. Meanwhile the man lies there with more holes in his body than a piece of Swiss Cheese. He lies there not able to utter a word or move a limb. He can barely breathe due to the blood that is rapidly filling his lungs. Blood gushes from his mouth by the ounce. He lies there with his eyes wide open, staring into the darkness. His breathing slows down by the second. Suddenly his eyes close into tranquility.

No need to worry about bail money. All of his worldly problems are now over.

Meanwhile a Few Cities Away

Mu-Mit and Latif sit parked a half a block away from Candy Kev's house. They've been sitting here patiently for the past hour and a half. After calling him all this morning and getting no answer, Mu-Mit decided to sit out here and wait for him to come out. At this point, he's pissed off with this matter.

Candy Kev has managed to make Mu-Mit look like a pure idiot in Latif's eyes. As much as Mu-Mit has told Latif about Candy Kev being like a younger brother to him and how he doubts highly that he would move out out on him, his negligence in answering the calls makes him look completely guilty. Mu-Mit still would love to give him the benefit of the doubt, but he can't. Candy Kev has now forced him to treat him like a stranger.

"I told you," Latif boasts. "No way in the world is this a coincidence. He's behind all this shit," Latif says, pissing Mu-Mit off even more. "He's in on all of this. A hundred grand loss for us, but a major come up for all of them."

"So, he thinks," Mu-Mit says.

"Oh, who that?" Latif asks while pointing to the porch. A beautiful woman and three small children walk slowly down the stairs. The woman lugs in her hands two small suitcases.

"Must be his wife and kids," Mu-Mit assumes.

"Hmmm, looks like somebody trying to get low," Latif says sarcastically. They both assume that Candy Kev is on his way out. "It's fucked up that we gone have to do him in front of his family." The woman packs the suitcases and the children into the van before she seats herself into the driver's seat. "She pulling off. I wonder where he at? Follow her. She may lead us right to the fag ass nigga." The woman pulls off slowly. Mu-Mit gives her a half a block head start before he tails her. "You can run, but you can't hide," Latif says sarcastically.

////// CHAPTER 108 //////

The Next Day

Tony and Dre sit in the entertainment room of Tony's lavish home. The room is filled with all state of the art electronics, a pool table, a ping pong table, and a miniature golf course.

Tony lays back in his recliner. In one hand, he holds an unlit cigar and in the other hand, he holds the Newark Star Ledger. He reads the article aloud. "Jamal Jenkins, 21 of Newark, found dead in a cell in Newark's Essex County Jail. Jenkins was taken into custody for the attempted murder of Attorney Tony Austin A.K.A. Tony Cochran after a shooting earlier this week.

Officers found Jenkins lying in a pool of blood with over twenty stab wounds. No motive or suspects have been found as of yet." Tony looks up at Dre, as he sticks the cigar in his mouth and spins it around to wet the entire tip.

Dre's mind is boggled. What the fuck is going on, he asks himself. Something tells him that his brother is behind all of this, but he will never admit to Tony.

"This shit is getting uglier and uglier by the second," Tony says. "You know this doesn't look good for us, right?"

"Phew," Dre sighs. "Yeah, I know. I mean, they can't charge us with it can they? We out here," he adds.

"Yeah, I feel you. They can't charge us with it, but it can definitely open a can of worms," he says nodding his head up and down.

Meanwhile at the Federal Headquarters

Federal Agent Dumber holds the exact same article in his hand after reading it thoroughly. "Who the fuck do they think they are?" he asks hastily.

"These niggas think they really have a great deal of power, huh?" Dumbest asks.

"That's what it looks like," Dumber replies. "But the reality is they only have as much power as we give them. We have to take control of this matter," he says as he dials numbers on his desk phone. "Hello, Diane? This is Richie! Good and you? Listen, you know Blackhead, right? Ok, I need you to get me a copy of his visit sheet. I need the name and addresses of everyone that has ever visited him in every institution that he's been in. I also need the names and addresses of everyone who has ever posted bail for him. I would appreciate it if you can get that to me, asap." He pauses briefly. "Thanks Diane! I owe you a million," he smiles. "Ok, later," he says before planting the phone onto the base. He looks at his partner. "All this time, we had nothing on him, but now the tables have turned. They've given us more than a lead to follow," he smiles. "See what being patient will get you? It's time to show them who is really in control."

Back in Watchung, New Jersey

"I've been working on this project for months now. As of right now, I only have your girl Angelique on board as a partner. It's a big project which will take a pretty penny to get it rolling. Although, Angelique and I can do it together, it would be a lot easier on us if we had another partner or so. The more the merrier. One more investor will help us to take this thing to the next level. Listen, there's millions of dollars to be made if this project is handled properly. This all works out perfectly. We need another investor and you have money that you need to invest. After our conversation, I've been busting my brain, trying to figure out what you could invest your money into to go legal and here it is right under my nose. This can be a very lucrative investment. I have all the bases covered."

Dre is already sold on the idea not because he has any idea of the business. His main purpose is to hide a couple more dollars. The fact that he'll be making a profit off of his money is all the better. "How much do I have to invest?"

"I can show you the spreadsheet with the projected income. I have no problem showing you what every penny will be used for. Manufacturing, advertisement, representatives, in total, $750,000.00. Put up 250 grand and in a matter of two years you will be a multi-million," he sings. "Legally, that is," he adds.

Dre doesn't hesitate to reply. "I'm in," he whispers.

"Ok, good," Tony replies while extending his hand for a handshake. "Partner. Trust me, this is the best investment your money can buy. You will not be disappointed."

///// CHAPTER 109 /////

The Mayor lays back on his cot, just lounging when his phone starts to vibrate. He answers it quickly. "What the deal?" he asks.

"Big Bruh, how you?" the caller replies. The caller is the Mayor's man, from the Essex County Jail. "You heard the news?"

The Mayor thinks quickly before replying. "Nah, what's good?"

"Aw man, Big Bruh, the young boy from the Trauma Unit came to the building the other day and he didn't last for four hours. They found his body in a pool of blood. Mufuckers carved his ass like a sculpture."

The Mayor listens closely to the shocking news. "Yeah?" he asks in a baffled manner. He wonders if his man made the move on the young boy.

"Yeah, like that, Big Bruh."

""Who the hell could have done something like that?" the Mayor asks attempting to talk in code.

The caller senses where he's taking this. "Nah, Big Bruh," he says sternly. "Rumor has it that them red niggas did it."

The Mayor realizes that the caller is referring to the Bloods. "For what?"

"Who knows, Big Bruh?"

Meanwhile In Inez, Kentucky

Damien Bryant a.k.a 'The Black Charles Manson' sits across his cot. He's just finished writing a detailed letter and now he's reading it over.

It reads: First and foremost I hope this letter reaches you in the best of health and spirits.

I'm sure you've heard the saying, one hand washes the other. I truly appreciate the fact that you didn't over react about our prior situation. I appreciate it just as much as the young homie does.

I understand how you could have reacted and being that you didn't, that has given me that much more respect for you. I have grown to understand that a man isn't defined by the power he has. He's defined by how he uses his power. Even a weak fool can destroy an entire country. I had a great deal of power, but I didn't know how to use it properly until I did my research on you. I did that as a token of my appreciation for you sparing my homie's life. So, from both of us, we thank you. I made the call, but he executed the move.

On a completely different note, word has traveled to me about a terrible matter and two of your men are in the middle of a disaster in the making. I am in no way connected to the opposing bodies, but I am only one phone call away from the superior who happens to not only love me, but he worships the ground that I walk on. This issue isn't an issue that should be ignored. We need to nip it in the bud before it escalates any further. Please get a representative to reach out to this contact. I have already handled the rest. The only thing that needs to be done on your end is for you to provide someone to represent you in this matter.

I'm sure you're probably wondering why I'm so eager to assist you in a situation that I have nothing to do with? Well for the most part, from gangster to gangster, I respect you. Secondly, I have a situation of my very own in which I'm in dire need of your assistance. As I told you before I'm being charged with capital murder. There is a huge chance that they may be giving me the lethal injection. I am a realist and I respect the game that I played. I realize that I must pay for my actions. I know there is no possible way that I'll ever see daylight again and I have no problem with that. I have already accepted it for what it is. My mind is already set on that. If they sentence me to 100 years, I'll sit back and do my time like the man that I am. My fear is them taking my life.

Fighting this battle with a public defender is a nightmare. I may as well kiss my life goodbye. My moms died before my second birthday and I have never had the opportunity to meet my pops. All my early years, I've moved from place to place. At the age of 14, I went off to raise myself. I say all of that to say, I have no love on the outside. If you could find it in your heart to link me with an attorney to represent me, it would be greatly appreciated.

Please do not take this as me looking for a handout. I'm no beggar. I have always worked for mine. Any help that I can be to you, I am more than willing to be there at your disposal. I think I have proven to you by now, what I bring to the table. In closing, I state to you that, I am a young black man in need.

He signs the letter, Damien Bryant aka The Black Charles Manson.

////// CHAPTER 110 //////

2 P.M. Friday

Several Muslim men fill this room, while the Muslim women are in a room of their own, upstairs. After hearing the hour long Khutbah (speech) on Eeman (Faith), Jumah is now over and everyone is making their way out of the building. Some walk slowly, holding up the crowd as they talk to each other, while others trot hastily.

"Brothers!" the middle aged man, who stands at the microphone, yells. "Brothers please? Can I get just two minutes of your time? I know you have to get back to work, but please? I only need two minutes." The brothers stop at the sound of his pleading. "Brothers and sisters, a member of our Umah (community), Brother Abdul Malik, his teen-age son is in Newark's University Hospital, where he's in critical condition. He needs all of our prayers. He's suffering from knife wounds. His lung was punctured two days ago as he was leaving a recreational center a few blocks away from his home. Apparently, they wanted his MP3 player. After brutally attacking him and stabbing him in his chest, they finally left. Brothers, when is enough? We stand here and say that we are Muslims, but what kind of Muslims are we? This has gone far enough. The savages have taken over our community. Our children are not even safe in their own communities. They can't even go to school in peace as they try and obtain an education. Our elders are afraid to come out of their homes. Our young brothers take these savages as their companions. Our sisters take them for their spouses. What has this religion come to? Islam has become a mockery! We call ourselves men? How can we, when we are allowing this to go on? It's up to us to stand up and take back our community. Some of us may say, 'it's not my son, so I'm going to mind my own business?' Yeah, it's not your child right now but who is to say that it won't be yours next? Others figure if we ignore the problem it will eventually go away. We've ignored it long enough, now look! It has only increased. We're already up to close to sixty murders this year already. When is the killing going to stop? It's not…until we put our feet down. We have to take our streets back. Any brother willing to aid in this matter, can meet me here tomorrow night after Asr Prayer. Allah says in the glorious Quran, 'and distinguish them from the hypocrites, to whom it was said, come fight in the cause of God or help in it. They said, had we known there is fighting we would surely have followed you. On that day they were closer to disbelief than to faith, saying with their lips other than their hearts concealed and God is all knowing of what they conceal," he quotes. "In closing remember this, Allah also says in the Quaran, 'it's only Satan who makes you fear his friends, therefore do not fear them, but fear me if you are believers.'   "As for our young brother, we're taking a donation because unfortunately, it has been a very difficult and trying time for the family. He's a part of our community which means it is our responsibility. A brother is standing at the door, so make sure you drop something in the bucket on your way out, Insha Allah? Give for the sake of Allah!"

Mu-Mit quickly approaches the bucket just as the brother says this. He dips around the brother in front of him, totally disregarding the brother's statement. As he passes the bucket, he lowers his head with shame. It feels as if the spotlight is being shined on him. He would love to donate, but his money is no good here. His money comes from drug dealing and murder which means it won't be accepted as charity. He feels terribly bad, knowing that he holds close to $8,000 in his pocket and he can't donate a penny of the Haraam money. He shakes his head with despair at the very thought of it.

""May Allah reward all of us who have contributed, and the ones who would like to contribute, but don't have the means to do so. May Allah guide all of us? May he reward us in this life and the hereafter? Ameen!"

"Ameen," the brothers shout out at the same time.

"As Salaamu Alaikum Wa Rahmatullahi wa Barakaatu!"

Mu-Mit walks out of the Masjid and stands to the right of the door. Seconds later, his wife and daughter walk toward him, dodging and weaving through the crowds of people that swarm the narrow sidewalk.

Both his wife and his daughter are dressed in full garb. Their heads are covered by brightly designed pastel colored scarves which match their over garments perfectly. Their jazzy shoes add so much flavor to their outfits. Mu-Mit stands there admiring their beauty. He's waited for this day when the two women of his life have wholeheartedly accepted Islam and are worshipping to the best of their ability. Now, if only he can get himself together, everything would be pefect.

Mu-Mit stands there looking as sharp as a tack as well. His all black over garment fits neatly over top of his jeans. His burgundy chunk Alligator shoes match the kufi cap that sits on the back of his head. His attire and his long thick beard make him look more Muslim than he actually is. Some brothers are Muslim by name and not in their hearts. They spend more time trying to perfect their look than they do in trying to perfect their hearts.

Mu-Mit's wife and daughter finally make their way to him. "As Salaamu Alaikum!" they greet simultaneously.

"Wa Alaikum As Salaam wa Rahmutullahi," he says perfectly. "What we eating, ya'll?"

"I don't know," his wife replies. "What you want?" she asks as she looks toward the daughter.

She shrugs her shoulders. "It doesn't matter."

"How about the Halal Buffet over in West New York?" he asks hoping they will agree. This is his all time favorite restaurant.

"Sounds good," the wife replies.

Mu-Mit steps ahead of them leading the way up the block. He stops short of the vendor who stands in the middle of the block. "Ya'll want Bean Pies?" he asks turning toward his wife and daughter. "Three Bean Pies," he says to the vendor. As he's reaching over to get his bag, he cuts his eye over his shoulder peeking at the heavy congestion of cars that fill the block.

He steps away from the table. As he's bending the corner on the way to the parking lot, he peeps his surroundings once again just out of habit. He can't help but notice the Chevy Lumina which is sitting still in the street, holding up traffic. Heavy horn blowing fills the air as Mu-Mit and his family step quickly. "Block, block, block! Gunshots sound off startling all the Muslims. They attempt to scatter to safety. Major trampling is taking place as everyone tries to get out of harms way. Mu-Mit looks in the direction of where the shots came from, only to see that the passenger of the Chevy Lumina is hanging out of the window aiming precisely at him. Block, block!

Mu-Mit's wife and daughter run closer to him for his protection. Block, block! He palm grips the tops of their heads and forces them to the ground. He drops to his knees, as well, using the car in front of him as a shield. As they're on the ground they hear several shots sounding off. Mu-Mit, his family and other people lie on the ground, nervously. The sound of tires burning rubber reassures them that the bandits have pulled off.

Screaming and yelling fills the air in place of the gunshots. As Mu-Mit is helping his wife and daughter onto their feet, he looks directly behind him, where he sees a crowd of people huddled up. "Call an ambulance!" the sister shouts hysterically. "Call the police!"

Mu-Mit runs over to the crowd and peeks over their shoulders. The sight brings tears to his eyes. There the elderly man lies gasping for air. "Who is that?" Mu-Mit asks the brother who stands next to him.

"That's Abu Bakr Sayiid, the Muezzin."

Tears drop from Mu-Mit's eyes. This is the worse situation that he's ever been in. He's sure this shooting was meant for him. He's positive that the Trauma Unit is behind this. Just to think that he's brought harm to the Masjid and a prominent figure in the community has been wounded because of his haram acts, makes him feel awful. The man Abu Bakr Sayiid has the most beautiful voice in the entire community. He damn near brings tears to the Muslim's eyes each time he recites the call to prayer. Now watching him lay here struggling for his life brings even more tears to Mu-Mit's eyes.
Several Miles Away

"Damn!" Trauma shouts from the backseat of the Chevy Lumina. "I can't believe you missed that motherfucker. You should have got out and ran right up on his ass. You could have popped his top, just like I told you to. Shit!"

///// CHAPTER 111 /////

In Yazoo, Mississippi/ Days Later

The Mayor reads the letter slowly, breaking down every sentence. From reading the last couple of letters from this kid, he has learned that the boy is quite crafty with his wording. He knows how to cop a plea and display aggression all in one sentence. The Mayor reads the letter entirely and for the very first time, he doesn't sense the slightest bit of aggression whatsoever. What he actually senses is a young man who really fears for his life. Reading the letter makes the Mayor feel a certain amount of pity for the kid.

This letter has answered all of his questions. The Mayor now realizes that the kid made the call to his underlings and had the Trauma Unit dude murdered. All in all, the Mayor has to admit that he underestimated the boy, but this display of his power is rather impressive.

The Mayor's hustler mind set makes him see a bigger picture. He's sure with that kid as an acting member of his squad, the sky would be the limit. There would be no end to the money that they can make together. Although this could be very lucrative for the Mayor, he is not only thinking of himself. By hooking up with the young man, he will provide a way for the man to be able to pay for an attorney to represent him with his case.

The Mayor picks up his cell phone and dials away.

At the Essex County Jail

"What up, Big Bruh?" the inmate whispers as he peeks around nervously to make sure no officers are anywhere around.

"Ay...what we discussed? Cancel it," the Mayor demands.

"Huh? I'm not understanding where you coming from."

"Yeah, the girl I wanted you to holler at for me?"

"Yeah?" the man mumbles.

"Well, don't. I'm giving her a pass. I found out she a little girl. She ain't ready for a nigga like me."

"You sure?"

"I'm positive," the Mayor replies. "It's all worked out. I'll kick it with you later," he says before hanging up the phone.

The Mayor thinks back to the letter the man sent him where he stated that he had close to 1,000 followers. That was quite some time ago, which means that his army has grown even more at this point. Multi-million dollar thoughts fill the Mayor's mind as he thinks of how he can use that to his advantage.

Meanwhile in East Orange, New Jersey

Federal Agents, Dumber and Dumbest sit secretly on the quiet block of

Arsdale Terrace. They watch the corner house, waiting to see any strange activity. They want to know who is going in and who is coming out.

The house that they're observing is the house of Tanya Richardson. Tanya Richardson is the messenger and mediator between the Mayor and his brother Dre. The Federal Agents got hold of the Mayor's visit list yesterday and they noticed that her name is the most consistent name on his list. This leads them to believe that she interacts with the Mayor more than anyone else. The purpose for her visits, they have no clue, but they're sure they are soon to find out.

///// CHAPTER 112 /////

The Next Day

Over twenty Muslim men sit on the Mucelli (carpet) listening attentively to the man who stands before them. Al-Khabir stands here with rage and fury in his eyes. Earlier today the Muezzin was called back. He was pronounced dead before the sunrise this morning. His death has touched the hearts of Muslims not just in this community but other communities as well.

They believe that he is guaranteed heaven just by the way that he died. Abu Bakr Sayiid died at the age of 77 years. Even though he's lived a full life, these brothers would have loved to see him live another 77 years. Truth of the matter is that, what they want doesn't count. Only what God wants really matters. Muslims are taught to believe that when and how things happen are solely under God's command, which means this incident with Abu Bakr was God's plan. Although they know and understand that, they still refuse to chalk up the loss of his life without making the murderers pay.

"These gang bangers don't value or respect anything!" the brother says with rage. "I never thought I would see the day when niggas don't respect Muslims. A lot has changed. You know why they no longer respect Islam? Because the same craziness that the niggas are out here doing, the Muslims are standing side by side with them indulging in the same activity. How can we speak out against these issues when we're committing the exact same crimes? Muslim drug dealers?" he asks sarcastically. "Friday Jumah prayer has turned out to be nothing, but a bunch of drug dealers who claim to be Muslim, standing in front of the Masjid afterwards, networking with each other and advertising their product. "Astighfuruallaah! In the new millennium, we now have Muslim gang bangers. There is no such thing! As Muslims we can not be a part of any other sect or group except for Islam! We are guilty of so much foolishness. We own Go-G0 Bars and everything else! Today we are no different from the Kufurs (non-believers). We have lost our dignity!"

Mu-Mit sits quietly with shame. His guilt makes him feel as if the man is talking directly to him. He's guilty of most of the above. He knows better to be indulging in this activity, but it's always been a constant struggle for him. He's been playing the religious tug of war for as long as he can remember. While in prison, he's able to stay on the right path because his distractions are very limited. He's able to offer the five prayers every day, on time, as well as study as he should. He lives his life as a devout Muslim. Once he gets on the street, he totally loses focus of all the things that he should be doing as a Muslim. He skips a prayer here and there and he hardly ever reads and studies. Lack of both, leads him to forget how important the remembrance of God is and that is when he begins to act like a savage. In prison his motto was, 'If you forget Allah, he will forget you.' Apparently he has forgotten his own motto.

The longer he sits here, the wetter his face becomes. He's sure that God is disappointed with him. He begged God over and over to set him free of the last charges. He in return promised God that he would live his life as a believing man should. God completed his part of the deal, but Mu-Mit didn't honor his own promise. The street life has helped him to totally disregard his promise. He's quite sure for that, he will be punished severely.

"Oh Allah, please bestow your mercy upon me? I know I have disregarded my promise to you," he whispers. "Please Allah give me the strength to change my lifestyle. I am not perfect, as you know, Allah. I ask you to have patience with me? I admit, I have not tried my hardest, but Allah please remove that sickness from my diseased heart?" he pleads as the tears pour from his eyes. He thinks of the fact that an innocent man lost his life because of him. The tears fall more rapidly with that thought in mind. "Oh Allah please forgive the brother for his sins and admit him into paradise. Me on the other hand, Allah I know the death of that man lies on my shoulders. I know I will be punished, but I beg you Allah, please bestow your mercy upon me as I'm being punished?" he begs.

The nerve of him. How can he expect God's mercy, when he has never been merciful with anyone?

"Brothers, we have lost our dignity which is why no one respects us anymore. Young drug dealers and gang bangers are impregnating our women. In the First Resurrection that would have never happened. They wouldn't even look at our women because they feared the consequences. Today there are no consequences which is why they are brutally attacking our children, dating and beating on our women and now even worse, they're attacking Allah's House. They have disrespected us gravely! They shot near our Masjid after Jumah prayer! They will never live to talk about this."

The man speaking, figures that this is an attack against Muslims, but it's not. It's actually an attack against Mu-Mit. Never in a million years will he admit that to them though. He doesn't know how they would react if they found out the innocent man was murdered because of a drug beef that he is in the middle of.

When the man speaks of the First Resurrection he's referring to the days when Islam was introduced to Black America. At that time they were following the teachings of the Elijah Muhammad, calling themselves FOI (Fruit of Islam). They were a militant group who used their teachings to elevate the black man, and bring him in off of the street corners and place them back in their homes to properly head their households. Many years later a great deal of these men switched over and started following the ways of the Sunnah. Al-Khabir is a Sunni Muslim with old school FOI militancy still left in him.

"Right here, right now, I'm declaring war on gang bangers! This here is a Holy Jihad! All in favor say I."

"I!" they all shout simultaneously.

"Takbir!" the man shouts.

"Allah u Akbar!" all the men shout simultaneously.

"Takbir!"

"Allah U Akbar!"

"Takbir!"

"Allah U Akbar!"

///// CHAPTER 113 /////

Dre leans against his Cherokee. Not too far away from him stands a man that appears to be in his mid twenties. This man happens to be the man whom Damien Bryant referred to in his letter as his contact.

The Mayor instructed Dre to reach out to him and that he did. They have been standing here chatting away for the past twenty minutes.

Mu-Mit and Latif stand close by Dre, just in case things start to look shady. With all the madness that has been going on, they trust nothing at this point. Across the street, by the man's Cadillac Escalade, there stands three other men who have accompanied him here. The tension from both sides is evident, but everyone attempts to act as if everything is cool.

Suddenly ILL Wheel's Cherokee comes roaring up the block. This is actually the moment that they all have been waiting for. Ahmir parks directly behind Dre's jeep. The driver and passenger door both pop open at the same time. Ahmir hops out aggressively. In each hand he grips a .40 caliber handgun. He doesn't know how this may end so he's come fully prepared. On top of his white t-shirt, he's wearing a bullet proof vest. He walks side by side with ILL Wheel who grips a gun in both of his hands as well.

The men on the opposite side of the street see the weapons they have drawn and they draw theirs as well. Not even a second later, both Latif and Mu-Mit have their weapons drawn. Nine men and seven semi automatic weapons can total out to be one huge bloodbath. The men start to step toward this side of the street.

"Yo," Dre says sternly. "Put the guns up," he says to Ahmir and ILL Wheel. The man looks to his squad and gestures for them to do the same. The look in his eyes forces them to conceal their weapons almost instantly. Ahmir and ILL Wheel are still quite hesitant to do so. "Young Cash, tuck 'em!"

Ahmir steps toward them while tucking his guns in his waistband slowly. ILL Wheel quickly follows Ahmir's lead.

"Young Cash, what up?" the man asks with a stone cold look on his face.

"You tell me?" Ahmir replies arrogantly.

The man pauses briefly before speaking. "All this is one big mess. We need to get to the bottom of it. A lot of Blood been spilled already. That ain't how homies supposed to handle inside situations."

Ahmir smirks at his statement. "From what I hear, we ain't on the inside. We food, right?"

"Let me explain that. Real talk, ya'll haven't been labeled yet."

"Yet? What the fuck that supposed to mean?"

"It means, your hood is under investigation. We got the word from Cali that ya'll hood don't even exist. It ain't official. We waiting on the paperwork to prove it though. The fuck boy, Ice wasn't even official. He ain't on record."

"Man, fuck Ice!" Ahmir shouts furiously. "This ain't about him! I been G'd up! I been busting my gun! Cee, you know me. Me and you done moved out with each other on several occasions. All of ya'll done seen me in action. I ain't no fucking dud! Then to move out on my man like that. I see that as a total disrespect. As much work as I done put down in this town, me and my niggas are supposed to be bulletproof!"

"I agree to a certain degree. It wasn't supposed to go like that. We never discussed that shit that happened. That was not planned. While at a meeting, ya'll names came up. The Homie Shotgun heard what he wanted to hear and took it upon himself to make his move. You know he be tripping off the 'Lean' and shit. The next thing I hear, he done some shitty shit that he shouldn't have did. I tried to jump on it asap. Before I can get with ya'll, my homies start getting hit and shit. You gave us no other choice, but to plan our retaliation. I feel ya'll. Ya'll did what ya'll was supposed to do as men. On the other hand, as a G, I feel violated. Young Cash, you right, I know you and just like I know you, you know me, too. Just one phone call is all that it would take to have this whole town shut down. I can import homies from Cali to tear the city up. I was two seconds away from doing so until I got the call from Kentucky, telling me to cease this war. That's why I'm here."

Mu-Mit and Latif listen to all this word for word and it's hard for them to believe that Newark has come to this. Hearing it for themselves forces them to see it as reality. They never thought they would ever see a day like this, when gangs populate this city.

"Although a few people have been touched, I'm still willing to charge it to the game. It's all a misunderstanding. What you got to say about that?"

"What I got to say?" Ahmir asks. "It ain't what I got to say. I'm not the one who was tied up, pistol whipped and robbed in my crib. They violated me by violating my Homie. It's all on what he says."

The man looks at ILL Wheel. "Well, what do you say? Can we get pass this?"

"Phew," ILL Wheel sighs angrily. He's pissed off but he actually does realize how dangerous this war can get. They really won't have any chance of winning if Cee presses the button. The fact that he didn't call the treaty still leaves him with his dignity. The only real loss is the money and dope they got him for. "Man, it ain't that simple. I lost 60 cash. That's a lot of Baby."

The man looks at Dre. "Nah," Dre interrupts. "That's already been taken care of."

"I already paid your man. As far as that goes we're even. I know you feel disrespected but so do we. Hopefully in no time, we'll all be able to get over that? Right now, we should just bury the hatchet. As far as ya'll set being unofficial, Charles Manson gone bless ya'll in under his Hood. That other shit will be erased. As far as we concerned, ya'll official now."

"I been official!" Ahmir interrupts.

"Young Cash?" Dre interrupts.

"Man, I don't need no man to tell me I'm official. Nobody ain't gotta bless me in. I move to the beat of my own drum. I go hard with the color or without!"

The man looks at Ahmir with a smirk on his face. "We getting pass this or what? Is it over?"

Ahmir looks at ILL Wheel who shrugs his shoulders as if to say yes. "Say it!" Ahmir shouts. "Yes or no? You wanna end it or we don't have to. I'm moving on your call. It's whatever for me! You already know."

"It's over," ILL Wheel whispers.

"There it is," Ahmir says as he spins around and walks away leaving ILL Wheel and the man doing their signature Blood handshake. Immediately after, ILL Wheel hops into the passenger's seat of his jeep and they pull off. Everyone else remains on the scene.

Fifteen minutes later, Lil Mama's jeep pulls up. "Here she goes," Dre says while pointing to the vehicle. "She has 500 bricks for you. That's 180 a brick, $90,000.00. I don't know what you're supposed to do on your end but I handled my end of the deal. How long do you think that will take you?"

"No time at all," he replies. "My network is crazy. I can distribute all this and then some in a matter of minutes. I should have the money in about a day or two," he claims.

"Alright, just hit me when you're ready."

The man walks to Lil Mama's SUV, retrieves the work and clears the scene quickly.

The Mayor and 'Charles Manson' made an agreement. The Mayor promised to supply them with the work and 'Charles Manson' promised he would use his army to circulate it in and out of town. Wherever they are Bloods, he claims he will be able to shake the dope. This is the best deal 'Charles Manson' has ever brokered. Hopefully in the event of success, in no time at all, he will be able to buy himself the representation that he needs to save his life. He will also be helping the Mayor to obtain his goal of going global.

///// CHAPTER 114 /////

Tony grips the banister tightly as he steps slowly down the huge flight of stairs of his home. He's not in as much pain as he's been the prior days, but his wound is still quite tender. He still should be honoring the doctor's orders by resting in bed, but him being the workaholic that he is, there's no way he would be able to spend another second at home.

Tony finally makes it to his garage where he positions himself in the soft leather seat of his convertible Cadillac XLR. Before pulling off, he pops the middle console open and grabs hold of a cigar. He peeks up at his bedroom windows before lighting it. Mocha hasn't allowed him to smoke not a single cigar since he's been home and at this point he's feigning like an addict. After lighting it, he takes two huge pulls before coasting out of his driveway.

Click…click. The camera sounds off as Federal Agent Dumbest snaps photos of Tony pulling off. Click, click, he snaps again. "Pull up to the house," he demands.

Agent Dumber creeps up to the huge castle type house. The house is luxuriously built. The cobblestone walkway leads to the extra high steps which lead to a huge mahogany door. "Beautiful home," he comments.

"Extremely beautiful," Dumbest replies as he continuously snaps shots of the house from every angle. "I can count a million dollars in just renovation work. Look at the doors and the windows. The houses in this area go for three million easily," he adds as he takes yet another shot. After taking about ten photos of the house he switches his focal point to the garage area where he lays eyes on Tony's exotic car collection. Three beautiful cars occupy the garage area. He begins snapping away. The first shot he takes is of the beautiful candy apple red Bentley GT Coupe. He takes two shots of that one.

"Ay make sure you get a good shot of the bullet holes right there on the front quarter panel," Dumbest suggests.

"Already got it," Dumber replies as he clicks away at a few shots of Mocha's platinum colored convertible Mercedes Benz SL55. "And last, but not least," he says as he clicks away at the milky white convertible Bentley GTC that the Mayor bought for Dre's birthday. "Look at that beauty! What a fool he is," he laughs. "The average man can't afford one Bentley, this fucker has two," he smirks. "Tony fucking Cochran," he laughs. "A three million dollar home and over six hundred grand in automobiles. What does that equal?"

"Uh, 3.6 million?"

"No," he says furiously. At the bare minimum, tax evasion and money laundering. I'm sure his books can't prove the amount of income he needs to live this lifestyle. Maybe if we dig further we can come up with a few more severe charges. We're not going to stop digging until we get this fucker disbarred. When we're done with him, he won't have enough energy or fight to defend himself, let alone defend a client.

Meanwhile in Newark

"Yo, ever since that shit was on the news, shit been crazy. Mufuckers coming all the way from V.A trying to cop this shit from me!" the man shouts with joy in his voice and in his eyes.

It's hard for Dre to believe that this is the same man who just a few months ago got into this same car looking as if the world was about to end. Now today, he's singing a completely different tune and has a different look in his eyes. 'After Party' has changed his life unbelievably. Knowing that makes it that much harder for Dre to tell him the heartbreaking news.

"Here," the man shouts as he hands Dre a plastic bag. "That's a buck, twenty ($120,000.00). I hope you got a lot of that shit on reserve cause shit about to go crazy!"

Damn, Dre thinks to himself. "Yo, Z, I got some bad news," Dre whispers.

"Bad news? What up?"

"I'm all sold out and the connect said he falling back for a second."

"Falling back? What you mean falling back?"

"I mean, once that shit hit the news, they got petro and now they want to let shit cool off before they hit again."

"Man, this some bullshit! I knew this shit was going to happen! I been fucked up all this time and now I finally get the chance to get my turn and now the bullshit happens. Got damn!" He sits there with anger rumbling in his belly. He should have known something wasn't right when he got here and saw Dre here instead of the girl. He hasn't seen Dre in quite a while. The only contact they had was through Lil Mama. Damn, I wish I would have known he didn't have anything, he thinks to himself. I could have held onto the money until he got something else. I could have flipped the dough with somebody else just to stay afloat until then. "Damn!"

"Z, it ain't on me," Dre lies. ""I'm waiting just like you."

"Nah, nigga you ain't waiting like me. You alright."

"Easy man, you act like the connect dried up. I told you, they just want shit to cool off momentarily. Give it a few weeks and we back in action."

"You sure man? You all I got."

"I'm positive. I got you, trust me."

"Alright man, I ain't got no choice. I'm banking on you. I ain't got nowhere else to turn. Don't forget me," he says with desperation in his eyes. "As soon as you get back right, make sure you hit me first. Please," he says as he exits Dre's jeep.

"Don't worry. I got you."

///// CHAPTER 115 /////

Candy Kev steps off the stoop casually. He's been staying here at this little hideout spot for a few days now. He feels much safer here. With no Mu-Mit or Trauma in his life, he's been able to breathe easy.

"Now," Latif says to Mu-Mit who gasses up at the sound of Latif's voice. In no seconds flat, they're within a foot of Candy Kev, who is opening the door of his wife's van. The sudden rush of the vehicle behind him snatches his attention. He damn near urinates on himself when he sets eyes on who sits before him. He stutters goofily before finally getting his words together. "As Salaamu Alaikum!" he says with a goofy look on his face.

Here we go with that Muslim shit, Latif says to himself as he looks over to Mu-Mit to see how he responds.

"Get in," Mu-Mit demands.

How the fuck they find me here, Candy Kev asks himself. "Huh?" he asks, but knowing exactly what Mu has said. Candy Kev really doesn't want to get in with them because he fears what they may do. He's sure if he refuses they will kill him right here on the spot. Damn if I do, damn if I don't, he says to himself.

Latif pops the door open and hops out. He pushes Candy Kev to the passenger's door. "Man, get the fuck in!" he says aggressively. Candy Kev gets in slowly. Latif doesn't even give him time to get his entire body in the car before he slams the door.

"Aghh," Candy Kev sighs as his leg gets caught in the door. Latif quickly hops into the backseat and Mu-Mit pulls off.

No one utters a word for a matter of three minutes before Mu-Mit finally breaks the silence. "So, you got something that you want to tell me?" he asks while looking straight ahead.

"Mu, come on, man," he whines. "Why are you taking me through this?"

"What?" Mu asks as he swerves the vehicle to the right. He parks and slams the gear into the park position. "Why the fuck am I taking you through this?" he asks as he damn near jumps into Candy Kev's lap. Mu-Mit is so close that he's kissing Candy Kev's forehead. "Keep playing fucking stupid, I'll knock your fucking block off right here! Them mufuckers that was blazing at us was them Trauma Unit mufuckers. Them mufuckers from your side of town, which means you was in on that shit!" He leans back into his seat. "I don't believe yo ass," he smirks. "I got something for you though," he smiles as he puts the car into drive and pulls off. "You wanna take the Kafa's side against the Believers?" he smiles a devilish grin. "I'm about to show you what happens to Muslims who do that. You went against your brother," he says as he taps his own chest. "For a filthy fucking Kafa? You motherfucker you."

Yes, Latif rejoices inside. This is the moment that he's been waiting for. He's never heard or seen Mu-Mit this angry. Judging by the looks of it, in a matter of minutes Mu-Mit will be giving him the word to blow Candy Kev's brains out.

Candy Kev is scared for his life and he should be. He's sure that it's over for him. He knew this day was coming. He wonders if he should just jump out of the car and attempt to make a break for his life.

Mu-Mit is speeding up the block with rage. "You wanna go against me?"

"Wallahi!" Candy Kev shouts before he's interrupted by a heavy force crashing into the back of his skull. "Aghh," he sighs.

Latif felt the need to interrupt because he fears that listening to Candy Kev speak may change Mu-Mit's mind. "Lawheed, my ass!" Latif shouts furiously as he draws back to smack him with the butt of the gun again, but Candy Kev ducks down low, making it hard for Latif to hit his target.

"Wallahi?" Mu-Mit asks. "Nigga, your Wallahi is a pork chop. That ain't gone save you today. Nigga save it for David," he rhymes. Mu-Mit turns onto Littleton Avenue and parks in the middle of the block. The quiet block is perfect to blast Candy Kev's brains out and leave him right here.

Nervousness fills Candy Kev's body. He realizes that it's going down. He has to say something quick that makes sense. "Wa," he starts to say again before quickly realizing how furious they got when he said it the first time. "Mu, listen, please? I swear, I didn't go against you. They set me up, man, word to mother. I was selling them bricks. The nigga Trauma ordered and I told him you were on your way. I didn't know he was off his bullshit," he lies. It was all a set up. Come to find out, it's not just a robbery. They got a personal beef with ya'll. The nigga Parlay? That was Trauma's man and his connect. After ya'll supposedly murdered Parlay and Tippy Toe, he was on some get back shit. He got the word that ya'll was coming for him next."

"Coming for him next?" Mu-Mit interrupts. "I ain't never even heard of that mufucker."

"Well, supposedly ya'll cut into me and was using me to bring him to ya'll. That way ya'll could get him out of the way and take over the town. It's like killing two birds with one stone.

"So, is that why you got with them and went against me?"

"Man, I didn't go against you. They put me in the middle of some bullshit."

"Nigga, you went against me. If it was up to you, I would have been dead already. You left me in the dark to be murdered. Nigga we like brothers!" he shouts with compassion. "You was supposed to tell me that shit!"

"Man, I wanted to tell you, but I was in a fucked up position. They applying pressure on one end, then I'm thinking, I have to tell Mu, but then again he using me on some stunt dummy shit to get to them. So, it's like damn if I do, damn if I don't," he says with sincerity in his eyes.

"So, it was just easier to sell me out?" he asks with tears in his eyes.

"Man, I ain't sell you out."

Latif can hear Mu-Mit's rage dying out and it's pissing him off to think that Candy Kev may have talked his way out of another situation. "Man, fuck this nigga. Let me knock his mufucking block off? Latif begs. "Word to mother," he shouts, mocking Candy Kev. "You gone take us to this nigga Trauma or else!"

Meanwhile

Ahmir cruises around in ILL Wheel's jeep with no determined destination. In just a few short hours Ahmir will be leaving New Jersey once again. His work here is done. In his pocket he stores two, one way train tickets to Baltimore. After listening to the Bookkeeper, he finally realizes that Newark holds nothing of any real interest to him. With his mother being in Atlanta now and Ahmad down in school in Baltimore his reasons for coming to Jersey is limited. The only future that the 'Bricks' hold for him is an early grave.

"Yo," Ahmir whispers to ILL Wheel. "I'm taking D with me."

"Huh?"

"I'm taking him with me. I got a ticket for him too. In that state of mind, this ain't no place for him to be. Shit too crazy out here to have him walking around like that."

ILL Wheel looks at Ahmir with a baffled look on his face. "Let me get this right? First you bounce on me and D. Then you come back and you wanna take the only mufucker I got, outta my life? So, you expect me to run around here dolo with no one to trust? What am I supposed to do?"

"Come with us?"

"Man, ain't nothing in country ass Baltimore for me! Man, all I know is the Bricks."

"Me too," Ahmir replies sarcastically. "When I went down there I ain't know shit about Baltimore either."

"Yeah, but look what you went down there to…a fucking Enterprise. What the fuck I'm gone do down there? I ain't got a fucking dime to my name."

"You don't need a dime. I got a few dimes. You ain't gotta do shit, but what you been doing."

"And what is that?"

"Be a friend when I need one," Ahmir whispers. "I ain't got none of those down there," Ahmir adds.

Those statements catch ILL Wheel by surprise and somewhat touches his heart. "Man, I can't come down there on ass, living off of you. I done got used to making a dollar for myself. I got to have my own."

"I'll help you get your own. Whatever you want to do, I'll set you up. A clothes store, record store or whatever. I'll put up the gwap and you just pay me back when you get the business rolling."

"Man, I don't know about that. It ain't that simple. I have to think about that?"

"Don't think too long cause in a couple of hours I'm out and D going with me, regardless. Like you said…you gone be up here dolo, bottom line."

///// CHAPTER 116 /////

Days Later

Tony steps out of Las Americas International Airport in Santa Domingo. The hot and hazy weather makes him agitated instantly. As soon as he steps foot onto the platform, his attention is stolen by the many beautiful looking Dominican women that are spread out around the area. As he stands there waving for a taxi, he feels as if he's under a microscope. It's all eyes on him. The Dominican women's 'American Man' radar picks him up instantly. Tony plays it cool as a veteran.

This isn't his first time in Dominican Republic, but it is his first time here alone without Mocha. They've been here quite a few times on vacation and one thing Tony has learned is, American men are treated like precious gems here. The times that he's been here, him and Mocha have literally had to fight the women off of him. As arrogant and self centered as Tony may be, even he realizes that it's not him that they're crazy over. Tony has traveled to many countries before and one thing that he's learned is everyone loves the almighty American dollar. In every country that he's been in, he's seen men and women who are willing to do anything just to get their hands on the American dollar. They are willing to provide services of carrying your luggage, to acting as a tour guide to manicuring your nails and massages for little to no money. They are willing to bend over backwards just to get their hands on a few Pesos. With the American dollar being equivalent to 32 Dominican dollars, these Dominican women are not only willing to bend over backwards but, some of them are willing to bend over forward as well. An American man can get sexual favors for 640 Pesos which only equals 20 American dollars. The poverty stricken country leaves some women with no alternative, but to make a dollar however they can, which is why they are willing to commit some of the acts that they do. Each woman hopes and prays that she whips it on the American man and impresses him enough to bring her back to the States, so they can live the 'American Dream.'

"Taxi!" Tony shouts.

"Ola Americano," the low, slightly hoarse but sexy voice whispers into Tony's left ear. He turns around abruptly. He gasps for air as he lays his eyes upon the beautiful woman. She appears to be not a day over 21 years old. Her long silky black hair falls down to her calves. Her caramel toned skin glistens from the film of sweat which covers her sculpted body. She stands at about 5 feet 6 inches tall and weighs approximately 120 pounds. Wearing only a halter top, cut off daisy duke jean shorts and $2.00 flip flops she's still as sexy as any video vixen Tony has ever seen.

"Papi, tu comprende Espanol?" Do you understand Spanish?

"Muy, muy poquito," Tony replies, telling her that he understands very little Spanish.

"No problemo, Papito. Tu familiar con Republica de Dominicana?" Are you familiar with the Dominican Republic?

"No," Tony lies.

"First time?" she utters.

"Si," Tony says as he nods his head up and down.

"No problemo. Don't worry," she says with a beautiful smile. "Yo habla poquita Ingles." She tells him that she speaks a little English as well. The taxi cab pulls up interrupting their conversation. "Papi wait," she begs. "No leave, please?"

Those words sound like music to Tony's ears. I can't, he says to himself. This isn't right. Please Mami, don't do this to me? Mocha's face pops up in his head. He can hear her last words to him clearly. 'Don't go over there and let them little Spanish skeezers get you into a situation that you can't get yourself out of. You worked hard to make it where you are today. Don't let lust be the cause of you losing half of everything to me due to a divorce,' she said with a satanic smile on her face. Tony knows her well enough to believe every word she said. Tony looks at the beautiful girl and for some strange reason divorce doesn't sound half bad at this point. I'm bugging, he laughs to himself.

"Papito, Americano no bueno. Mucho mucho problemo," she warns as she points around the surrounding area, telling him that Americans have a lot of problems here in the Dominican Republic. "Loco Papi,' she whispers. "Be careful. Papi, me you eyes. Me watcha for you," she offers. "Ok?" she asks as she points to the taxi cab, gesturing if it's alright for her to come along.

Shit, Tony thinks to himself. Without hesitation he replies. "Si."

"Papi," she says as she sticks her index finger high in the air as if to say one minute. "Mi amiga," she says as she points behind her. Tony looks in that direction and his focus is drawn to another gorgeous vision. A woman just as beautiful as her, but 30 pounds heavier which makes her thicker and twice as voluptuous as the first girl. Her hazel eyes stand out boldly against her dark cinnamon complexion. Thick and beautiful sandy brown hair falls just past her shoulders, draping over her full triple c cups. Full but toned thighs extend from her daisy dukes. She turns away from Tony bashfully. This gives him a view of her backside. Tony has to double take. He's never in his life seen so much ass attached to such a tiny waist. Her thighs and calves look as strong and lean as a race horse. "Mi amiga?" she repeats as she points to the taxi.

Tony stands there in awe. He has to pinch himself just to make sure that he's not dreaming. He quickly thinks it over, trying to find a good enough reason to bring the two fine women along with him. Although he's familiar with D.R., he's unfamiliar to the particular area that he's going to. The times that he's been here before, he has never left the grounds of Punta Cana Resort. A tour guide or two really would be helpful to him. This is all innocent, he tells himself. They offered to be my tour guide. I can't help the fact that they are extremely gorgeous, he utters to himself.

"Papi, por favor?" she begs. Please?

Damn, how can I resist, he asks himself. Fuck it. He shakes his head up and down. "Mamita, ben aqui!" he yells as he guides the first girl into the taxi. He slides in right behind her. The second girl squeezes him in the middle.

The cab driver pulls off quickly. A Spanish sandwich, Tony says to himself smiling from ear to ear. The girl to his right dazes into his eyes deeply. Mami, muy bonita," he says telling her how beautiful she is. She blushes deeply. She lowers her head with shame. "Uhmm, uhhmm, uhhmm," Tony utters under his breath.

Meanwhile back in the States

Cindy hops into her car and pulls off driving like a maniac. She zips up the block recklessly. Judging by the way she's driving, she's rushing to a dire emergency.

She blasts the tunes of singer Monica's 'Why Her,' as she zips up the block. She sings along paying no attention to her surroundings. What a mistake that is? The loud music and her anxiety makes her totally disregard the Chevy Impala which is trailing behind her a few cars back.

Federal Agents Dumber and Dumbest follow her lead attentively. They checked Dre's file and found that Cindy's address is where he's been paroled to.

"This bitch must be late for a funeral," Dumbest says.

"Or a dope deal," Dumber replies with sarcasm. Both of them are wrong. The emergency that Cindy is rushing to is her hair appointment, which she is already ten minutes late for. "Hopefully, she'll lead us to a piece of the puzzle?"

In Dominican Republic

Tony sits in the luxurious office. He leans back into the plush leather chair while exhaling a lengthy train of smoke from his mouth. "The draw is great," he whispers. Just as the smoke begins to clear, he holds the cigar up high in the air. "This is it," he says as he twirls it around viewing it from every angle. "This is the best one by far. The taste is awesome," he claims as he smacks his tongue against the roof of his mouth. "Yeah, this is definitely the right blend right here."

The Latino man sits on the opposite side of the desk, leaning back in his chair. He listens closely as Tony praises the cigar. This man here is Tony's cigar manufacturer. His reason for being here in D.R., is to solidify his business deal for his cigar line which is the project that he talked Dre into investing into. "I'm glad you like it."

"What are the specifics?" Tony questions.

"Ah ah, ancient secret," the man teases. "If I tell you that, I'll have to kill you," he smiles. "Just kidding. The Maduro wrapper is from Nicaragua. The filler is from Honduras and the binder is Dominican. It's all hand rolled of course. The tobacco is 15 year old tobacco," he adds.

"Good combination, I must admit," he says before he takes another drag of the cigar. He exhales slowly. "Sweet taste," he utters as the smoke exits his mouth.

"I need to know what size you want to go with?" the man asks.

"Ah, me I'm a Churchill type of guy, but I think I want to go with the Solomon. It looks so much sexier," he smiles.

"Then Solomon it is.

"So, about how long will it take for production?" Tony asks.

"Ah, right now, we have so many projects in process. If I shut the plant down and put all my manpower on your project we can have you ready to enter the cigar world in no time at all. Do you have your band?"

"I sure do," Tony says as he digs into his briefcase and retrieves a disc. "Here," he says as he passes it to the man. "The artwork is on here."

"Good, what name did you come up with?"

"I came up with the name Euphoria. That means a feeling of well being or an abnormal feeling of buoyant vigor. When cigar aficionados smoke my cigar, I want the experience to be euphoric. Euphoria, it's not just a cigar. It's an experience," Tony says as if he's advertising on a commercial. "My Platinum Edition will be the stronger one and the Gold Edition will be the milder one."

"You sound excited," the man smiles.

"Of course I'm excited! Aren't you?" Tony pulls the check from his briefcase and lays it face down onto the desk.

The man flips the check over and looks to the corner. It reads: $500,000.00. His eyes light up with joy. $500,000.00 will go to manufacturing and the other $250,000.00 that Dre invested will go to the marketing of their cigar.

"Now, I'm excited," the man smiles.

"Good. Now shut the plant down and let's make this thing happen!"

///// CHAPTER 117 /////

It's 10:30 p.m., just a half an hour past the Isha (night) Prayer. All Muslims should be indoors by now unless they have reason to be out. The two caravans that are riding back to back are filled with a total of eight Muslims. They have all the reason in the world to be out right now. The reason in their minds is Holy Jihad. In just a few short minutes hopefully they will have gotten some type of revenge against the murderer of Abu Bakr Sayiid.

All the brothers present have traded in their over garments and Kufi caps and sandals for army fatigues, ski hats and combat boots.

Mu-Mit peeks around at the men who occupy this van. All these men can be looked at and underestimated by the naked eye. They appear to be humble, devout Muslims, but many, many years ago in the world, they were all considered to be vicious criminals. Through Islam, they have been able to change their lives around and put all the devious acts behind them. Deep down inside there has been a rebel lying in their souls just waiting for the opportunity to be unleashed, but fortunately they have been able contain it. This is the perfect excuse for them to let that beast explode from within.

The driver, an older brother who goes by the name of Abdul Kareem cruises up the block in silence, but he prays silently to himself. Suddenly he speaks aloud in Arabic language, but in English, it means. "In the name of Allah. Oh Allah we ask you to bestow your mercy and blessings on us? Oh Allah we ask you to guide us? Oh Allah we ask you to give us the strength to fight in your name and make us victorious over these non believers? Ameen!"

"Ameen!" the other men shout all except for Latif and Mu-Mit. Latif sits quietly just listening. He feels like a foreigner. He has not a clue of what they're talking about. All he knows is one thing and that's murder.

Mu-Mit sits in silence because he feels horrible. Here it is, these men are willing to kill and die for a cause that they not know. In their hearts they believe that they're retaliating because of an attack on the Muslims, when in all reality the dope dealers were attempting to attack Mu-Mit over a drug war. A part of him wants to reveal the secret, but he could never admit to them the fact that Abu Bakr Sayiid died over a drug war.

"Here we go ya'll," the driver whispers as his heart races. Mu-Mit looks up the block and sees a group of young men huddled up on a street corner. Mu-Mit pulls his gun from his waistband and all the others grab their weapons as well. Heavy artillery is the words that best describe the weapons that these men are holding. In total they have about ten guns in this van alone and the revolvers that Mu-Mit and Latif have are the smaller and less dangerous ones. The most dangerous one of them all is the AK47 that Al-Khabir holds. He's the perfect man to operate this weapon being that he's a trained Marine. The other weapons range from Uzi's to Mac 10's to Sk47, to M16's.

"Ya'll ready?" the driver asks as he inches up to the corner. The van behind them tails them closely. The driver stops short. "Go!" he shouts. The double doors slide open and the Muslims pour out of both vans.

"Allah U Akbar!" Al-Khabir shouts before firing a half a round at the crowd of men. People scatter in all directions. Some get away, but others are not so lucky. They fall to their feet, tumbling over face first. The words 'Allah U Akbar' echo loudly over and over again.

Approximately two minutes later, the men return to the van with a prisoner of war. There are two more POW's in the van behind them. Mu-Mit dumps the man into the van. He lands on his head. "Go!" Mu-Mit says as he slams the doors shut. The driver pulls off and the van behind follows closely. One Hour Later

The Muslims all stand around in the basement of the abandoned house. The three captives stand, stretched against the wall side by side, shoulder to shoulder, fingertips to fingertips. All of them are completely naked. Their bodies are badly bruised from the torturing. They stand there with blood dripping from the corners of their mouths and many other wounds. The most blood comes from their hands which are bleeding severely. The three of them have been nailed to the wall by way of three inch carpenter nails drilled into the palms of their hands. This was all Al-Khabir's idea. His militancy has taken over.

The two men on the ends are nailed facing the wall while the man in the middle looks toward the crowd of men who are watching him being tortured. His position is far worse than theirs because he can actually see what type of torture is on the way before the other two men can.

"Go ahead," Al-Khabir instructs the man who is carrying two buckets of water. The man passes one bucket to another brother and they both toss the hot water onto the captives. "Ya'll like disrespecting Masjids, right?" Al-Khabir asks before lashing the man across the back like a slave.

"Owwww!" he screams as the extension cord rips into their soak n wet flesh.

"Shut up! I'll teach ya'll to respect Islam!" he shouts as he lashes the man on the opposite end.

"Aghhh!" he screams loud after the cord tears into his buttocks.

"Look at ya'll! Hung up like the prophet Esa that ya'll call Jesus. May peace and blessings be upon him. You actually believe that Jesus died for your sins? Astighfuruallaah! Then why are ya'll up here being crucified now?" he asks before lashing out at the man in the middle. "Who would invent such a lie against Prophet Esa, peace and blessings be upon him?"

"Owww!" the man screams before the cord touches him. "Owwwww! Owwww!" he screams even louder once the cord cuts through his cheek directly under his eye.

"Shut up, I'll teach ya'll savages how to act civilized," he smiles a wicked smile.

"Come on, my turn!" a man shouts from the back of the room. He walks up holding a bucket of his own. The lashing session is now over. It's now time for the next phase of their torturing. The man in the middle looks with fear. He can't imagine what could be in the bucket, but he's sure whatever it is only means more pain for them.

The man begins pouring the contents onto the man in the middle first. As soon as the contents splash onto his body he screams at the top of his lungs. The green rubbing alcohol seeps into his flesh wounds sending a burning sensation throughout his entire body. The other two men start screaming before he even gets to them. Once he finally gets to them they scream and cry even louder.

Mu-Mit sits back and watches. Torture is not his game, which is why he's letting them handle this part. He's just waiting for the murder part so he can do him. They planned to torture the men hoping that they will tell them everything that they want to know. Mu-Mit prays that they don't tell everything they know. Then his secret will come out that he's behind all of this.

"Enough!" Al-Khabir shouts as he steps closer to the man in the middle. "Ok, now it's time to play a game," he says sternly. "In this game the end results can only go one of four ways. One way is, all of you can continue living your lives. Two, one of you can continue living your life, while the other two die here. Three, two of you can continue your life while the other one of you dies here. Four, all of you can die here. I think those are the rules of the game," he laughs. "It doesn't matter. It's as simple as this, all of you can live or in the worse case all of you will die in here. It's all on ya'll and how ya'll play the game. Now let me explain the rules of the game to ya'll. Listen carefully cause I'm only going to ask the question one time. I have two questions to ask and I'm starting from this end. You fat boy, if you're lucky, the game will be over before I get to you. If your teammates play fair and cooperate, you'll be lucky enough to get the chance to answer the bonus question. Mustafaa!" he shouts.

"Yes Sir," the middle aged man shouts as he comes running into the room. In his hands he holds a Black and Decker power saw. He revs it up as he steps into the room. At the sight and the sound of the saw roaring, the man in the middle actually defecates on himself, stinking up the room terribly.

"Shut it off so they can hear me!" he shouts with rage. "Contestant number one!" he shouts. "Who fired the shots at the Masjid? You got two seconds. Mustafaa, start it up!

The power saw revs up loudly scaring the man almost to death. "Shawn Jones," the man shouts out without hesitation. "They call him Dirt."

"Good answer!" he cheers. "Contestant number two, where does he live?"

"On 16th Avenue and 14th Street, in the apartment building!" the man shouts louder and more quickly than the first contestant.

"Very good answer! Contestant number three!" he shouts over the loud noise of the saw. "Where can we find Trauma?" As bad as the man would love to answer this question in order to save his life, he can't. He does not have a clue. Although he hangs out on the same block as these guys, he's not an official member of Trauma's Unit. He's more like a Trauma Unit wanna be. He just hangs out there trying to look as if he's actually down with the crew. The answer to the question, he does not know, but he's more than positive that they don't want to hear that. "Three seconds, starting now. Two!" he shouts.

"I swear to God," the boy cries. "I swear, please? I'm not part of the Unit.

Ask them? I barely know Trauma like that!"

The man gets quiet for a second giving Al-Khabir enough time to get a word in. "Mustafaa, shut it off! Contestant number one, is this true? Answer quickly!" he demands as he looks at the man's arms. He notices that contestant number one and two have the letters TU branded on their right shoulders, while the third contestant does not. He assumes that the man may be telling the truth. "Where your T, U at?" he asks as he grabs his shoulder, almost yanking it out of the socket.

"I ain't part of the Unit," he cries.

"Contestant number two, is this true?"

"He be with us," he replies. He's not trying to save the man the least bit.

"Ok, well which one of you is willing to help him? He doesn't know the answer to his question. Help him. Maybe it will be beneficial for the three of you. Mustafaa, start it up!" he shouts. Not one second later the loud noise starts up all over again.

"William Street in East Orange. 134!" the man shouts nervously.

"Good answer, number one! Now that's teamwork!" he shouts as he turns toward Mustafaa. He gives him a slight head nod gesturing for him to go ahead. Mustafaa steps toward contestant number one. He stops short a half a foot away from him. The man in the middle starts screaming at the top of his lungs while closing his eyes in fear of what he may see.

The saw gets louder and louder. "Game over!" Al-Khabir shouts. "And the winner is?"

"Allah U Akbar!" Mustafaa shouts.

///// CHAPTER 118 /////

The Next Morning

Tony awakens from a deep sleep. As soon as his eyes open, they're greeted by a stream of jet black silky hair which is plastered to his face. He looks over only to find the beautiful Dominican woman asleep in his arms. She's nestled up in his chest as if she actually belongs there. Their nude bodies fit together perfectly like pieces of a jigsaw puzzle.

The tugging of his right foot steals his attention. He looks to the bottom of the bed where another nude woman sits on the edge of the bed, filing his toe nails. Tony shakes his head from side to side. The more he thinks of last night's wonderful experience, the more guilt he feels. Damn, he sighs to himself. I should have been a little stronger, he says. It's way too late for him to start thinking about what he should have done last night. What's done is done. The situation would have been tough for any man to withdraw from. Who would be able to deny three extremely gorgeous women catering to his sexual needs and desires? Tony replays the night over in his head. No one would ever believe how fantastic it actually was, he says to himself with a smile. This was a dream come true for him. Suddenly the guilt pops up again. Damn, I'm a married man. If Mocha finds out she will kill me. He replays her conversation back on how she would take half of everything from him.

A third woman enters the room, holding a first aid kit in her hand. She's nude as well. This woman here is the final installment of the edition. They met up with her at Club Macumba late last night. Supposedly she is the cousin of the initial girl. The initial girl insisted that Tony allow her to come along.

She's equally as gorgeous, but in no way does she look similar to the other two girls. She's a 'Big Girl Lover's dream come true. Her plus size figure is sculpted perfectly. She stands 5 feet 11 inches tall and weighs approximately 200 pounds, all solid woman. Hips, ass and breast make up all 200 of her pounds. She's thick and voluptuous and far more sexy than any Ashley Stewart model that Tony has ever seen. Her long thick, curly black hair falls to the middle of her back. She has chinky eyes, puffy cheeks and baby doll lips. Her tiny but puckered lips are to die for. They scream out 'kiss me.'

Tony is so glad that they pressured him into letting her come along because this mami was actually the star of the show. Tony watched with awe as she performed stunts that he's never even heard of. He watched her twist her huge body into positions that are probably not known to man. The way she maneuvered her body she would put any petite woman to shame.

Once again Tony thinks of Mocha's threat to him. Then his mind goes back into last night's foursome. Just thinking about it, Mocha's threat really isn't that horrifying. Just having only half of what he has in the States, he will still be able to come here and live like a king. Uhmm, he thinks to himself. That is something to think about it. Never in his life has he ever been taken care of like this. These women have catered to his every need. They have taken care of him from head to head to toe.

"Buenas Dias, Papito," she says as the words roll from her soft and sexy lips.

"Uhmm," Tony utters under his breath. He bites his top lip in order to keep from kissing her. The woman in his arms awakens. She rolls out of his arms and out of the bed. He watches with admiration as she steps to the bathroom. Through the wide gap between her thighs, he can view the entire room. Damn, he says to himself as he looks down at the other woman who is still filing away at his toe nails. Then to his right, the woman slowly takes off his bandage and begins scrubbing away gently at his bullet wound.

He looks back to his left where he sees the other girl walking back toward him. Shit, ya'll got a nigga fucked up he says to himself as he smiles a wide toothed grin. "Listen Mamis," he says slowly. All their eyes zoom onto his lips so that they can read them carefully with hope of understanding what it is that he's about to say. "Whatever happens," he says slowly as if he's talking to someone who is hard of hearing. "In Dominican Republic," he says slowly. As he's talking, the women sound out his words, moving their mouths as he is moving his. "Stays in Dominican Republic. Comprende mamis?" he asks with a smile on his face.

The woman standing there with the file in her hand translates what he's said to the other two women. She may not be able to speak or understand English well, but she knows enough to use context clues. Smiles pop onto all of their faces after she's made the translations. "Si, Papi, comprende," she replies. "No problemo."

"No problemo," he smiles as he reaches over and strokes her hair. "No problemo." This is the best sixty-dollar investment that I've ever made, he says to himself.

Meanwhile in Brick City

Candy Kev walks cautiously toward his wife's van. He's just dropped his daughters off to school on Seventh Street and 15th Avenue. Candy Kev's wife had a doctor's appointment and couldn't take the girls to school, which forced him out of hiding.

In just a few short months this nightmare will be over. After school is finished for the year, he plans to sell his house, pack up his family and relocate to Atlanta. For now, he has to slip and slide as he's been doing for the past few days. He feels a certain amount of safety being that neither Trauma nor Mu-Mit knows his whereabouts. He and his family were staying at his brother's house, but after Mu-Mit caught him there, he switched his location to his mother's house. He doesn't have a clue on how they found him at his brother's, but he figures they just caught him coincidentally. He does not realize that they followed his wife there. In any event, he's sure they will never find him now.

Candy Kev sticks the key into the lock of the driver's side door. As he grabs the door handle, he hears, "Candy motherfucking Kev!" Oh my God, he thinks to himself. He recognizes this voice instantly. He turns around slowly. A cheesy smile appears on his face like magic. "Trauma what up?"

Trauma looks straight ahead, while rubbing his hand over his face. "I been looking all over for you," he whispers. He displays a distraught look on his face. He hasn't slept a wink and it's evident. "Shit crazy B, three of my lil niggas got kidnapped yesterday," he says sternly. "I ain't heard nothing from them yet," he says as he fumbles around his lap secretly before raising his nine millimeter and extending it out of the window.

Candy Kev's mouth drops wide open and his feet become glued to the asphalt. Boc! The first shot sounds off loudly before crashing into his forehead. His head snaps back and bangs into the roof of the car before it bounces forward like a basketball. Parents and children attempt to disperse into safety, running for their lives. As his body is sliding down the side of the van, Trauma busts four more shots, aiming directly at his target. Candy Kev's body lands in a fetal position. "Go!" Trauma shouts and the man peels off recklessly.

After sitting at his house for hours last night with no success in catching Candy Kev, Trauma quickly remembered that his daughter's attend this school which happens to be only a few blocks away from their base. They sat here for an hour hoping that he would bring the girls to school. Luckily he was the one who brought them because today they were not discriminating. They already had their minds set on murdering who ever came first, whether it was him or his wife.

"Bitch ass nigga!" Trauma shouts with a great amount of satisfaction. "You touch one of mine and I will murder all of yours!"

///// CHAPTER 119 /////

The Next Morning

Dre stands at his balcony unable to move. The terrifying words that he's just read in the newspaper article have him frozen stiff. The article states that the heads of three men were found nearby a tree in Newark's West Side Park yesterday morning. They were able to match one of the men's dental records and what they found out is that the head belongs to a member of Newark's Trauma Unit.

A couple of lines later is where the madness begins. The writer reiterates the previous articles about him and Tony being shot at and the Trauma Unit member being murdered in the Essex County Jail. The part that made him damn near faint is when the writer states that officials believe that all this is stemming from the Blackhead brothers/ Tony 'Cochran' situation. From the looks of the article, any person that can read would believe that Tony and Dre are linked to all of this and the Mayor ordered the hit. The truth of the matter is Dre has no idea who would be as raw as to not only behead three men, but to carry three heads and dump them in the park. He sits there quietly for a second. Maybe he does have an idea?

Meanwhile in Brick City

The man hops out of the Hummer H3 in the parking lot of IHOP on Bergen Street. He hops into the passenger's seat of Lil Mama's Infiniti. "What up, Girl?" he asks while already knowing that she is not going to respond.

She hands him the bag filled with 'After Party.' This is the last 300 bricks that Dre had. Dre has been holding onto these especially for him, due to the fact that he's paying cash for them instead of expecting consignment like the rest of the team members. "That's 300," she whispers.

"And that's 54," he replies. "Later! Tell Dre, I'll hit him!" he shouts as he gets out and slams the door behind him. Lil Mama backs up and zips out of the parking lot. The Hummer trails closely behind. Once they get a half a block away a third car exits the parking lot and follows their lead.

Lil Mama approaches 12th Avenue quickly. Just as she gets to the corner, the traffic light changes from yellow to red rapidly. She speeds through, totally running the light and the Hummer zips through right behind her.

The third vehicle gets caught by the heavy traffic which pours down 12th Avenue. A Newark Police car, which is cruising in the opposite direction happens to witness the two vehicles run the light. The driver stops short in the middle of the street and makes a wild u-turn. He turns his sirens on as he speeds up the block. He too runs right into 12th Avenue's heavy traffic. He pulls up to the corner and slams on his brakes. He looks up ahead at both of the vehicles which are stuck one traffic light ahead. The officer hits his sirens with hope that the drivers will let him pass. The driver is shocked to hear another siren sound off to the right of him. He looks to his right where he sees the driver of the Chevy Impala waving his hand out of the window fast and hard. The man rolls his window down to see what it is that he's talking about. "What's up?" the passenger of the police cruiser asks arrogantly.

"Are you in pursuit of that Infiniti and H3 up there?"

"Yeah," he replies with a cocky demeanor.

The driver of the Impala flashes a FBI badge out of the window. "Let 'em go," he says in an aggressive tone. "Keep it moving."

The light changes and the Chevy zips through the intersection, leaving the police officers at the light angry and quite humiliated. They quickly catch up to Lil Mama's Infiniti which somehow has gotten behind the H3. She makes the quick left onto West Market Street while the Hummer continues straight. The Chevy is now about two cars away from the H3. "Why did you let her get away?" Federal Agent Dumbest asks from the passenger's seat.

"Ah, let her go. No need to worry about her," Federal Agent Dumber replies. "Where is she going? We know her whereabouts. We can get her whenever we choose to. If we grab her, that will alarm the rest of them and may stop us from getting an even bigger sting. Right now, he's a valuable piece to our puzzle."

"You don't think that will alarm them?"

"Nah, if we put the right amount of pressure on him, he won't utter a word to anyone. If he cooperates he will never want anyone to know that. That will give him the incentive to keep his mouth shut. The key is to make him cooperate. Go ahead, call it in."

What they just witnessed is all the evidence that they need. They have sat out in front of Lil Mama's house waiting for her to come home, but she never did because that was no longer her house. After sitting for days they decided to investigate and what they discovered was a landlord who explained to them that she was no longer residing there. They were left with only one link which happened to be her light bill. When she moved she didn't discontinue the service, she only transferred it to her new apartment. Being that her last apartment was in a working class person's name that confused the agents, stunning them slightly.

How did they find out about Lil Mama? Let's just say a scorned woman is a dangerous woman. While the agents were lurking around Cindy's place hoping to catch Dre doing something camera worthy, they had her house phone tapped as well as her cell phone. As they listened, hoping to hear Dre calling someone with juicy business lingo, instead they overheard Cindy talking to a girlfriend. She cried on and on about how she hated Dre and hopes that he dies or goes to jail for doing what he did to her. They then learned of a girl that he allegedly left her for. They figured they could capitalize off of the hate she holds for him. All they would have to do is further enhance it by exaggerating about Dre and the other woman's relationship. They were sure that would make her tell them anything they needed to know.

One early morning they caught Cindy leaving for work. They pulled up on her and introduced themselves. They threatened her before asking of his whereabouts. She immediately told them everything they needed to hear about the other woman. She did so not out of fear because Dre taught her many years ago how to operate under police pressure and she has never forgotten that. She very well knows how to handle herself with them. She told everything out of pure revenge. Although they know that she holds hatred for

Dre, they still couldn't take the chance of her warning him or even discussing this with anyone. That caused Agent Dumber to apply some dirty tactics. He warned her that if she told him or anyone else about their meeting, she would be charged with conspiracy and go to Federal Prison. He then told her that they will be following her everywhere. He then named the location of her job and the beauty parlor she goes to, to show her that they have followed her. He also told her that both of her phones are tapped and if they even hear her speaking with him, she's going to prison. They even spoke of a few things that she's said over the phone just to instill fear in her. They warned her that if she wants to avoid a conspiracy charge, she should never be in the same room with him and if he calls, she should hang up on him instantly. They are sure that she will have no contact with him at all due to the fear that they instilled in her. If that wasn't enough they threatened to take her son from her.

Federal Agent Dumbest grabs hold of the walkie talkie. "Yeah, we're in pursuit!" he shouts. "We're going East on Bergen Street and Central Avenue, black Hummer H3, tinted windows, Massachusetts license plates."

"Got you," the voice replies.

Minutes later, the driver of the Hummer H3 waits impatiently for the Dodge Durango in front of him to move. He's just a few feet away from the ramp of Route 280. The light has changed a half a minute ago and the truck is just sitting here. He mashes the horn continuously. "Move motherfucker! We got the light stupid ass!"

Suddenly a Chevy Suburban zips around to his left side at the exact same time as the F-150 pick-up truck swerves close on his right side. They have him trapped with nowhere to go. He's deeply frightened at the many white faces that he's surrounded by. He already knows that he has a problem. "FBI! Don't move!" Agent Dumbest says as he flashes his badge with one hand and points his gun with the other. "Hands on the dashboard in front of you!" he shouts as he makes his way to the driver's side window. Agent Dumber runs quickly to the left side, snatching the door open. All the other agents surround the truck as well.

Agent Dumber retrieves the bag which sets on the passenger's seat, while Agent Dumbest opens the door and snatches the man out of the vehicle like a rag doll. He slams the man onto the ground violently. He turns him over, cuffing his hands behind his back.

Agent Dumber opens the bag and sees the supply of the After Party. He walks over to Agent Dumbest and says, "Got it." "What do we have here?" he teases as he kneels down over the man. "Look what we have have stumbled across? We have the kingpin distributor of the Killer Heroin."

The man lies on the ground. The words Killer Heroin and Kingpin send chills up his spine. He's heard that word Kingpin several times throughout his prior incarceration and it always ended with life in prison. His life flashes before his eyes. Damn, he thinks to himself. How the fuck did they get onto me? I know Dre didn't set me the fuck up?

"10 states and over forty noted homicides," Agent Dumbers says as he shakes his head from side to side. "Are you in trouble?"

Fuck that, he says to himself. "Yo, this thing bigger than me. I'm just a pawn on this chessboard. I ain't the Kingpin!"

////// CHAPTER 120 //////

Tony hops into the passenger's seat of Dre's jeep. "What up baby? Tony shouts joyfully. "Man, I got the best news of a lifetime!"

"I got the bad news of a lifetime," Dre mumbles, as he exits Newark International Airport.

"I bet you my good news will wipe out your bad news. Wanna bet?" Tony asks while putting his pinky in the air, like a small child.

"I'm willing to bet everything, but I don't want to take your life away from you," Dre whispers. "You first?"

"Ok, you know your brother's court date is real close right? Well, I checked my messages and a Federal Prosecutor friend of mines gave me the heads up that they're under pressure. Everyone there is all stirred up. They have no grounds for conviction, no witnesses and no co-defendants. They can't seem to come up with anything that can actually stick. If we play our cards right, he'll be coming home. He has over eight years in already on the weapons charges. At the worse case, he may have to do another two to three years maximum, but at least he will not spend the rest of his life in prison. Now isn't that good news?"

"Great," Dre replies with no enthusiasm whatsoever. "My turn, now, right? Here, you read it for yourself," he suggests as he hands Tony the newspaper article.

Tony reads it slowly, letting it all marinate inside of his head. "Oh my god!"

Meanwhile in Asbury, New Jersey

Mu-Mit and Latif just step foot into Salaam's house. He's been calling every couple of minutes telling them that it's imperative that they come and see him.

"Yo man, you bugging," Latif says with agitation. "I told you we had something up the way to handle."

Salaam interrupts hastily. "That's fucked up, ya'll. That's really fucked up. I bring ya'll down here and roll the red carpet out for ya'll and that is how ya'll do me?"

"What the fuck are you talking about?" Latif asks.

"You know exactly what I'm talking about! How ya'll gone just cut me out of the operation and start giving the work to that nigga?"

"What nigga? What the fuck is you talking about?"

"The boy, Eternal. Ya'll telling me ain't no work right now, meanwhile he tearing the town up with that After Party."

"Eternal?" Mu-Mit questions. "I don't know no fucking Eternal!"

"Well he got After Party! Somebody know him!"

Mu-Mit and Latif's wheels begin turning. They wonder who he could be linked to in order to get his hands on the work. More important than that, Dre told them that he's falling back for a couple of weeks. Maybe he hasn't fallen back? Maybe he just told them that so he can cut off his ties with them? Mu-Mit saw something in his eyes the last time they met. It was as if Dre really doesn't want to be bothered with them due to the confusion that's going on with the Trauma Unit. The devil whispers into Mu-Mit's ear and he's listening with his undivided attention. Maybe Dre linked up with someone from here and passed the work onto them to cut Mu-Mit and Latif out of the program. "I know that Fuck Boy ain't playing like that," Mu-Mit whispers to Latif. "I know he don't wanna play like that?"

A look of frustration pops up on Latif's face. "You think he would do that?"

/////// CHAPTER 121 ///////

Days Later

The Mayor paces back and forth throughout his cell. He hates having to depend on people to make things happen for him. The worse part of him being incarcerated is the feeling of helplessness. He hates to ask someone to do something and have to wait until they decide to do it. At this point he feels like he's at Dre's mercy. He's been receiving call after call from potential clients, but he can't make it happen. His new found connection with the 'Bloods' has so much potential, but he can't make it happen on his own, from behind the wall. His hands are tied. He can't seem to talk Dre into moving out the way he would like him to. Instead of Dre supplying the heavy demand, he's gone into cruise control mode. The news about the Killer Heroin has Dre scared out of his mind. He's now forced to believe that him and Dre are in no way cut from the same cloth. "Bitch ass nigga," the Mayor utters under his breath.

He dials his brother's number. He's sure Dre will get mad at him and start yelling at him for calling his line direct, but at this point he couldn't care less. Something has to be done. There is so much money to be made and the Mayor won't be happy until it is made. He listens to the phone ring for a matter of seconds before the generic answering service comes on. Damn, he sighs to himself before hanging the phone up.

"Hmphh," Dre sighs as he looks at his cell phone. Just seeing his brother's number, he's sure that he knows exactly why he's calling. He refuses to answer because he's sure this call will be no different than the last calls that he's answered.

Dre feels that the Mayor's greed will be their downfall. Although the Mayor is in total control of this operation, Dre realizes that he has to put his foot down and draw the line no matter how his brother feels about it. He will put 'After Party' back on the market when he feels it's safe to do so and not a minute before that.

"As I was saying," Dre says looking Chico in the eyes. "Ya'll gone have to hold me down for a second. I'm holding out on 'After Party' and only getting 'Death Certificate' put together for ya'll. That 'After Party' is bad news right now. I'm gone let it cool off for a minute, that's it. Then when shit clear up, I'll come back."

"No problem, Primo. We got you. I'll do anything for you. You know that already. Whatever you need me to do just let me know."

"Nah, I'm good. I just need ya'll to shake the dope. My only source of eating will be ya'll for the time being, feel me?"

"Don't worry. I'll make sure you eat."

That I'm sure," Dre says with a smile. "Check, my little girl is about 30 minutes away. She bringing 4,000 bricks for ya'll. Alright?"

"Cool Primo. You want this money or do you want me to give it to the girl?"

"Nah, I'll take it."

"Here," he says as he hands over the bag of $310,000.00 for the last 2,000 bricks that he fronted them. "So, I'll be here waiting for her. If you need me for anything, just give me a call," he says as he exits the vehicle. "Later!"
Back In Yazoo

Ok, here we go with this shit again, the Mayor thinks to himself. He thinks he just gone do what he want to do, while ignoring what I want to do? When will he learn that I run this show? The Mayor is fully aware of the 4,000 bricks of 'Death Certificate' that Dre received yesterday. The connect tells him Dre's every move.

The Mayor's ego makes him forget why Dre isn't ordering the 'After Party.' Instead, he's busy concentrating on the fact that Dre is still making moves. His stubbornness makes him feel like he's in competition with Dre, when in reality, every move Dre makes benefits the Mayor more than it does Dre. His arrogance has him blindfolded. He just loves to see everything done his way. I see I'm gone have to pump the brakes on this shit once again, he says to himself. Why the fuck he can't do what I ask him to do?

///// CHAPTER 122 /////

Latif pistol whips the man gruesomely. "Nigga shut the fuck up!" The man's girlfriend and two small children scream louder and louder with each blow. The man is hog tied to a chair, sitting in the center of the room. Latif strikes again. "You better tell them to shut up," he mumbles from under his ski mask. "I'm telling you!"

The woman crouches in the corner of the room. She puts her hand over the children's mouth, to muffle the sound of their crying. "Shhhh," she whispers as she buries their heads into her lap so they don't witness the brutal attacking of their father.

"Please man?" he begs. "Not in front of my family, please?" he pleads.

"Nigga where the dope at?" Latif asks.

Under normal circumstances they would have to kill him in here, but today they have his back against the wall. He fears for his family member's lives and also he doesn't want his kids to be traumatized by this. "Please man, I beg you to take them out of the room. I'll cooperate. I'll give you whatever you want. Please just take them outta here?"

Latif looks at Salaam and gestures for him to take the woman and children out. Salaam grabs the woman by her hair and drags her onto her feet. He pushes her out of the room hastily. She leads both of the children by their hands. They're weeping with each step.

As Salaam is passing by the victim they happen to lock eyes. Oh shit, the man says to himself. He knew something about this particular man seemed familiar. He just couldn't pick up on who he is until now. The mask may cover his face, but he would be able to spot those eyes anywhere. The twitching of Salaam's left eye is a dead give away. Not only does it twitch, the pupil is noticeably smaller than his right pupil. Fucking Salaam, he thinks to himself. I should have known. I can't believe this shit. He always had a funny feeling about Salaam. He got the feeling that Salaam was slimy, but he overlooked it, underestimating Salaam as a slick ass crack head. He considered him to be harmless, but Salaam has proven him to be incorrect. Ok, he thinks to himself. Realizing this is Salaam is even more reason for him to cooperate so they allow him to live. That way he can punish Salaam for all of this.

Salaam slams the gun into the man's face. "Fuck you looking at?" Salaam asks in a muffled voice. He attempts to disguise his voice, but little does he know, it's way too late. His card has already been picked. "Don't you eye fuck me!" he shouts as he slams the gun against the man's head.

"I want everything," Latif says with aggression.

"Look in the closet over there. In the Timberland box on the shelf." Mu-Mit takes off in search of the box. He opens the closet door and quickly locates the box. He opens it and there he finds a box full of bricks. His curiosity leads him to grab hold of one of the bricks. Just as Salaam said, the stamp reads 'After Party.' Because Mu-Mit knows his product, he picks up on the stamp's defect quickly. The print is slightly different and their print is a tad bit smaller than the official 'After Party.' Mu-Mit can definitely see how customers could mistake it for the real thing though.

Mu-Mit steps right in front of the seated man. He's furious. He hands the bag over to Latif who buries his head inside the bag. "Where you get this from?" Mu-Mit asks in a muffled voice from under his mask.

"Huh?" Eternal asks.

"Where the fuck you get this from?" Eternal sits there quietly not knowing what answer Mu-Mit is waiting for. Mu-Mit slams his gun onto the top of his head. "Where the fuck did you get this from?" He still does not reply. "Oh, you just gone sit here and act stupid, right?" he ask before ramming the gun into the man's face repeatedly. Blood pours rapidly.

Salaam watches from the hall, while Latif rips through the closet. Salaam comes back in a matter of minutes, holding another bag. Latif shoves it into Mu-Mit's face. Both of their eyes are lit up as they view the many stacks of green backs. Latif then gives Mu-Mit the sign that their work here is done. Mu-Mit doesn't hesitate to reply. Boom! Boom! He fires, hitting the man in the center of his forehead. Screams from the woman and children sound off loudly from the other room. The impact forces Eternal and the chair onto the floor. Blood and brain matter gush from his head, as he lays there stiffened. Mu-Mit fires once more. Latif stands there as cool as ice but Salaam backs away with fear. He's never seen anything this gruesome in his life. His stomach can't take it. He's getting queasy.

"I guess he ain't Eternal, after all," Latif says with a smile.

"Come on," Mu-Mit instructs to them, as he leads the way out of the room. They run at full speed right pass the woman and the children who are still screaming at the top of their lungs.

Latif leads the pack as they exit the apartment. Mu-Mit is in the middle, while Salaam is in last place. By now his stomach is doing flip-flops. The sour taste fills his mouth warning him that it is about to happen. He can no longer hold it down. He stops in the middle of the hallway where he bends over and throws his guts up onto the floor. Both Mu-Mit and Latif stop with confusion. They're shocked to see him reacting like this over a murder with as many capers that he's claimed to have been a part of.

"Come on, let's go," Latif shouts as he snatches Salaam by the collar, leading him onto the porch. Mu-Mit follows closely behind the both of them. They all trot quickly to their get away car. Latif hops into the passenger's seat as Salaam grabs hold of the door handle of the backseat behind the driver's seat. Boom! Boom! Salaam drops to his knees before falling flat onto his face. Mu-Mit stands over Salaam's lifeless body. Boom! He fires again.

Minutes later, Mu-Mit steers onto the Parkway. "Damn, Salaam!" Latif shouts. "Bitch ass nigga. Always talking that tough Tony shit though! Throwing up at the sight of murder," Latif says slowly. "He had to go, right?" he asks as he turns toward Mu-Mit. "If he was that weak, you know he would have told under pressure."

Mu-Mit nods his head up and down. "Damn right. His DNA would have led homicide to him and he would have brought them right to us. I had no other choice."

///// CHAPTER 123 /////

In Fort Dix, New Jersey

Benderas opens the envelope and reads over the balance of his account. Tony just deposited his monthly allowance of $500.00 the other day. At this point, Benderas has any and everything that any inmate could ever want, the Mayor continues to shower him with money and gifts. Benderas has asked the Mayor to stop on many occasions, but he refuses to do so.

Benderas misses the Mayor. He loves him like a son and he hopes and prays that he will be ok. The Mayor wrote him the other day telling him, that his freedom date is coming close. Benderas wishes nothing but the best for him, but he's sure the Mayor has not learned his lesson. He gets the feeling that prison means nothing to the Mayor which means he does not respect the system. Benderas knows what happens when you don't respect the system. You end up coming back, or even worse than that, you end up not able to come back. With the Mayor's huge ego and pride, Benderas doesn't think the Mayor will last on the streets. With that being said, he will never admit this to the Mayor, but deep down inside he doesn't want the Mayor to be freed because he fears that he will die on those streets.

Meanwhile in East Orange

The elderly woman and a young woman sit at the kitchen table engaging in gossip when a loud boom sounds off. One second later the back door caves in and six masked men run into the apartment crazily. Both women scream at the top of their lungs. The noise brings a middle aged man out of his bedroom to find out what all the noise is about.

"What?" he manages to get out of his mouth before the Desert Eagle Nine Millimeter crashes into his mouth, knocking his dentures out. He falls onto one knee holding his mouth as blood drips from it like a leaky faucet. The women's screams are getting louder by the second.

"Shut up!" Al-Khabir yells from underneath his mask. "Shut up, or he dies!" he threatens before he kicks the old man in his face with his steel toed combat boots. The man attempts to block the blow, but with Al-Khabir being a third degree black belt he's rather swift with his feet. He stomps him several times as the man lies there absorbing the pain.

A masked man who we know as Latif stands at the center of the table with a gun in each hand. He aims precisely at both of the women's heads. "Both of ya'll shut up," he barks viciously, trying to intimidate them.

The other four men run back into the kitchen. "He ain't nowhere in here," one man shouts.

"Where is Trauma?" Latif asks as he extends his guns closer to each of the women's heads. Instead of replying, the women scream even louder.

Al-Khabir snatches the old man onto his feet by his frail neck. He damn near strangles him to death. "Trauma is your son, right?" The man nods his head up and down with fear as he gasps for air. Al-Khabir loosens his grip. "Where is he?"

"I don't know," the man replies while breathing extra hard. His circulation is cut off once again. "I'm going to ask you, again. Where is Trauma?"

"We haven't seen him," the young woman shouts in an attempt to save the old man's life.

"Who are you? His wife?"

"No, his sister," she mumbles while crying.

"Where is he? Tell me before I strangle your daddy to death," he threatens. The man's eyes bulge from his head. He gasps hard because not enough air is coming in. Al-Khabir loosens his grip. "Somebody tell me something?"

"Honestly, we have not seen him since last week. Go and check his room. His clothes are gone," she cries.

Al-Khabir speaks again. "Mother dear, where is Trauma? Tell me before I kill the love of your life?" he threatens.

The girl isn't lying. Once Trauma's soldiers were captured, he relocated with fear that they may have told where he lives. Correct he was. Moving was the best thing he thought he could do when he thought of bringing drama to his parents and his sister. By doing so, he has done his family a terrible injustice. He's left them here all alone to fend for themselves.

"One more time and that's it!" he says as he snatches the old man by his collar. "Where is Trauma?"

"We don't know," the girl cries once again. Latif plants the guns onto the back of their heads. Mu-Mit eases to his side. "No women and no children," he whispers.

"Listen son, please?" the old man pleads. "We don't have a clue of where he is.

"Nah?" Al-Khabir asks as he pulls him closer. He plants the gun against his left temple. The old man's eyes spell out fear. "Well, ya'll tell him, I'm tired of looking for him. Tell him it's his turn to come find me." Bloc! He fires and the old man's body falls free of his grip. The women scream at the top of their lungs as they watch the old man fall to the floor landing on his back. He squirms around in pain with his eyes still wide open. Bloc! The man stops moving and breathing at the same time. Bloc! Bloc! He fires two more shots at the already dead body.

///// CHAPTER 124 /////

Mocha's flip flops smack onto the cement loudly as she walks swiftly down the steps of the porch. She grasps her satin robe tightly in order to keep it from opening up and exposing her nude body. In her free hand she lugs a huge garbage bag. She struggles with the bag until she gets to the curb where she dumps it in line with the other garbage bags that are lined up along the curb in front of every other house. She quickly trots up the stairs and runs into the house.

"Pull up there," Agent Dumber says. They sit a half a block away from Tony's house just observing the surroundings with hope of seeing something worth sitting out here for.

Dumbest zips out of the parking space and cruises up the block. Once they get to Tony's house, Dumber speaks again. "Let me out." Dumber hops out of the car. He peeks around from side to side as he steps toward the curb. He snatches the bag and steps quickly back to the car. He dumps the bag onto the backseat. Just as he's getting into the car, Mocha busts the porch door open. She watches in a baffled manner as they pull off.

Five Minutes Later

"Wife, what up?" Tony asks.

"Tony, the weirdest thing just happened. I cleaned up a little bit, right?"

"You cleaned up?" Tony interrupts. "Yeah, that is weird."

"Tony, this is serious. Stop playing. Listen, I took one garbage bag out and placed it on the curb. As I was bringing the second one out, I see a man drop our garbage into the backseat of his car and pull off."

"Wife, you're bugging. You're telling me someone stole our garbage?" he laughs.

"Yeah. You laugh, but I'm dead serious."

"Mo, take it down, Ma." Tony figures that Mocha is seeing things. Ever since he got shot and the newspapers started printing articles about him, she's been under a great deal of pressure. She's scared out of her mind that they will try and drag Tony into their madness. It's one crazy thing after another with her. "Wife, listen to me. Take it easy, ok? Check, I just got here. I'm walking into the spot right now as we speak."

"Tony listen?"

"Mo, please? I just had a terrible flight. I'm tired. I have jet lag. I have not got over the jet lag from the D.R. trip and here I am all over again." D.R., he thinks to himself. Wow! Just mentioning those letters to Mocha, makes him feel extremely guilty. "I'm going in here to get this straight and I'm back on the first flight outta here, ok? You take it easy. You're taking this way too serious. We're good. Hold it down. I'll see you in a few hours. Ok? Later!"

"But?"

Agents Dumber and Dumbest pull over on the quiet suburban block. They both get out simultaneously. Dumber carries the bag over to the dumpster that sits behind the deli. He dumps the contents of the bag onto the ground and both of them dig through the garbage like savages. They're in search of anything of value to them and their case against Tony 'Cochran' and the Blackhead brothers. They pay close attention, looking for phone bills, light bills, bank statements, credit card bills and anything else that may have a paper trail which may lead them to houses or apartments that they know nothing about.

Tony sits in the visiting hall of 'U.S.P. Big Sandy.' Tony is so exhausted that he can barely keep his eyes open while sitting here. Inmates pour into the room one at a time. Tony looks at each man to see which one he's come here to meet. Suddenly a face appears at the doorway that somewhat matches the photo copied mug shot he holds in his hand. Tony waves him on and the man steps toward him. Tony stands, as the man gets within reach of him. He extends his hand to the man. "Attorney, Tony Austin," he says loud and clear. Tony looks the young man over and can't believe that this is the man that has been labeled a menace to society. If he didn't read over the paperwork himself he would never believe it. To him this man appears to be harmless.

"Damien Bryant," the man replies. They both take their seats across from each other. The Mayor sent Tony out here to Kentucky to meet with 'The Black Charles Manson.' Reading the young man's letters and hearing his cry for help forced the Mayor to send Tony to his rescue. The Mayor paid the fee for the man already, but he's told him that he will have to pay him back once the work is back in circulation.

"Listen, I read over everything," Tony claims. "I gotta be honest…they got you by the balls. I'll be lying to you if I were to sit here and tell you that I'm going to get you outta here. That is out," he says with compassion. "We both can forget that. My goal is to get the lethal injection request denied. Can I promise you that? No," he says with sincerity. "But what I can promise you is that I will fight my hardest."

"What more can I ask for?"

///// CHAPTER 125 /////

Mu-Mit tip toes through his dark bedroom. The sun hasn't even risen yet. It's part of his everyday regimen to be up and out of the house at this time. He leans over his bed and plants a soft kiss on his wife's forehead as she lays there peacefully. He then walks out of the bedroom and throughout the apartment carefully so that he doesn't bump into anything.

Mu-Mit's day begins with him offering the Fajr prayer at the Masjid everyday at this time. He then immediately goes to pick up Latif and they start their adventurous day from then on.

Mu-Mit grabs the keys off of the refrigerator before opening the door as quietly as he possibly can. He steps right foot first onto his porch, while reciting the translated words of 'In the name of Allah' in a low whisper. "O Allah, I seek refuge with you from Satan," he utters as he walks down the staircase. As he steps foot onto the ground he hits the remote starter button and the truck starts up automatically. He walks slowly towards the truck. Suddenly he makes an abrupt about-face turn due to the shadow that flashes over his shoulder. A huge spark lights up in front of his face and brightens up the entire block. Boc! Boc! The back to back slugs crash into the bridge of his nose and penetrates his skull, sinking dead into his brain. He's knocked off of his feet, stumbling backwards until he lands on his back. Trauma and another gunman stand over him and begin firing away. Boc! Boc! Pop! Pop! Pop! Boc! Pop! His spirit exits his body and soars away into the sky as his body bounces high off the ground, flipping and flopping after every shot. Twenty shots later, they run off, leaving a bloody corpse.

It's noted that any good thing that happens to a man, comes from God and any bad comes from one's self. Mu-Mit rest in peace, or will he?

An Hour Later

Mu-Mit's wife and daughter stand there with their faces full of tears as the coroner pulls off with Mu-Mit's body. Neither of them can believe that this has happened. Both of them are still in a state of shock. Mu-Mit's daughter awoke after hearing the shots. She assumed it was a dream until she ran to the window and saw the lights of her mother's SUV, with a body laying behind it.

Latif stands in between both of them. He holds each of them under his arm, trying hard to comfort them. He's the first person that Mu-Mit's wife called, even before the police. "Come on ya'll? Ya'll gotta be strong," he whispers. "Stop crying," he suggests as the tears drop from his eyes faster than theirs. "Come on. Ya'll gotta be strong."

Latif unloosens his grip of them, when he sees two detectives coming toward them. He steps off subtly before they can get over to them. "Mrs. Muhammad," the young detective says. "Detective Rodriguez. Uh, we would like you to come down to the precinct with us."

"For what?" she asks with concern.

"For questioning, maam?"

"Questioning? Questioning about what? I don't know anything. I was in the bed asleep," she cries as her daughter pats her back.

"Just come with us, please? We have a few questions to ask you. Who knows, maybe you know who your husband's murderer is and not even realize that you know. The culprit may be right up under your nose," the detective says as his attention is drawn to Latif who stands a few houses away, leaning against a house. "You never know?"

///// CHAPTER 126 /////

Federal Agents Dumber and Dumbest step off of the elevator and walk toward their left. The gold plated tag that's posted on the door is at eye level. It reads: Attorney At Law, Tony Austin. Agent Dumber pushes the door open hastily.

Mocha is startled by their boisterous entry. "Mocha Austin, we're here for your husband," he says as he flashes his badge.

Oh shit, Mocha says to herself. How the fuck do they know my name? The agents storm right pass her. "Excuse me, wait. You can't go back there. Wait!"

"My ass," Agent Dumbest replies as he walks toward Tony's office.

Mocha grabs hold of the telephone quickly. "Tony!" she shouts. "Tony, the Feds are on their way in your office," she says nervously.

Tony lays back with his feet up on his desk puffing on a cigar. He hopes that he's heard her wrong. "Huh?" he asks.

"The Feds," she says just as Dumber forces the door open.

"She said the Feds are on their way into your office," he says with sarcasm. "Hello, Tony Cochran."

"Hello," Tony replies as he sits up, planting his feet onto the floor.

"Tony. Long time no see," Agent Dumber says.

"Ah, the Cohiba Siglo 6," Agent Dumbest says. "I see you have good taste when it comes to cigars, huh?"

"Tony, how have you been?" Agent Dumber asks.

"I been ok. May I ask what brings you to my office? And what gives you the right to bombard your way in here? Do you have a warrant?"

"A warrant?" he smiles. "What do we need a warrant for? We're not searching your office. We're not arresting you. What is the warrant for? We're just here paying you a visit. Just conversing, that's it. May we take a seat?" he asks as he sits down. "Tony Cochran," he sings. "If there was an 'Attorney of the Decade Award,' I would be the first to present it to you. I'm so proud of you," he claims. "I watched you take your career to the next plateau. I was there when you were just a kid coming out of law school with hopes of being a high profile attorney. And look now, you have blossomed into one. Mr. Tony Cochran," he sings. "I watched you, case after case and I must admit you are quite clever and tactical," he smiles. "Everything you have, you have earned it. The three million dollar home in Watchung.

"Four million dollar home," he interrupts arrogantly.

"Ok, four million dollar home, forgive me? The two Bentleys, the Cadillac and the Mercedes. You deserve it all. You work hard so you should play hard."

Tony smiles while blowing a huge cloud of smoke into their faces. "Yeah, sometimes I work entirely too hard. Why just last year, I represented an average of 10 new clients a month at a minimum of $7,000.00 per client. Do the math, that's over $800,000 on the books. Not to mention that a few of those clients I represented during murder trials. You know $40,000.00 here, $70,000.00 there. Some appeals you know? Overall, I had a busy but, very lucrative year. Just in case you're insinuating that I don't make the money to live a certain quality of life. Try earning that type of income for the past six or seven years. Damn, I'm bullshitting," he smiles. "When I think of it, I realize that I'm actually living way below my means. I must stop being so modest and step my game up," he says arrogantly.

The agent's face turns red with fury. He ignores all of Tony's statements. Tony can see that he's angry and that makes him act that much cockier. "Speaking of trial, we hear that things are looking good for the Mayor. Congratulations is in order. Looks like you're going to pull off another victory. They say it's a shoe in. I heard you already have the victory in the bag."

Tony smiles. "You heard that? This is my first time hearing that," he lies.

"Yeah, it's true," he smiles. "I got ears. I hear things. This victory will put you in the history books," he smiles. "Ex- drug dealer turned high profile attorney," he says with sarcasm.

"Excuse me?" Tony pardons.

"You have one hell of a story, right?" Dumber asks as he looks to his partner.

"Sure does," Dumbest replies. "Brought tears to my eyes."

"Raised by a single mom. Overcame the obstacles of the street life and was able to turn a positive into a negative by paying his own way through college and law school with drug money. Now look at him. His way of giving back to the community that he helped destroy is by representing his drug dealing friends. I have to admit…you beat the odds."

"Excuse me? What are you talking about?" Tony asks before taking a huge drag of his cigar. "As a matter of fact, can you both please exit my office?" he asks as he duds out the cigar.

"No problem," Dumber says as he stands up. Dumbest stands up right after him. "I know you've made all of your loved ones proud of you. Especially your Aunt Lorita."

Aunt Lorita, Tony repeats in his mind. Where the fuck has he gotten that from? "I'm sure that she's nice and proud of you? Too bad her only son Kareem wasn't as fortunate as you. He was murdered right?" Oh shit, Tony thinks to himself. His armpits begin to tingle from nervousness, but he sits there as cool as a cucumber. "That is, if I'm not mistaken," Dumber continues on. "Correct me if I'm wrong."

Tony's mind races in chaos. He's astonished at what he's hearing. What is he insinuating? How does he know all of this? Oh shit, Mocha wasn't tripping. Maybe it was them snooping around at the house. Tony's mind goes back to the early nineties. The scene plays vividly in his head as if it's happening presently.

Tony closes the door of his apartment, while throwing the money filled duffle bag over his shoulder. He turns around only to be greeted by his cousin Kareem who stands a few feet away aiming a gun at Tony's head.

Tony draws his gun quickly and he aims straight for his cousin's head. Tony can still remember how he felt that day. He was scared and confused.

To see his cousin standing here ready to end his life over money hurts him. How could he be so grimy? Maybe he's just trying to scare me into giving up the money, Tony thinks to himself. Nah, look at his eyes. He's blazing right now, Tony analyzes. I really don't think he will kill me. Maybe he will. Boom! Tony fires a clean shot to his cousin's head which forces him onto the floor. Tony stands there in shock as his eyes are glued onto his first cousin who lays there dead, still holding his own gun in his hand. Tony's childhood flashes before his eyes. He remembers Easter Sundays at church sitting side by side with each other, wearing extra slim white suits and white shoes. He remembers him and Kareem panty pumping in the backyard with the neighborhood girls. That was their favorite game, 'catch-a-girl-get-a-girl.' A couple of years later that game changed to 'hide-and-go-fuck." All the good times that they shared, who would have ever thought that it would come to this one day? Not Tony. Tony hears a creaking above his head coming from the apartment upstairs. His heart races a mile a minute. The door cracks open and Tony dashes out of the hallway. He exits and hops into his Porsche without being spotted or did he? His mind replays his long ride down Route 95 South to North Carolina. Tears pour from his eyes the entire ten hour ride.

"Mr. Cochran," Dumber says, snapping Tony back into reality. Tony just stares at him as nonchalantly as he can. He regains his confidence and poise. One thing Tony knows about the Feds is 90 percent of their game is mental. They try and get into a person's head and manipulate them. They shoot high, threatening to send a guy to prison for a particular case that they know they have no power to do so. The guy in turn is afraid to face that amount of time, which makes him admit to his actual crime thinking that he's better off admitting what he's done and getting less time than going to jail for something that he didn't do and getting the maximum. Either way he loses. Tony also knows that the Feds only know what people tell them. Once they get enough concrete information from what people have told them, they try and scare a man into admitting what he's done. Never, Tony thinks to himself. "Nephew, everybody has a past," Dumber says. "Please don't make me bring yours to the present and fuck up your future," he says as he steps toward the door.

"What the hell are you talking about?" Tony asks while trying to play it cool and calm.

"Oh, you don't know? Beat that case and I'll show you what I'm talking about," he smiles. "Setting him free will cost you your freedom. Good day!"

///// CHAPTER 127 /////

Mu-Mit's wife and daughter stand in the center of the room, surrounded by four Muslim men. They've come here to the Masjid to set up the funeral arrangements for Mu-Mit. This has been a tough experience for the both of them. Although they were aware of what type of lifestyle he lived, they never imagined having to bury him.

"Sister, I'm sorry. We got word last night what all this chaos is about. Your husband's death is a result of a drug war. Your husband was a drug dealer. I'm sorry, but I refuse to wash your husband's body and I will definitely not pray over him. I'm sorry."

"What?" she asks in a high pitched voice. "Brother are you denying that brother his rights to be buried as a Muslim? You owe him that. We owe him that. If you deny his rights to have a funeral prayer, then you will be held accountable."

"Sis, this is one sin that I will have to take. I can't do it. In fact it may be hard to find someone who will perform the Jaanazah. The word has spread throughout the entire community. Your husband brought Fitna to Allah's house. Our Muezzin has been slaughtered because of him." He pauses momentarily. "As Salaamu Alaikum!" he shouts before leaving the room.

She's now stuck not knowing what to do or where to turn. Suddenly Latif comes to mind. Maybe he can tell me what I should do, she says to herself. Or maybe he can direct me to someone who will perform the ceremony. She pulls her cell phone from her purse and starts dialing.

Meanwhile In North Newark

The sound of Latif's IPOD rips through his earphones damn near bursting his ear drums. The music is so loud that he can't even hear his phone ringing over and over again. He starts bopping his head crazily as he listens to the same song for the 100th time. He stops bopping his head for a few seconds just long enough to bury his nose into the dollar bill filled with dope. He takes a huge sniff of the heroin. This particular heroin is the work that they scored from the robbery/homicide in Asbury. It may not be the official 'After Party' but if he sniffs enough of it, it will surely get him as high as he wants to be. That is if he doesn't overdose first. He has over 200 bricks to go through at his own leisure.

Latif was doing good. He's been drug free for over two years and now this had to happen. He takes another sniff. He shakes his head from side to side, while pinching his nostrils. He then immediately starts singing along loudly with Rapper AZ from the group Mobstyle. "They killed my man!" he shouts. "I watched him die," he whines. "I started bugging. I started to cry," he mumbles with passion. "I started getting high," he says raising his voice by a few volumes. "Off my own supply. Wondering why and why and why? This beef ain't over til somebody die. A mother...a brother...a sister? Mobstyle, I'm taking no prisoners!"

///// CHAPTER 128 /////

Tony sits in his office as Dre walks in. "Tone, what up? I got here as fast as I could." Tony gets up and starts walking toward the door. He gestures for Dre to follow him. He refuses to talk inside this office ever again. He doesn't trust those two agents the least bit. For all he knows they could have easily bugged his office and be listening to every word that is said. Tony is feeling so paranoid at this time. They have him walking on egg shells.

Once they get out onto the parking lot, Tony begins to speak. He peeks around nervously. "We have a problem," he says as he peeks around the parking lot. He gets the strange feeling that they're being watched.

"What up?"

"The two agents who have been on your brother's ass for years paid me a visit today. The good news is they confirmed the fact that we are in store of a victory. They have nothing solid to stick to your brother. Bad news is, they've been to my house and checked out my vehicles and everything. They're all up in my shit," he says. "That, I'm not worried about."

"Well, what is it that you are worried about then?"

Tony pauses before speaking. "Dre, I have never spoken a word of this to anyone," he says before pausing again. "Dre, this is from my mouth to your ears," he says with a stern tone in his voice. "Dre, I have not always been a clean cut, legal eagle type of guy," he claims. "Before this, I too played the game. I didn't touch the quantity of money that you do, but I did head my own organization. Ten kilos here, fifteen there, at the height of my short career. To make a short story even shorter, the Feds have dug into my past and what did they find out? They found out the biggest secret of my life and if they shine light on that incident, I may not only lose my license to practice law, but I could easily spend the rest of my life in prison."

Dre listens attentively and wonders what it is that Tony could have hid for all these years. He's absolutely shocked at all of this. He remains silent, but he's awestruck.

"Dre, they threatened to dig my ghost if I show up in court to represent your brother. They said, his freedom will cost me mines."

Damn, Dre sighs silently. He always feared a day like this. It's as if he predicted it. He always feared the day that Tony would be pressured into testifying against them and forced to sell them out, which is why he always warned his brother about telling him all of his business. Now the nightmare has come to reality. With all the knowledge Tony has of their operation, he can have them buried. Dre is sure of one thing and that is Tony has worked very hard to get to where he is in life and he will never put that in jeopardy for them. That means if he has to roll over, Dre is positive that he will. Right now, Tony is highly dangerous to them. Damn, I may have to press the button and get him touched, Dre thinks to himself. The timing is perfect right now with all the chaos going on. All the news about the Trauma Unit can work to his advantage. The heads in West Side Park, Mu-Mit's death. It could easily look like another Trauma Unit attack? They already shot him once. Murdering him next time won't be unbelievable, Dre thinks as he looks deep into Tony's eyes. Damn, I can't do that. He has a few hundred thousand of mine and millions of my brother's money. How can I get hold of the money so I can make my move on him? I have to come up with something and quick. I have no time to waste. Our lives are in this bitch ass nigga's hands.

///// CHAPTER 129 /////

Ahmir, ILL Wheel and Dusty sit along the docks of the waterfront at Baltimore Harbor. They sit side by side on the bench just eating seafood. ILL Wheel slurps the last of the raw clams. "Aghh," he growls as he stands up. He walks to the edge of the platform and tosses the clam shells into the air. He looks around slowly, just enjoying the beautiful view. He had to admit to Ahmir that he's really glad that he came down here. Since he's been here he hasn't had to watch over his shoulder at all. He's had peace of mind and that gave him time to really sit back and think. He realizes that Baltimore really isn't that bad of an idea. The change of scenery may be better for him.

ILL Wheel walks back over to them. "Thanks," he whispers to Ahmir.

"For what?"

"For making me think outside of the box. Man, real talk…Cee a sneaky mufucker. Ain't no way in the world he was gone let me get away with killing that girl or none of that other shit. They would have pushed me the first chance they got."

"True story," Ahmir agrees. "I'm just glad you came cause on the real Bruh, I ain't never going back up that mufucker!" he laughs. "If the Bricks didn't kill me that last time around, they ain't never gone get the chance to cause I ain't never going back," he smiles.

"I heard that," ILL Wheel replies.

"For old times sake," Ahmir says as he extends his fist in front of him. ILL Wheel extends his fist, touching Ahmir's. "Three the hard way!" Ahmir shouts as they hold their hands in the air awaiting Dusty's fist. Instead of sticking his hand out, he sits there rapping under his breath. He points his fingers in the air as if they're guns. His face is stone cold. As they watch him, he performs his mini-rap concert. "Psst. Two and a half the hard way," he laughs.

Meanwhile Back in the Bricks

Two Muslims push Mu-Mit's body to the front of the Masjid inside of the unfinished pine box. He can not be seen due to the fact of the box being closed because of religious custom. His funeral is quite empty. A few of his friends line up in the front row, while his wife and daughter stand in the back of the room with the rest of the women who are in attendance. Latif and Dre sit on the floor on the opposite side of the room.

After searching high and low, Mu-Mit's wife finally found someone who was willing to perform the ceremony knowing the circumstances. He said regardless of what, they have to send him away as a Muslim and only God can judge if he was a good Muslim or not.

The Imaam begins the procedure by placing his hands close to his ears. "Allah U Akbar!" he shouts. The other Muslims follow his lead. He stands over the box with his arms folded over his chest. He remains in silence as he prays for a matter of less than a minute. "Allah U Akbar!" he shouts before going back into the same stance. He prays for another 30 seconds. "Allah U Akbar!" he says before folding his arms once again. After praying this time, he looks to his right and says, "As Salaamu Alaikum wa Rahmatullahi." Immediately after that the brothers roll his body out of the building.

"It's over already?" Latif slurs slowly. The dope has him as high as can be.

"That's it," Dre replies. "It's over."

"That is the fastest funeral I have ever seen," Latif slurs. Latif has been high ever since Mu-Mit's murder. This is how he's been coping with the loss. If not for the dope, he would have turned into a mad man already.

Everyone exits the building and watches the men struggle to pick up the box that houses Mu-Mit's body. They dump the box into the back of the Cadillac hearse while Mu-Mit's wife and daughter hop into the backseat. Seconds later, the hearse cruises away slowly. Dre and Latif watch the car until it's out of their sight. So long Mu-Mit," Latif says. "It's over for my boy."

How wrong he is. This is just the beginning. Now it's time to pay for his sins.

/////// CHAPTER 130 ///////

Tony sits across from the Mayor in the visit hall. The Mayor listens to Tony carefully so that he does not miss a word of what he's saying. He looks into Tony's eyes and he sees stress. Tony claims that he's exhausted from the traveling he's been doing lately, but the Mayor knows stress when he sees it.

Finally, Tony stops speaking. The Mayor sits quietly for he knows not what to say. This close to freedom and now this, he says to himself. It's down to me or him and who do I think he'll pick? Him of course, the Mayor says to himself. My shit is officially over. I'm really about to spend the rest of my life in prison. Damn.

The Mayor's silence is ripping Tony apart. He wonders what it is that he's thinking. He can't take another second of it. "So, what do you have to say about that?"

"What can I say?"

Several Hours Later

It's 10:30 p.m. and Dre and Latif are here in Harlem, New York. "Wait right here," Dre instructs Latif who sits in the passenger's seat. Ever since all of the mayhem began, Dre has been quite skeptical about moving around alone. The murder of Mu-Mit has reassured him that he has all the reason in the world to be skeptical. He feels the need for protection. He believes that the Unit will strike again, but he just doesn't know when. He just has to be on point and ready whenever or wherever it happens. Keeping that in mind, he's forced to do something that he's never felt the need to do. He now carries a gun on him.

Throughout all his years of hustling, he's never even owned a gun, but today he realizes that it's the law of the game. He knows that he's no gunslinger or marksman, but he just wants to have protection if trouble comes his way. He just needs a little something to get him out of the hole if he's forced into a tight situation. He has the ideal tool for that.

Dre grabs the 5 shot nine millimeter Dillinger from under his thigh and jams it into his sweat jacket pocket. The gun is so small that no one would be able to tell that he has it on him. It could easily be mistaken as a toy or a cigarette lighter. It may look like a toy, but the bullets are the same deadly bullets that fit into an ordinary nine millimeter and trust and believe, if those hollow tips rip through the flesh of his enemy, they will bear witness that although it may look like a toy, he isn't playing.

Dre hops out of the jeep and rubs his hand over his jacket pocket just to smooth out the small bulge from the gun. He then looks down to make sure that it can not be seen. "Let me holler at these mufuckers real quick," he says to Latif as he's closing the door. Dre is here to meet with the connect. He had to come to them this time because they refused to come to Jersey because of the widespread news of the killer heroin. He tried to come up with all types of neutral meeting places that he felt was safe, but they rejected every last one of them. He refused to come in the daytime because he feared the business of these streets would distract him. He figured it would be much safer to make his move at night in the dark.

He takes off trotting across the street, not even realizing that the door has not closed all the way. From the sound of it something must have gotten jammed in the door. Latif leans over the seat and finds Dre's wallet jammed in between the door. He forces it open and snatches the wallet. As he's pulling the door shut he looks down at the wallet and Mu-Mit comes to mind. This is actually the exact same wallet that Mu-Mit carried. It still hasn't completely sunk into Latif's head that Mu-Mit is dead. Each day at sunrise, he still waits for Mu-Mit's call. He does so out of pure habit. Losing Mu-Mit took a big chunk out of Latif. A part of him feels empty without his partner in crime. He feels lost without Mu-Mit. They've been together night and day since they initially linked up. Moving around without him makes him feel a sense of emptiness.

All Latif's life, he's been somewhat of a follower. He's always been in need of a leader. Once he finds one he clings to him for dear life. He doesn't have a mind of his own which means he needs someone to direct him to what he needs to do. All his life he's bounced from team to team. Lack of loyalty is not the reason for his hopping around. He's always been linked to guys who only use him and never show him love or even care about him. They normally use him until he can no longer be used. Being a part of this squad has been a totally different experience for Latif. This is the first time in his life that he actually felt like the loyalty factor is mutual. This makes it that much easier to put his life on the line or go to that extra edge for his teammates.

He's grateful that the Mayor and Dre gave him a shot to be down with the 'A Team' as he calls it. Bringing him in has changed life as he knew it. He's been able to do any and everything that he's wanted to do. Because of them, he's been able to keep money in his pocket and live a lifestyle that he's never imagined living. With all the love they showed him he has no choice but to reciprocate.

He lost his main man and feels horrible about it. He just wishes he was there to save him. Every second of the day he thinks and plans his next attack. He will get even with Trauma even if it's the very last thing that he does. He realizes that he has to be smart though. At the end of the day, all he has is Dre right now and protecting him is his main concern right now. He may have lost one, but he refuses to lose another.

Latif digs into his pants pocket and retrieves a bag of dope. He splits the packet along the edge and buries his nose inside. "Sniff..sniff..sniff," he sniffs the bag entirely. He immediately pulls another bag from his pocket. He sniffs this bag in just one huge sniff. Before he can get the drain from the first two bags, he pulls another bag out and totals this one out as well. He rolls the window down and tosses the packets out to remove the evidence. The last thing he needs is for Dre to find empty bags in his car. That could result in him being fired.

As the drain drips from his nostril passage onto the back of his tongue, he lays back, anticipating his high. Being a dope addict for most of his life, has given him a very high tolerance which is why one bag doesn't even come close to getting him high. Unless of course it's as potent as the official 'After Party.' Latif has yet to get his hands on it due to the fact that there has been no 'After Party' around since he's been getting high again. Today may be his lucky day though. He plans to get his hands on some of it one way or another. He can't wait to find out if all the hype that he's been hearing is really true or is it just overrated. Dre already informed him that he's only getting a small amount of work. Latif doesn't know how he's going to persuade Dre to give him a few bricks, but he will definitely come up with something.

Minutes Later

Latif is good and high now, but he's able to remain cool and calm. He has to do so just to keep Dre from seeing him in that state. Latif watches as the garage of the house Dre went in, opens up.

Lil Mama backs out of the two car garage onto the opposite side of the street. She stops directly in front of Dre's jeep. She makes the right and cruises down the block casually. Latif looks in Lil Mama's face. She looks so young, sweet and innocent. No one would ever look at her and think that she's transporting dope around, but she is and lots of it.

Lil Mama's vehicle is packed with enough dope to tear down an entire state. She has ten kilos for Imamu and one thousand bricks of 'After Party.' Dre hated to get more of the killer heroin, but the Mayor insisted that he at least gets 1,000 for the Blood homies. The Mayor wouldn't take no for an answer and Dre knew exactly what that meant. As usual, it's his way or no way.

Once Lil Mama gets halfway down the block, a late model Mitsubishi Montero pulls out of the garage and cruises down the block in the same direction. Dre walks out of the house and makes his way across the street. As he's approaching the jeep, Latif lifts his head up slightly; peeking into the visor mirror to make sure his nose is clean of any dope residue.

Meanwhile Two Blocks Away

A late model Chevy Lumina sits parked discreetly down the block. The passenger has a set of binoculars glued to his eyes. Through the binoculars he has viewed the entire episode. "Showtime," the Federal Agent says as he watches Dre get into the jeep. The agent drops the binoculars onto his lap and picks up his walkie talkie. "Let's go!" he shouts over the radio to all the other agents who are sitting parked around the entire vicinity of the neighborhood. They all have been waiting impatiently for this call.

One Block Ahead

Lil Mama sits at the traffic light when a late model Ford work van cuts her path abruptly. The van swerves recklessly before crashing into her SUV. Three white men bust out of the back doors. "FBI! Don't move!" one man says as he flashes his badge and points his gun at the same time.

LIl Mama looks around in shock as Federal Agents and DEA swarm her car. Unmarked cars come from every direction. "Hands out of the window!" the agent yells aggressively. "Now!" She peeks around nervously as she raises her hands slowly. All she can think of is the abundance of heroin that she has in the vehicle. The tears start falling from her eyes instantly.

Her door is snatched open and she's dragged from the vehicle with no consideration for her being a woman. As she's pinned to the ground, face down, she looks to her left where she sees the agents slamming the driver of the Mitsubishi Montero in the back of an unmarked car. That man is the transporter of the dope. He's the man who gave Lil Mama the work and in turn she gave him over $800,000 in cash money.

While the man is being put into the car, another agent searches through the Montero. In no time at all, Lil Mama sees him walking away from the car holding her duffle bag. At this point she realizes that her life is over. One agent steps his foot onto her back as another one cuffs her hands behind her back tight and uncomfortably. She cries a river silently.

"What about me?" the Spanish man asks from the back seat of the unmarked car. He moves around real nervous and hyper. "What about me?" he asks again with major concern. "I'm going to jail too, right? Ain't I? Ya'll taking me to jail too right?"

"Shut the fuck up!" The Federal Agent says. "You done talked enough, now shut the fuck up!" he snarls. His partner hops into the passenger's seat. "I been doing this shit for 20 years and I never heard a guy talk as much as him. There is a such thing as too much information." The man in the backseat has done exactly what they said. He has cooperated to the fullest. He has not left out one detail. He sits back wondering how his future will play out. I have cooperated so will they cut me loose or will they still lock me up forever? If I'm lucky they will just deport me back to my country. His mind races a mile a minute. "What about the other guy? They got him yet?"

The partner grabs hold of his radio and chimes in. "What's the situation?"

There is no reply for several seconds before a voice cuts in. "Heavy pursuit, but we're on him close. Apparently he spotted everything and he made a quick detour right into Radcliffe. We're on him, he'll never get away."

Dre peeks through his mirrors nervously. His focus is on the string of cars that are behind him as he speeds up 125th Street. After seeing Lil Mama's truck and the Montero being boxed in by the Feds, Dre knew it was over for them. Luckily he was able to make a quick right turn, just one block away. In his mind, he thought that he had gotten away without them seeing him. Little did he know, they were already on him as well. Lil Mama's innocent looking face pops into his mind. He feels horrible that he's gotten her into this mess. He's sure that she's frightened to death right now.

Latif sits on the edge of his seat peeking around nervously as well. All he can think of is doing a lifetime bid. He knows for sure that there is no coming back for either of them with the excessive amount of dope that Lil Mama has in that vehicle.

Dre realizes what the Hemi engine in his truck is all about as he stomps on the gas pedal. The engine roars loudly as he speeds up the block recklessly. Damn, he thinks to himself. Please God, help me get away," he pleads. All he can think of at this point is going back to prison and spending the rest of his life there. Fuck that, he says to himself as he stomps on the gas pedal even harder. The back of the truck lowers closer to the ground as the front lifts up. The engine roars even louder.

Sirens sound off loudly, frightening both Latif and Dre even more. "Oh shit!" Dre shouts as he sees three Crown Victorias in his driver's side mirror. They're zooming up the block on the opposite side of the street.

Latif looks behind and his heart skips a beat when his eyes set on the speeding cars. The whole scene is playing like a movie that they've seen. The only difference is that they're the stars of the movie. They both know how it's going to end because the bad guy never gets away. "Go, go!" Latif shouts desperately.

A few car lengths ahead, a bunch of cars are stuck at the traffic light. "Dip around them!" Latif shouts. Dre does just as he's instructed to. He dips around onto the opposite side of the street, just barely missing the car that is facing them. He regains control by swerving to the right. At the intersection, a Lincoln Navigator speeds through. Dre has to dip to the right to miss it as well.

Both of their hearts are pounding. More and more sirens echo throughout the neighborhood. "Oh shit!" Latif shouts as he looks down the block to his right and sees yet another set of cherry tops blazing. The raggedy work van bounces up the block at high speed. He looks to the left and there he sees another set coming from that direction. Apparently they were attempting to trap them off.

At this point Dre is stuck. He has not a clue of which direction he should go. With him not being an expert driver, he's sure that they will eventually catch up with him. There is no way that he will be able to get away from all of these cars. He slows down at the next intersection while gripping the steering wheel, rocking it back and forth indecisively. "Go!" Latif shouts. "You gotta step on it!" And that he does. He stomps the gas pedal harder than he's done before.

Dre's jeep flies up 125th Street. He looks behind him and sees approximately seven vehicles with their lights blazing. This gives him the incentive to drive faster. A small Toyota cruises in front of him. He mashes the horn as he dips around and gets in front of the slow moving car. He makes the quick left without using the slightest bit of a breakdown. The truck slides into the cement divider. "Damn," he sighs. He realizes that he can't let that slow him down. His future suddenly looks brighter as he sees the ramp to the West Side Highway. He mashes his horn loudly as he runs the red light and hops right on. He looks behind and is happy to see that not a single Fed car is behind them as of yet.

Dre looks ahead and is also happy to see clearly up the highway except for a few cars that are spread out in the lanes. His adrenaline is pumping from fear. He looks at the speedometer which reads 105 miles an hour. He then looks in his rearview mirror where he sees a string of police cars coming onto the ramp a few miles behind him. He mashes the gas pedal even harder and the speed accelerates by ten miles almost instantly. Each time he looks into his mirror and sees the Feds behind him, he gets more frightened which in turn makes him stomp the pedal harder. He now looks at the speedometer and it reads 120 miles an hour. He's passing by vehicles quickly as if they're standing still.

Latif peeks behind them. He's scared to death. He attempts to count the cars that are coming. In total he's already counted ten cars before he stops. He realizes that the chances of them getting away are slim. "Turn off your lights," he demands.

Dre does as he's instructed to. Good idea, he says to himself. He's now speeding up the highway in the dark. He dips in front of a few cars with hopes of confusing the Feds who are still speeding up the highway as well.

"Step on it!" Latif shouts frantically. Dre mashes the pedal and the jeep increases speed rapidly. He dips into the middle lane where he rides for a few feet before cutting back into the first lane. He looks up ahead where he sees a string of vehicles in his lane. He speeds up to catch up with them. Just as soon as he approaches them he cuts into the left lane and dips right back into the middle lane as soon as he passes them. He just misses the first car by a hair. Heavy horn blowing sounds off.

"They're gaining on us!" Latif shouts as he notices that the distance between them is decreasing. Dre becomes even more scared now. He peeks in the mirror and sees it for himself. He then looks ahead of him and becomes frightened as he sees several automobiles cruising in all of the lanes causing congestion. Damn, he thinks to himself. He catches up to the cars in no time at all. He immediately starts mashing his horn as he's glued to the car in front of him. Stupid motherfucker!" Dre shouts. The driver in front of him cruises along out of spite. Dre gets highly frustrated. He bangs his jeep into the back of the vehicle and pushes it up the highway until the driver finally pulls over into the next lane. He now has the lane to himself for a few miles. He decides to cut into the middle lane, just to stay out of the Feds' vision. He's looking behind him at all the lights that are shining in the windows behind him. He cuts over onto the middle lane and a powerful force bangs into the passenger's door. He loses control of the jeep. He was so busy watching his rearview that he didn't pay attention to his blind side.

Dre's jeep soars across the highway uncontrollably until it smacks into the divider head on. Both airbags explode into the faces of Dre and Latif. They both sit there in shock for a matter of seconds before the sound of the sirens revive them. Dre forces the driver's door open and he jumps out of the jeep. Latif attempts to open his door, but it's jammed from the crash. He quickly climbs over to the driver's seat and exits from that side. He follows Dre's lead as he runs up the highway. The sounds of sirens are echoing louder and louder making them run faster and faster. How long do they think they can manage to run before the Feds catch up with them?

Suddenly, Dre runs across the pitch black highway without even looking out for speeding cars. Heavy horn blowing sounds off as the driver of a Mercedes just misses him. Tires screech as all the drivers slam on the brakes to avoid hitting Dre and Latif. Dre pays no attention to them at all, but Latif runs carefully, trying hard not to get hit. Dre looks back and is shocked to see that not even a mile away, are the string of Feds. He peeks around nervously, not knowing what exactly to do. At this point, the only thing on his mind is prison. He's made the vow never to go back there and he plans to stick to it. The sounds of the sirens are getting closer and closer. He then looks at the body of water which sits to his left and with no hesitation he looks back at Latif and says, "I'm going in!"

Latif hopes that he's heard Dre wrong. "What?"

"I'm going in! Fuck that! I ain't going back to prison!" he yells as he jumps onto the railing.

"You crazy?" Latif asks.

His question is answered when he sees Dre dive over. "Oh shit!" Latif shouts aloud. He can't believe his eyes. He looks behind him and he sees the Feds are now closer than ever. He looks to the water and there is no sign of Dre, but what he does hear is the huge splash that sounds off when Dre's body hits the water. Latif thinks of getting caught and taking all the weight of this crime. It takes him no time at all to make up his mind. He hops onto the rail and one second later he dives into the Hudson River as well.

Seconds later, the cold water awakens his body as he splashes into the river. He's somewhat shocked at all of this. He begins swimming with all of his might. He looks up ahead for Dre. He can't see him, but he can hear his hands splashing against the water with each stroke.

The powerful force of the water is way too much for Latif, but he continues to swim anyway. Dre gasps as the abundance of water fills his lungs. He coughs hard to clear the water from them. This may slow him down, but he refuses to stop. They both refuse to be captured. They swim up the river like two runaway slaves attempting to make it to freedom.

///// CHAPTER 131 /////

The Next Day

Tony hops into the backseat of the Lincoln. "Hey Ralph," he says to the chauffeur.

"Hello, Mr. Austin. Women's Detention Center, right?"

"Correct!" Tony shouts. "Hmphh," he sighs. He's exhausted. All the traveling and back and forth flights are beating him down. He's tired, but he can't complain. He'd rather be tired from work, than to have no work at all. "Aw shit," he says aloud as he suddenly remembers that he's left Miranda's paperwork in his office. "Got damnit," he says aloud. That defeats his purpose in coming here. Maybe I can get Dre to fax the papers to me? He pulls his phone from his pocket and dials. Dre's phone doesn't ring not one time. It goes straight to his voicemail. Tony hangs up and dials again, but the same thing happens again. He now begins dialing his office.

"Attorney Tony Austin's office," Mocha recites in her most pleasant voice.

"Wife, put Dre on the phone."

"Dre is not here."

"Not there?" Tony questions. "He left out?"

"No, he never came in," she says with a huge amount of sassiness.

"Did he call in?"

"No," she says slowly.

Hmmmm, that's odd. That is not like Dre at all. "Anyway do me a favor? Go into my office and get." He stops short. Something important just came to mind. In the exact same file cabinet where Miranda's files are, Tony stashed the phone number that belongs to the girl from Dominican Republic. He enjoyed the time that he spent with them so much that he disregarded the old 'hit and quit it' 'touch and go' method. He couldn't let her go without taking her number. Then how would he get in touch with her when he's in D.R. for business? Something tells him that those cigars will have him spending a great deal of time there. Well at least that's what he's told Mocha as he attempted to prepare her, so it wouldn't come as a complete shock to her. "Ah never mind, you'll never find it," he lies. I hope not, he says to himself as he thinks of the penalty he will have to pay if she even gets hold to that number.

"You sure? What is it?"

"Don't worry bout it. Never mind. It's nothing. I'll see you tonight!" he shouts before hanging up in her ear. As soon as the phone is hung up, he immediately dials Dre's cell phone again. The answering machine comes on once again. Tony gets a funny feeling in his gut. "Damn, this ain't like him," Tony utters aloud. "Something isn't right."

One Hour Later

Miranda sits here quietly while anxiety fills her belly. When she called Tony two days ago, he told her the decision is in. When she asked him what the final decision was, he told her he would rather not discuss it over the phone. In her mind, that could only mean bad news. She assumes it must didn't work out in their favor.

Miranda looks in his eyes attempting to read him. Her heart pumps nervously as she looks into his baggy eyes. Baggy eyes are a sign of no sleep, she says to herself. She figures that he must be stressing over the decision.

Tony sits there quietly, shaking his head from side to side. "Miranda, Miranda, Miranda," he says with saddened eyes. This is the icing on the cake for her. She starts to shake her head from side to side as well. Her eyes become glassy looking. "They went for it," he whispers.

"Huh?" Miranda asks. She thinks that she's heard him wrong.

"I said they went for it," he repeats as a huge smile spreads across his face, brightening up the entire room. "We're in. I talked to them early yesterday. All we have to do is meet with them, sign the paperwork stating that you are willing to testify. Tell them who he is, pick him out of the mug shots and we'll gamble from there," he whispers. A smile two times as big as Tony's pops up on her face. This is the first time Tony has ever seen her smile. He gets caught up in her beauty momentarily before snapping back into the reality that this is his client and he should never be looking at her in that manner. "Miranda, be cool. Don't get too excited. We're only halfway there. It's not in the bag yet. Let's just keep our fingers crossed," he says as he crosses his fingers on top of the table.

Miranda follows his lead and crosses her fingers. "They're crossed."

////// CHAPTER 132 //////

In Yazoo, Mississippi

It's 7 a.m. bright and early. The Mayor leans back on his cot with his phone glued to his ear. He hasn't slept a wink. He's been waiting all night for 7 a.m. to come because he knows that is the time that Tony normally wakes and turns his phone on. "Hello!" he shouts anxiously.

"Yeah?" Tony replies in a groggy voice. He's still half asleep.

"Say it ain't so?" The Mayor begs. "Please Bruh, tell me it ain't true?"

"Huh? Tell you what ain't true?"

"Tony, don't bullshit me? Don't try and sugar coat it for me. Keep it real with me Bruh? I'm a grown ass man."

"Yo," Tony says with his voice dry and crackling. "What are you talking about?"

"About my brother? Is it true?"

Tony gets alarmed. Judging by the tone of his voice he's sure that bad news is about to follow. No wonder, I have not heard from Dre. But why? He's almost afraid to ask the Mayor what it is that he's heard. "What about Dre?"

"I heard he's dead," he says as his voice cracks.

A huge lump forms in Tony's throat. He tries to swallow it, but he can't. He gulps a few times before he's able to speak. "D,dead?" he mumbles.

"Yeah, word is he drowned, trying to get away from the Feds. Please tell me that it isn't true? Big Bruh is the only blood that I got left," he cries.

"Listen," Tony interrupts the sentimental moment. "I just got back into town late last night from Miami. I have yet to hear anything." Damn, maybe it's true. This is why I have not heard anything from him. I knew something wasn't right. Damn, I'm getting the feeling that this may be true. If it is, there is no way in the world I will be able to break the news to the Mayor. "Where did this suppose to happen at?"

"He supposedly drowned in the Hudson River, near Harlem." The Mayor can easily believe this rumor because he's familiar with the area of where Dre allegedly drowned. That house is the exact same house that he would go to from time to time to meet with his connect. No one actually lived there, but it's where they've been conducting their business for years.

"Let me get out and about and see what's going on. I'll get back with you as soon as I can? Alright?"

"Asap! Tony please! Get back with me either way. Good or bad news! I need to know right now. I'm waiting on your call, man!"

"I got you," Tony says before he hears the click in his ear. He's dumbfounded. He doesn't know where to start. He hops out of the bed and tip toes down the stairs. He snatches the door open slowly. As he looks down at the newspaper his heart pounds like a drum. He's afraid to pick it up. In his heart, he feels that it's true. He bends over and grabs hold of the paper.

Suddenly everything seems as if it's playing out in slow motion like a scene from the twilight zone. As soon as he flips the paper open, the first words that he sees are Ex-Felon Drowned. There goes his confirmation. His heart is now beating out of control, making him feel very uncomfortable. His stomach gets queasy and his hands start to tremble. The newspaper rattles loudly from the vibration of his trembling hands. He reads the full headline. Ex-Felon Drowns in an Attempt to Flee From FBI. Now come on Tony, don't jump the gun, he says to himself trying hard to be optimistic. This could easily be a mix up. It doesn't have to be Dre just because they said Ex-Felon. He reads further. Ex-Felon, Andre Blackhead, he reads before the sour taste fills his mouth. He's quite frightened to read the rest, but he does so anyway.

Tony reads the complete article over and over again and still he doesn't want to believe that it's true. Damn, he thinks to himself as the water drips from his eyes. Now for the biggest task. How am I going to break the news to his brother?

///// CHAPTER 133 /////

Three Days Later/ August 27, 2007

Tony sits upright on the bench in the front row of Churchman's Funeral Home. He just stares at the closed casket as he's been doing for the last hour. To his right sits his support system, Mocha. Throughout the many ups and downs Tony has had in the last few years, Mocha always seems to be his rock. No matter what he's gone through, he's always been able to depend on her to have his back. Tony looks at Mocha and is so grateful to have her on his team. Just to think that he almost blew a good situation. Back when he asked his client Suave to introduce him to her, he automatically bashed her and tried to talk him out of it by stating what type of gold digging street chick he perceived her to be. Luckily Tony didn't stop pursuing her because of that. If he had he would have missed out on one of the best things that has ever happened to him. Even his colleagues were against Tony marrying Mocha. They didn't believe that she was the right chick for him.

Tony looks at some of their marriages and wonders if they believe that they have the right women for them. All of their wives are shallow women who have always been sheltered. They don't have the slightest clue of how to fend for themselves if they had to. Tony looks at Mocha on the other hand, who is a hustler at heart. She's tough and will find her way out of any situation. Tony has always believed in marrying on his level, and although she's not on his level financially, she's on his level mentally. He always felt that it is far better to be with a woman that has been through the struggle as opposed to someone who hasn't. At the end of the day, Tony is sure that she's strong and won't fall for anything. On top of that he realizes that she's been in the world and had the chance to experience meeting with different dudes. That in return makes her know what is really out here for her. She's told him on many occasions the types of dudes that she's experienced being with. With Tony knowing that, he feels comfort in knowing that she appreciates him wholeheartedly.

He remembers clearly Suave telling him that Mocha is the opposite of him and that is exactly what he loves about her the most. She keeps him in check and also grounded. Suddenly the guilt of his D.R. trip kicks in once again. He thinks of how he betrayed Mocha. As he analyzed the situation, he's now come to realize that he wouldn't trade his Mocha in for ten of those women. All he can do at this time is be thankful to have her by his side. He looks over into her eyes and whispers, "Thanks."

The Mayor made sure that Tony put his brother away the proper way. He lays inside the beautiful cherry colored marble coffin, wearing a beautiful pin stripe Zegna suit and his body will be put to rest next to their mother in a huge mausoleum.

It tore the Mayor to pieces to hear that his big brother and the last one of his immediate family tree is no longer. The worse part is the Mayor wasn't allowed to be here. Tony did everything in his power, and his funeral visit was still denied. They claim that their decision was based on all the activity with the Trauma Unit, but Tony believes that it was done purely out of spite. They knew how much it meant for him to be here and they got satisfaction in denying him the privilege.

If the people only knew what hideous sight lies inside that closed casket? A person would have to have a stomach of pure steel in order to bear that sight. Identifying Dre's body was one of the worse things Tony has ever had to do in his life. His body was swollen the size of two Sumo wrestlers and his head was quadruple the size, resembling the head of a fear-provoking monster. Lying dead in the water for all those hours blew his body up enormously. All the while, Tony stares at the closed coffin, envisioning the hideous sight. For days now, he hasn't been able to shake the memory. He goes to sleep with the vision in his head and wakes up all night long to the same vision. Every silent moment, the vision pops back up in his mind haunting him.

Tony shakes his head from side to side to attempt to shake the vision away, but it goes nowhere as usual. He turns to his left, only to be greeted by Federal Agents Dumber and Dumbest who are staring at him with the coldest looks ever. Tony then looks to his right where he sees an elderly couple accompanied by two men and one woman. This is Dre's Uncle Fred and his family yet Tony has not a clue of who they are. Sitting behind them is the Mayor's girlfriend Liu Ching and her mother.

The Mayor's co-girlfriend, Megan made her cameo appearance not even twenty minutes ago. She dashed in and out in record breaking time. As much as she would have loved to stay to pay her respects, she knew she couldn't attract any attention to herself. She came in fully disguised by a big wig and dark shades just to throw Dumber and Dumbest off. Although they didn't recognize her, she felt paranoid just being in the same room with them.

Tony peeks behind him and finds the rest of the room completely empty. From the looks of the room it appears that Dre was only loved by few, but Tony knows better. As much love that Dre spread amongst his crew they had no choice, but to love him. He changed the lives of everyone who came in contact with him. He didn't discriminate. He made it possible for everyone to eat. His motto was 'if I eat everyone who deserves to eat, will eat with me.'

A woman dressed in all black and dark Dior shades comes walking into the room escorted by a woman on each side of her. They step elegantly as if they just entered a club instead of a funeral. They walk up to the coffin stealing everyone's attention. The woman in the middle carries one long stem rose in her hand. As she's making her way up to the front of the room, the tears are already dripping down her face.

They make it to the coffin where the woman stands there just staring at the coffin. As she's standing there, tears as big as drops of hail fall onto the coffin. Tony automatically assumes that this is Dre's ex-girlfriend Cindy. She grabs hold of his picture and brings it close to her face. The tears drop even faster now. She plants a kiss onto the framed portrait before placing it back onto the coffin. She then lays the rose across the top of his coffin. Her head drops low and the weeping begins. She's no longer mourning in silence. Her cries echo across the quiet room. "Why?" she asks, as her escorts lead her out of the room. Tony stares at her curiously as he thinks of all the things Dre has told him about her. He's forced to wonder if her mourning is genuine or is she performing for the people.

Meanwhile In Yazoo, Mississippi

The Mayor sits across his bed, just skimming through his locker. He digs deep in search of anything that reminds him of his brother. He's been sitting here reading letter after letter from Dre and he hopes to find more. From now on, his brother will have to live through these letters and the few photos that he has of him.

The Mayor feels responsible for all of this. He feels like he set his brother up for failure. Not only did he pressure him into going over there to get the work to supply the Homies, he also feels bad for introducing Dre to the connect in the first place. One thing that he's learned from this situation is that no one can be trusted and everyone has a breaking point. You can never tell what the next man will or will not do. After hearing Tony tell him how the ordeal took place, it broke the Mayor's heart to know that he plugged Dre into a connect who was the cause of him losing his life.

The Mayor feels he should have known better. He remembers a time when he was in the house with his connect one particular time and there was some mayhem going on. The connect feared that the Feds were on to them. They were just about ready to pack it up and vacate the country, but the Mayor was there trying to talk them out of it. As the connect was explaining their side of the story to the Mayor, he saw a look in his eyes that he will never forget as he said the words. 'I have no family here. I can't go to jail here.' That statement bothered the Mayor terribly. At a young age he realized that jail comes with the game and he couldn't understand how they thought differently. After hearing the connect make that statement he should have known then that it was time to break away from them, but he didn't. His greed forced him to continue on and now look, he's lost his brother. What a terrible price to pay, he says to himself.

Tony explained to him that the connect got caught with over 100 pounds of heroin a week ago. The Feds then found out that they were the head of the 'After Party Empire.' They then offered him a deal if he could turn them onto something of value. It was then that he gave up Dre.

The Feds on that case had nothing to do with Dumber and Dumbest in the beginning. That case had nothing to do with the investigation that they were trying to put together with Dre. After the connect gave the Feds Dre's info, they found out about the investigation that he was already under. Then everyone joined forces in order to bring down the entire organization. Tony told the Mayor as of right now, he has not gotten word that they have anything solid on the Mayor.

For years the Mayor has safeguarded that connect and done everything in his power to keep them out of the spotlight. He's had so many opportunities to flip on them, but he didn't even though he could have lessened his time.

Now to think that he protected and preserved them just so they could roll over on his brother, makes him feel horrible that he put his brother in that position. No one could have ever told him that it would end up like this.

He looks to the bottom of his bed, where he has several photos lined up. He has them organized from the earlier ones to the more recent ones. The photos are dated back to the seventies, long before the Mayor was even born. The others are of Dre when the Mayor was known as Junebug to everyone. Then there are the photos of Dre that the Mayor actually remembers.

The Mayor smiles happily at some of the old school pictures where Dre was wearing silk BVD t-shirts, Cazal glasses, furry Kangols, tight jeans and shell toe Adidas sneakers. The Mayor look at the photos and realizes that Dre wasn't always the modest, conservative low key type of dude that he's grown to be before he passed. In this photo he's wearing a huge 14 karat gold Dookie Rope with a medallion of the New York City skyline attached to it. In his mouth he has 2 gold fronts on his front teeth and on his finger he wears a three fingered ring which has his initials spelled out across it. The Mayor thinks of all the times Dre would get mad at him for wanting to floss. He now realizes where he got it from. He must have inherited it from his big brother.

The photos progress showing his elevation in the game, where he's wearing velour custom made Gucci sweat suits, Gucci sneakers on his feet and a Kangol cap on his head. Instead of Dookie Ropes, he's now sporting a super thick Herringbone necklace and a nugget watch on his wrist. The Mayor laughs at this particular photo. He can remember it as if it were yesterday; the day Dre passed that watch down to him. In this same photo, there are dudes standing around with huge radios in their hands, but the Mayor assumes that even then Dre was way ahead of his time because he's not carrying a radio. He's standing next to a Candy Apple Red Jeep wrangler which is piped out with custom made leather Gucci interior. The tire on the back is Gucci covered too with the letters 'Dre Money' printed boldly. The Mayor pays close attention to the dude standing next to Dre in this next photo and is surprised to see that it's Cashmere. There they stand side by side. Dre stands in front of his Jeep Wrangler while Cashmere stands in front of a 190 E Mercedes Benz. He's Louis Vuitton down and so is the interior of his car.

The next picture shows more elevation. This photo is of Cashmere sitting across the hood of his 300 E Mercedes while Dre sits on the trunk of his 535 BMW. The Mayor gets hyped just looking at them doing them. They're dressed in matching Pierre Cardin velour sweat suits and Prince sneakers. The next photo is of Dre pointing to his steel grey M3 BMW, while Cash points to his red 300 CE Mercedes. Dre is wearing a bright colored Gerry ski-jacket and suede Timberland boots on his feet, while Cash is wearing a short lambskin shearling jacket and chocolate brown, 40 below, Timberlands. The very next photo they're standing together side by side wearing matching Fila velour sweat suits and Fila tennis sneakers.

The pictures begin to look more and more up to date. This particular photo is of the two of them wearing Sergio Tachinni nylon sweat suits, Le Cog Sportiff sneakers on their feet. Apparently they've stepped their game up because they're both wearing 24 karat gold Rolexes on their wrists. Dre stands by his 850 BMW pointing to his treasure trunk, while Cashmere sits on the hood of his S500 Mercedes.

This photo sparks thoughts in the Mayor's head. He remembers clearly disrespecting Cashmere calling this same car a Dinosaur. He feels like a complete idiot right now. He laughed at Cash driving around in the old style Benz when he first came home, but little did he know the legacy behind that 'Dinosaur.'

He now understands what Cash meant when he told him 'You a rookie. I'm a veteran to this shit.' He now understands those statements to be true. He now realizes that in all actuality the joke was on him. He was way too young to respect their gangster. The Mayor acted as if he invented the game. The fact is that they both were doing them long before the Mayor came along.

Dre always told him that the game is the same only the players change. How right he was, but the Mayor refused to take heed. Right now he wishes he would have listened to them and took in some of their wisdom. The reality is, it's too late now. They're both dead and gone.

The Mayor holds the photo in his hand as the tears drip from his eyes. "RIP, Dre Money and Cashmere."

///// CHAPTER 134 /////

Two Months Later

A terribly nervous Miranda gets sworn in. Today they are holding court and proceeding with trial although the murderer is not present. The prosecutors hate the fact that they agreed to this but at this point there is nothing that they can do. The paperwork has already been signed on both ends.

Miranda looks over at Tony who sits on the bench as cool and calm as he can be. She wishes some of his casualness would rub off on her because she can't seem to get it together. She's as nervous as can be. She realizes that it's all or nothing for her. The outcome of this can change her life forever. Either she can regain her freedom or finish herself off for life. The jury can find her innocent or they can find her guilty. The dangerous part of this is the fact that she has to open up and put everything on the line. She'll have to admit to playing certain roles in this murder, which may make the jury go against her. However it goes, she will have to take it however they give it.

"Defendant, state your name."

"Miranda Benderas," she whispers.

"Now in your most audible voice tell us what happened on the night of December 23, 2004?"

Her heart thumps throughout her entire body. This is the moment of truth, she says to herself. It's all or nothing. 'Miranda, your life is on the line,' she can hear Tony saying to her loud and clear in her mind. 'Go, girl,' she tells herself before she begins. "It all started the day me and the love of my life, the man who I foolishly thought I was the love of his life, came here to Miami to visit my mother's gravesite on her birthday," she begins as her voice cracks nervously. The judge and jury listen attentively as she tells the details of her entire stay in Miami.

Tony was smart enough to pick a mostly female jury. He figures at some point and time in their own lives they have dealt with an abusive man or they've known someone who has. Knowing that, he plans to capitalize off of that by having Miranda embellish about how scared she was of him. She's sure they all can relate to that. Tony also told her that he would pay special attention to the ages of the men that he will choose and make sure to pick the younger ones. He's sure no young man can get pass her beauty. He doesn't think any man in his right mind would want to see a girl as beautiful as her get sentenced to life.

Tony watches with admiration as Miranda performs like the actress she is. The highlight of the show is when she starts to cry as she relives the murder scene. She sits up there sobbing away for minutes at a time.

An Hour Later

Tony and Miranda stand side by side. The both of them tremble like two lonely leaves hanging from a branch. Tony secretly holds Miranda's hand in comfort. He looks around to see the expressions on the people's faces. He's just wondering what the jurors are thinking. Did they believe her story or do they think that she's bullshitting? In Tony's years of practicing law, he's made an observation. He's learned that it's a good sign when the jurors come back into the room and can look the defendant in the eyes. Normally that means they didn't finish the defendant off. If they come back into the room and can not look at the defendant, oh well. He sneakily watches the juror box and is somewhat glad to see that each and everyone have taken a look at Miranda. "Please, he thinks to himself.

The judge stands up slowly. "Miranda Benderas, on the behalf of the state of Florida, I find you not guilty of murder, but guilty of conspiracy to murder.

Tony sighs from relief. Yes, he thinks to himself as he squeezes her hand gently. It all worked out as discussed. As long as they stick to their word, on the day of her sentencing the judge will sentence her to five years in which she already has close to two years served. She will have to do another year before she's eligible for the halfway house program, where she will do the rest of her sentence. Once her prescribed time is completed, she will be sent somewhere far away to a witness protection program, where she can live her life happily ever after.

"Miranda Benderas, you are ordered to return to my courtroom two weeks from today for sentencing," he states. "Court adjourned!"

"I told you," Tony whispers. "Put it all on the dead man," he smiles.

///// CHAPTER 135 /////

One Month Later

The small cigar shop is packed. The room is one big cloud of smoke due to all the smoking that is going on. The layout is beautiful. Plasma televisions, plush lounge chairs, area rugs, expensive paintings and brass ash trays set the tone remarkably. It's the perfect setting for a cigar launch party.

The word Euphoria is posted all over the room. Posters and cardboard stand-ups are scattered everywhere. The slogan 'Euphoria is Not Just Another Cigar. It's an Experience' is posted everywhere as well. Tony is the host of the party and he looks good doing so. He sports a black satin smoking jacket which has the Euphoria signature on the pocket. Every club member is wearing this jacket as well. He's made sure that everyone in the room will never forget the name of his cigar.

Tony passes out cigar after cigar to every member of the club and they are enjoying and appreciating them totally. This is the perfect place to launch his cigar because all walks of life step though this door, including doctors, lawyers, politicians, actors and musicians. They all have one thing in common. They are cigar smokers. Tonight they're not smoking though. They're enjoying the experience. The look of pure pleasure is displayed on their faces and that makes him extremely proud.

Another walk of life has just entered the room. "Phew," Tony sighs. He should have known they would be here. He puts a huge phony smile on his face to conceal his true feelings. He grabs hold of two cigars and steps toward the door. "Hello," he greets. "Welcome to Sanj's Smoke Shop. I'm here today launching my new cigar, Euphoria. Have one," he says as he passes a stick to the two men who stand side by side. "I hope you enjoy the experience," he says with a smile.

Federal Agents Dumber and Dumbest both snatch the cigars without replying. The look of hatred covers their faces. The envious looks on their faces combined with the look of enjoyment on others, makes Tony proud. He just wishes Dre was here to appreciate the moment as well. He looks to the small cardboard poster which sits on the counter. It's a picture of Dre. It reads: In loving Memory of Andre Blackhead. R.I.P. "RIP," Tony mumbles under his breath.

The sound of a creaking bed echoes from miles away. The loud thumping makes the bed sound as if it's going to crash through the floor any minute now. The sound of sexual moaning and groaning rip through the walls. The sweet smell of hot and steamy love making fills the air.

The woman sits in an upright position as she rides her mate like a feisty cow girl. She throws her body around sadistically as if she's being thrown around by a wild bull. Beads of sweat are flung from her body with each jerking motion. Her body is covered with so much sweat that she looks as if she's been in a sauna. Her hair is plastered to her head. Her eyes are half closed and her lips are slightly parted as she moans with ecstasy. "Angghh," she grunts as she bounces up and down as hard as she can as if she's on a trampoline. "Yes baby! Yes!" she shouts as she rubs her hands over her cantaloupe shaped breasts. "Give it to me daddy," she begs. "Ooohh," she sighs. "Say it," she growls as she grinds on him hard and as fast as she can. Her body mashes onto his causing extreme friction. "Say it motherfucker," she whispers in a sexy voice.

"Ass is not ass," the man whispers.

"What?" she barks. "I can't hear you," she says as she bounces hard onto him. "Say it again," she demands as she grinds, short and quick, but hard strokes. "Say it!"

"All ass is not the same," he says loud and clear. "Aghh," he grunts as every muscle in his body contracts violently. As soon as he releases, he resents what he's just said to her. Suddenly he feels as if he's lost the battle.

Her body quivers uncontrollably. "Oh, Dre! Dre," she cries. "Dre! Oh!" she shouts as she sits still for a second savoring the moment. She hops off of him abruptly. She slaps him in the face gently before rolling over beside him. "I told you all ass is not the same," she brags.

They lay there in silence for no more than two minutes before her snoring starts up. "Angie," Dre whispers. As he lays there his mind wanders. The scene of that night plays clearly. He still remembers the look on Latif's face when he told him that he was about to jump into the Hudson River. He remembers looking back a few times and seeing him, but at one point he lost sight of Latif. He never saw him pop his head up again. It's obvious that he never came back up because he drowned.

As much as Dre wanted to go back and rescue Latif he couldn't because his own freedom was on the line. Dre owes his life and his freedom to the boat filled with young ballers, who allowed him to climb aboard. If it were not for them he would have died right in the water as well. He wishes he knew who they were because he would surely compensate them for their deed. Even with all the helicopters soaring in the air and sirens sounding off, they still pulled him in which was a lifesaver for Dre.

The Coast Guards shut everything in the water down checking for Dre. At that point he felt like it was a lost cause. It took hours before they allowed anyone to move again. Dre hid on the small boat, hoping and praying that he didn't get caught. Suddenly his prayers were answered. Once they found Latif's body their search was over. Either finding one man was enough for them or they thought there was only one escapee, Dre will never know. There is one other thing he will never know. Newspapers and news castings stated that the body was so swollen that it was impossible to identify the body. The only way they were able to identify him was by the wallet they found in his pocket, stating that he was Andre Blackhead. Dre still to this day can't figure out how Latif got hold of his wallet or why he had it. At this point, it doesn't matter because it saved his life and made him able to remain a free man. Damn, Latif died so I wouldn't have to, he utters to himself. How grateful he is.

Dre has been thinking of how his brother may be dealing with his death. He wishes there were some way that he could reach out to him to let him know that he's alive just to ease his pain, but he's sure that will not be a good idea right now. He feels it's best to lay low for a while before he resurfaces. He's sure his brother will be alright. He'll get over it someday, but for the time being he plans to hide out here in D.C. with Angelique until things simmer down. Then he will reach out to his brother and Tony. His main concern right now is the money that he's left with Tony and his uncle. With them thinking that he's dead he assumes that they are probably running through it like a marathon. That is one reason that he may have to come back to life sooner than he wants to. "Angie?" Dre whispers to the sleeping beauty. "Angie?"

"Huh? What baby?" she replies in an aggravated manner.

"You have to promise me you won't mention a word of this to anybody... not even Tony."

"Dre, baby for the last and final time. I will not mention it. As bad as I wanted you and now to have you all to myself, do you think I would do anything to lose you? No," she whispers in a reassuring manner. "You have my word. It's our secret."

///// CHAPTER 136 /////

Months Later

The Mayor sits in the front row of the courtroom with his eyes glued to the cuffs that are on his wrists. After all these years of listening to Tony, he actually believed he would be a free man again. Now it breaks his heart to know that these shackles will be a part of his life for as long as he lives it. Damn, he sighs as he shakes his head from side to side.

It's already 9:30 and Tony has not arrived. The judge is giving him the benefit of the doubt, thinking that he's late as usual, but the Mayor knows better. In no way is he expecting Tony to show his face. He can't blame Tony though. He did the very best that he could do. He fought his hardest at all times, never showing any sign of weaknes in any battle. The Mayor is sure that he would have been a free man under any other circumstances. The Feds knew so too, which is why they had to throw the monkey wrench into the program. Presenting the information about Tony's past is the only tactic they could come up with. They were desperate and they needed something.

The selfish part of the Mayor wishes Tony would just put everything on the line and get him freed, but the realist side tells him that isn't fair for him even to expect that. How could he expect a hard working man to put his livelihood on the line to get a hardened criminal freed? How could he be so selfish as to expect a man to lose everything he's built, to free a society destroying criminal? Truth of the matter is, he can't. He knows in his heart that it isn't fair.

Throughout their years together, the Mayor has grown to love Tony like a brother. There is nothing that he wouldn't do for Tony. In fact, his own brother was jealous of how close they were to each other. He always told the Mayor to keep in mind that it's only business. The Mayor never looked at it like that and now look, those words have bitten him on the ass. He'll mark it down as just another one of life's valuable lessons. Dre continuously asked him if he actually believed that an attorney would put his livelihood on the line for two felons. The foolish part is the Mayor actually believed so. Dre was right again. The Mayor will just charge it to the game.

The selfish part of the Mayor cries out saying 'fuck it, if he frees me and they bring up his past we can fight his way out of it. I got money. I'll get him the best attorney that money can buy. So what if he loses his license. I got enough money to do whatever else he wants to do. I got money, he says arrogantly to himself. Damn, how can I expect this man to give up everything for me? What kind of man am I to even want him to do that? I created this situation for myself. I made my bed now I have to lay in it. The shit I did to get me here was done way before I even heard of a Tony Austin. Why should he have to pay for something he had nothing to do with? He shouldn't be but the gesture sure would feel good to hear right now. It would really feel good to know that Dre was wrong about our relationship and, it wasn't just about

Tony milking me for the dollar. At the end of the day it is what it is, he tells himself.

He looks over to Federal Agents Dumber and Dumbest and for the first time the looks on their faces actually matter to him. He finally feels like they beat him. They've managed to do exactly what they said they would do. He could have given up a long time ago and not only saved time and money, but his hope as well. Yesterday he calculated how much money he's spent on fighting these cases. His first attorney took him for $250,000.00. Once he hired Tony, he's blown almost $400,000.00 with him in total.

It broke the Mayor's heart when Tony offered to pay him back every dime that he's given him. What Tony didn't understand was the fact that it's not about the money, it's the principle. The Mayor looked at him like a brother when Tony only saw him as a client.

Damn, the Mayor says to himself as he stares back at the agents who are smiling and taunting him. Damn, these bastards beat me, he says to himself. "Fuck ya'll," he whispers, figuring he's already lost the battle. There is nothing more they can possibly do to him. Damn, these bastards beat me.

"Mr. Blackhead!" the judge shouts. "It's now 9:40 and as usual your attorney is late. I have several other cases. The Mayor looks over at the agents again. They're still smiling from ear to ear. It's over, he thinks to himself as he shakes his head negatively. "I have no choice but to proceed."

Suddenly the doors open wildly, stealing everyone's attention. The Mayor is hesitant to look back. He believes that his mind is playing tricks on him. The sound of the shoes banging onto the floor is familiar. "Your honor, please forgive me for my tardiness," he pardons as he always does. The Mayor is sure that it's not in his mind now. He spins around slowly in his seat only to see his main man Tony strutting gracefully down the aisle.

The Mayor looks up at the judge whose face displays hatred. He then looks over to the Federal Agents. Their mouths drop to the floor, not believing that he has the balls to show up here after their threat.

Tony winks at the Mayor as he's approaching. Once he gets there he extends a closed fist as he always does. "What up?" he asks as they dap each other.

Suddenly the Mayor's life has hope again. He really does give a fuck about me, he thinks to himself. And I give a fuck about him. I give a fuck enough not to let my man lose everything he's worked for and risk spending the rest of his life in prison for murder because of me. Fuck that, he says to himself as he stands up. "Your Honor!" he shouts loud and clear. Everyone focuses on him wondering what he has to say.

Tony looks at him with a look of confusion on his face. "What up?" The Mayor rolls his eyes, turning away from him.

"Yes, Mr. Blackhead?" the judge questions with a look of confusion on his face as well.

"Your Honor, I wish to fire my attorney at this time."

The entire courtroom has perplexed looks on their faces. No one can believe that they've heard this; not the judge, the agents and definitely not Tony. "What's going on?" Tony whispers. The Mayor ignores him as if he hasn't said a word. "Listen man, please," Tony pleads. "Don't do this. You're making a big mistake," he whispers.

"Fuck that," the Mayor whispers just loud enough for Tony to hear him.

"You're gonna end your life. Please, don't do this? I worked too hard for you to do this to me," Tony states.

The judge interrupts Tony's pleas. "Uh, Mr. Blackhead. It's your decision and I'm granting you the right to do so, but for the record, may I ask on what grounds have you dismissed your attorney?" Tony looks at the Mayor with disgust before hanging his head low. The entire courtroom is awestruck. Everyone waits impatiently for his answer.

The Mayor stands there pausing for a brief second. "Real niggas do real things!"

THE END

ACKNOWLEDGEMENTS

First and foremost I have to thank Allah for allowing me to be in a situation to produce another book. I thank you for bestowing your mercy and blessings upon me. I also thank you for the strength you've granted me to endure the many trials and tribulations that have been presented before me. In closing I beg you to have patience with me and continue to shower me with your blessings, Ameen.

I have to thank my supporters from near and far. Without you there would be no purpose in me writing. You've held me down from day one and I appreciate you wholeheartedly.

To my readers in the penitentiaries from Otisville to Yazoo Mississippi; thanks for holding the kid down. I do what I do with ya'll in mind. Your support motivates me to the max. Your letters keep me on point. Each letter pushes me back into the lab. I may not be in a position to respond to each and every letter but know that I've read them line for line. I'm in the lab constantly hour for hour trying to create another hot joint to help you through your struggles. I'm always asked why I've never made the Essence Best Sellers List and the only answer I can come up with is, maybe I'm too raw for Essence. I'm True 2 Life! No cut, no watered down fairy tales, no plastic storylines. 'They can't handle the truth!' F.k 'em! Who needs their recognition when I'm triple platinum in the hood, where it really counts. Real recognize real! Ya'll stay up and get ya minds right. I'm living proof that it can be done. We come from the same gutter. I treaded through the same trenches. I am you. I just switched my focal point and so can you. They say, God changes the conditions of a man, once the man changes the conditions of his own heart. Let's change our conditions? Eliminate plan A, which is normally negativity and replace it with a positive plan and let's see how far that takes us?

To my brethren in faith; do not believe for one second that I wrote the segments in this novel to expose our sins or to make a mockery of our religion. I wrote these segments as a reminder of what we should or should not be doing as Muslims. Sometimes when on the highway of life, speeding 200 miles an hour it's hard to see how critical things really look. Hopefully, seeing it in black and white makes things look that much clearer for us? As Salaamu Alaikum!

To my loved ones; I have to thank ya'll for keeping me focused. As ya'll know this has been an adventure for me and I'm grateful to have myself surrounded by ya'll. All your support has been extremely beneficial to me.

Ma, keep the kid in your prayers. God knows I need it. I been through it! Telly, I love you. You at that age now. Gotta stay on point. You can either soar to the top or fall to the bottom. All it takes is one wrong decision. Stay focused. I love you.

To my fighters; my days of getting in that ring are over. I can only live my dreams through ya'll. I'm passing the game down to ya'll the way it was given to me. Watching ya'll put those combinations together, slipping and dancing, gives me motivation and keeps me focused in doing what needs to be done. Al-Malik, Amin, Razor, Spank stay focused. To Lil Sadee, and Kareem, keep doing what ya'll do. Dreams do come true.

I breed lions and tigers. You can call me the zoo-keeper. Over twenty hours a week, I'm in the cage with them; depriving them of food, but feeding their mental as well as their physical. Anyone who dares to step in the box with anyone of mine, I must warn you. There's a chance that you can lose your life. I'll press the button and sit back and watch them pick you apart piece by piece before I signal them to devour you in whole. "Get 'em!"

Kenneth and Fireman-Bo, we got a good thing going on! Thanks for the opportunity.

Sorry to have to ruin the vibe but I have no choice. To my haters; Back in 2003, when I first stepped into the literary world, there was a comment made. "He wrote a book? What he got to write about? Who gone read it?" Well, it's four years, five novels, several hundred thousand books sold, later. Now I would like to ask you, would you like to retract that question? Don't hate me, hate your mother for giving birth to your goofy ass!

One more hater needs to be addressed; To the half a man, who I hear is running around the town making comments about a situation, he knows nothing about. You don't know the least bit about me. Girls gossip, not men. You should keep my name out of your mouth. You may have a few people fooled, but not me. You're plastic. I can see right through you. Stop hiding behind your projects. It ain't where you from, it's where you at! I knew you before the big watches, big cars and your Fed beef. You was a b…h back then and you still a b…h in my eyes. Don't make me pull up your skirt and expose you in front of the world. And you claim to be Muslim? I love you for the sake of Allah. Let's keep it like that.

To my man Joe Rugilio, what title do you want? You do it all from graphics to internet marketing, to business structure. I know your worth, baby! Everybody wins, bottom line! To my brother, Naeem, True 2 Life Forever! You already know! To my cousins, Friend or Foe, huh? Lately ya'll been finding out there are more foes than friends. I told ya'll but you had to find out for yourselves. Better late than never.

Tonisha, you a lifesaver! Need I say more?

And last but not least to my heart; there's been a huge strain on our relationship. They're determined to break up what we have. They're jealous and they also know how much you mean to me, which is why they would love to take you out of my life and shatter my world into little pieces. Little do they know about the vow that you and I made to never let anyone break us up, regardless of what. I know forcing a six year old to make a promise like that was not right but I was desperate and fearful that their plans may one day come to life. Daughter, I love you more than life. Right now, you are too young to understand what is going on but one day in the future you will. One day you will realize that I am not the man you were told that I am. My name has been slandered and my flesh has been eaten in front of you. When will they realize that the more energy they exert in turning you against me the worse their lives become? They run around town kicking my back in to anyone that will listen to them. How beat are they? They burn the ears of individuals telling falsehoods from corner to corner, avenue to avenue. What do they attain by doing so? They can tell lies to a few folks in our city but I can tell the truth and spread it across the world. Would I be more of a man if I expose their weaknesses in black and white for the world to see? I have a platform of millions of readers. You're local and I'm global. Stay in your lane before I embarrass you in front of the entire world.

O Allah despite the negative influences that my daughter Fajr has around her, I beg you to raise her up to be an obedient, devout servant of yours. I beg you to give her the best of this life and the Hereafter? I beg you Allah to take the veil off of her eyes one day and help her to realize that I only want the best for her. O Allah I thank you for sending her to me for she is the reason that I chose to change my life around. O Allah, I beg you to help us maintain a strong bond regardless of what hurdles we have to climb over. Ameen!

Fajr, I love you! As Salaamu Alaikum!

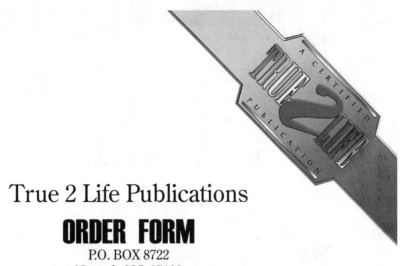

True 2 Life Publications

ORDER FORM

P.O. BOX 8722
Newark, N.J. 07108

www.True2LifeProductions.com

Also by the Author:

No Exit

ISBN # 0-974-0610-0-X $13.95
Sales Tax (6% NJ)   .83
Total $18.63

Block Party

ISBN # 0-974-0610-1-8 $14.95
Sales Tax (6% NJ)   .89
Total $19.69

Sincerely Yours

ISBN # 0-974-0610-2-6 $13.95
Sales Tax (6% NJ)   .83
Total $18.63

Caught 'Em Slippin'

ISBN # 0-974-0610-3-4 $14.95
Sales Tax (6% NJ)   .89
Total $19.69

Block Party 2: The Afterparty

ISBN # 0-974-0610-4-2 $14.95
Sales Tax (6% NJ)   .89
Total $19.69

Block Party 3: Brick City Massacre

ISBN # 0-974-0610-4-2 $14.95
Sales Tax (6% NJ)   .89
Total $19.69

Shipping/ Handling for 1 -3 books
Via U.S. Priority Mail $ 3.85

Each additional book is $1.00

Buy all 6 books and Shipping is Free.

True 2 Life Publications

P.O. BOX 8722
Newark, N.J. 07108

www.True2LifeProductions.com

PURCHASER INFORMATION

Name:_____

Address:_____

City:_____

State:_____

Zip Code:_____

Books

No Exit:_____

Block Party: _____

Sincerely Yours: _____

Caught 'Em Slippin': _____

Block Party 2
The Afterparty:_____

Block Party 3
Brick City Massacre: _____

HOW MANY BOOKS?_____

Make checks/money orders payable to:

True 2 Life Publications

(handwritten): Kings of South Beach — Mark Walberg